MY KILLER DID NOT COME

"A" Final Investigation

Inspired by Events That Really Took Place

By

Ene'es ELIGREG

This is a work of pure fiction although derived from real events. Names, characters, entities, places, events, and incidents are either the products of the author's imagination or used in a fictitious manner. Most resemblances to actual persons, living or dead, or to most real events are purely coincidental.

To my mother and daughter, who do not realize that all the energy the good Lord endows me with, pours through them.

To my sister Mrs. Chassaing.

To Magney O'Leifins

Table of Contents

INTRODUCTION *9*

PART ONE *19*

CHAPTER 1. .... *21*

A Microphone In The Coffin 21

CHAPTER 2. .... *29*

A Quickie at Labadee 29

CHAPTER 3. .... *37*

Lysius and "Grandbaby Doc" 37

CHAPTER 4. .... *45*

Crime Inc. 45

CHAPTER 5. .... *53*

History Channel and Morgan Freeman 53

CHAPTER 6. .... *59*

Bloody Sunday 59

CHAPTER 7. .... *68*

Born Among the Dead 68

CHAPTER 8. .... *77*

The Fall Of 1991 In DC 77

CHAPTER 9. .... *89*

That Day In History 89

CHAPTER 10. .... *99*

Killing The Cat In Cell 8 99
CHAPTER 11 .... *121*
A Load Of Tchako 121
CHAPTER 12 .... *138*
As We Were Saying - The Interview 138
CHAPTER 13 .... *153*
The Editorial 153
PART TWO *179*
The Investigation 179
CHAPTER 14 .... *181*
A Double Date In Washington, DC 181
CHAPTER 15 .... *195*
Quantico 195
CHAPTER 16 .... *205*
The Ball Drop 205
CHAPTER 17 .... *211*
A Chance Encounter 211
CHAPTER 18 .... *221*
A Kinky Welcome 221
CHAPTER 19 .... *240*
The Other Welcoming Committee 240

CHAPTER 20 250

Sex On The Beach? 250

CHAPTER 21. 259

The Platform 259

CHAPTER 22. 275

On The Sofa 275

CHAPTER 23. 299

A Political Calm 299

CHAPTER 24. 323

The Assassination 323

CHAPTER 25. 348

A Protective Exile 348

CHAPTER 26. 362

Inaugural Crowd 362

CHAPTER 27. 377

It's The Fight In The Girl 377

CHAPTER 28. 387

President Josaphat Hurries 387

CHAPTER 29. 401

Fall Out 401

AFTERWORD 419

ABOUT THE AUTHOR..421

GRATITUDE...423

INTRODUCTION

Exceptionally few things could be more realistic than the assassination of this man. On April 3, in the year 2000, Anno Domini, journalist Jean Dominique really died an unfortunate and despicable death. This work of pure fiction, solely with cinematic entertainment value, is but a writer's attempt to recreate the tragic events along with the environment in which this iconic journalism figure existed. Today, that environment is still a petri dish for violent crimes against other journalists.

By inclination and formation, I am interested in the film industry. I was always fascinated by storytelling. As a child, I would think of stories to entertain my friends and folks who often wondered where I got them from or if I made them up myself. So, in a theatrically hilarious way, I would be pointing to my buttocks as I answered that my stories come from my head. I previously authored this story in the form of a screenplay as I drafted other stories to push them through Hollywood via, of course, a literary agent. As a result, this, like my other stories, is rich in dialogue. Also, the standards call for short, consequential exchanges with subtexts, all geared to advance and profit the plot and storyline. As these efforts were getting in the way with school, I have stopped after a few submissions. JEANDO, the working title of the story, has done well in some contests that could bring together up to 50,000 or more screenplays. I was still involved in film school, and I wanted to complete it at all costs, in time and money. I also held a healthcare job to make ends meet when something remained after incurring my expenses toward my education.

Since I had previously tried to send other writings, I grew aware of the time and effort it takes to funnel a movie script to Hollywood producers. I only had time to be busy at my place of employment and school. School involved of being on a set shooting something or at the soundstage or in an editing bay molding the craft.

For we always had a shoot somewhere, we, students, were given the task to team up to cook up the stories or concepts we would decisively choose from to work on as class projects. Need I tell you that I always had my fix? Through the other obligations at work and from the other professors, I kept my chin down and wrote a few stories. Some stories were long, some short. Some I completed and others, to this day, still unfinished. Nonetheless, I kept writing. I did not preoccupy my mind with what would come of what I was writing, considering the shelf life of a movie script in Hollywood.

The only worry that haunted me was that case the assassination of that man would finally be solved, putting an end to this injustice and impunity. At the same time, the closure would be making all of my writings and thinking about the case irrelevant and obsolete. If you are reading this today in 2020 A.D., it is for sure the death of journalist Jean L. Dominique remains shamelessly unsolved. No one has been held accountable for the savage killings of that fateful morning. Murders? Jeando was not assassinated alone. His employee, Jean-Claude, was also sifted through with the criminals' bullets. As this book was in the process, the fear was that some of the actors of the real shit that inspired it would suddenly die, with impunity wrapped as a parting gift, under the weight of "Almighty age."

I did not even finish college when Dominique's assassination occurred. The case dragged from one prosecutor to another. It is as if their wings melted for venturing, like Icarus, too close to some "powers that be?"

My generation grew up listening to Jeando on the radio, his station; and we developed a great love for him. Of today's, most ignore who he was. However, thanks to YouTube and other media, public opinion is widely stacked detrimental to some of those real actors who took part in the events. At some points in this fictitious story, one can equate my achievement to only the way I works with or dispose of the alphabet's twenty-six letters. I talked to many people. Even those who would admit they never knew the journalist, blatantly accuse. Citing the "internet," this generation has an exact belief about who pulled triggers, who ordered Jeando killed, and who paid for the bullets. Criminals' planning. The man certainly has had his imperfections, and people who have worked alongside him can attest to the many mistakes he made in his life. Jeando, by a long shot, was neither saint nor angel; however, this book does not try to count the things for which he may be held accountable. This is not such a book. When and if proper, the author does not hesitate to point out, though subtly, the one most prominent accusation Jeando has carried into his grave. Never did I think I would find in that man's assassination the materials to satisfy my love of storytelling. As some would and may believe freely, storytelling to make a dollar, that is for sure. However, the real satisfaction is not at all financial. It is the fact that the story is told and is out there, be it in that genre.

Like I previously stated, this is a work of fiction that stems from a very true and real story. The meat of this tale is as accurate as it can be. I would not have enough brain noodles and materials to imagine the assassination of Jean Leopold Dominique and conceive of the behavior of the authorities toward it. The authorities at the time, as well as those that subsequently followed to this day. Among the realities that one cannot neglect within this labyrinth, there is, at times, especially at the approach of each anniversary of the murder, the single voice of Guyler Delva. Also, a young journalist, before joining subsequent administrations, he continued to demand justice, thus risking the same fate as Icarus for venturing too close to the "sun?"

However, on the twentieth anniversary of his assassination, Jeando "appears" to die again of some shit apparently not natural. If not in the authors' mind and certainly in the hearts of his loved ones, there was not a thought about the journalist.

One should not categorize this book as a cheap accusatory tool. Indeed, some parts may appear "truer than the fiction" of which it is professed to be the work. Pure coincidence or suspicious truth. Participants in the real events constituting the meat of this work, therein may recognize shrapnel of the truth and particles of which the author himself is not readily mindful. Remember, the author first wrote the story with Hollywood in mind. Also, in Tinseltown, conflict, sex, and blood make the world go round. When we star as the audience in the movie business, we are ready and self-predisposed to believe it is all real though we know it isn't so. However, there are two instances where I could not conjure up fictitious blood. The plasma Jeando and Jean-Claude spilled were all too real and are kept such in the story. On the other occasion, there was enough blood, in that school used as a polling location, to fill a river. As a journalist and radio station owner, Jeando covered that election day in 1987. One should hear his rant on the air the day after.

In this book, the author forgoes any of the due diligence, which requires to contact critical figures therein mentioned. The information and the belief surrounding the assassination of Jeando have reached public domain status. Some real characters, along with their real names, are mentioned, for there is no fictitious way around that fact. Self-effacingly, some names are withheld. Some actors in the actual events that inspired the story have become such political giants that an insignificant pseudo or false designation could not bypass. The author considers it fair game if they have already passed or have held positions thrusting them into the public domain. Jeando's assassination comes in, perhaps, like an equalizer.

The jury may still want to stay out of this one. However, that small enclave does belong in the land's near 11,000 square mile area. The inhabitants of Cazale sure exhibit the traits of some foreign ancestry. The white genotype has not faded away entirely amid this Afro-Caribbean population.

Genetics tells us that race-mixing did indeed take place in that region of the country. Those foreigners were not settlers, and they did not arrive on a cruise ship as tourists either. They came to execute someone else's dirty bid as soldiers. Just like centuries before them, many outlaws and outcasts, who did not have anything to lose, elected to accompany Christopher Columbus on his audacious, blood spilling, women raping and diseases and pestilence spreading voyages rather than finishing their miserable lives in that little brat Isabella's dungeons. Bartolome de las Casas put aside. There had never been any humanity within the subsequent European expeditions to this part of the world. And, these few words could expand out across all the African continent and still prove right. The who's who of Spanish society did not show up on the shores of the New World but the scums who would have no other way to treat the peaceful humans they encountered there. Columbus, for one, was nothing short of a dick (Neil De Grasse Tyson). The "navigator" would use his knowledge of astrology to terrify the natives on the beautiful island of Hispaniola and extort from them the things he needed for his voyages.

With reason, many regard Toussaint Louverture as one of the greatest black men who ever lived. Such consideration, sometimes, is mostly in contrast with how his twin freedom fighter Dessalines is himself seen. Jean-Jacques Dessalines was receiving stripes on his back as a young field slave, Louverture was reading and dreaming about becoming Spartacus. He was a house slave but a slave, nonetheless whose final aim was freedom for his race. Louverture may be regarded as the brain, the careful risk taker in the fight. Instead, Dessalines is the muscle, the pragmatic force. He is hell-bent on reprisal for whiplashes across his and the backs of the other black slaves in the world. An insolence. A dare or impertinence that would have posteriorly, bought him a priceless assassination and perhaps, would explain the current situation of the first black nation on earth. The brazenness to propose to his counterpart in the United States, at the time, to buy the freedom of all the African slaves on the land, might have done it.

After the ceremony of Bois-Caïman, the real birthplace of the slaves' revolt, in 1791, Toussaint bravely saved the lives of many white colonists like his old master and his entourage, and their possessions. Malcolm X and some would call that "House Slave Instinct or Mindset." Knowing the man. Perhaps that earned him recognition, the French citizenship, and respect. By contrast, young Dessalines that same year probably, was still receiving from the white masters' whip the same scars across his back as were the other revolting slaves. He resolved to have no more of that shit and swore to proclaim it in writing using the skin of the white man as paper, his blood as ink, his skull as inkstand, and a bayonet as a pen. In no way, that would earn anyone other recognition but that of a butcher when the vanquished retained the monopoly of writing the story. Most of this has not been written anywhere in the History of France. Their defeat at Vertières, Saint-Domingue, in November 1803 never happened. It's a total blackout date. The eighteenth day of November 1803 has never seen the day. Perhaps, it is because the real French army or part thereof was M.I.A. in Saint-Domingue that day. A worthy analogy. "Were Haitians alone given the task of writing the history of the World Cup, on June 15, 1974, Italy would have had to lose that game one goal down, and nothing else had happened."

Napoleone di Buonaparte, his real Corsican name, was at the time master of all of Europe, giving foreign lands to cousins, friends or countries to women he wanted to lay. His armies were vested in conquests far more critical than the shoelace that the colony of Saint-Domingue was providing for the metropolis. It was a substantial shoelace, however.

Around the time that the slaves were fighting for their freedom, Poland was under the control of Prussia, Austria, and the Russian empire and, by 1795, had undergone three partitions. Many Polish soldiers, officers, and volunteers emigrated, mainly to Italy and to France. They practically sold their souls to Napoleon, who would use them on foreign soils because the French constitution did not allow the use of external soldiers within the hexagon. Here is how nearly 6000 Poles were indeed sent along with Swiss and German troops to Saint Domingue to crush "the Haitian rebellion."

The enclave, Cazale, would look different today with a whole other feel to it had all of the Poles survived the tropical diseases foreign legions encountered in the Caribbean. Historians report that around 4000 either succumbed to yellow fever or the brute force of the Haitians fighters who followed the orders from Dessalines. Treatment of the captives left the Haitian leader with a reputation issue in need of polishing. Enter the few remaining Poles (about 150) who were disgruntled, to begin with after participating in other Napoleonic campaigns hoping to gain France's assistance in restoring their country's sovereignty. Still, until 1802, Napoleon has not made a move in that direction as a condition of the Poles joining the French cause. That would ultimately happen only in 1807.

Presumably, Dessalines' directives were to eradicate everything white from their midst should the slaves wish to become free. Symbolically, he even ripped the color white off the French flag, thus creating the Haitian flag. The idea the General would ask his troops to show leniency for the Poles is far-fetched. However, it is well conceivable that those Poles grew straight from being disgruntled with Napoleon to apparent frustration and despair after losing about 4000 of their dedicated military personnel. Yes, these 150 Poles have switched sides in the battle, for they understood that the Haitians were fighting for the same reason they sought Napoleon's assistance that he had not honored still. So yes, they did stay in Haiti for the remainder of their lives and lived in Cazale. Everything else in the story smells like a myth buoyed even by Dessalines himself. At the time, he experienced a severe deficit in convincing the rest of the world that, in fact, he was human despite the vilifying brush strokes the vanquished of Vertières offered of him.

PART ONE

"The important thing to know about an assassination or an attempted assassination is not who fired the shot, but who paid for the bullet."

Eric AMBLER *(A Coffin For Dimitrios)*

CHAPTER 1.

A Microphone In The Coffin

It may be for some reason, or some other uncommon human predispositions that we have yet to explore. During the memorial ceremony at the stadium, Dorothy McLintaugh could not take her eyes off President René Préval. Her husband, Ed, without any prior arrangement, chose to visually dissect former presidents Michel François Gibéa and Jean-Bertrand Aristide, all in attendance with the Salesian and Gibéa sitting together as always-inseparable buddies in good and evil deeds. One of those past presidents could command the other to stand on one foot, bark like a dog, do the hokey-pokey, and whatnot. What would follow are pure obedience and execution with between the legs tuck tail. As he stared, Ed felt like he was communicating with and reminiscing his always-quizzical late father of the behavior of most of the country's presidents and political leaders. Before he died, Aristide and his pal Gibéa had the most glorious privilege of being the subjects of such amused puzzlement on the part of the elder McLintaugh. To the left of her husband, sitting right across from former president Aristide, Dorothy, either deliberately or with professional instinct, intensely observed René Préval. The Americans did feel that heat under the gazebo in the stadium. In mid-April, when they left Washington to attend the funeral a day prior, Dorothy still needed a light jacket. However, it was remarkable that the usual humidity on the field cooperated that day during the time of the service only. The caretaker had to wet all his clothing to prep the ground for the afternoon and evening games.

A multitude of thoughts came rushing simultaneously through the couple's minds. To this day, investigations after investigations have come to abrupt standstills. Dorothy never registered the reason she made a mental note to tell her students of the disturbing pattern of serial killers to be nearby as the authorities discover the gruesome scenes of their crimes. And still, a few of those psychopaths include in their modus operandi their remorseless presence, be it at some distance of the victims' funerals.

Physically in the stadium, Dorothy was mentally taken back to sometime after the military ousted Jean-Bertrand Aristide. Subsequently, the journalist, in the coffin, who had feverishly campaigned for the former priest a year earlier, had no place within the scheme that would play out in the country throughout the following three years. For a second time, he went into exile in the United States. Had he not died, Jeando had promised to designate one by one all those who would have harmed him. That, he said, as mentioned in a later chapter, would have been the last thing he'd have done before going into exile for the third time. Many in the country believe that Jeando had designated his killers. Like bits of short movies, she relived the instant Jeando, at his age then, played hide-and-seek around their home in Washington with her son. Observing the President, she believed to have heard the giggles of both Jeando and the boy calling each other by the same name as though the illustrious journalist were near his age. To witness their joy at play, it was probably the other way around.

She recalled the long, tiresome, and eventful trip she and Ed took to the country thirteen years ago.

Ed sat fixated behind his dark shades as he looked at his friend in the coffin, and the next fraction of a second, his eyes would not leave the former presidents. His field of view allowed him to switch back and forth with ease and speed between *punctum proximum* and *punctum remotum*. He needed no panning or tilting of his head to visually dissect Aristide and Gibéa while looking at Dominique's lifeless façade. At that precise instant, he thought of that television advertising for a photographic camera, which claimed that only the human eye focuses faster. He revisited the day his father came home, announcing he had been asked to contribute in the investigation into the death or disappearance of James Riddle Hoffa. The President of the International Brotherhood of Teamsters Union from 1958 until 1971 merely vanished around late July 1975. He knew that only a muscled investigation would bring his friend's assassins to justice. He also knew he could not even volunteer his expertise or talk about such a case. To whom? To President Préval, perhaps? In Ed's mind, that President had always come across as dangerously too laid-back or as a master procrastinator. To Aristide? On the ground that maybe he would be interested? No, since he had in many settings refrained from telling Jeando compromising things about his great "friend."

Ed knows his father was never fond of that President. A CIA contact had told his father of that young priest who badmouthed the United States at his parish near that impecunious neighborhood in Port-au-Prince. He also put in danger the lives of the young missionaries from the Latter-day Saints Church, equating them to spies of the Central Intelligence Agency. The elder McLintaugh called it irresponsible and reckless. However, Ed remembered that, at the time, Jean-Claude Duvalier was in power. He recalled his father mentioned a high-ranking official who may have thought he could rat out the priest to the CIA operative acquaintance of his father's. In that official's mind, both young Gibéa and Aristide would fit inside Papa Doc's definition of his detractors. The other question on his scientific mind near Jeando's coffin will have to brazenly, not because of itself, wait for twenty-three years to play itself out and provide an answer. In that country? President Michel Gibéa never crossed his mind. Ed thought he was old news after breaking his teeth during his term and would never consider another stint at the presidency like the others.

As Jeando's sister stepped aside after kissing her brother, President Préval caught Dorothy's stare. She thought then that she had just paid dearly for forgetting her stylish shades at home and for neglecting to pick one up as a duty-free airport item. He internally panicked. He wondered how long she had been staring, if she thought he did it or, at least knew the assassination was going to come down and who were plotting it.

"My God!" President Préval quietly implored veiling his eyes with a hand to display his distress to have lost that caliber of a friend in that brutal and coward slaughter. "Maybe she thinks…Ah!

Anyway", his mind kept chewing, "had it been her husband staring, perhaps, there would be cause to "swim to escape and dodge" what may come."

He did not know that Ed, on his part, was dissecting the former presidents. The current President cut that impractical contemplation short because some subtle noise had had the American shift her eyes away not to resume her stare. After that ceremony, a short period of socializing was in order, and President Préval walked up to Ed to greet him and Dorothy. Préval and Dominique had kept their relationship with the McLintaughs very confidential and discreet. Not even Aristide knew who they were. A year prior, in legacy-preserving mode, Préval had been purportedly concocting and fostering Jeando for a possible run. They had made several trips throughout the innermost countryside. On one of these excursions, Ed was with the party. Socializing, President Préval introduced the McLintaughs to Jean-Bertrand Aristide as his friend but not as Dominique's. Politics. Jeando was a fortunate individual to have had such discreet relationships even deep within those rough regimes of the Duvaliers'.

In the hot but comfortably humid shade under the tent, the President invited the Americans to ride with him in his motorcade to the site by the river where Jeando's ashes were to be discarded after cremation. That was undoubtedly the cultivated politician at work. Perhaps, he presumed that he could tacitly unearth the mystery behind Mrs. McLintaugh's stare during the ceremony. En route to the river, the atmosphere in the vehicle proved to be gawkily quiet. The President could not break the ice past his welcoming and his thanking the couple for accepting to ride with him. Shyness or good manners, Mr. Préval never liked to offend even his political opponents. He had not been able to lead the Americans into a topic of conversation that could tip them to the reason he offered the ride in the first place. At the other end, the silence had turned out to be somewhat more cautious than klutzy. They had managed to take control of the conversation and keep its foci trivial to and from.

As an officer started to honor Daniel Butterfield and pay tribute to the journalist on the trumpet, standing to the right of Mrs. Jeando, Dorothy thought of sending her illustrious friend off with something he loved. When McLintaugh Sr. had passed away, Dominique made the trip to America for the funeral. At Arlington, he heard these words sung for the first time in Dorothy's beautiful voice, which, by the way, had gotten Ed all "Dorothized" the night of that play in high school.

DOROTHY'S VOICE

Day is done, gone the sun,

From the lake, from the hills, from the sky;

All is well, safely rest, God is nigh

As she sang the lyrics of "The Taps", amazed heads turned to discover whence that booming and beautiful singing voice originated. The thought came to Ed's mind that the President had been too quiet for a first since he had known him. Many a time that the three of them had met, Jeando would turn it into a betting game to have the President drunk before either Ed or him. Although they were not addicts, the journalist and the President exhibited professionalism of the glass and bottle. Jeando, fake sipping, would make sure he loses and for a reason. Then the President would just let loose and talk about anything and everything. Trusting? Keeping his glass in check, Ed ends up learning a load of shit about this country from the mouth of its own President. And one could learn a lot from that President, sober or stoned.

The makeshift urn, "makeshift, not fancy" as the deceased would have wanted, made the round from hand to hand until it had gotten at the bank of the river. As Jeando's ashes were being poured out of the urn, a light breeze blew. It carried the smallest and only to Michele visible particle of ash all the way to Dorothy's left shoulder. It rested there all throughout her voyage back until she hugged her son, who started sneezing until he developed a slight sinus allergy for a half hour. The journalist was maybe thanking Dorothy for her elegant send-off. By the same token, he chose to bid farewell to the boy he had loved so much. In her first broadcast alone, without her husband, Mrs. Jeando was dead right when she said that her husband was not dead, that he had merely used one of his spells to disappear. She was confident that he was being seen at that instant somewhere else smoking his pipe.

That exact day, in Washington, Dorothy's son started a new habit to hold his pencil like one would a pipe as he goes about his schoolworks. However, a character in the story bluntly equates Mrs. Jeando's disappearing spells remarks to something true as in the country's folk saying, "Even in hell, there' is favoritism." When nobody knew of his whereabouts during the infamous torments of members of the media by the Duvalier regime shortly after Reagan was elected, in November 1980, Dominique did not disappear. He was merely a well and better-informed journalist. No spells could have kept him off the grid from November 28th, 1980 thru January 6th, 1981, when he finally left the country. His wife had been forced out a month prior with the first group of journalists expelled by the Tonton-macoutes.

Deep within the Duvalier regime, Jeando had far-reaching tentacles, most, probably among the many of his genotypic makeup populating the administration since the marriage of the President for life, Baby Doc. He was informed. He knew of everything every time the power would be about undertaking anything. He practically walked into the Venezuelan embassy until the circumstances allowed for his safe exit in the first days of January. One of these internal "limbs" (revealed in a later chapter) might have had to drive him to the airport himself. Not his appointed chauffeur, but the high-ranking official in-person took Dominique to the diplomatic lounge at the airport.

CHAPTER 2.

A Quickie at Labadee

Labadee, Haiti. December 17, 2022

For a significant period of time, the word "Haiti" in the caption was suppressed or neglected. Royal Caribbean holds a ninety-nine-year lease from the Haitian Government to exploit Labadee for a meager percentage per tourist visiting the location. However, many have never realized that they were not told on which island they were. A marketing decision indeed, but other intentions and preconceived complexes were also in the mix. When the Marquis de La Badie settled there centuries ago, exploitation and pillage were on his mind. At least, the locals were participants, even if they were the "things" exploited in the pillaging of what mattered.

Whether one was on board any of Columbus' ships in 1492, or Royal Caribbean's "Anything" of the Seas ships in 2022, one thing is a given: As one nears the shores of this beautiful island, a small part of the mind goes numb to any other stimulus to believe that one has indeed reached paradise.

This day, *Freedom of the Seas* nears the beautiful island and from the deck; the tourists observe the beautiful water and coastline of white sand. Some of the passengers pull out their cameras to snap or record images. It is a festive atmosphere. At least, those tourists are aware of which island in the Caribbean that oasis is. The country's Department of Tourism might have finally stepped in and complained after an investigative journalist had trashed the company for how business was conducted. The reports gave the impression that once at Labadee, the visitors' freedom was limited like it was the case for the followers of Jim Jones' cult in Guyana. The locals were kept at bay, and the visitors were not allowed to venture out or have any contact with them. The fenced premise is continuously under surveillance by armed personnel.

If you are there to investigate, you do that. But if you leave your nine-to-five cubicles, breadwinner gig, and your home to have fun in paradise, then Labadee is your primary destination. However, it is part of an impoverished and tumultuous land. A land of contrast, a slippery ground, they say over there, where weird shit occurs as though it is the norm. That could, in a way, stand for a reason the cruise line withheld the country's name from the visitors. In 2022, much has changed in Haiti, and way too much has stayed the same. At arrival, the visitors are impatient to feel the white sand between their toes without thinking of what is happening at a few bird's wing flaps away in Cap Haitien. For that matter, in the whole rest of the land. Folks are being intimidated, beaten, and even killed as they exert their right to vote and their right not to have their vote dictated or stolen.

After years of political chaos, corruption, and a terrible integrity deficit, Haitians have found a messiah in thirty-eight-year-old Lysius Geffrard, a retired professional athlete-turned-politician who was twice re-elected to the country's most critical Senate seat. Should one tell those tourists that this day is an election day in the country, not one who is familiar with the notion, would believe it. In fact, it is Election Day, less bloody but typical nonetheless because, in some hot spots, there are the usual reports of fraud and violence.

The Haitian elite and Washington actively back the son of the late President Jean-Claude *"Baby Doc"* Duvalier. Unheard of, the other twenty-one candidates terminate their campaigns to join the vast majority of the country to support Geffrard as the unique candidate with the best chance to defeat Duvalier. As the Washington establishment sends signals that it would welcome a potential Duvalier win, the new American President sure hopes otherwise. The first Latino to be elected US President, David Sosa, before becoming a senator, had spent a considerable amount of time with Lysius Geffrard. The two men were roommates at Yale after Geffrard had stopped his athletic career to pursue his international law degree. That is to be in line with all the men in the Geffrard family. Closed associates entertain the belief that the two were having pizza in their dorm room when news broke that journalist Jean Dominique had been assassinated. At one point, according to many in their circles, the future US President fell on tough times, and Geffrard's family had him in Haiti one summer. By the following semester, Geffrard Sr. would have paid all of David Sosa's expenses at Yale. It was with reason that the United States' President made clear his warning to the establishment about meddling this time around in Haiti's elections. "That sorta thin' hurt the others in the world too," Sosa wrote on Twitter to remind them what they felt a few years back. Vladimir Putin allegedly helped Donald Trump perhaps to avoid any bone picking with a particular woman with whom he (Putin) was involved in a passionate hate affair. Others alleged it was a blatant fear on his part of the emotion. Then, fear and love must, indeed, be opposites.

The tourists, here at Labadee, are unreservedly oblivious to all the politicking going on beyond the fences surrounding them. Who would not be with this welcoming and entertaining music by the troubadours who bring Altieri Dorival back to life with his famous song *Ti Ca*? By the end of the 1970s, Dorival was this troubadour folk artiste who alluded to the female private anatomy likening it to a cat, a pussycat, or some other caring and lovable animal. In the song, he begs a woman to let him borrow, rent, or buy so he could have his way with it. This song, forty years ago, had had its way on the Haitian airwave. This June/December couple, however, hears it probably for the first time. They sure enjoy it, but it's not much of a hit to keep them in that small crowd of gringos trying to dance to this music like Mexican dancing horses. They quickly make their way out of the hall.

A million and one things cross their minds after leaving the gathering. Peter Ekstroem thinks of his prominent position. He thinks of the high profiles like Senator Franken, Harvey Weinstein, and even of President Donald Trump. He reflects on Jeffrey Epstein and all who have had their names associated with the wave of sexual misconduct accusations a few years back. Sixteen to twenty women accused Donald Trump alone. On her end, Heather thinks about the "Me Too" movement that prompted and generated a wave of new accusations. This intuitive process would be to remind the adults that they are in charge and can always pause and reconsider.

One would think it is violence in this hotel room, but it is not as the young twenty-something voluptuous woman bounces on the bed after she was tossed on it. It is another thing instead. And considering her giggling leaves very little room not to figure that what is about to take place in that room will not involve two kindergarten children. We will call it "lust." The sound of the troubadour music stops abruptly as the man pulls the door shut behind him, thus giving the room the quiet atmosphere that the designers had imagined at conception.

"Goodness!" she shouts!

The young woman inserts her thumb and pinky finger in her mouth to remove the gum that she has been chewing since she was on the *Freedom of the Seas*. She also reaches for a tissue in which she will wrap it after pulling the trash container near her beside the bed. Multitasking, she also grabs the TV remote control.

"It is lovely and peaceful here; on this island," she continues.

The director of the FBI, now in free fall in the new President's trust, has become a regular at Labadee. Sixty-six-year-old Peter Ekstroem has heard that comment countless times. Heather, the young woman on the bed, is not the only assistant or intern who had ever been at the forensic lab. Royal Caribbean was taking its first trips to Labadee around the time a younger Ekstroem dazzled his bosses, who unanimously promoted him as Head of Forensics. Each time he hears this comment, he remembers the first and the only time he took his wife to Labadee to celebrate that promotion. He probably had done it with more vigor, but the routine wants him on his knees on the bed. Instinctively, all the women would join him on their knees, and they would start to pray. Hmmm! Pray may not be the exact word here.

Ekstroem did not feel a need to answer to the comment. He will certainly not explain his hesitation as he recalls the numerous times his wife and his dates to the oasis have all made the same observation. However, he is pretty familiar with what is beyond Labadee. He is aware of what day it is, as well. He knows what is happening at just a rock's throw away as bra, shirts, and panties fly across the room onto the armchair, covering the watchful lens of the woman's photo camera.

"I just recalled my promise to you near that water cooler", he mumbles.

"What was that promise," she asks?

"The first thing I ever told you was that I would take you to paradise."

The young woman kisses him passionately, ignoring that she is not the first bull in this rodeo.

"Yes, you did, and we are still alive," she says as she reaches and grabs the remote off the pillow.

The television turns on to an aerial shot of the presidential palace under construction for which thousands of Haitians have volunteered their time and little money they have. The broadcast shows them as working with the purpose to meet a deadline. They sure would like to place either Geffrard or Duvalier in that new palace by inauguration day.

REPORTER

Haitians will have a double celebration this next February. The reconstruction of the presidential palace destroyed in that devastating earthquake of 2010 is now nearing completion. Also, it will be completed just in time for the inauguration of the country's next President, either thirty-eight-year-old Lysius Geffrard, the nephew of a former president with the same name, known here just as "Lyzou" since high school and his days as a footballer, or, listen to this, Nickesse Duvalier, also aged thirty-eight, who is the son of none other than the former President Baby Doc. They are both well loved in the country. Still, Lysius enjoys a much higher endowment with a wealth of political maturity that overshadows the recognition of the formidable name of "Duvalier" and the nostalgia of its Macoutes followers. Geffrard may well be the favorite here. Candidates, except the two from the parties of former presidents Aristide and Michel Gibéa, have dropped out of the race to join the people in his support. Later, they understood that none of them, even their unlikely alliance, could defeat either one of the younger candidates. They have quietly abandoned, with no fanfare, one by one. Geffrard is a man who claims to be able to combine his charm, competence, and eloquence with those of the likes of Bill Clinton and Barack Obama. He would add a touch of "the Senator's own words" Anderson, the persistence of the Rudy Giuliani of yesteryear, to govern his turbulent nation. The world will not be immediately ready to forget his war of words as a senator with our former President Donald Trump for his treatment of his fellow compatriots. Then Senator Geffrard urged the American people, after that infamous Helsinki summit, to get rid of their President, put him in prison, or send him into exile to his boyfriend. The world, Anderson, will not forget that.

The young blond seems to be interested as the reporter enumerates Lysius' accolades and talks of his wish to cut the name Christopher Columbus from the country's history. The Senator always argued that the worst thing that happened was this relentless and blood-spilling Italian, with his band of low-life rejects, setting foot in Quisqueya. Half-Italian, Ekstroem is not in the mood. He stretches out on top of her beautiful chest and takes the remote from her hand to turn the TV off.

"Did we come all the way down here for this shit?" The Director says impatiently.

CHAPTER 3.

Lysius and "Grandbaby Doc"

After the other candidates had dropped out, the younger ones, Duvalier and Geffrard, kept an uncluttered, cordial, and respectful relationship, though, at times, they appeared to be politically at each other's throat. Like Joe Biden about Barack Obama or George H.W Bush about Ronald Reagan, in one campaign stopover, Lysius enumerated his opponent's qualities and competence as a good and decent man. However, he ended his remark saying that the only one thing that will do Grandbaby Doc, the Senator's electoral nickname for Nickesse, no justice was his "motherfucking" last name. Geffrard never apologized, but Duvalier forgave. However, despite the little irregularities and violence reported among a few of their respective surrogates and supporters, they have conducted themselves unlike typical politicians of their country. They have had several private meetings. They have appeared together in public. Duvalier and Geffrard met after Lysius publicly condemned a television ad depicting two-year-old Nickesse wearing the Macoutes' blue uniform in the company of his presidential parents to celebrate the National Day of the Tonton Macoutes on a 29th of July.

"Let us condemn my opponent's father and grandfather," the Senator/candidate told reporters. "As a matter of fact," he continued, "let us fuck them up, let us hang them again and again.

Bring our car tires and our gasoline out. Let us cook the fucking Duvaliers [sic]". Stunned reporters braced themselves.

As a pit bull who would not let up, the Senator charged, "Let us do that shit each time it can put food on tables, send parents to work, kids to school. Let us also kill the Duvaliers' son and grandson, ex-wife, daughter, and former collaborators if that could guarantee proper health care, better infrastructure. Let us keep up with that fucking crap [sic] if it can ever contribute to the betterment of our lives."

Of course, he has drawn much criticism since the many large organizations supporting his candidacy sponsored the ad. Long before he got his feet wet in the game of politics, Lysius had learned in the game he played to rub it up his critics' noses with his athletic performances. Like a refined and well-advised politician, he managed to preserve these groups' trust in him intact and score significant points well within Duvalier's base. As it has never happened in the country, Nickesse Duvalier himself came to Geffrard's campaign headquarters and got on stage with Lysius to congratulate him on his victory. That action on Duvalier's part raised his political stocks both abroad and in the country that can now breathe more comfortably after this much-heated political season. Throughout the land, as in the case of this plush living room, the same television broadcast is being watched.

REPORTER

Of course, Anderson, with this victory, Lysius brings a host of ambitions to the office. The most controversial being the reopening of the investigation into the assassination of the country's most prominent radio journalist, Jean Dominique, which occurred two decades ago. When he does deliver it,

Anderson, it is cranked up to be, as Norman Schwarzkopf and Colin Powell would say, the mother of all victory speeches.

Moïse Josaphat, the outgoing president, was not on the ballot. The law of the land did not allow seating presidents to seek immediate re-election. He will, however, go out with many credits to his name, of which two play out on this same election night. He had worked tirelessly to modernize the electoral system to do away with the long wait before polling results can be made public. And, he has restored the country's power grid to guarantee "round the clock electricity". The immense and euphoric crowd, at this hour of the night, in front of the podium historically shared by the two presidential rivals, stands as a reliable testimony that President Josaphat had managed to keep some of his master campaigners' promises. As usual, Nickesse Duvalier moves around with a posse and countless, let us call them, groupies. The followers of Nickesse are a sample of the youth of the country. They are the children of a nostalgic generation who heard of "Duvalier" for good and evil. But they have not had any good antidote to their fanaticism since his father left the country in 1986. When Jean-Claude Duvalier returned, he appeared more like somebody who came back to die rather than to realize the wishes of many former Macoutes and their progenies, of course. Another politician would degradingly call them "ratpakaka or chimè." This night is no different when he arrives at Lysius' campaign headquarters to concede and gracefully ask his followers to unite in the celebration with the supporters of his new friend. As he puts it, the President-elect is a political half brother from the same mother, Haiti. He did not need to say a word tonight when he appeared on that stage side by side with

Lysius. His presence signals this generation has decided to part with its elders and ancestors' tradition that called for chaos and outright bloody carnages at similar stations in their history as a people, as a nation.

DUVALIER

"It is not without purpose that Lyzou and I, arrive at this juncture of our nation's history at the same age with similar political ancestry. Were we to stay true to our ancestors' tradition, we would not be side by side on this stage at this moment. Our generation needed to decide, and that decision fell on our shoulders this day. My compatriots let my handshake and my raising of our new president's hand tell the rest of the world that this land is moving forward in peace and unity."

Many in the political arena and the media questioned the sincerity of Nickesse Duvalier even as he speaks alongside his more fortunate opponent. They insist on calling them "former opponents," though he now calls Lysius his friend and political brother.

Sitting with the sharks of his campaign, after results have poured in, Lysius knows he has the victory in the bag. He is getting ready to step out onto the podium. He waits only for his wife, who had physiological feminine urgency when the strange commotion occurs near him. Lysius stood puzzled and dazed for a second as he felt left out in the dark, deprived of any information. What was happening around him when the earpiece-wearing sharks ran out, leaving him alone on that sofa? The commotion was caused by Duvalier and his dedicated posse as they make their way through the massive crowd of Lysius' supporters. Only a handful, realized that Nickesse Duvalier walked among them.

Lyzou! Lyzou! A young female member of his entourage calls running in from the exterior. As no one told him what was happening, Lysius held his frustration by turning to the wall behind the sofa. He looked at portraits and charts he's seen many times already. The aide is midway toward him when his wife appears from inside the restrooms. His attention is instead drawn to the young and beautiful aide by whom, at last, he thinks he is going to be informed. He turns around with his million-dollar smile. A thoughtlessly jealous spouse would find the material here for groundless grievance.

"What is going on?" he asks. "Has the sky fallen out there?"

"Mr. President," answers the first person ever to address him with that title with it meaning something, "you won't believe who's out there coming in to meet with you."

Much earlier, as Nickesse was only mulling his possible stint at the presidency, a supposed friction transpired between him and a top aide on that very front. This aide had accused Grandbaby Doc of letting that "Mr. President" shit get to his head.

"Mother of Dragon," Lysius shouts. "What the fuck!"

The future First Lady is, of course, less surprised than his aide, who, also at a hearing distance from Lysius, is shocked to hear that from her boss. As the aide starts to answer the President-elect's question, some of Lysius' staff lead Duvalier and his entourage. Lysius recognizes Nickesse as they appear at the turn of the long hallway. Thus, Lysius' instinctive utterance as he glances down the hall.

After the concession, Duvalier shakes Geffrard's hand and raises it in victory to the crowd before they lock in a hug to the appreciation of the sea of their supporters. With Nickesse Duvalier on the podium, Lysius exhibits an extra boost of confidence to talk of one of the issues he championed all during the campaign. Nickesse only showed his mindfulness of the rift that had existed between his family and the journalist.

LYSIUS

And now, my compatriots, you know, since I was a student, an athlete standing for our country, or a senator, I always keep my word. Tonight, my brothers and sisters, the elections are over, and this proud and glorious nation has made its voice heard loud and clear. I am incredibly grateful to my opponents for their patriotism in dropping out and backing me. I invite them all and, of course, my brother Nickesse Duvalier, in the enormous tasks ahead of us. I thank the people sincerely for selecting me to be their President in these challenging times. This promise, my fellow Haitians, is "not" the typical "On Day One" politicians' rhetoric.

Lysius takes a three-breath pause that the crowd translates as a cue to go wild in ovations. And with the determination of a horny teenage boy, he charges on with the words imitating Bob Dole's running mate Jack Kemp in his debate with Vice President Dan Quale.

I went to school in America. I studied American history, and our Jean Dominique is no Jack Kennedy. I will task my transition team to gather all the pieces on the table. We shall solve the puzzle of his barbaric assassination alongside his employee within my first month in office as your president.

CHAPTER 4.

Crime Inc.

Peter Ekstroem and his young date had already sailed away from the oasis. Contrary to the FBI official who never overstays at Labadee, but in one sense, alike since this Dutch septuagenarian also is an enthusiast. He is a prolific novelist who has made the port his place of inspiration. How much different is he from Ekstroem? Well, since the late 1980s, Ljudvig has brought the same and only girl to Labadee. He calls his wife "his muse." From time to time, they sail to other ports, but he prefers to stay in Haiti, where they hop from bar to bar.

Ljudvig and Briijeet have developed a profound friendship with Maurice, who's been a server at the hideaway since his thirties as Royal Caribbean was setting up shops. The couple carries a little calendar of the bars, with the days and the times they go to each. Years prior, Ljudvig and Briijeet along with Maurice would have met tonight at a place like the Adrenaline Bar. Aware of the political climate, the older visitors gather at Columbus Cove. Despite the cruise lines' efforts, few have become interested in what is beyond the oasis. They have chosen not to sail to the next port to follow the broadcast.

On the counter, Maurice slides the Tiki mugs toward a much younger couple at the end that has ordered Labadoozies.

Maurice and the older couple have made it a habit of commenting on and discussing the country's politics. Looking at the mugs slide to the other end of the counter, Ljudvig makes a mental note that he needs to include sampling that beverage in his bucket list. Still, the thing on the tip of his tongue as he watches Lysius deliver his victory speech begs to come out.

"Maurice," says Ljudvig, aloud, "'t seems that significant changes will come to Haiti…"

"And they will be good ones," replies Maurice, audible enough more to himself and Ljudvig, as he already prepares another drink.

Still elsewhere, in the country's capital city as it probably is in any remote location, the feelings are out there in the "cloud," the "emotions cloud," that is. In this modest dwelling, this father, just a bit older than the new President and Duvalier, lectures his teenage son on how he now feels about the developments. He and his family volunteered their time to work for Geffrard's campaign. Only a few hours since his election, a latent sense of frustration already sets in. Even groups that supported him feel edgy. The wealthy folks in the mountains above the capital city wanted and had hoped for the victory of Duvalier, whom they think betrayed them for the manner of his concession to Geffrard. A smart politician, Lysius will nonetheless have all the people's support as days go by.

"Bah! This is getting to his head," the father complains. "Lysius should remember his real friends and take care of us. This talk of reopening Dominique's case is alarming and smells like shit."

"Father!" the teenager interjects in open disagreement. "He promised."

"Fuck Jeando," the man tells the boy. "He's dead, and the bastard ain't coming back. I remember the load of shit that motherfucker used to talk on his fucking radio [sic]. Fuck him. Shit!"

"Son," the father adds, "I've supported Lysius up until now. But..."

Again, the boy interrupts his father. This time, however, in a plea.

"Don't give up yet, father. Lyzou's a good man."

Again, the higher and more profound one ventures up these mountains, the more affluent, the more remote from a cultural standpoint folks get. Imagine the Dutch novelist from Labadee blindfolded and merely placed in this luxurious living room with the same people watching the TV broadcast of this election's night celebration. Ljudvig would quickly and speciously determine that he is in some well-to-do household in his native Holland or anywhere in Europe.

No. Mr. Labadee, you are not in Holland or nowhere else in Europe. Only one person in this company reminds you of your pal, Maurice. He must also tell that you are still in Haiti with that five-star Barbancourt he fills his glass with every minute. He is sixty-five-year-old Daniel Toumain, and the jovial atmosphere you got dropped into is, in no way, a celebration of Lysius' victory.

Rather tonight, Toumain is Tito's guest to celebrate the reception of their latest delivery, which arrived earlier in the afternoon. As no one in this room pays attention to Lysius' speech, but at some occurrence, one can say that elections night just happens to be tonight.

Tito Massim, the sixty-two-year-old host, is a white genotype Haitian of Lebanese and European origins. He is a direct descendant of the original refugees fleeing the Middle East.

Sailing toward Brazil, they ended up on Haiti's shores at the turn of the twentieth century when Germans, British, and French mostly owned all the businesses. Those tenderfoots engaged in odd jobs and trades to make ends meet. At night, they slept on the floor or on cardboard in front of the established businesses in the commercial section, which earned them a peculiar nickname that has not stuck to them. Still, their descendants are referred to as "The Syrians" with no regard to the actual place of their origin.

Late in the afternoon, Tito had asked Toumain to come and check out the latest devices one of his sons had deemed necessary to have in this day and age. With no questions asked, Toumain guaranteed his presence.

Daniel Toumain emerged timidly out of nowhere onto the scene sometimes in the nineties as Jean-Bertrand Aristide struggles to affirm himself as a real leader despite his overwhelming popularity. He gained in significance around 1992 when de facto Prime Minister Marc Bazin was at the head of a consensus government. From time to time, the country would see an onslaught of political slaughters and extrajudicial assassinations by death squads. That environment served as a petri dish fostering the killing of thousands of civilians and created around 300,000 Internally Displaced Persons or IDPs, causing thousands more to flee across the border to the Dominican Republic. This period could very well be when Toumain solidified his relationship with Tito Massim, whose crime business boomed within the ten years included between 1991 and 2001. One of the duo's most talked-about criminal undertakings happened in March 1995. They would cooperate in Port-au-Prince for the very suspicious murder of a young, fashionable female attorney. That assassination will serve forever to demonstrate how lethal was the criminal partnership of Toumain and Tito. On orders from a higher power, these partners whacked this woman. They masterminded it to suggest a drug deal score-settling.

Overnight, Tito's men invaded the home of the young attorney's driver, threatening his family at gunpoint. They ordered him to call out sick for the day and offer to send his brother in as a stand-in. The driver announced that everyone in the young lawyer's entourage knew he no longer had a brother since the fatal morning of the coup by General Cedras, Biambi, and Michel François.

"I guess you've just made me your uncle," said Tito's prime cutthroat, Chapo, with a gun glued to the driver's temple. "By sunrise, I am going to make you a fucking cousin."

The assassination of Mireille carried the price tag of a contract killing from the highest stratum entrusted to Toumain and Tito, who were provided with cars and weapons to see it through. FBI investigations later revealed where the vehicles and guns came from and who supplied them. Late that night, Tito received a call from his men telling him of the brother-less driver. Right on the phone, Tito recalled an unsettled score with one of his pushers who had double-crossed him. Tito just decided to make a widow of this poor man's wife because the time has come for him to render unto the Syrian. In the middle of the night, he made an unexpected phone call that boils the guy's bowels. He woke up Eddy, aka "Ed Badass," offering him to let bygones be bygones if he agreed to run an errand for him. An errand? He must start by going on the spot to the attorney's driver's home and see his man Chapo who will further instruct him.

The next morning, March 28, a well-dressed, freshly clean-shaven Eddy reported to work on behalf of his cousin. The substitute driver impressed the lawyer. Tito thought of striking an emotional chord with his plan when he asked that the "The Badass" wear a shirt that the attorney had offered the real driver recently on his birthday.

"Ask the son of a bitch to give Eddy his favorite shirt," Tito told Chapo on the phone.

This genetic proof may have worked as Tito expected. A melted young woman sold by the shirt idea went naively about her usual daily routine. Throughout the day, Eddy kept running his narco-chicken pea brain. He wanted to make sense of it all. Why had Tito offered him this sweetest of sweet deals to forget every biff between them? The well-connected Toumain had words from above. The lawyer was expected at a location to sign off on a massive amount of cash to drop a case about a powerful entity later in the afternoon with a set time of 4 pm at the latest. There is no way in hell Eddy would have known that, in Tito and Toumain's playbook, he is employed as a disposable prop in the lawyer's slaughter.

At the end of September 1991 already, they had found themselves drawing lots. They needed to decide who would head to Les Cayes with Gibéa and who would get to do the Port-au-Prince job as they were asked to separate. Tito drew to go to Les Cayes but arranged with his partner on the ground he had a personal score to settle in the capital.

Toumain had become an essential fixture in the country's politics. However, he never held a government position or any elective post. He has always been in the "know" business. He knows people and knows all about them. He has dirt on everyone who is anyone in the country. He is a kingmaker. He places his protégés at every level of the government, of businesses, and of the country's social makeup as a whole, and that made him more powerful than the sum of his placements. Many even say that if Aristide chickened out to lose the elections in 1990, Toumain was, somehow, going to make him the president. But Aristide was not about playing games. The people wanted him as president and were going to elect him come whatever, wind, rain, thunder, or high tide. Toumain is, however, the type of man who doesn't take chances. He made sure the members of the electoral council were folks who ate from the palm of his hand.

In the palm of Tito's hand sits the smallest ever and the latest drone out there on the market. The NSA and the CIA swear by it. This one had been changed and customized to drop a lethal dose of C4. His son had just arrived from his rendezvous trip in Bogota, Colombia, for the clan's other dealings and to receive delivery of the tiny and terrible flying object. The damage and terror the bee-like device can cause equate this gathering to that of any terrorist organization. In fact, the past behind each, in no way, would have them pass for choirboys. The brave people of the country have nicknamed Tito Massim "Saddam Hussein" naturally or by ethnicity-derived sarcasm, turning his mercenary twin sons into "Uday and Qusay."

They have welcomed the nicknames and taken a liking to them. Tito turns to his guest, who just about now pays enough attention to hear what Lysius says about his contentious campaign promise.

"Dani," says Tito as he presents the drone to Toumain, "this will be our eyes in the sky."

The device flies around the room as Tito gives a demonstration to his guest. Like a pro, he guides it out of the living room and into Kenskoff's crisp open air as they all come out gazing up to follow the drone.

Toumain gets close to Tito, who looks like a teen gamer with the console.

"Lysius is not bluffing, Tito. We must not underestimate him."

"Ha!" the Syrian says dismissively with a hand. "Nini's butt. Rat shit behind a box."

Much to the amusement of Tito, Toumain has never laughed as hard and loud. The Massim twins, now in an empty lot on the property following the drone's red and green lights in the dark sky, yell out to their father, aware that Toumain has been heavily drinking all evening. In fact, at that late hour in the night, Tito will have to convince Toumain to stay the night over or let one of the twins drive him home

"Is he okay, dad?" yells out one of Tito's sons from the dark.

CHAPTER 5.

History Channel and Morgan Freeman

After the United Nations officially ended their mission in the country, the upsurge in violence and the potential for fraud at the onset of the electoral season led the Security Council to adopt a resolution calling for the sending of its peacekeeping troops back to Haiti. A move that will later be the catalyst behind the collective decision of twenty-one presidential candidates to drop out of the race and join the rest of the nation in support of one uniquely qualified candidate. Many criticized the U.N. contending that the organization could not, in good faith, guarantee a peaceful outcome since they have displayed favoritism toward Nickesse Duvalier with whom they have, on occasion, wined and dined in New York City.

"Ha!"says an officer. "Opening that case again? How many commissioners have been sacked while biting on it? Three? Six?"

Throughout the day and well into the night, the feelings have also been mixed at the police headquarters. They have not made any comment about politics up to now as one officer just started his shift. They would not dare in front of the peacekeepers here to give them a hand for the occasion. The words of the president-elect called for the older officer's blunt comment with sarcasm, causing a younger officer to laugh.

"Good luck as well, Mr. President," the older man says.

Age has started to work its number on those much older officers' hearing. They always insist on being the closest possible to the TV set or in the front at H.Q. meetings. In the police force, the slightly older of the two is known as History Channel, for he is a living, breathing, kicking history book. His younger partner is a movie enthusiast who has watched all the movies starring Morgan Freeman, whom he emulates both in actions, looks, and vocals. The way the pair works is simple. History Channel supplies Morgan Freeman with the stories they tell together at the headquarters.

"Eight actually," says Morgan, "if you count those who lived, and the one agent forced to leave the country."

"This Jeando gets all this attention," says this twenty-three-year-old French soldier sitting with them. "Who was he anyway," he asks.

The young Frenchman just handed a blank check to Morgan Freeman. The officer does not need History, though "The Channel" will heavily contribute since the partners were in the heart of the story he is about to tell. It is like Diana Ross handing a microphone to an eight-year-old Michael Jackson. She later complained the child would not have returned it had Joe not stepped in. As the broadcast is nearing its end, everyone in the hall gets the feeling that History and Morgan would seize that occasion and make it something none would forget.

They all gather toward the front. Picture the real actor on History Channel.

"Under the dictatorships of Papa and Baby Doc", Morgan starts, making sure he has the foreigners' attention, especially the young Frenchman and pointing to the younger U.N. soldiers.

"If you young bloods should know, those were respectively Nickesse's grandfather and father. Under their reigns of terror, while other journalists were bought to be quiet, intimidated, or only chose to stay calm."

"I wonder sometimes," says History, "how Nickesse turned out as such a presentable young man." Something, just only hours ago before Duvalier's atypical concession, none who would have voted for Geffrard would conceive this in his or her mind.

Like the actor tells of the date Andy Dufresne came to Shawshank, Morgan takes his audience back to a night in a few neighborhoods around Port-au-Prince in 1987. A little more than a year before that, Jeando had finally come back to Haiti from exile and worked extremely hard to restore his radio station, Radio Haiti Inter.

"They might have been drinking," he says, "and had gotten the matchbox damp. After the truck stopped in the darkness, the box was thrown away. A cigarette lighter failed many times to ignite, and a stifled voice emanated from inside the vehicle."

"Yo!" called the voice. "Tito! Hurry up, man!"

Tito Massim is twenty-eight years old when he starts earning real money on the Haitian crime landscape. When he finally lights the Molotov cocktail, the flame reveals his most significant employer at the time as the letters F.A.D.H. become visible on the side of the truck behind him.

He throws the cocktail in a store window. He steps on as the truck starts to drive away in the sponsored darkness manufactured on demand by the electric company. That night was no different from the others since the start of that November month. As it was clear the entire country engaged in that final dash toward the first post–Duvalier era elections, the military's higher hierarchy, hell-bent on keeping the power, began an aggressive intimidation and terror campaign. At his youthful age, Tito Massim became the mastermind and the principal contractor.

Indeed, he must have proven himself earlier at an even younger age.

Before many factors combined to drive businesses out of the section of Port-au-Prince known as Croix-des-Bossales, Petionville was a peaceful, well-to-do residential neighborhood on the hills overlooking the capital with a European feel to it right in the middle of the Caribbean. Before that night, nothing but peaceful and joyful living happened in La Coupe, as Petionville was called soon after it was founded. The sun already started to peak on the beautiful houses on the hills as rooster crows and machine guns combined for a peculiar "gun-certo." Nocturnal fires would break out everywhere in the capital. In the morning, as regular life restarts, corpses were discovered lying on the pavement. Frequently, students needed to jump over cadavers they had not imagined finding on their routes.

Tito introduced the military to the corpses' intimidation tactic. Bob Lemoine, that other giant on Haitian radio space, had never discovered the artistry behind these corpses. The legend presented the streets of Port-au-Prince in his morning spots. He never realized that these were placed long after rigor mortis had set in. And only Tito and a select few knew that the blood on and near the corpses was not theirs and most often was that of animals. History would stop his partner to tell the recruits that this same tactic was tried by part of the opposition to the outgoing President.

"However," he says, "they did it like miserable amateurs."

In fact, in 2019, that ill-advised, internally flawed, and divided opposition left it out or just was ignorant of Tito's method. That opposition accused Josaphat of killing protesters. "Protest organizers," the old officer adds, "brought cadavers around the perimeter of the presidential palace that they tried to beset. In their midst at the time, a sitting senator who folks said appeared unhinged and, in an urgency to become President by any means and hide from something or some other shit."

"According to the opposition," the old man continues, "President Josaphat would have hired foreign snipers who would shoot protesters in the head. That allegation would a tad later find some legs as some officials were named in aiding a few armed foreigners apprehended by police." "One of those officials," the officer adds, "would have gotten shot in another unrelated deal. Yet, no trace of fresh or coagulated blood on the pavement or anywhere near the stiffs."

Morgan tells his audience that the people were determined to elect Gérard Gourgue. That notion must have scared the shit out of some power-angry folks. And "the powers that be" decided to wash that idea off the voters' minds with blood. A pool of blood that the people will have supplied graciously, bravely, and abundantly.

"Same shit," History adds, "would have happened for Aristide had the people not learned and gotten smart."

"The whole Cyrano de Bergerac and Cleopatra's nose theory," he says, "could have applied for Gourgue and Haiti." "Afterward," he continues, "Aristide? What a fucking moron! I'm just saying."

"Ah, partner!" Morgan quickly replies. "That was not called for."

The partnership of History and Morgan has only one boundary that it never crossed. That limit it is Jean-Bertrand Aristide about whom they do not talk. That comment almost puts an end to Morgan's show. Morgan, who likes Aristide, asks his partner to respect the former President, be it only as a man.

"Shit!" History says. "That motherfucker ain't shit. I ain't scared of him. Bring that old fart up here, and I will tell him right to his big mouth that he is a fucking piece of shit."

To the French soldier, History whispers that his biff with the former President is in part, about money he lost in some financial fraud the President had championed. But, only to have a bunch of crooks buy real estates in countries as far as Taiwan. He will not say that to Morgan, who will defend the President.

"Folks should also ask where is that fucking money," he would tell Morgan.

CHAPTER 6.

Bloody Sunday

That date," officer Morgan Freeman starts hoping to calm his partner down, "will remain as a nightmare in the recollections, hearts, and minds of the people. An image of death and slaughter that brings havoc in the collective consciousness and psyche. The carnage was the type of shit a reasonable person would never fathom. Nobody with a full deck would think it could ever occur. Let alone imagine that the minds of human beings could conceive of such." At the same time, History silently speaks the same words. He is aware that his partner paraphrases a journalist from Jeando's radio station in a broadcast on the first anniversary of that massacre. Many thousands of Haitians, that journalist narrated, decided to take the destiny of their country into their own hands while holding a voter identification card. At least, that was their hope. But with the courtesy and murderous cooperation of the army, folks in the streets would see and experience the unthinkable. So much for getting in lines to vote for whom they thought would help change their condition and the country's destiny. The army's tanks would be shielding gangs armed with all sorts of weapons instead of protecting the people.

The voting cards the people carried in their hands were symbolic of all the changes they had hoped for regarding the outcome they collectively sought. They had hoped for freedom of speech, a better life, better education, justice for all, and a holy host of other grievances. Honky-dory, right? But should one ponder former president Martelly's analogy with the experience of another musician like himself, how would Mr. Gourgue measure up within such a man-eater of a system?

Though they all had a terrible and sleepless long night on the eve with endless gunshots of intimidation all about them, they came out in droves. All these hopes were to be crushed in a matter of minutes. The mercenaries would assail the people on many fronts at the voting centers. And, many of them will testify that they saw the military engaging in the barbaric and deliberate act of slaughtering their brothers and sisters.

From all the polling stations, many voters were reporting what they witnessed in the streets. Early in the morning, many had voted at a precinct in Delmas housed in a religious school, amid the nerve-wracking gunshots from a suspiciously moving vehicle. A few minutes after, that vehicle would be identified at another polling place where it got bloody and deadly very quickly. Civilians who went asking some military for assistance and protection were told that they could not even defend themselves. Though it was not the only place where the blood ran along the streets, Rue Vaillant will forever be the symbol of that massacre, which took place in three separate chapters. Reports mentioned that early in the morning, a passing car opened fire on the crowd waiting in front of the school of Argentine Bellegarde for the precinct to open. Propitiously, no one was hurt, but a Dominican cameraman, Carlos Guyon, died on the spot. Later, one election official declared that he was perplexed. A "white woman," he did not know at the time was Mrs. Massim, had lobbied the Council on the idea of retaining this particular school as a voting center.

By now, it is already water under the bridge. The old officers had decided long ago before this date that they had been partners in the force longer than the former priest had been involved in the country's politics. In fact, even before he was ordained, the two, with all their hair and virility, were breaking their teeth under Nickesse's grandpa, chasing "The Kamoken." His adversaries were coming at him from all sides. Duvalier, the elder, had thought of a brilliant way to have the free preparedness, cooperation, and determination of a not-so-bright populace to help him fight them. Putting faces on his many enemies, Papa Doc embedded in his definition of the term Kamoken: "Individuals who only wanted to plunder and violate the commonality." He also took care to incorporate in his description the raping of wives and daughters. Who would not subscribe to become a Volunteer of the Security National?

Words such as the ones History used to disparage the former President, have flown past and between the partners before. They proudly carry some mental scars proving they survived even the tumultuous and fragmented presidencies of the ex-Salesian. They had resolved that their respective opposite feelings toward Aristide can, in no way, part them. In that vein, History approaches Morgan and whispers in his ears.

"I had heard of the place numerous times," Morgan resumes with the second installment of the carnage. "Including the time Granddaddy Doc ordered that massacre there. Nonetheless until that Sunday morning, at Rue Vaillant, I have never met anyone from there."

"It was around 6:10 in the morning. I stopped at the turn of the street," Morgan adds, "to light a cigarette near the sign with an arrow that read: BUREAUX DE VOTE."

"This was," says Morgan, "when I noticed that thousands of people dressed in white had already formed the line that goes up the block to end at the angle of John Brown Blvd (Lalue). Earlier at the end of March of that year, Haitians thought they needed to purify the country from Duvalier or anything and anyone related. They had established a new constitution that the consensus called the people to dress in white to vote in a referendum. This morning also they are in white, symbolic of their final divorce with dictatorships, or so they thought."

At the very end of the line stands a young pregnant woman of almost a blond skin complexion with green eyes who runs her hand onto her belly. Morgan and History had agreed to meet at this exact corner. Since foreign journalists overran the country, in particular, the capital, the partners, at first, assumed that she could be one. As they approached, they noticed that the woman wears no identification badge as visibly do the members of the press. As the officers speak with her, they are surprised to detect no manner of a foreign accent. She tells them she is just a Haitian girl from Cazale. She is eight months into her gestation. As Morgan speaks with her, History is puzzled at the way she looks deep into his eyes as she smiles. *Was she flirting or just posing for a close-up portrait? A strange behavior*, the policemen later agreed.

"Some strange shit," History told Morgan.

The precinct had opened. The line starts to move. The officers now are about their "duties," and by the time the pregnant woman gets at the gate, it's close to seven o'clock. She sighs as she finds out the line of voters turns around in the front yard, and many voters had joined behind her since the time the police officers spoke with her when she was last in the line.

It should be a sunny day, and the heat and humidity are starting to be felt. The street vendors are now all about offering their merchandise yelling out "papita," patés, roasted peanuts, etc. A man with a blue V-neck shirt under his white dress shirt gives a five-gourde bill to a young man who hands him a bottle of Cola, which he sends down with one shrug. With the wisdom or senselessness that thirty-six years can add to a man, History must have imagined what he now takes over from Morgan to tell the gathering. As a disclaimer, he warns that he could not have seen the army General sipping his Barbancourt before phoning these macabre orders to this young man, Tito Massim. The two partners remind their audience that they only attest to what they witnessed as two lowly and helpless officers at the time. They will also tell the audience how they felt when Jeando opened a can that embarrassed them for being part of the police force, that tragic day. The two of them are incomparable, but History is impressive in telling this part as he vividly remembers every little detail and even insignificant things he does not convince himself to have seen that day.

A single line of sweat glistens near the pastry vendor's eye as he walks along the path of the voters in the street with a yellow straw basket under his arm,

"Hé Patééés! Patés!" yells the man just before a voter in the line calls him.

The vendor moves the basket to his left forearm and pulls a red piece of cloth to wipe the sweat off his face. As he now walks back, facing Lalue, toward where he was called, a truck full of masked men in black outfits turns at the intersection and speeds up the street firing at the people in the line.

Inside the gate, panic sets in as the people are now familiar with the tactic aware of what can occur as they are boxed within the walls of that school turned polling center. A young man who had just voted comes out of the precinct. He appears ecstatic, not knowing that both his euphoria and first-time vote would count for zilch and not even a rat's ass.

"Yeah!" he shouts before kissing his inked thumb and raising his arms in victory.

He takes a step and receives a bullet in the middle of his forehead. He falls with his head on the ground and his legs up the steps. The commando storms the yard as the voters scream in horror.

"Roye! My God! My God!" the voters cry. "Jesus, Marie, Joseph!"

Moans and groans here, there, and everywhere. Blood splashes the walls as the voters fall all about the yard.

"I know him. Chapo is not his real name," History says, introducing the gathering to one of Tito Massim's most loyal and blood-angry acolytes. He was Tito's classmate when he showed up in school with a hat claiming Papa Doc himself came to his house and placed it on his head. And just like that, this name stayed with him, and in 1987, he still wears the hat.

Like his boss, Chapo is also twenty-eight years old of a deep dark skin complexion with one front gold tooth that he licks periodically. After he shoots that young man, he takes off his hat, pulls off his mask, and brandishes a machete. Another voter starts running by and passes him toward the gate but trips and falls to the ground. Chapo pulls out his gun, steps over the voter, and blows his head off, gushing blood over his own face.

He runs his tongue on the gold tooth as he wields the machete above his head as if to ask who's next. He pans the yard with his eyes while in the truck near the entrance, behind the wheel, Tito puts on a mask and gets out with a machine gun. Tito needs the cover that allows him to continue being one of the country's most law-abiding businessmen who should be in good standing with everything on the surface. By trade, the Massims are all in the pharmaceutical business. Be it just a front, they maintain a good relationship with society to the point of even giving free medications to the poor who cannot afford to pay for them. Saddam Hussein has been an excellent papa for most.

Like a man on a murderous mission, he walks toward the voters and shoots right in the street. Standing in the middle of the courtyard, Chapo looks for his next kill as he sends a frightening smile in the pregnant woman's direction. Now, the woman is midway toward the office entrance. With the mercenaries around, what are her chances and anyone else's ever to reach it and go along with the people's resolution and elect Gerard Gourgue? Not a chance in hell. If Rue Vaillant was not already hell, wherever those thugs came from was and they brought to that schoolyard a big chunk of it with them.

In the eyes of his boss, Chapo is a legend, and he is about to prove it. Perhaps Tito had the time to notice the pregnant woman at approximately the same instant Chapo's intense attention is drawn to her. Maybe, he was trying to save her. And if not really, the dash Tito suddenly takes to get to Chapo does not suggest otherwise. Tito rushes past a voter who had probably thought of being a hero. The man had found a slice of a cinder block that he could use as a weapon. He raises his hand to strike Tito in the back of the head. Had he, the Syrian would be done for. Maybe in the upper corner inside his dark sunglasses, Chapo perceived the movement behind him. Without hesitation, he turns around and fires a shot that breaks the rock and destroys the voter's hand in the process. Tito quickly turns around and shoots the voter while Chapo keeps his momentum on the way to assaulting the woman. Afterward, Tito remembers he was about to save her. But she is already on the ground.

"You're one sick fuck," shouts Tito. "But…thanks."

"Yeah," says Chapo, ignoring whether his boss acknowledged him for saving his life or for whacking the young woman.

The massacre lasts from three to five minutes but leaves a carnage that would require a longer time of military hand-to-hand combat. This was, however, an unfair combat pitting voting card versus guns, machetes, and other types of weapons.

As the voters fall, the white wall rapidly changes to a macabre red with blood spatters. That blood flows beneath a pile of injured people, some already dead in the middle of the yard with voting cards scattered all about.

"In the street," History continues, "a skeletal dog eats the pastries from the lifeless vendors' baskets. A vendor lays face down with a hole in the back of his skull and blood running from his mouth."

Tito and his men would come back for the third episode of the bloodshed. They had to finish off the wounded they left in a rush to go kill more voters at a nearby station as they crossed paths with the first responders at the angle of John Brown and Vaillant. Witnesses reported that at that corner where the partners first laid eyes on the pregnant woman, an army truck was parked apparently to monitor the mercenaries. The door opens hastily before the Red Cross minivan stops. The paramedic descends as he thrusts his foot into a trickle of blood flowing along the gutter. With difficulty, wounded, out of breath, and in pain, a young boy, probably a more inexperienced street vendor, stumbles and arrives at the van. The rescuers start to administer medical care to him. Suddenly, the boy points toward the pregnant woman who is barely moving and asking for help.

"She lives!" the boy yells. "She lives... she's alive!"

CHAPTER 7.

Born Among the Dead

It is Monday morning. They had been traveling for three hours but had not gotten much far from where the trip departed. The chest of this beautiful 30-year-old voluptuous blond is one of the things inside the Wagoneer that could tell of the condition of the poorly if ever, maintained dirt road they are traveling on. The American couple must hang tight, obliged by the sudden and dangerous movements of the vehicle. Visibly, they had never ridden on such bad roads in their entire lives. The driver, however, is the least concerned about the road's condition. As a member of the disbanded army of the country, he's driven the FADH trucks to and from Les Irois on numerous occasions. Today the born-again former Tonton-Macoute is a churchgoer. He serves as the driver for this couple, the friends of a friend from the congregation. To that friend, he offered to take the visitors to that remote locality considering the dangerous driving conditions along with the electoral and political climate.

Dorothy McLintaugh jumps everywhere on the seat.

"You-know-Ed-Ah!" Dorothy says in her "bad roadly" fractured voice. "Pity. Ah! We couldn't have the child with us."

Like Peter Ekstroem in December 2022, this FBI agent is well aware of what is happening around him in Haiti in November 1987. He knows it is an election weekend but the reason that has him and his wife in the country could not wait and would not have them in the capital. For that purpose, they have chosen to get off the grid. They needed to disconnect from all irrelevancy with what has commanded them in Haiti for these five days. From the driver and others around them, they sort of understand that things went exceedingly bad in Port-au-Prince the day before. Now, Dorothy's husband, who is in the front seat, scans the radio dial for news. At this hour, he is perhaps searching for one familiar voice.

"Sweet…heart," he says, "the Lord knows why we're childless. He will provide… Won't he, my brother?" he asks the driver.

"Praise the Lord, Brother Ed," the driver answers with a thick Haitian accent.

Edward McLintaugh is a twenty-nine-year-old third-generation FBI agent. He is not on vacation in Haiti with his wife. The adoption case summoned their presence in the country at approximately around that time in November. The Caribbean nation is not the "first world" they are used to where one learns of the gender, and the exact date babies are to be born months in advance. In the United States, his colleague Peter Ekstroem and Ed work with Edward Sr., Ed's father. They toil on inventing a high-tech method that will use memory distortion through hypnosis in investigations.

In that remote part of the country, one thing is sure for a woman in gestation. When the time comes, it does not matter if it's windy, sunny, or stormy. The baby will come out. She is going to pop, no matter what. The couple expected to rush back to the United States with the pregnant young mother. They had intended to finalize the adoption as mother and child would be receiving the urgent and intensive care they need. They had strictly followed the advice of the doctor they sent to visit the teenage gravida 1 para 1 that finally resulted in a stillbirth over that boisterous weekend. Ed remembers the pain and suffering they witnessed in Les Irois. He sets the dial and sits back.

The jingles and sound bites that kept Richard Brisson alive long after he was killed early in the 1980s now fill the cabin. The vehicle enters the last portion of this road from hell toward the capital city. As the couple speaks and writes the French language, they feel more at home now as the station is about to present the morning editorial. They try to accept the fact that they will go back to DC childless as they left, hopeless to ever conceive due to a particular medical condition.

RADIO

The events of the world. The pulse of the nation. The Journal of Radio Haiti…

The lyrics of the jingle are oft confounded with the emperor's "Call to Arm." Duvalier's Tonton Macoutes had grasped them as theirs. Poor thing. They have never been that. In French, they loosely translate as "All the news of the entire world on Haiti Inter and for all Haiti." These sound bites usher onto the airwave the voice that probably almost the entire country awaits every morning. Today, perhaps, the whole nation plus two look forward to what journalist Jean Dominique aka "Jeando," will say of the massacre that yesterday halted the dream of forever divorcing from Duvalier. The "two" on that list being Edward and Dorothy McLintaugh, who know Jeando on a personal level since his father introduced him to Dominique many years prior. The elder McLintaugh and Jean Dominique met in Paris as the former perfected his craft as an agronomist. That was perhaps the reason why Jonathan Demme, the director of *The Silence of the Lambs*, had titled his 2003 documentary on the career of Jeando *The Agronomist*.

Jean Leopold Dominique was the owner of the country's first independent radio station, Radio Haiti-Inter, which he founded in 1960. Months earlier, after the July 1987 massacre of peasant farmers by landowners and some Macoutes in the northern region, Jeando allotted considerable airtime to it. The country expects he will devote as much time and examination to Rue Vaillant. Despite the military's attack on the station, Jeando does not disappoint.

JEAN DOMINIQUE

Good morning! It is seven o'clock. Yesterday, at Rue Vaillant, hundreds of brave voters, armed only with a voting card, have fallen to criminal machetes and bullets. If no one dares say it, I, Jean Leopold Dominique, am accusing "them..." The military and their accomplices unjustly slaughtered those poor and brave men and women. As citizens of a sovereign nation, they fell yesterday in the exercise of their God-given rights. In this massacre, ladies and gentlemen, everyone can see the hands of Generals Namphy and Regala....

The road is now flat. The Wagoneer drives in a dry powder in front of a massive and impervious cloud of dust.

Mid-afternoon. The journalist had long ended his broadcast. Jeando comes out of the station and walks around the front end of his car when the jeep covered with dried mud, and dust pulls up next to him. Jean turns around as Ed gets out and walks toward him with his arms open, and they hug.

"What a carnage yesterday, huh!" Ed says in French as he exits the vehicle.

"Those bastards," Jeando replies. "The military. They want to stay in power."

Ed places his hand on Dominique's shoulder in a compassionate gesture.

"In a hurry, Jeando?" he asks.

"To a particularly unique and sensitive case," Dominique replies. "Yes, I am."

"Ride with us," Ed invites. "We agreed to meet yesterday. The events and our adoption case kept us in Les Irois longer than we planned."

They hop in. The doors close, and the vehicle drives away.

Hopeless and worn out, Mrs. McLintaugh had fallen asleep ever since they had reached the paved road. Perhaps her mind played that weird trick on her. She had started sleeping a little after Jeando came on the air. As Jeando spoke on the radio, the brain may have placed her in the studios with Dominque and Michele who stands behind her with a hand on her shoulder. As the journalist presents his rant of an editorial, she sees herself in the flesh, in his wife's seat, assisting and listening. She would finally wake up to the man sitting next to her in the back seat, talking to her husband. Well, the driver has never gotten that close to Dominique as he confesses quickly to the radio icon. A born-again Christian, he reveals the only time and the closest he has gotten to Jeando. "It was," the driver says, "seven years ago." He drove an army truck filled with the soldiers who were ordered to shut his station down in 1980 during Baby Doc's reprisal.

Sensing the driver implores his forgiveness, Dominque reaches out to tap him on the shoulder in a comforting fashion with his right hand.

"Like the lavender, my friend," Jeando soothes him with class and elegance, "I leave my perfume on the heels that crush me."

The kids stop their street soccer game so the automobile can pass. It drives through and turns left as Dorothy wakes up completely.

"Oh, Jeando!" she exclaims. "I've been sleeping for how long, Ed?"

"Long enough," answers Ed. "Long enough, dear."

Late in the afternoon, the day before, Dominique and his staff took to the streets to survey the extent of the army's carnage. This or fate brought him to the school at Rue Vaillant, considered by most to have received the brunt of the day's premeditated violence. Once there, Jeando finds himself embroiled in a rescue effort assisting a doctor trying to save a bleeding baby boy from within a severely injured young woman. That rescue could not wait to be done even at the nearest medical facility. Doctor Pierre accomplished that feat right in that court as other rescuers helped the victims still alive, and the others, not so fortunate, were wrapped and conveyed to the morgue.

It is sweltering, and the odor is horrible. Jeando and Ed are walking very fast, and behind them, Dorothy grapples to keep up as she appears astounded by the poverty around her. Many of the wounded from the eve's massacre still fill the hallway hoping for care. The insalubrious environment jumps at the foreigners' eyes. In these situations, Jeando always feels awkward as he questions his country's worthiness of being the first independent black nation on earth. Deep in his guts, the journalist is sickened. Everywhere, at any level, the country displays such deficiency, commonness, and above all other things, the leaders' unrepentant disrespect for human lives, for human dignity. "A brazen disrespect," he calls it, "for the lives of our fellow natives."

Doctor Pierre, who speaks only French, meets them halfway. Jeando takes off his signature black leather cap, shakes hands with the doctor, and introduces Ed and Dorothy.

"How is she today?" Jeando asks.

"Not well," answers the doctor. "Horrible, Mr. Dominique."

They get near the bed where the young woman is unconscious with a weak signal on the heart monitor. The condition of the young woman reminds Dominique of the awkward conversation he just had in the car with his American friends about the loss of the infant they had hoped to adopt.

"And her child?" whispers Jeando to the doctor.

Nonetheless, Jeando's inquiry is perceptible enough to Dorothy. She suddenly becomes excited, forgetting the awful roads, the trips to and from Les Irois, the painful stillbirth, and the loss of the infant. Already, she is running in her mind the thousand and one things that could.

"Can we see the child?" she asks with the excitement of a little girl.

Through the window of the makeshift NICU, the doctor looks at the young woman then at Dorothy as if he could read the love the blond woman was sending out.

"I birthed the boy in that yard near many dead bodies," says the doctor. "The blade that sliced the mother also cut his little finger. He'll be okay with a lot of care and love."

"Any family came looking for her?" Jeando asks.

"No one. The girl lives…"

The segments on the heart monitor flatten out on the line, and the doctor swallows the rest of his sentence.

"Well," he rectifies himself, "she was living alone in the city. One girl here who knew her says she was from Cazale, you know, that old Polish town, and was a maid in some mulatto [sic] folks' house in Petionville. She was let go after she became pregnant."

Ed bites his lips, and under his breath, he lets out simple words: "Poor girl! She's dead."

"Ed, we could care for the child," suggests Dorothy.

Ed also runs a million things through his mind but wordlessly reminds Dorothy that he is, at the minute, the lucid one in the association.

"That's an idea, Jeando," he says. "But we leave tomorrow. No time to do it legally."

"Not if you go to the US embassy now," Dominique replies.

"I can give them a letter," adds Dr. Pierre, who leaves as the employees get in to take the corpse away. Jeando stops them. With moist eyes, he looks at the body. He is reminded of a passage he read a long time ago from one of Victor Hugo's works when another Jean, Jean Valjean, towered over a dying Fantine. Without noticing it, he plays it out.

"Though I never met you in life," the journalist says, "I give you my word. Your child will be in good hands."

He turns to Ed, who also looks familiar with this part of *Les Misérables*. However, Victor Hugo is the last thing on his mind now that he sees a chance to have his wife's sanity back. To have this blond Haitian baby finally in the United States with them as their child.

"McLintaugh," says Dominique, "go to the embassy right away. I'll take care of everything on the Haitian side for him to be your child by tomorrow."

As a journalist, Jeando knows well the ins and outs of the system. He knows whom to call in any situation. He has done favors for Mrs. Jean-Philippe, the head of the Social Welfare Institute, the institution that oversees such matters. These favors probably include many that neither Mr. Jean-Philippe nor his female counterpart would be too delighted to read about in this book. Today, she must return the favor.

The American couple walks quickly toward the exit when they meet the doctor, who hands an envelope to Ed.

"And the funeral?" Ed asks, a bit too excited and loud for the setting as he turns to Jeando after two steps.

"Mind the child. I'll see to it," says the journalist.

The Americans take off running.

Dominique sits on the edge of the bed, takes off his hat, and runs his fingers through his hair. He gets up and goes to the door and looks at the employees carrying the corpse away.

CHAPTER 8.

The Fall Of 1991 In DC

It was not such a long trip, after all. But the leg from JFK to Dulles lasted two eternities in Dorothy's mind that could not wait to see herself home with the infant finally hers. Legally. That would have to wait. The circumstances had her monitor the infant with the help of a young Haitian nurse from the Georgetown University Hospital who traveled to the country to vote for her former professor, Mr. Gourgue. Dr. Pierre had requested his niece's assistance in flying with the baby and the McLintaughs. After much lifting on Jeando's part and the parts played by all his essential contacts and connections, they arrived at the international airport in Port-au-Prince quite a bit late, courtesy of all the formalities. The baby's condition and the telephone call from this influential and affluent friend, who had never left the country after the fall of Duvalier, constrained the airlines to buy them an extra forty minutes. Usually, flights from PAP to JFK go smoothly.

However, they were mid-flight aboard their connection to Dulles when the baby started to exhibit the signs of extreme cyanosis. Made aware, the flight captain arranged for an ambulance to be on the tarmac as the plane lands. Ed, Dorothy, and the nurse rode with the baby in the back of that ambulance to the Children's National, Georgetown University Hospital. The infant was rushed straight to the Neonatal Intensive Care Unit near which Dorothy spent most of her time in and out of the AT&T telephone booth. Despite their privileges as parents, they opted to let the nurse, Dr. Pierre's niece, in with the medical staff. They were petrified of going through with the frightening sight of their tiny bundle within this forest of wires and machines, helping him breathe as well as with other vital functions.

"Don't you worry too much, sweetheart," Ed said.

"Why do you say that?" Dorothy asked.

Like his father, Ed held a Ph.D. in Psychology, and both received their Master's in Forensic Sciences and Electronic Engineering. He was quick to observe how his wife had been behaving lately. Like a chain smoker would light up, she had made calls after calls to folks she had not talked to in years telling them selective part of her good news. She displayed the signs of a person under overwhelming pressure or fear from the ordeal concerning the baby's condition.

"The folks that you talk to on the phone," he replied, "sure can hear the excitement in your voice. Me, on the other hand, I'm here witnessing your immense fear."

Dorothy offered him just a smile when Ed pleaded with her not to worry too much. And, back into the booth, she would go. Later, some of Dorothy's phone calls paid dividends. The couple and a nurse led two visitors, her sister and brother-in-law, toward the neonatal ward, and they were allowed only to view through the glass window to which Dorothy did not object.

The visitors, Ed, and Dorothy gazed at the babies through the glass window. The sign on an empty incubator in the room read, "LEOPOLD MCLINTAUGH."

A blond nurse walked in, followed by the dark-skinned nurse who carried the blond baby, with his left hand wrapped in a blue dressing.

"Here he is! Oh Lord!" Mrs. McLintaugh said excitedly. "Our Leopold!"

The blond nurse caressed the cheek of another baby as bliss filled Dorothy's eyes through the window. Baby Leopold would spend close to two months at the hospital as Ed and Dorothy alternated to shuttle between their professional activities and the NICU ward. They praised and showered with gifts the Haitian nurse who had cut her vacation short to return to work. She would practically be, at the same time, medical staff and babysitter when Ed and Dorothy were away.

Meanwhile, in Haiti, the officials were hard at work. They tried to instill a false sense of security in the population who had not stopped echoing whatever accusations most of the "politickers" disclosed concerning the massacre at Rue Vaillant. The mysterious nocturnal fires no longer broke out around the capital. Although Tito Massim and acolytes remained on the payroll, they must have been asked to lay low. No more corpses in the morning until another actor, Roger Lafontant, would return on the political panorama and also enlisted the criminal expertise of the Syrian perhaps strengthened by praises and recommendations.

A lower rate politician, Constant Pongnond, took pleasure in calling him "the Hippo." But this beast, this monster, Leslie Manigat, was not a lightweight. No premeditated witticism intended. He is still and forever will be the unprecedented "political animal." Not anyone else.

Papa Doc himself acknowledged it. When he drove Manigat into exile, he admitted there was not enough room in the enclosure for two mammoth dogs at the same time.

The consensus was that many of the consequential candidates would boycott the elections the military announced for the month of January immediately following the massacre. In the early hour, "the beast" blends with the many calling for the boycott. By the late hour, he'd reversed. Manigat is all about a push. A Louverturian drive, he insisted as he justified his decision to suddenly be taking part in the subterfuge election.

"Masquerade, it was called," History reminds.

The date ultimately arrived, and the people needed no particular convincing to stay put. The generals and company carried on, and Leslie François St. Roc Manigat was elected President.

History is anxious to point out that there was a mistake somewhere in electing Manigat as the country's President and some rectification became a tall order. Who needed to rectify? The people? Manigat or the army? Although the new President was not unpopular, a functional fragment of the populace wanted no part of it. And that would not equate its nonparticipation to a mistake. Manigat's inaugural speech revealed a massively naïve "political beast." From that time forth, he failed to see his political stocks nosedive never to recover. A few years later, he could not outdo even the relatively mediocre René Préval in some future elections. "The keyword here," History clarifies, "is 'relatively' since Préval has proven to be one shrewd politician by completing two full terms plus some days as President. Something that the most self-opinionated, popular but contentious Aristide could not do 'twice' for himself.

Nevertheless, both Préval and Aristide failed as they tried to have their respective protégés elected. The latter could not have the country swallow his mum's pill of sorrowfulness, Celestin. The former choked regretfully with Maryse as a presidential candidate. Josaphat, a newbie on the block out of nowhere, knew how he got to be President. His predecessor, perhaps, dropped a better horse in the race. Now, was the mistake on the part of the army or 'the powers that be'?"

"Some in the know," History tells the peacekeepers, "would argue that the powers that be would never allow this noxious triangle to form right under their noses. Fidel Castro in Cuba, Carlos Andres-Perez, and, or later, Hugo Chavez, an emerging figure in Venezuela and Manigat in Haiti. Morgan, on his part, thinks that opinion regarding Manigat resulted from a damaging courtesy of Papa Doc. The generals made the political blunder in January. They rectified when they ousted Manigat in a coup d'état in June."

Meanwhile, in Washington, DC, Leopold rapidly grows up as though mother Nature put his pituitary gland in overdrive. He goes about doing it as fast as the political events unfold in his native country but behind a genetically guarded secret. People in their immediate entourage knew he was an adopted child but did not have the slightest idea of which country he was from. In eyes and minds, this blond infant could fit within the Bruce Springsteen's song. Besides, neither

Ed nor Dorothy is about carrying a sign vaunting that information.

Fast-forward a few years later. The political climate had taken many unexpected and surprising turns. The army generals Namphy and Avril gave the impression that they could restore the dictatorship. Perhaps we are wrong to think so, the elderly officers point out. No matter what he will later say in the books he writes and excuses he offers, Prosper Avril will have thrown a dictator's playbook at a future Prime Minister during the occurrence stamped "The Prisoners of La Toussaint." He made an example (Giulianism) of three dissidents among whom that eventual PM. Nowadays, many believe that could be a tall order to combat the rampant disrespect, the blatant lawlessness, corruption, and anarchy. During the past few years, societal values have practically disappeared and swapped with an unabashed deficiency in morality. Many openly wished the return of "the good ole" days of Papa Doc Duvalier, Nickesse's granddaddy, the officer reminds them.

"Now in 2023," Morgan adds, "the lesson in dignity, in political adulthood, and morality from the two young presidential candidates should be regarded as an excellent scourging to this generation and the ones before."

"I will credit," he continues, "Nickesse Duvalier. He gives a much-needed boost to the Duvalier repute with his concession to Lyzou."

He probably is the most ostentatious, pompous, zealous Tonton Macoute of the last days of the dictatorship. Roger Lafontant unheeded the soul-article of the newly adopted constitution banning him and all Macoutes from the country's politics. A colossal mistake repeated after the second overthrow of Aristide that the country will continue to pay for dearly. He returns with the pretentious rationale he had all the right to claim anything or something in that slippery post–Duvalier era.

Ask History. The foul mouth older police officer will tell you "that nobody said or did shit" about the return of Lafontant, which was a gamble in itself. He was, instead, allowed to even run for President. He tried to bully his way through the process at the onset of which he downplayed Aristide's popularity. With Tito Massim, he terrorized the priest's supporters. Massive explosions were heard at nightfall, and by sunrise, Tito's cadavers resurfaced throughout the streets of Port-au-Prince. He was ultimately proven to be no match for the former Salesian, who is no pushover. Roger grew desperate. After Aristide's victory and before his inauguration, Lafontant thought he would resort to the ill-conceived coup attempt against President Ertha Trouillot, the woman who was assigned to organize the 1990 elections.

Had he succeeded, drop by drop, the funnel would scatter out Macoutes from every hole where they went to hide in 1986. The first Duvalierist who would come back was in Paris, possibly in touch with Roger Lafontant up to the minute of his whacking in September of 1991, as you will read in a later chapter.

As the proud and happy parents of an adopted child from the country, in Washington, DC, the McLintaughs follow the events in Port-au-Prince closely. They have the highest esteem for their friend, the journalist who had helped them adopt the infant. With reason, they named the boy after Dominique's middle name, Leopold, and who has grown up to become one spoiled toddler. Ed and Dorothy would stop at nothing to give him anything. Leopold spends almost all his waking hours on the front lawn. There, the parents have installed a lovely and lively playground with a ton of different amusement toys, with the kids of his parents' close friends and, of course, Consuelo the Mexican nanny. Since it is already September, the main feature of that super playground is its disassembling ability, which had allowed the contractor to come this day and relocate it indoor. A clause in the contract calls for such twice a year until Leopold turns fourteen, long after the boy will have lost all enthusiasm for this type of things. However, it is a beautiful day, and while the men busy themselves about the playground, the toddler resorts to the first tire swing that Ed had hung on a tree branch. For some reason, anyway, the child has always shown his preference for the old-fashioned tire swing.

Dorothy smiled that afternoon when she looked at Ed pulling on the cord attached to the tree branch to secure Leopold on the swing.

"Hang tight now, big boy," Ed told the child who insisted he could swing the set alone.

"I can do it, daddy."

Dorothy closed the book in her hand. She adjusted her readers on the bridge of her nose and looked on anxiously as

Ed made believe that he was getting away as Leopold had wished.

"Ed! Don't leave him," Dorothy pleaded.

"Honey...," Ed assured her.

Ed pushed the swing a little and walked over to his wife, who felt that something had been bothering him from the look on his face even though he was all smile while he played with the child.

At the FBI that day, Peter Ekstroem hit the ceiling when the Bureau finally endorses the MIM (McLintaugh Investigation Method). After the sudden death of Edward McLintaugh Sr., the son continued on with the experimental work at the Bureau. For a good part, Ekstroem collaborated and consequently acquired a great deal of experience and knowledge. Enough to think he could branch out and undertake the invention of a similar method involving the mind and the memory in matters of federal inquiries. All the time he collaborated with the McLintaughs, Ekstroem also secretly worked alone to develop his version of the MIM. At that point alone, the two were similar. At the time he left and announced to the Bureau that, he too, was working on his own method, Ed Sr. thought of experimenting with sketch artists. They would quickly render from what an operator would read aloud to them. Such were the information and knowledge Ekstroem had from his collaboration with the McLintaughs.

In some circles, the belief is that the reason Satan gives so much importance to the human soul is that he does not know how to create one. Therefore, he cannot create a human being as well as he can create or conjure up an animal that does not need a soul. It is said that Lucifer had already quarreled in the preexistence and gotten expelled down to earth before man was. He had already had the opportunity to be taught how to create animals. Not humans. And, indubitably, not how to give them a soul. That is where we find Peter Ekstroem a bit after September 1991. He lacks the data, the recipe to bring to life his version of the method. Another variety of that belief spills into the folklore of the native country of Jeando and Leopold. Folks there will tell you that the wasp had bitten the bee right after it had learned from it how to make the comb. The bee got mad and took off without ever teaching the wasp how to produce honey.

At the unveiling, Peter Ekstroem grew uncomfortable when he discovered the innovations the younger McLintaugh had brought to the invention. Ekstroem had left McLintaugh to break his teeth alone in trying to invent his method with the limited data he had gathered. While Peter's invention still lingers with artist-rendered sketches, the MIM has projection capabilities onto TV monitors or giant wall screens. The information flow would come on the screen as it did in *The Matrix*, a 1999 Hollywood film. An operator would wear a gargle that transforms this data into vivid images that can be recorded and printed. Somewhat cumbersome. The MIM uses the properties of chemically modified electrodes or CME, like the ones used for medical purposes such as EEG, ECT, and ECG. They are also attached around the subject's head, heart, and mainly communicating with the limbic system before attempting hypnosis. Then, the operator practically gains access and can do as he wishes with the infinite number of mnemonic drawers within the mental universe of the subject. The patent application triggered some five or six congressional hearings, and it was made unlawful to change the subject's memory, but to distort it remained legal and commonplace. Positively, Peter could swear that he had heard the McLintaughs discuss CME. Still, he was kept aloof as to which properties of the electrodes were suitable for the invention.

Of Ed, Dorothy, and Peter. These three had known each other since high school and part of their college years. In fact, Dorothy and Peter were sweethearts two or three years before the football team QB swept her off her feet and away from Ekstroem.

Ed gave up pushing the swing as if to obey the orders of his boss, Leopold. He walked over to sit by Dorothy. She welcomed him with a smile, put an arm around Ed's neck like she was waiting for the moment to sit together for once to cherish their toddler.

"Some' wrong, honey?" she asked. "You look pissed."

"That prick, Ekstroem," Ed replied, "trying not to show anger or anything negative the boy's subconscious may pick up from how they, as parents, express them." He resorted to whispering near Dorothy's ear as he sat next to her.

"Peter's been a jerk since high school," Dorothy said. "What did he do now? Twelve years now, and he's not gotten over my marrying you instead of him."

"He's furious that the Bureau endorsed the MIM."

"Wow!" she exclaimed, hugging her husband. "Congratulations! That's good news. I thought the two methods were similar...."

"Yeah!" Ed replied, "Until he stopped working with me. His version needs sketch artists. And by now, you know what our system does."

They both looked at the boy struggling to swing alone. Dorothy got up and walked toward Leopold then turned around observing the face that the toddler made. A telling look that he was about to also scream at her: "Back off, I can do it."

"Ed," she said, walking back toward him, "Peter will stop at nothing to get even and get his method endorsed no matter what or how long it takes."

"These were his words, this afternoon," replied Ed with his arm on Dorothy's shoulders.

Dorothy returned to the swing, kissed the boy, and gave a soft push.

"Thank you, mommy," said the toddler, gently.

Ed quickly turned around with a somewhat suspicious gaze toward the two. Dorothy opened her arms and boastfully smiled.

"A woman's touch," she said.

CHAPTER 9.

That Day In History

Just a minute ago, Ed was again thinking of himself as a superhero or Mr. Universe. From the instant he jumped on the spin bike in his luxurious basement gym earlier in the cold DC morning, the thought has invaded his technologically rotten mind. Ed sure felt like a superhero too. For a few seconds, his mind told him that he was *Conan the Barbarian*, or precisely Arnold Schwarzenegger, pumping and buffing up in preparation for the role in the actual movie. Anyone else, who is that much of a fan, would put on a VCR tape of any film starring Arnold. Not our Ed McLintaugh. He interrupts his workout to take a half bath rapidly and with a bathrobe comes to sit at his desk in his study with a book he authored a few years earlier. As his mind ran rampant on the bike, he thought he would brush up on the hypnosis techniques about which he and James talked the day prior.

It was still before seven. Ed's moving about might have awakened Leopold, whose youthful mind may have connected with that of his father's in their superhero little adventure. Ed had quickly gotten deep and so fast into the gadgetry chapter he'd wanted to go over that he did not hear the toddler's little footsteps as he jumped down each stair. He might have had the idea that the child was coming down, but the thought quickly vanished from his mind. When the kid got down on the third stair to the last, Ed realized that the sound of the next footstep was taking longer. He instinctively lifted his head only to see Leopold striking the superhero pose, with his blue Superman sleeping suit and a red towel tied around his neck as a cape—red of the same hue as Ed's robe. Ed quickly realized that the boy's foot was on the towel. From that stair, the child had already jumped when the father precipitated to catch him for he thought he would fall hard. The child fell in front of Ed and flexed his small muscles. Ed had thought Leopold would cry because he saw that the boy did fall hard.

"I am Superman!" Leopold yelled out loud, and convincingly.

Ed startled when Leopold bent his little knees in preparation to jump to the living room floor. Thinking and fearing the worse, he had put down the book on the desk to rush to his help and catch him.

"Superman must fly, you know," Ed said.

Instead, Leopold giggled out loud as Ed picked him up by his flanks and flew him above his head like a miniature human airplane. He opened his little arms like the wings thereof. The father walked around the living room with the child in the air who imitated the sound of a jet engine. From Leopold's perspective, he was an airplane flying over a big city represented by the spacious living room. When Ed decided to return to his reading, he flew him toward the desk, which Leopold perhaps perceived as an airport. And, the image of an airplane on the cover of a book would amplify the child's make-believe. However, as they neared the desk, Leopold remembered that this was not about being an airplane. He clenched his fist forward and shouted again that he was Superman.

Ed put him back down so he could continue to research in the book whose cover read: *Forensic Hypnosis, Memory & Gadgetry* by Ed McLintaugh.

He pinched Leopold's cheek and whispered a mission into his ear.

"Now, little man, go wake mommy up."

That mission was hurriedly aborted in Ed's mind when he lifted his head and realized that Dorothy probably watched the whole Superman/airplane flying scene. She watched from upstairs with a door half-opened. When she heard her husband give the command to Leopold, she quickly but softly shut the door, thinking she would now engage Leopold in a hide-and-seek adventure. As Leopold ran up the stairs to Dorothy's room, Ed's mind quickly took him to Port-au-Prince. Especially, to the Friday before as the Haitian President delivered his provocative and explosive rant upon his return from his first trip to the United Nations.

During Moïse Josaphat's first UNGA trip in 2017, New York's Haitian diaspora gave him a piece and fragment of their minds. Quite the contrary, Jean-Bertrand Aristide, in 1991, was welcomed and spoiled in the Big Apple by the authorities and Haitians from almost everywhere on and near the US East Coast. Ed thought that perhaps the grand reception and Aristide's wandering mental perception of his performance at the UN podium had gotten to his head. He might have believed that he had conquered the world and that it was legit to give that scornful speech telling his supporters to follow their guts and do as they pleased. In McLintaugh's mind and in that of followers, such statement registered as the President suggesting looting. When they needed food, shelter, and even fresh air to feel free to go up the mountains around the capital and breathe like "them." Take all of what they need. Ed found it repulsive and reckless for a country's President to ask his illiterate, violence-bent supporters to give "them" what "they" deserve. Despicable it is when a President alludes to "the pleasant" smell of human flesh burning in gasoline-drenched car tires.

Ed remembers a visit with Jeando that he and his parents took when he was much younger as a freshman in college. He recalls the road to Petionville covered with flamboyant green trees that becomes a red ceiling over the street around the summer months. These trees helped drop the temperature considerably on the road to and from Petionville. The city's temperature was also cool and, at times, crisp. Today, it is not the case. A freaked out and paranoid President might have ordered the trees cut so choppers above could follow his motorcade as he travels along the Bourdon road. Petionville has become foul-smelling, dirty, and hot as hell. When one looks up the hills around the capital, the ugly panorama, the clusters of pathetically built slums, stands as a loud reminder of all the ugliness in that post-UNGA rant of 1991. *What a fucking moron!* Ed thinks soundlessly. He wonders why his mind jumps so much this morning without him making an effort to take control. Is it that he enjoys it?

Leopold had gone up the set of stairs very fast and gotten inside Dorothy's room, and the second the door was shut, the telephone rang. Perhaps, a bit too loud for this quiet morning.

"McLintaugh!" Ed answered. "Ah! Jeando!" he continued as a short moment of silence ensued.

"Gee! Another coup?" he asked.

This morning, the military had just ousted democratically elected President Aristide in what by the minute was turning into one of the bloodiest coups in the region. Army General Raoul Cedras aided by Biambi and Police Chief Michel François assumed the control of the country. Ultimately, they would leave the power to the most ancient judge. In the receptor, the machine guns were going off as Dominique begged his friend to listen to what was happening in Haiti, around him.

"Do you hear, McLintaugh?" Jeando asked many times. "Do you understand, McLintaugh? Do you listen? Those bastards, those sons of bitches are shooting at my station."

Ed was saddened by what he heard from his friend, but as Aristide went, he could not help but utter the words: "The son of a bitch had it coming." Like father like son. The elder McLintaugh believed that had Cedras not kicked the bastard out, he would have been perceived as less than a military man. As he listened, Ed untangled the long telephone cord that ran from the base in the adjacent room. He also made a mental note not to voice to the journalist all his feelings toward the ousted President whom he despised. Jeando was a personal friend of the priest and had actively campaigned for him less than a year prior. The time for the cooling off of that friendship had yet to arrive

"That interview," History says, "which would turn their friendship sour and upside down will inevitably take place. Stay tuned."

Ed reaches for the remote control, and a news broadcast comes on. Morgan Freeman sends signals that he, too, would dismiss the death of Roger Lafontant in the wake of that September 1991 coup as did and still does the rest of the country.

No one seems to care about how this man died. Nobody inquires as though no one gives a rat's ass. In fact, Lafontant's death will not be the only assassination with political overtones at the time of the coup. A few diplomats must intervene and negotiate with a pack of wolves. The object: to spare the very life of the President as Daniel Toumain, along with former president M.F. Gibéa, heads to Les Cayes. Their intent is clear and straightforward. To kill Sylvio Claude, the most popular leader in the country. The reverend has the following capable of scaring the "heebie-jeebies" out of the deposed Aristide, or anybody the now powerful and arrogant weapons men may impose as a puppet president.

Morgan Freeman favors this part as it explains Sylvio Claude's assassination because it does not directly involve President Aristide. Notwithstanding, his buddy Gibéa, has really made the trip to Les Cayes. Every time History would try to accuse the President, his partner would make it clear that a Haiti without Sylvio Claude was most profitable to the military. Toumain and the former President had a field day. They made it look easy to take down Sylvio. They easily whacked a man who had commendably weathered the Duvaliers before feeding him to a bitter, pro-Aristide mob eager to carry out what they had gathered from their "leader" in their vernacular language, only three days prior. As spoken as understood, it is said of the Haitian Creole language: the mob set fire on an already dead man.

Many, History included, attempted to pin Sylvio's death on Aristide on the sole basis that Toumain had always been in cahoots with the President. He may have issued such an order, they contend. An anti-Aristide, History could not feel at ease when Morgan almost totally exonerated the "priest-president." He would then insist on the other wrinkle that President Gibéa's taking the trip alongside the criminal entrepreneur added to the events.

It is inconceivable, Morgan thinks, that the President could have given such order. Aristide was in the middle of a predicament with the army general and his gang as, practically, they were deciding whether or not to kill him. Folks familiar with the events believe that when the general found the character a bit too cumbersome, he would ask his surrounding what they would have him do. "Kill the piece of shit," [sic] a quasi-unanimous reply would echo from within the rest of the pack. Supposedly, even the low-ranked soldiers wanted him killed. Perhaps to sell a human face like Dessalines may have done with the Polish story, General Cedras might have told that part to the world. That he personally saved the President's life that night in the thick of it all. Toumain and Tito were paid by the backers of the coup to eliminate this player, Sylvio, who would not put up with any of what the military would put the country through for the next three years. However, only Toumain and Gibéa traveled to Les Cayes. Mr. Massim had a special rendezvous at the national penitentiary with a high-profile guest there.

The older officer insists that before these elections, Nickesse's mother might have been on to something when she declared that the pastor did not die on her husband's but on Aristide's watch.

Ed McLintaugh had returned to his reading after talking to Jeando. Dorothy's door opened. She came out up to the last top stair with Leopold behind her. She looked concerned when she asked her husband why he had unusually turned up the volume while reading. But he had not been reading for a good while. Instead, Ed spent the last several minutes without reading a single word.

"I'm following the events out of Haiti," Ed told his wife. "There's been another coup by the military, and they threaten Jeando. He's considering leaving the country."

As Dorothy was about to ask another question, a photograph of Roger Lafontant appeared on the TV screen. Ed motioned her to wait, but he could not help uttering his disgust for the former Tonton.

"That son of a bitch," Ed said, to which Dorothy silently protested, jerking her head with her eyes aslant from Ed toward Leopold.

"Edward!" She yelled swiftly and softly.

Dorothy went back inside the room, and Leopold followed her. Ed continued to watch the broadcast announcing the death of Roger Lafontant, the former strongman of Nickesse's father, in his prison cell at the national penitentiary. If Lafontant came to prominence in the 80s, his first rodeo was not only then. Early in Baby Doc's dictatorship—"early" meaning as of November of 1972—he became the Interior and Defense Minister. Still, because of his political ambitions, he was handed a golden exile when he was sent away as an emissary to Montreal, in Canada.

As he watched the broadcast, Ed crossed his arms at first, then brought his right fist under his chin. Probably, at that exact time, he may have been the only person perhaps who cared to wonder who, why, and how that bastard got whacked on the day of the coup against an elected popular president.

That morning, before the rumor mills conceded to factual information, the capital was somewhat asleep but would soon wake up under an unmatched aftereffect. A bit before sunrise, *Word of Mouth TV* was on the air via the few remaining domestic telephone lines in the country. Folks learned of the coup against the President, who only the Friday prior was inciting his devotees in his incendiary rant when he returned from the UNGA.

"Winston Churchill once said," Morgan continues, "'Show me your prisons, and I shall say in which society you live.'" The elderly officer justifies his use of that quote with the fact that only a handful of occasions in the partnership he and History have been apart. They both seem unable to provide the exact periods. They insist though that Morgan was on duty at the prison when army General Cedras, "Sweet Micky" (not the musician), and Biambi overthrew President Aristide. The only proof they offer is the tendency of anyone who hears to believe the vivid and detailed account Morgan Freeman gives of that night and dawn at the pen. The citation stands as he tells his audience of the prison's demographics, a duplicate, or a representation of the societal makeup of the country at large and mainly what is the capital city. The nameless prisoners pack small cells that house ten, twenty of them in subdivisions. The divisions are given names like "cite Soley," "Lasaline," "Portay Leogane" after the worst or impoverished parts of the city. A cat like Roger Lafontant receives all the special treatment in the world. He was condemned a few months prior for his attempt to topple the government that piloted the last elections that saw the former Salesian ride a hefty 67 percent of the vote to the presidency. He enjoys a refrigerator and a TV set in his cell. The illustrious prisoner gets his daily newspaper delivered along with the menus from the various restaurants around the city. He gets to choose his meals. The block where his cell is located is named after Petionville, that city on the hill where most well-to-do families dwelled long before that President encouraged his supporters to invade places where others seemed to live better. For safety concerns also, businesses moved in. The wretchedly built shantytowns on the hills near and around Petionville bear witness. The midtown area that used to be a clean and quiet residential space is now a noisy, stinking marketplace. Beautiful Petionville is now home to a horde of people who were not born there. They ignore its culture and history and do not give a flying fuck about keeping the town clean as in the time of Max Penette, one of the city's past mayors.

CHAPTER 10.

Killing The Cat In Cell 8

Today, at the request of the warden, Pacho must run another telephone cable from his office into Roger's cell who expects for this night some crucial conversations with some folks in France. This Nigerian's real name is Uhuru Agwadewi. Because of his impressive physics, he tacitly commands respect from the other inmates who would not bother even to approach, let alone quarrel with him. He does not speak the country's language and, at first, did not know much of whom this pampered prisoner in cell number 8 is. He does not give a fuck. A friend of the warden's, the captain of a military prison and ally of the president, suggested that Pacho is put in charge of cell number 8. He is not likely to be intimidated either by the bald doctor or by the other inmates. Later, that captain will offer to testify that the president personally gave him the order to eliminate that guest. Uhuru, therefore, serves as a housekeeper, a distant companion, and a handyman to Roger Lafontant hence the long cable he'll run from the warden's office to facilitate these crucial conversations.

How Pacho ended up in the country and particularly in prison is an unbelievable yet actual story. The fall of Duvalier created the power vacuum the Colombian drug lord long sought to ensure the transition of his product into the United States. At the time, Pablo Escobar, who controlled more than 80 percent of the world's cocaine market making him $60 million richer every day, was scouting around the Caribbean for a route through which he could move some commodities. He needed a way station with the right mix of political instability, biblical poverty, and bribe-greedy officials. In his sight, post-Duvalier Haiti is the best option that will check out. Effectively, in a relatively short period, the Haitian military built and monitored the much-needed infrastructure, an airstrip outside Port-au-Prince for kilo-loaded planes. The cartel worked directly with Lt. Col. Joseph-Michel François, who, in 1987 alone, safeguarded 70,000 pounds of Escobar's nose candy through Haiti to America. For this, he earned a reported $4 million *(The Rise and Fall of Haitian Drug Lord Jacques Ketant by Kyle Swenson).*

When Uhuru landed in Medellin, he had one objective and was ready to do or risk anything to realize it. He flew there from New York City to somehow meet Pablo Escobar, hoping to work for him. What were the odds? Fortuitousness robbed him, that night, of the chance to do any of what he psychically readied himself to undertake to attain his aim. Pablo Escobar came to him after he took care of a particular lingerie affair. Pure coincidence had the drug lord pick him up at the airport. It was raining cats and dogs when he walked out of MDE onto the curb, expecting to hail a cab. The bulletproof SUV stopped, and he was invited in by Pablo Escobar himself just because of the monsoon. At least, this is the story he tells his folks back in New York and Nigeria. He perhaps also invented the name change, should a series of interviews he may have given Jeando be trusted. According to the version to which he stays blindly faithful, the drug kingpin always referred to him as "Pacho." Escobar believed he resembled the former head coach of the country's national soccer team, Francisco Maturana, except he, the Nigerian, had a more impressive physique to display.

Then came that time Escobar was looking around the Caribbean for that secure transit hub for his nose candy. He sent many of his minions to court the Haitian newly appointed officials. Supposedly, the Nigerian had gone way up the ladder of Escobar's trust. He became one of the people he sent to Haiti, where a certain colonel was the first of the bribe-angry military personnel who met with Pacho as he was introduced. No matter the level of his trust in somebody, Escobar always devised a sure way to have the last word. For Uhuru, it was never clear what Pablo had up his sleeve. Pacho rubbed the Haitian President the wrong way. Escobar may have refrained from pissing off the newly elected popular leader. Aristide, at first, gave the impression he could be somewhat a prickle, a nightmare for narco-traffickers considering his past rhetoric. Many officials in the first three months of the new administration mistook Pacho for a local operating on behalf of the drug industry and the military part of the junta for the last four years after the fall of Duvalier. Some placed a tight watch on the airstrip to the displeasure of the army men who were generating millions off that chapter of the industry. Ultimately, Pacho was apprehended and sent to the national penitentiary, but he stoically never questioned Escobar's silence and indifference.

This night, separately from running the telephone cable into Roger's cell, Pacho had been ordered to open the five adjacent cells to the right of number 8 and to briefly relocate their occupants elsewhere in the pen. The cell itself is always open, and that prisoner roams freely about the prison's perimeter, even stirring fear, intimidation, and, above all, with his known audacity, commanding respect from the inmates. Pacho, who did not know who the cat was, did not give a rat's ass and would not give in. Therefore, he was put over him and often would straighten him when he would try to be bossy as he is used to. That relationship worked perfectly. Roger could not say shit, and Pacho did not give any.

By the time the first shots were fired to signal that the coup to topple Aristide was in progress, Pacho had already done all that they had asked of him except opening the five cells. At times, Morgan would include a thought to taunt his anti-Aristide partner. Here, he would add that he couldn't think that at that precise moment, the president would be thinking of a list of folks to have whacked as the army's plan to depose him is underway. Morgan believes that President Aristide is innocent. The blood of the doctor and the reverend are not on his hands, although, in other cases, his suits' sleeves might appear drenched up to his elbows. If History could read through Morgan Freeman's mind, that cocktail of a belief would, at the same time, tear a crevasse straight into his heart and console him.

History wants either Aristide, Gibéa—"the two-headed snake"—or "sneaky" Cedras to have given the order to whack Roger. In private discussions, possibly after reading Gilot's take on the matter, he had lectured Freeman on why he thinks Aristide gave the order. Roger died three times; he would tell him with the former lawmaker's very words. When he failed to realize that he was alone in undertaking the forceful takeover of January 1991, he fuckin' died. He died again when a revenge-thirsty president stuffed a bogus courtroom, placed him and his accomplices in front of a partial judge, jury, and Lutetia "the blind woman." They were given only five recently graduated law students as their defense team. Lastly, but ironically, perhaps he had started to die his final death long ago when the father of Nickesse conceived of a wish early in his dictatorship. A military brotherhood instigated the coup. Feasibly, this was what Jeando meant when he told Aristide and Préval not to trust the army General and the others who surrounded him. They were from the same promotion of which Baby Doc handpicked the members among the sons of his father's friends in order to have military officials near his age after the death of Papa Doc.

"Do you think," he'd ask Morgan, "it was a marriage between Cedras and Aristide, or was it a political blunder on the part of the former?"

That question from the officer, or exactly what Jeando wondered in the editorial that, in part, may have pissed off that senator who may have also been part of that promotion. Although Roger had the repute of not being too fond of the army, he had probably facilitated the entrances of many into the academy. In turn, they would gratefully depose an elected Aristide and literally walk his number one foe, from the Pen to the palace. Aha! Thus, giving legs to this other speculation that would have Dr. Lafontant shot on the steps of the presidential palace putting on the trigger the finger of an uninformed military who smelled a mutiny at a glance.

History maintains that is where the order originated to the captain, who will write a report about it at the price of a few years of his freedom. The foul-mouth officer would contend that the military would have had not one tooth left to bite this ripe banana.

Tito, he would argue, had prior knowledge of the coup. He arrived in front of the prison at about the same time as the little squad sent by Sweet Micky. Why? To fetch Roger? Possibly to only free him out of gratitude or even, aware of the man's arrogance, to allow him to take charge of the coup? Micky did not elucidate that wrinkle with the army branch of the operation. The killer waits quietly in his vehicle as the correctional officers block the entrance, not allowing the Cafeteria squad to enter. They move on after a radio communication he could not hear, but he witnesses it. When the Cafeteria team comes back, it is too late. Here again, that rumor would have the Cafeteria squad bring Lafontant's lifeless carcass back, leaving the corpse in the yard in front of his cell. Rumor aside, the killer, the piper, had already gotten paid. This cat would have already died his final death.

Again, in private discussions, Morgan Freeman remembers the Cafeteria Squad grew in numbers when it came back. From within the squad, the new member, a soldier, walked straight and open one cell that was not in question that night. Out stepped a man who will cross the Dominican border within a few hours. In a matter of days, he will reach Florida. History knew the man. It was he who told his partner that man started as a lowly soldier to become Duvalier's driver from father to son. A French soldier tells the older officers of a seemingly fabricated story, he was told, that circulated in Paris. It was around the time a young priest was becoming an emerging figure on the country's political scene. The story alleged that some voodoo priests, advisors to Jean-Claude Duvalier, contacted French authorities with a bold prediction. Those men would have had Baby Doc sacrifice 700 young people from each of the country's departmental regions to remain in power. Those Haitian "Nostradami" predicted that Jean-Bertrand Aristide would be elected in 1990. He shall be an instrumental president who would revive an extended historical matter between his country and France, specifying that it'd be detrimental to the former colonizers. The Europeans apparently bought blindly into it.

Silent until now, the young local recruits, start to ask questions about that story they had never heard or read about. Officer Morgan, who had been in quite a few gatherings among the elite where things like this are often talked about, remembers having vaguely heard such an account. He deems himself clued-up enough to take a whack at the young local's query. However, he feels he could cruise through to get back to his account of that night Roger Lafontant was killed. French Intelligence had justly determined the predicted president could only bring to the surface the funds that France had extorted from his country. They knew that they had indeed crippled that young nation economically, socially, and globally. Though France put forth all sorts of bullshit, even recently through François Hollande, they secretly knew that such a claim would have some legs to stand on and continue its course. The verdict? Pre-emptively eliminate that threat, be it physically before he gets elected.

"Ha!" exclaims another recruit, "Then that could explain December 5th, 1990, in Petionville."

"I hope you can tell us more," says another.

"Alright!" says Morgan and sounding exactly, minus the Haitian accent, like the Morgan in *Shawshank*, as he formulates his response.

"Let me tell you some', my friend. 'Hope in this country is a dangerous thing.' Roger Lafontant enthralled himself with helping Jean-Claude Duvalier return to the country. To achieve that, he needed money, lots of it, and everyone knows that after his exit, Baby Doc was darn loaded. JCD would give anything to return to the country he loved so much, or so he thought. He must have gladly and guilelessly supplied the 'Plata.' However, greedy Lafontant wanted more and thought he would promise the French, for a fee, to get rid of the little priest before the elections of December. Supposedly, collateral came forth, and disbursements were made.

Perhaps to extort him as he pleased, he had even suggested a prearranged divorce from the former First lady as a *sine qua* non-condition for his return. Michelle was not the only problem or the sole reason JCD could not remain in power. Morgan believes that the persona, the humanity that made up Michelle was never a problem. Her greedy and heartless father was." History does not refute Freeman's claim. Instead, Morgan's partner would reference Mr. Bennett's bouts with Jeando each time the journalist would call him out in his editorials. So, the plan called for Lafontant to come back to Haiti and prepare Duvalier's return as president, at least. The "for life" coating would come maybe subsequently. But along the way, Duvalier genuinely felt swindled. Roger.Lafotant went after the presidency for himself, leaving Baby Doc high and dry on the curb holding the bag and submerged in debts. The officer cruised through his last words to resume his recounting of the atmosphere at the pen.

"Could Jean-Claude Duvalier also order Roger's death since he felt double-crossed?" asks another local.

"Yes, definitely. But not when the former dictator had only the skin on his butt and trouble paying for shit as he dragged his old mother's ass everywhere. Now, where was I?" he quickly asks as a way to dodge other rapid questions from the younger Haitian policemen and the United Nations' foreigners.

"Oh, yeah!" Morgan hurriedly utters. "Pacho was exhausted after the chores of the long night. Amid the orchestral *ra-ta-ta* of the military's machine guns, the gigantic Nigerian catnapped in the hallway near the night officer's quarter. Before he had fallen asleep, he'd tried to talk the me into letting him in on why he was asked to perform all of these chores."

Naturally, the night officer, presumably Morgan Freeman, did not have a clue. He invented a bullshit story that, in turn, Pacho will tell the prisoner with the red Che Guevara beret later. When he finally gets to the last cells, he was to open; the occupant thereof places his hand on the lock. It is not to prevent him from doing what he was told but to have his attention so he could ask him what the words were around the joint and whether some big shit was about to go down. Among all of Lafontant's prison neighbors, Pacho had a lot of respect for Serge. He had confided in him that during his time as a free man, he was a radio talk show host at his own station. Perhaps, the storytelling police officer could not know whether Serge told Pablo Escobar's former confidant who financed Radio Liberté. He even allowed the African to wear his beret for entire days. If Pacho learned facts about the country and the guest in cell number 8, it was thanks to Serge, who had always been reputed for having a big mouth.

Long before dawn. Few inmates had managed to snooze through the gun-certo accompanying the ouster. They were awakened by the loud and arrogant voice of the prisoner. He was now on his fourth of the night and possibly the last telephone call of his life. To this day, the older officer maintains that the first three calls that all lasted very long seemed to have been from the same person whom the prisoner kept referring to as "Excellence." Morgan thought of the only person this particular inmate could call such. Around that period, in France, Baby Doc was bathing in red ink and faced with lawsuits for unpaid rent. Indeed, it was then murmured by close associates that he even more seriously contemplated his return to the Caribbean. Nickesse's father ran up a huge telephone bill to achieve that goal, which he posteriorly abandoned. All the prison guards attest that the prisoner had received numerous calls from that "Excellence" character.

Jean-Claude was plagued. His hope to return to his home country faded. His unpaid rent, restaurants' checks, and huge telephone bills piled up. The lawsuits, the constant moves with his eighty-two-year old mother to cheaper and cheaper cribs that he couldn't pay, And, last but not least, there was the ouster of Aristide. His wife had already left and remarried; taking the kids. All these components shared one item in common: time. Not as in how long they lasted but in their completion.

If Pacho and the other inmates dozed through the telephone calls, Morgan should not and did not on duty. That is how he figured out that Baby Doc might have called three times that night and had all throughout his incarceration and perhaps. The Nigerian is awakened. Not by the prisoner's voice, but by the officer who hears a subtle footstep with a tempo that had never been heard at the prison before at this time of the night or morning already. However, it could have been the commotion created by the prison guards on the way to block the entrance to Micky's squad. Morgan wakes Pacho up and reminds him of opening the cells and relocating the inmates.

The feel throughout the entire facility changes. The killer entered the prison and will encounter no obstacle because the plan called for a quick two-minute job hence the tasks attributed to the African. According to what he overheard, the substitute night officer believes that whoever was on the fourth call knew the killer was coming to whack Roger.

"Shh! Be quiet and follow me," whispers Pacho as he opens Serge's cell while the killer's footsteps become more audible as he nears his target.

At intervals, the stillness at the prison is palpable when the bald prisoner allows his counterpart the time to put in a few words. When he does take over, Rosny Desroches, in his office at the College Bird, could have heard his loud tirade. The African hurried the five prisoners to make up for the precious minutes he lost snoozing. Probably, the intruder's image had had the time to be impressed on the outside periphery of Serge's retina, he being the last inmates following Pacho to their temporary cells to walk past the staircase's reinforced framework. James Madigan's forensic expertise would be instrumental in establishing that fact if Serge were alive today to sit on the couch. If no one cared to know who whacked that prisoner, it is interesting to remember that the complete image of that killer was, that morning, engraved on the retina of two inmates. One of them being relocated as one of the neighbors on the right to keep them heedless and let the killer work calmly. Pacho was instructed to lead them back to their cells via an alternate route. The word, however, quickly got out as soon as the prisoners returned in the cells. They heard the gunshots. There were plenty, but none recalled the bloody carcass in the yard near the prison cell where it was later photographed. In the realm of rumors, it could have really been dropped there by Sweet Micky's squad when it had later returned?

This has been the most prolonged period of silence since Baby Doc supposedly made his first call. Silence? Not really. The footsteps of the self-assured professional assassin still reverberated throughout the prison as an unusual, subtle noise. Beyond the prison's walls, gunshots sporadically go off in the distant yet near Port-au-Prince environs. The relative silence could be the result of R.L. actively listening rather than forcefully barking his thoughts through the telephone. Roger briefly looks at the phone as the caller may have announced that he's been beleaguered. His back is against the wall. The French feared the somewhat compromising dilemma they might find themselves in now that the army will retake the power in an announced bloody coup. History would remark that Mr. Lafontant may have learned of the coup through the last two callers, namely, JCD and whom, he contends, may have been his last finance minister. The former also deliberately proclaimed that Roger was just a sitting duck in his prison cell. Any moment now, that caller told him, someone he might not wish to see may visit him.

"Ah! Roger, Roger, my friend, why?" the caller asks. "Why are you mad at me?"

"Why? Why am I mad at you?" Roger replies angrily, wigwagging. He turns to face the wall, his back to the cell door.

Little did Roger know that the killer was nearer than he or the last caller thought. Gosh! He will not have a single minute to query about who his approaching killer could be. Cold sweat. Whoever was on the phone with him warned him. Although Roger has a Master in handling the endocrine system, cold sweat is all he can do about what's at hand.

"Imbecile, traitor, you knew. You fucking knew everything, and you convinced me to take the money. You led me into coming back here. Now, you ask me why? Still, now, I have not paid your guy. You'll pay for this, idiot!"

Roger fumes with rage as he violently hangs up and swiftly turns around to face the shiny barrel of a stainless gun. That horrible surprise, in less than a second, turns his life upside down, heating and moving the content of his stomach down to the very last section of his small intestine. All that internal movement in such a short span creates some heat-generating friction. Naturally, what's got to give must be in the form of sweat. The kind that, when passing through the pores, feels like a basketball being cogently shoved down into a golf hole. The resulting sweat rolls down his face and slowly dropped to the floor with the sound and impact of a ton of bricks, if one could hear it.

"Massim! Who paid you? Why you?"

This fatal surprise gives the shudders to Roger, who had never been at a loss for words but could only find these. He feels alone and isolated. He wishes he had not hung up now that his dispatched killer is before him in his prison cell. The two older officers agreed between them to find an explanation as to why Tito Massim found himself behind that gun in the cell. They understood then that it would take some deep digging to get to the bottom of it. And, they dug.

Since the rule of Baby Doc, teenage Tito enjoyed the friendships of all the influential folks who surrounded Nickesse's father. The officers believe that should all assumptions hold regarding the identity of the last caller, it makes perfect sense. That ex-official has indeed been very close to the Massims on both socioeconomic and genotypic standpoint. In fact, he is the absentee godfather of Tito's son, known as Qusay.

A European professional assassin was initially slated for the job, and the Secret Service would pick up the tab. He was supposed to land the night before, take a stroll around Petionville, spend a few hours in the casino at El Rancho, and be in the cell by breakfast in Paris' time. All the key players were to play their part to a T like Pacho. That "Made in Paris" deal involved Roger, one or both the callers, and the secret service. Upon his return, Mr. Lafontant found out very fast that it was not the same environment that he knew. He had faced great difficulty honoring his end of the bargain with the Europeans. He had used up the entire fund allocated to him and was not even able to pay Tito with whom he had a few nasty word fights.

R.L. had started to lose in blessings when he failed to kill the priest-candidate in Petionville, eleven days before the prediction of Duvalier's Nostradamus found a renewed importance. Jean-Bertrand Aristide became the first democratically elected president by the favors of some massive Toumain-sponsored irregularities. However, the priest's popularity alone would secure his victory. Even History, who witnessed it first-hand, agrees that Aristide proved it time and time again. On his own, he could have conjured that 67 percent of the electorate he rode to the presidency. The man commands tremendous popular support.

Nonetheless, Toumain needed assurance. His thumb tips the scale all the way. Over the following years, the prediction would mimic the CAC 40 accordingly with events in Haiti. It started to take in some water when the coup occurred within only his few months in office. His original return in October 1994 and the completion of his term were causes for the prediction taking in some more.

However, behind a slogan, not at all dear to his predecessor and to journalist Jean Dominique, Aristide was again "elected" in 2000. These elections carried the seeds of what would cause dire economic hardships on all fronts. The president would play his joker hand as he did revitalize the contention the French had justly guessed years ago. According to History, Tito obtained that his pal in Paris lobby on his behalf so he could fill in and take care of the Roger account for slightly less moolah. At this point, no one else in the Pen supposedly had laid eyes on the killer or knew who he was. As for Roger, he is practically psychosomatically dead, for he can no longer control his bodily functions. That fatal encounter causes him to urinate and defecate in his pants.

Conversely, the son of a very affluent businessman "earned" the right to sojourn in the cell to the left of Roger's. Morgan Freeman has, in the past, done this mulatto some consequential favors when he was assigned at the customs. The officer receives a stipend from the family, which he refrains from naming, to keep an eye on him in prison. Not that anything would have ever happened to him in the cell adjacent to R.L.'s on the left. The first reason he was safe in that part of the prison is that all the inmates on the block are of the highest echelon, either political or economic. The second reason checks out as well since the kid is a "cool" cat. Though by his socioeconomic status, he was not expected to mingle with the general population, he does. He goes to them bearing goodies and shit. Shit can mean that sort of candy that put him in the can in the first place.

Turf war. Long before Jacques Ketant, this young cat was the first civilian in the country to have ever attempted to cash in after the corrupt fringe of the military hierarchy had put the narcotic infrastructure in place. Well, that airstrip just immediately outside the capital city. Because of his deep pocket and ability to smuggle the merchandise into both the United States and Europe, he drew some competition from some compelling and corrupt officials. Twice and a half, the wealth of his loaded father could not have saved him from prison. He has told Morgan that, although a tough nut to crack, the colonel was his most moderate competition before that "bowl of soup," whatever that means. The others, the likes of Sweet Micky, again, not the musician and future president, and countless others were all real hardcore nitwits and outright worthless nincompoops. The latter only arrested him. The former made sure that "little mulatto's" lousy ass was sent to prison. Sweet Micky's will be done was the way of life at the time.

The young, wealthy mulatto had not been able to rest all night. Beyond the confines of the prison, sporadic gunshots kept him awake and entertained. He likes the sound of guns. Next, to his cell, Roger ran the mill on that rotary telephone continually since 9:39 pm. So, he heard many things and had gathered a lot of information for free. Probably from the first or the second conversation before midnight from someone in France who apparently could not fall asleep due to, perhaps, his many unpaid bills. The young inmate is sure to have overheard Roger asking if his caller knew about any scheme to have him whacked. He had somewhat heard that from the person who will call him last tonight. But the young inmate is not sure about the answer his neighbor got. Maybe JCD, if indeed he was that caller, had promised him that he would find out and call back. That explains the calls from around midnight.

He remembers Roger talking about breakfast with the last caller. Based on what the young drug trafficker revealed to his prison protector, the former finance minister or the last caller was having breakfast in Paris at the time of the call or had just done so. From that call, he clearly heard that someone would be coming to pay Roger a visit of the kind he'd never wish for. He then had another incentive to stay awake, and he did. He started to put together why his protector, Mr. Freeman, had asked him earlier to avoid being seen in the cell and to be observant throughout the night. The young man heeded and spent half the night in the corner behind a luxurious, pricy and out of place leather chair. His TV set stayed off, and with his pillow under his butt, he pressed his right ear on the wall to eavesdrop on Roger's conversations, at least his side thereof.

Roger had reprimanded him before, accusing him of snooping. The cat from the block across was his driver in his days as Interior and Defense Minister for Nickesse's father and just recently during his senseless comeback in the country's complex political landscape. He had told his former boss about the young mulatto, as a show of his continued loyalty.

The arrogant doctor came charging at the young man right into his cell. Roger probably assumed he could intimidate the youngster. The lad held his own and managed to push him out and held his bald head in a half-nelson until Pacho and the day officer pulled them apart. Had he been present, that would have been the only time Morgan Freeman would have earned or justified the side wage he receives from the young inmate's relatives.

Though Pacho took all the precautions to open the cells, to lead and temporarily relocate the five neighbors, the foreseeable and unforeseeable did occur. The five inmates did not keep quiet until Pacho reminded them that he was in charge. Squeaky cell doors, feet dragging, and the assassin got inside the prison before the prisoners were relocated. Like a blind man, the young inmate resigned himself to only imagine what was going on though, at times, he fought his strange desire to crawl and take a peek. He achieved that to a certain degree. He stayed put. The noises that Pacho and his gang make are nothing new. Tonight, Roger's abnormally loud voice is added to the mix. Still, that is not out of the ordinary. Roger had, on many a night, had lively conversations on the telephone. On a similar night, that cat, like his boss, condemned for the coup attempt, saw the young man with his ear glued flat to the cell wall while Roger intensely gestured on the warden's borrowed telephone. After the killer got in, however, a new set of little noises contributes to further ignite the young man's curiosity. From the corner he hides, he monitors both the rage, the conversation of his neighbor, and the assertive footsteps of the approaching intruder. As his lack of maturity takes over, he gives in. He decides to crawl diagonally across the cell to get an angled view of the right side of his pampered neighbor's cell. According to what he later tells officer Morgan that would be the worst timing of everything he had done in his entire life.

Roger was uttering his last cusswords and vulgarities at Fanfan, conceivably his last caller's nickname, before he brutally ends the call in a vapor rising rage. When the young man lifted his head just a bit higher than the lowest bar, a man he knew very well was entering his neighbor's cell armed with a shiny stainless-steel gun. This was when the fatal glimpse happened and shall remain ingrained in the basement of his brain, the hippocampus. Their eyes briefly meet. The young trafficker panics and runs under the bed, mistaking his mouth for his ass. Fear causes him to shit, urinate, and throw up as he listens in on what is happening next to him

"Shit!" he inaudibly repeats as he soils himself under the bed. "That motherfucker saw me," he complains to himself as he confounds the smell in his pants with that which is in his neighbor's.

He covers his mouth to reduce the noise his vomiting makes but, in the process, gets the shit all over his face. He knows very well what that man is capable of, including whacking him right after he accomplishes what he came for. However, for now, his father's friendship with Tito is buying him, we shall see, a short extension on his lease on earth. Amid shit, urine, sweat, and vomit, deadened with fear, he pays close attention as he listens.

Not necessary, the young man hears through the wall. Worry instead about whom you are paying now, answers Tito imitating a French accent. Perhaps as an attempt to refresh Roger's memory of the money he received in France for which the last caller had served as collateral.

"Shh!" Tito continues with his index finger on his lips. "Shh! Not relevant who paid or sent me."

He looks at his watch, for he had promised Roger's last caller to visit his boy by breakfast. Paris' time. It is only a coincidence the coup happened that night at around the same time. Morgan would, once more, take the opportunity to clear Aristide's name and, at the same time, allow his partner History to cast his doubts. However, the actor's emulator believes that coup or no coup, Roger would have gotten whacked anyway that night. President Aristide is not even a chunk of meat in that soup, he says in the country's vernacular.

You see, he claims, the former president had practically nothing to do with this asshole's assassination. Long before the coup, plans were being drawn to facilitate his meeting with his maker. That arrangement only got cheaper and more expedient when the man he talked with last petitioned to have his pal Tito as the substitute assassin. Saddam Hussein got paid for a crime he would have committed for free on his personal account anyhow. Tito played the part entirely even to the attire he wore for the occasion. Khaki Bermuda pants, Hawaiian shirt, and dark shades lifted upon his forehead. He wanted to make sure Roger understands he was before him in that cell on two accounts. That of the French moolah and his own for his criminal services in intimidating the supporters of presidential candidate Aristide. He looks at his watch again.

Heard you hum *La Marseillaise* at breakfast. Well, in Paris, it is breakfast time now.

The next cell's prisoner's jaw drops in shock. The only difference between him and the guy in hole number 8 is his ability to still control his bodily functions albeit the earlier accident. But he is scared as shit because he is aware Tito has seen him and knows that he may be listening. He knows that at any minute, he could come to his cell and kill him first.

Tito whistles to the tune of the French national anthem as he aims then sings the first words,

"Allons enfants de la Patrie… Sing doc," he orders Roger.

Like a guilt-ridden lousy ass child, Roger Lafontant drops to his knees. Maybe he begged for his life and pleaded for mercy with his arms and hands opened at first, then clamped together as his knees touched the floor, he starts to sing with his voice engulfed with fear.

"*Contre nous de la tyra …* Ah! No, Tit—!"

Tito did not come at the Pen to linger. He fires two shots splashing the wall with blood. Roger slumps to the floor in the corner of the cell with a hole in his forehead. Another one in his heart spills his blood onto his white T-shirt transformed into see-through by the amount of sweat, his fear, and surprise of seeing his killer had generated. The final gunshot is for later. Right after the second shot, Tito remembers that the young, wealthy prisoner in the next cell had seen him. He thinks of doing something about it right there and then. The orders and plan called for him to kill one man precisely. That one man only happened to be on his personal shit list. The young drug trafficker had no other dealing but nose candy with Europeans and would hardly be a bystander victim should he whack him in his cell now. On his account, Tito certainly thinks, that sucker is dead. With the clean corner of a white handkerchief attached to an arm of the rabbit ear antenna, he wipes a tiny drop of Roger's blood off the gun. Tito leaves the cell, thinking of sending a warning and a terrifying look in the adjacent cell. That, he swiftly does.

From his point of view, Tito's gaze, however, appears to meet an empty cell. Gripped with fear by the unbearable short silence after the second shot, the young prisoner had crawled even deeper under his bed. Little did he know he populated that silence in the killer's mind. By the third gunshot, the young prisoner was at the other corner near the cell to his left which was empty. Back in Florida, after his parents bought his release, he told his folks that night he prayed to all the saints in heaven and all the devils on earth to spear his life. He did not have a long lease extension because soon after, he would become young Qusay's first kill. Then a student at Florida International University, he received the order from his father, Saddam. That young student shot Roger's ex-neighbor in prison in front of what would years later become the scene of a horrific massacre, The Pulse Nightclub.

From the corner where he hid deep under the bed, he caught Tito's quick and threatening glance into the cell. Hearing the killer's footsteps as he gets away, he hurries from under the bed. He crawls on paws and knees to peek through the bars at the exit but sees only a leg of the killer leaving his field of view.

CHAPTER 11.

A Load Of Tchako

Haitians need no special occasions to change a simple event into a blown-out street carnival with their guitars, drums, and their makeshift trombone made with bamboo trunks. They do that for religious matters, politics, and, of course, international soccer rivalries. As for their own, a victory for the Brazilian or Argentinian national team is cause for celebration, and the aficionados of either take to the streets to celebrate the loss of the other. Likewise, during the 1994 World Cup, they morphed their celebration for a superb Bebeto of Brazil into an outright demonstration demanding the return of the ousted president. Raoul Cedras did not like the lyrics one bit that day. Tonight, however, is no simple event. Folks who are never brought to the streets are out celebrating and it is all about peace as they are glad to join the supporters of both Duvalier and the president-elect Geffrard.

For the peaceful celebration all over the country, the crowds seem to attribute much of the credit to Duvalier because they knew Lysius as an aggressive field athlete who wouldn't shy away from a fight. In politics, Geffrard plays from the Clinton book. Like Bill and Hilary, Lysius the politician seems to want to eat the competition for breakfast. Few years prior, Donald Trump was staring straight at Hilary's political incisors and would have been nothing else but just a forgettable roadkill had it not been for Vlad. The Haitian people fathom his never-die and never-surrender approach regarding his opponents. Everyone knows he would have given Duvalier his money's worth had he or his supporters tried to disrupt his victory as wished for by the wealthiest fringe of his backers who now see him as weak dismissing the greater gain his concession has brought him and placed in the bank for a probable run in the future. Short vision. Nickesse Duvalier is a young man. In the gospel according to Lysius, there are merely no unreturned gifts in politics even though his motto is: "Be eaten alive or eat 'em first."

Even President Moïse Josaphat is excited about how all had turned out. People close to him report that when came the occasion to call and congratulate the winner, he inadvertently dialed Duvalier's number and thought he'd called Lysius. Those people attest they overheard Duvalier's reply through the receiver: "No, Mr. President, it is not Lyzou. It is Nickesse." At the start of the electoral season, Josaphat appeared unwilling, shaky and sent the signals he would play strictly in favor of the candidates from his party like his predecessor and the ones before him and before. Those candidates were nonetheless among the last to drop out before the ones from that other party after some serious and heavy political muscle flexing and persuasive prowess on Lysius' part. This elections' night, the outgoing president is all smile and has reasons to be. At least for two aspects of his most commanding achievements. The results of the presidential and senatorial elections are, for the first time in the country, electronically tabulated and published the night of the polling. All this including the festivities late into the night are made possible thanks to his tireless effort to modernize the electoral process and, dear to his heart, to restore the country's power grid to guarantee “round-the-clock electricity all throughout the country.

The meeting hall at the headquarters now looks more like a place outside the country since most of the local policemen, eager to join the rest of the people and witness the euphoria in the streets, had left the minute the broadcast ended. They also knew that it would cost them absolutely nothing to push the replay button and the old officers will be more than happy to fill them in on whatever they’d have missed tonight. And they knew much of the stories anyway. History Channel and Morgan Freeman never miss out on any chance they find to give a show the kind of tonight’s.

By now, the partners had told the young soldiers much about Jeando from the time he came back from France when he started his radio career, bought the station to the post-Nickesse’s dad’s era when he returned from his first exile. These are things the locals who were previously in the room knew well and could afford to forgo. Anyway, just as with the real American institution, The History Channel, rerun is the norm. Morgan and his partner must have told them the same stories countless times. But the foreigners wish to learn how the journalist reacted after the coup of September 1991. Both the peacekeepers and the two officers seem not to offer much importance neither to the celebration in the streets nor the late hour of the night. The older men tell their young audience that at their age, they would have been awake anyway and they have already spent years sleeping. Just one night without could, in no wise, dig their graves while they do what they love.

History had never given a jack dooky about Michel Gibéa as a member of the parliament or an occupant of the national palace. He never gave a shit about Aristide even throughout his Salesian years at the parish of St. Jean Bosco. And not even a tiny portion of a fuck did he give when and after he became a twice ousted president. He believes that Jeando had stopped being an esteemed icon the minute he announced his blind support behind the former priest's candidacy. Before that, History would have vowed a cult to Dominique. What has never changed though is the utmost respect he has always nurtured for the man. Whereas he seems to suffer from the Tourette syndrome when it comes to Aristide, he presents with the maintenance of perfect equilibrium wittingly forgoing the fetidness of his lingo toward the journalist even after his post–Rue Vaillant rant. He calls himself a presentable old fart.

"Not much of a reaction," History interjects. "The son of a bitch took off."

And before he could add anything else more reasonable, officer Morgan rebukes his partner as he always had done when History or anyone else shows a lack of respect for his buddy Michel Martelly, President Aristide, René Préval, or any other high-profile individual of the country. Strangely, Morgan never takes the defense of Gibéa as he seems to practice what he asks of everyone: respecting the presidents.

He had considered his partner MIA the morning of the coup as he was leaving the prison after a shift filled with occurrences and had, perhaps, unknowingly taken part in the assassination of a man. He understands that many may have ignorantly murdered Roger. For instance, he maintains that even Pacho did not know why he had to relocate Serge and the other four prisoners who occupied the cells to the right and why, the heck, not the ones to the left of Roger's cells. At that point, the officer ignored the identity of the killer until he had talked to his young protégé who saw and recognized Tito Massim. All of Morgan's calls to History's house were either unanswered or resulted in busy signals. Morgan thought then that, for sure, the rumor mills network was operating. The officer was right. He decided to call his partner's lady "friend on the side," they call that. He alone had that number among the colleagues in the police force and, of course, the man in "the flesh" answered, unaware of what had happened in Port-au-Prince overnight. Did he and his mistress stay off the grid for the weekend and stay in during that monsoon the day before the coup d'état?

History's reference to Dominique taking off or hurriedly leaving the country in the wake of the coup, quite frankly, does not stand on its legs. It has none. That could be attested by Ed McLintaugh whom Dominique called in Washington around the time of his morning broadcast from the station. And Ed did hear the gunshots when Dominique told him that the bastards were shooting at the station's building. Of course, Dominique left and gave many interviews in the United States, and the one we will not forget soon was that he gave to Charlie Rose when four-year-old Leopold recognized him.

A second time. The charmer whom Dr. Pierre birthed in the yard of the school, Argentine Bellegarde, at Rue Vaillant amid the carnage left by Tito, Chapo and their mercenaries on orders from the generals, is already seven years old. Bill Clinton is now the President of the United States who is hell-bent on restoring democracy to Haiti. Ed Sr. had always felt the desire to debate the POTUS' real intent. He wanted his son to understand that Bill Clinton did not give a shit about Aristide whom Bush Sr. saw as a cumbersome character with the deck missing a few cards. One sure thing about that POTUS, he will be in a room filled with people, and if he must talk to every one of them, he will make every single one feel important as though he or she were the only person in the room or in his universe. On the other side of the coin, Aristide tends to wish everyone herald him and know that he is the shit, the one and only, the Almighty. So, Bubba does what Bubba does. Each time they met, the President made Titid feel that he is the shit. The Haitian leader bought it every time.

Later, Jeando himself had become a whistleblower or a worrywart. He took on denouncing the Clinton administration's apparent resolve to destroy the Haitian agriculture while championing his love for the country and its people on the insinuating that he and Hilary spent time in Haiti as newlyweds and went to mass at the new Cathedral. What?

"That was a load of 'Tchako,'" History claims.

He cared about the business aspects of his dealings, the elder McLintaugh told Dominique. And when he managed to get himself sent to the country as an envoy from the United Nations, History could not help but tell anyone with a working pair of ears.

"That's a load of crap. Motherfucker comes to cash in."

Jeando grew desperate and frustrated as the country's officials presented their deaf ears to his editorials on the matter as he confided to his friend McLintaugh Sr. who had suggested that he not poke it much for his safety. Ed Senior pleaded with Jeando. Likewise, may have done their mutual friend, President Préval. In one famous editorial, Jeando called his friend, President Aristide, stubborn. Like attracts likes. Did Dominique heed? Subsequently, the horse himself would admit in front of a public gathering that his administration has, indeed, done a lot of wrong to the Haitian people. On that matter, History once confided to his partner that he will never forgive those members of the opposition to Moïse Josaphat who went as far as to completely exonerate Bill Clinton putting what he had confessed on Josaphat's shit column.

Repentance? That was before even Nation of Islam's leader Louis Farrakhan, in no way advocating for Donald Trump during the 2016 US presidential elections, wondered whatever happened to the enormous amount of money raised and donated to rebuild that Caribbean country after the 2010 earthquake.

Ed and Dorothy were enjoying a board game with their son, whose attention span called for channels surfing when the child thought he might have seen a face he recognized.

"Daddy, Jeando is on TV," Leopold cried pointing to the screen. And Dorothy instinctively took the remote command from the child who had already switched to *Scooby-Doo*, to *Barney*, and past the *Teenage Mutant Ninjas*. She surfed a couple of channels back for she believed that she too, may have had a glimpse of the face. The McLintaughs understood that the journalist was exposing to Charlie Rose all the hypocrisy with the so-called "Democracy to Haiti."

DOMINIQUE

"And if you read the NY Times or Washington Post, you'll realize the American Government was involved deep, deep in the coup. One voice, President Clinton saying, 'DEMOCRACY IN

HAITI!' and the other voice, the CIA, telling General Cedras 'Stay in power... He's bluffing."

Verbatim, Morgan offers the young UN soldiers what he heard from Dominique's broadcast the morning of the coup, when he too, getting home, heard through his vehicle's receiver as the army shot at the building of Radio Haiti after the journalist directed a question toward the military. A question that pushes Morgan to mimic the journalist's voice.

"With the enormous profits from drug trafficking... even more so when you are in power, we can understand the idea of a coup. But, good God! Why slaughter so many innocent people?"

The rumor mills were already unbearable for the military of which the plans for the coming three years could not have included a coexistence with "Le Marquis de Delmas," as Serge liked to refer to Jeando, at the time an unwavering supporter of Aristide, running his mouth at his radio station. A few hours after the coup, the death machine intended to send that chilling warning to Dominique who startled a bit but stayed at the microphone as gunshots rained down breaking windows and piercing bullet holes visible on the façade up to the time of its demolition after the earthquake of 2010. He was reporting and commentating on the numbers of people the military had killed in various pro-Aristide populated regions and neighborhoods.

The young UN peacekeepers wonder if the stories that they are told are real or if officers Morgan and History are only darn good storytellers, as Morgan prepares to recount the events that he claims to have witnessed in the streets, early in the morning and by midday after the coup. The officer could, in no way, have seen all of the things of his assertions. His itinerary after leaving the prison suggests it is believable that the officer did witness the first scene that he asserts happened on his way to pick up his monthly stipend at one of the stores owned by the father of that young mulatto at the pen. Of course, he found the place closed for as one of the backers of the coup, among countless others, that affluent man had advance knowledge. The tight community of wealthy mulatto businesspeople grew very tired of Aristide's shit and agreed to put their money where their mouths were by financially sponsoring the coup.

"With a small radio receiver in his hand, the young man emerged from a narrow path between the rundown dwellings of the slum. He could be, let's say, seventeen years old. At his age, he should have hidden at home knowing that the military was firing at anything that moves. The orders from the high hierarchy were clear and simple: "If it has two feet and moves in the streets today, shoot it." The young man wearing a #11 jersey of the Brazilian soccer team bumps hard into the policeman's vehicle as he speedily tries to make the sharp turn onto the street from the narrow corridor. As he runs out to inform the crowd, Morgan, an inflexible fanatic, cannot help but notice Romarió's name handwritten in the back of lad's camiseta amarella.

The crowd chants and beats on cans, pots, and everything metal. They had begun to assemble sending vulgarities toward the army as a whole and especially toward Raoul Cedras whose men are already sweeping the streets. In some select areas where the blind supporters of the president's live, armed commandos actually comb the slums house by house leaving behind them trails of blood.

As the young man gets near, he shouts, and the crowd quickly disperses, everyone running into corridors like roaches run into cracks in a New York City apartment when the light is suddenly turned on. The old officer figures that the young man must have been on the roof of the only high building in the area monitoring the length of the single street that leads to their slum. To get to that building without encountering what he heard from Jeando on his small transistor, this youngster had gone to and from through a maze of the city's corridor system, running, jumping over all sorts of obstacles on his path. Of course, he caused some anger-prone folks to throw water, urine, or other objects at him as he jumps over their boiling coffee pots or their infants moving their bowels in what they don't call bed pans over there but little plastic vases which come in a variety of colors.

From the rooftop of the building, he realized that Jeando's reporting was, in fact, taking place and the shit was coming toward his slum. A line of private cars, perhaps furnished by the anti-Aristide elite, drives up and down the streets ever so dangerously slow with the radio of one red truck tuned to Jeando's broadcast.

JEAN DOMINIQUE

"However, in this botched coup, initiated by Michel François, taken over by General Cedras, "on demand," it seems, there are two questions, which could, one day, be asked for me, or any other journalist in this country... Those questions, ladies and gentlemen, are: "Who killed Roger Lafontant in his cell earlier this morning and who killed Reverend Sylvio Claude in the city of Les Cayes? Who?"

From the moving vehicles, machine guns spray everyone who ventures out in the streets. These assassins make it seem like a well-orchestrated drive-by at first. The first slums they patrolled earlier were lucky for the higher authority had not yet given the orders to follow the protesters deep inside their miserable dwellings after they ran away.

On the back seat of a pickup truck, Morgan recognizes Chapo with his dark sunglasses and famous hat. He appears that he is listening to what Jeando is saying but he is only looking to kill somebody, anything, and anyone as Jeando continues on the radio.

"Roger Lafontant is dead, or is it better to say he was whacked by the military to make it appear as though President Aristide ordered it?"

A man pushes open a gate, and a dog runs out onto the street. He takes two steps and mercilessly, Chapo riddles him with bullets. The dog panics and starts running fast to cross the street. Overstepping the order only to kill what has two legs and moves, Chapo shoots the dog by the vehicle's right rear bumper. The sheer force of a bullet that bounces off the ground sends the animal flying and landing on the hood of a parked tap-tap, splashing its blood over the windshield. The officer did not have anything to fear because he was in uniform and had actually thought of saving the young man's life by letting him into his car as he runs by back into the corridor from which he first emerged. Morgan later tells his audience he regrets that he did not.

"Is it a conflict among Macoutes?" the journalist wonders on the air. "*Is it the old strife Aristide vs. Lafontant that dates*

before the last elections? Or, is it some deal gone wrong with few folks in Europe?"

The word is out. The military patrols the streets and probes the slums. They unleash the repression against the supporters of Aristide. Nonetheless, they are out there organizing themselves into a somewhat resistance until they hear the first shots nearby or see a suspicious car coming. The officer's vehicle had probably been thought of at first to be one of these sent by the military. It was then evident that it was not since Morgan had stopped to avoid harm to the young man who ran out of the corridor. Some in the crowd that the young man needed to warn of the likely arrival of the death squadron would at least vaguely remember to have seen the officer in that car probably, every month, on his way to picking up the stipend for as long that young mulatto has been in the can.

A cathedral of thick black smoke rises behind a barricade where a crowd of protesters wave few posters of President Aristide. The pickup trucks do not come to a complete stop yet that the armed men already jump off. The sound of their boots hitting the ground sends chills to people inside their homes as they know better not to venture out to witness the demonstrations and the military's reactions all throughout the country, as the officers attest. The crowd of protesters disperse. The armed men chase after them, following them even inside their homes, pulling them out or killing them.

Eager to kill and to spill more blood, Chapo advances slowly in the corridor rolling his eyes. He pushes a door and gets in slowly. It's a one-room dwelling, a small castle made for the poor where things are in order and neat. His out-of-the-ordinary sense of hearing tells him that the woman he chases after does not have any other escape route. He, like a predator, can hear and feel her breath. Perhaps killers like him have special powers. From beneath the bed, the woman surveys "silently" Chapo's boots as she protects her baby infant and as he moves cautiously and rolling his eyes from corner to corner throughout the small room and many times, looking at the neatly made bed because only one thing occupies in his mind at this point. He is going to rape her on that bed.

Finally, the woman must have felt at least a sense of relief, but to what degree is terrible luck reasonable for a person? Notwithstanding the conviction that the woman could be nowhere but inside the room, he decides against his killer nature to leave and to let live. Chapo walks out. Under the bed, the woman sighs thinking she could conclusively take her hand off the infant's mouth so he can breathe and two or three steps outside after crossing over the dwelling's doorstep, the infant starts to cry.

Chapo violently lifts the bed exposing the terrified woman who covers herself and the infant with a towel on which is hand-drawn the likeness of President Aristide. As a demon before a crucifix and with no humanity, Chapo fires a round at the sketch on the towel and blood flows from underneath the cloth with a spatter onto a small area of his steel toe boot. On his way out, like his boss in Roger's prison cell a few hours earlier, he reaches for a hand towel on the table. He puts his foot on the seat of a chair and wipes the trace amount of blood off his boot before he gets out. However, as he cleans, the trickle of blood on the floor had reached the rear end of his other boot soiling the heel. As he leaves, he pays no attention to his bloody heel print following his every step to the truck where only the driver awaits. The other gunmen probably followed some other protesters into the other corridors. The sounds of their shots corroborate.

On his way to the store, Morgan traveled that route as he had done many ends of the month. He heard Jeando's reporting on the radio about the massacres going on all about the city throughout the morning. It is also alleged that it was the same in many other parts of the country. The officer gave no second thought as to whether it was safe for him to follow through with his plan to brave it out since he needed the money. He was in uniform but that could be unsafe. The police chief whom Jeando referred to so many times in his rant was his boss. Perhaps he was the one who ordered the shots he heard live on the air as the journalist spoke unmoved by the assault on his building. Hence Dominique's mindful idea of making a call to have a witness other than his audience listen to bullets smashing on the façade of the radio's building. Jeando called his friend in Washington, DC, Edward McLintaugh, who may have advised him to consider leaving for a temporary exile. The notion of Jean Dominique running away does not stand for it is a "holy" idea. Not the kind of heaven's saints' holiness but a concept that is not waterproof because it has holes all over.

Disappointed that the store is closed, Morgan decides that he would drive back along the same route thinking that the army's angels of death had already passed. This was when he beheld what will affect him for years since he believes that he thought then of saving his life by inviting him in his car. In the middle of the deserted street, a body lays face down on the pavement. He gets off and walks around the front end of the car.

He could read the handwritten name on the back of the jersey, but the number 11 is drenched in the young man's blood with his mouth open and bleeding.

History had often pleaded with him that he let go, but it is no easy task even when he asks Morgan to ponder the order side of the coin. He had repeatedly reminded his partner, at his remorseful moments, that the kid was listening to Jean Dominique on the radio incriminating his boss as one of the coup's masterminds who was behind most of the senseless slaughters of many innocents.

"For God's sake, Marcellus (Morgan Freeman's real name), seeing you in that uniform, 'You fucking think the boy would get in your car?" History would argue.

Morgan oddly stays quiet to that question.

"Shit!" History would add. "Maybe he'd call the others to set the car ablaze with you in it. Just like their prominent lip leader told them to in his bloody speech the Friday before."

Late hour. History thinks they should let the foreign soldiers go by now that everyone else had left to either join in some celebration or merely head home straight after one long and eventful day. Think he'd say "Ite Misa es"? Not without adding a story of his own.

History was not at work the entire weekend. The last duty along with Morgan whom, he knew, was to fill in at the prison these three nights, was mainly at the international airport overseeing some young recruits as the president was returning from, in his mind, his conquering UNGA trip. The partners actually parted right after the ill-reputed speech. History understands that he had missed much of the event but does not regret any of it. He insists his "young" woman was taking too much good care of him. He could not bother with the pettiness among Cedras, Sweet Micky, and a man, a president he certainly never liked. History will incriminate both Aristide and Gibéa every chance he gets but for some reason, he seems to recount something either president had probably no business in, and even he could not prove. He had told many of his audiences many unbelievable atrocities he states to have heard from what he calls "The Talking Mouths" in the country's vernacular. The weirdest of these are, of course, the two stories he retains the foreigners to tell. The older officer never offers a shred of proof when he alleges that the president had once threatened to murder his daughters should his wife ever leave him. Like many in the country who think everything on the Internet must be accurate, the old man would cite YouTube or other sites.

"Massenat, shut the fuck up," Marcellus would respond in Aristide's defense when History places the president in a macabre scene in a room at his villa.

"Now motherfucker," Morgan objects, "that's some shit. Have you seen the president with that fucking baby in his hands with your own eyes? Don't repeat shit like that. The Jean-Bertrand Aristide, the Titid, the president I know did not murder and grind an infant child. That is fucked up shit, Massenat."

On his way back from his mistress, he learned from the street what was happening around him and decided to check on his old pals that he usually plays dominoes with on Sundays very late into the night.

The night of the coup, they indeed played and cooled the Prestige without him. He says that when he finally gets to their house, the dominoes pieces were scattered around covered in blood that dripped from the table where it appeared that somebody had been dragged inside the house. A bloody handprint's smear on a door pane told the story.

Like Chapo followed the woman into her home, the army-waged mercenary came up to the dominoes table where he stabbed the man. Being followed, he ran to the house of the officer's older friends because he knew that their door always stays open and he usually goes there to watch the older men play. He did not make it to the door. The thugs stabbed and projected him onto the ivory dominoes where he bled a good deal before one of History's friends deemed it safe to venture out and see what had occurred.

CHAPTER 12.

As We Were Saying - The Interview

"I am deprived of my microphone, of my radio station. I am in exile here, in a political exile in the US because a bunch of thieves, drug dealers, the military took over my country."

Jeando appears to lament and complain during that TV appearance. Dorothy comes to sit on the couch next to Ed and Leopold as the American journalist interviews Jeando. Ed crosses his arms and looks at Dorothy, who points him to Leopold glued to the TV as he focuses on Dominique's face. Of course, the journalist knew a great deal, too darn more than the military would want him to know of what had made the existence of the landing strip necessary. As a good journalist, he did not need extra muscles to mollify the impressive Nigerian who gladly gave him a succession of interviews. The lamenting, however, will be over soon. It will make room for the reason that will prompt actors Tom Hanks, Danny Glover, Anthony Hopkins, and late film director Jonathan Demme to call. They will congratulate Jeando after the station goes back on the air fully functioning.

For that to have been possible, Bill Clinton had deployed thousands of marines with helicopters adorned with the Haitian flags and lots of massive fire toys. Like a door-to-door transportation service, the Yankees drop-delivered "democracy" right on the steps of the presidential palace, packaged in what looked like a bulletproof glass box with a microphone inside. Every time the partners relive this event, they are reminded of a trip the police force had sent them on to South America, in

Argentina. They remember a policewoman there telling them a story. A South American dictator had thrown in prison a radio journalist after shutting down his station because of his rants and diatribes against him in his political commentaries and editorials.

Dictators like Duvalier needed aid during the Carter era. They faked the existence and the respect, in their respective countries, of the freedom of press and expression. During that time, Duvalier and his cronies staged parliamentary elections to stuff the chamber with zealous loyalists and sycophants, suffering a crack here and there for one "dissident." The officers contend that the meat of that electoral stuffing was of far better quality than the humdingers of mediocrity and low personalities that, of late, populate the country's legislative bodies. The burden rested on the candidates to sell their brand of loyalty to the regime. But the dictator usually handpicked the winners from a pool of high fabric and moral standing in their respective communities. A losing candidate might have run with the slogan: "Joseph X, Ferocious Defender of Duvalierism." In the United States, folks would have had a genuine fear of seeing the likes of D.N. for Congress, "Greatest Enabler of D.T.," or again, for the US Senate, M.M., "Straight From D.T.'s Ass." The partners agree on one thing. One cannot compare the fiber of one Rony Gilot, Victor Nevers Constant to that of most of the hacks who populate the den by the sea today. Morgan, especially, always had the utmost respect for those two, although Duvalier handpicked them.

Nonetheless, despite the easing, the government would, for instance, periodically harass Fardin and the journalists who usually penned in his weekly paper. Before November 1980, when the Macoutes became seemingly emboldened by Ronald

Reagan's winning the US presidential elections, the media took advantage in various ways of the situation. Jeando, at his radio station, on the other hand, did the other thing. Radio Haiti stopped all news information concerning the country's political climate. What the radio did, however, turned out to have been far more lethal to the administration of Nickesse's father. The station made it a cult to broadcast information about other embattled dictators in the country's creole language to permeate the collective psyche.

The damage had been done already when Nickesse's dad decided in November 1980 to crack down on the so-called freedom of expression championed by Jimmy Carter. History thinks the station sowed the seeds for the inevitable popular uprising. Contrary to their thick-minded oppressors, the silently listening population registered. They made the connection amongst these various dictators. They heard what the people did to topple them. The masses learned to link that information with what they had at home and what they could likewise do.

So, it was when Jimmy Carter insisted, the Argentinian policewoman told them, that the dictator thought he would free the political commentator after three years in prison. But when he visited the journalist with that prospect, he laid very clearly the condition of his release. The political commentator was to affirm never to criticize the dictator on that particular show again. He gladly took the bargain and was freed.

A week later, his radio station announced a "new" kind of show entitled *Como Deciamos Antes…* or in English, (*As We Were Saying…*)

That story she told the partners fittingly frames both the ousted President and Jeando within that particular political bubble.

Such to create, Washington orchestrated the exits of Cedras, Sweet Micky, and Biambi to make possible the POTUS' sponsored return of "Democracy." In some circles, most still deem it one major setback for the country. The reinstated soft-spoken President, History contends, did not display the sort of wisdom worthy of a head of state.

"Besides that grievance," asks the young French peacekeeper into whose ears History had whispered about the loss of his savings, "for what do most people reproach the former President?"

Morgan, who has anticipated History's response, tries once more to protect the dignity of the man, for he knows what his partner's vulgar lips can do. That officer, although History thinks otherwise, is not really a fan as he is of Michel "Sweet Micky" Martelly, but he will always set things straight. Mr. Freeman would not let anybody disparage a fellow Haitian in front of any foreigner and much less to entertain those pencil-neck geeks from the United Nations. About Martelly, however, Morgan did not give a fuck, he'd say. He merely enjoyed his music and peppery jokes. But as President, he would add, he couldn't care less. Conversely, he appreciated how Micky rebuked the empty-suits journalists who got under his skin. Morgan has always condemned how the former president and second-episode musician conducted himself regarding a particular radio journalist. Herself, the policeman thinks, had many a time gone too far within the man's personal affairs and even into his young son's calamitous misfortune.

If you have a biff with the man, deal head-on with him and leave his fucking kid alone. Morgan would so speak privately with History during long-winded discussions regarding that radio journalist. That lady has done quite a 180 on journalism. She now talks a bunch of shit during the time slot that should have been allotted to actual news for the sole purpose of undermining whatever governing administrations undertakes. In their private discussions still, History would refer to her as "a pyromaniac." Strangely, his partner would not protest. For circles familiar to Morgan, she was initially arrested in 1980, and the charges might have been of arson. Many of that same organization are prone to set ablaze any good thing in the country. That journalist who collaborated with Jeando around the time he had announced his blind support for Aristide never outgrew the party's ways. Jeando did. Perhaps, that was at the cost of his life.

Shit! would History say about her complaining about the number of flies and the piles of garbage in the streets? She ought to know, the officer thinks that there are even more flies around 4 pm every day as she spews her shit on the air. Morgan disagrees.

"She is "'Fake News,'" History would add, imitating former President Donald Trump.

She heralds the lousy condition of the roads. Everyone knew she was politicking as though all that shit and streets' conditions were the making of all other administrations but the one of the political "family" of her adherence. Morgan Freeman would want you to believe that he never took the defense of Aristide. Still, he will always stand up for the dignity of the office that until recently, only a select few could ever attain. On the other foot, History would tell the unpleasantness of the President's character and eerie appearance. Likewise, Morgan will not shy away from disgorging a bunch of shit about or right to Sweet Micky's face. Thin-skinned, Aristide may not be able to take it from History. But Morgan is quite confident that his thick-skinned "buddy" Martelly can and will opportunely return the shit back at him or at anyone for that matter. "He neither cares nor does he give a rat's ass as he sings it."

***

"Nowadays," History continues, "there are plenty of folks whose academic proficiency does not overlap their shaky ability to write their fucking names. When they are running away from something, they think they'd run for the protection given to members of the den by the sea. And once there, these hacks think they are presidential materials. Poor thing."

However, despite his years in the Senate, neither Morgan nor History really knows much about this newly elected kid, Lysius. Officer Morgan almost needs a sign on his forehead to broadcast that he was a classmate of Lysius Geffrard Sr., the president-elect's wealthy father. History could boast he had witnessed on television Lyzou's debut in international sports in Paris at the age of fourteen. But they both have, like the majority of their compatriots, great hope the young man will return honor and dignity to the office. After Nickesse Duvalier's gracious concession to Lyzou, most now think he would have been much different from his daddy or granddaddy. That would also stand against those who ruled before Lyzou. To a much lesser degree, Nickesse would surely be different from the outgoing President, Josaphat.

"There is no doubt," History argues, "the affection and hope the population manifest toward Lysius today are nothing compared to what we gave to Aristide. I, for one, had thought very highly of him though I was never a fan. After a few months of his first election to the presidency, even his detractors would agree there was another atmosphere, a new feel to life itself in the country."

"I think," he continues, "he was improvising, for he did not know jack about governing or politics. He was fresh out from his religious vow of poverty. And speaking of poverty, Aristide did struggle to gather the fees that came with declaring his damn candidacy. He was somebody who supposedly would not care about getting rich and who wouldn't engage in the embezzlement of the nation's meager assets. He was the best thing the country had in hope for a contrast with the years of Duvalier and the four lost ones when the tail tip of that snake struggled to stay alive."

"The tail of that snake," Morgan adds to support his partner who has not uttered a single vulgarity, "had not realized that its head had been gone."

But, before he got into politics, the priest made powerful enemies—among them, Uncle Sam to whom he will sell his soul to return to power in 1994, three years after his bloody overthrow. That had never happened before; after a coup d'état for the ousted President to return. "When you are gone, you stay gone, or your ass be gone," as would say Ving Rhames in Tarantino's 1994 film *Pulp Fiction.* As a priest, he often used the pulpit to condemn the American way as a deadly sin. Recently under Donald Trump's powerful spell, that would probably earn "father Titid" a valuable place beyond President Bush's the axis of evil although Trump has no respect from Dubya.

Ironically, in lieu of capital or mortal sins, imperialism and capitalism conveniently became virtues, or means to an end. Bill

Clinton fell under the spell of the soft-spoken man who, only four or five years earlier, as a priest disparaged his country every chance he got. The deposed president had rallied quite a line-up to his cause. Many world celebrities also fell for it. However, Bush Sr. was pretty straightforward as he deemed the ousted Haitian mentally deranged and unstable.

"What we blame him for is simple," History says." "If my partner, here, did not know me for a long time, I am sure he'd label me a nostalgic Duvalierist. He would, in many instances, be right because I, for one, miss the time when our children could get up early in the morning to fearlessly take the streets and go to school. My boys could spend half the night studying under a streetlight post."

Morgan wants to interject, and before he could stand, History ironically calms him down.

"You be quiet, young man," he says.

"The truth." History resumes. "Aristide had changed this fucking country for the worst. Since his presidency, there has not been any control or any restraint over his supporters. He unambiguously had urged them to look around and take shit they need to sustain themselves. Before that earthquake that displaced a significant number, that man had encouraged an enormous flux of internal migration. Folks would abandon or sell their properties and come to the capital or migrate to the nearest suburbs without any apparent expectation of what they would experience or do once there. With overpopulation and intermingling, crime was introduced inevitably. The internally displaced needed to make a living. By any means. It is not that it was not so before, but it had all started with a glaring lack of respect for the individual. Today, most believe that the democracy that President talked about allows them to do everything their way with manifest disregard for the comfort and the right to the peaceful existence of their neighbors.

"There are no more quiet and peaceful neighborhoods," he adds. "They must think that stands normal. To come in front of a citizen's residence, in front of their young children. To pull, bend down, and spread to urinate in public. How can our children concentrate and study in the hell of noises offered them by their unfit neighbors? Each generates his or her set of clatters. When confronted about their common ways, these folks usually find the audacity to reply that the streets belong to the state. And as their father had told them, they are rightful owners also. But, the motherfucker never reminded them it's their responsibility to keep their shit clean.

"However," the old man continues to curtail Morgan's reaction after the foul outburst, "that is not entirely characteristic to Aristide. Long ago, folks said that shit about Nickesse's father, but the roads were clean. Papa Doc, supposedly patrolled the streets at night as a habit he had developed when he was a public health official in past administrations. For crying out loud, motherfuckers were stopped for walking the streets barefoot or shirtless.

With no clear and real plan to create employment for them after he invited them to the cities, these people quickly would find out they had to fend for themselves. In many cases, fending meant a husband who had left or sold his possessions, options to shine shoes while "wifey" sells roasted peanuts throughout the streets. When they come back to their shack, their only pastime takes place on something they agree to call a bed. They copulate thus procreating what we have now: The Ratpakaka Generation, one that has neither values nor morale. An ignorant generation that only knows how to burn tires and shit and whose parents' old possessions now belong to powerful and corrupt members of Parliament.

Aristide is the only person with such charisma. He could entice anybody to like him instantly. The little priest had had the most honor and chance to change the country for good since the people's butchered hopes in Gerard Gourgue. He deceptively has, not once but twice, managed to fail the people so miserably. I believe I told you that he did not show much political wisdom. Well, the minute the Marines dropped his behind inside that glass box, instead of uniting the country, he offered a threatening and divisive rhetoric. He might have advocated differently in Washington before his return."

"Since he was the one calling the shots," the officer asserts as he continues, "it appeared that he single-handedly disbanded the army. In Aristide's defense, I, History, reckon the mood of the populace was all about that. They were the ones suffering the brunt of the repression of the last years. Later during that face-to-face interview, Jeando would ask him if this disbandment was initially called for in the English language."

History is confident that the President is no fool; he had to catch the core of that question from the journalist. Morgan stands perplexed as he could not believe his ears. History taking the defense of that former President is unheard of. Many of his disparagers unjustly accuse Mr. Aristide of single-handedly disbanding the institution. Some of its rotten members, indeed, could not see themselves in his politics. On the other hand, a significant number did not approve of his arming, mostly young thugs, (irony) to go about his dirty rancorous deeds.

"The years away from power, most believe, have turned him into a distrustful, cynical, retribution-predisposed freak," History explains. "However, if one tries that shoe on the other foot, Aristide, Préval, and Gibéa will be no different from a Nickesse Duvalier. This cat will get in your face and deal with you on a leveled field. Both Aristide and Gibéa could be like the president-elect who has sucked the political lives off of all his opponents. For Pete's sake, his political motto would fit the former priest-president like a glove. Not President Gibéa, however. The vast difference lies in the humanity and wisdom displayed by the two younger politicians."

"Furthermore, my young friends," History adds, "most reproach him his barefaced hypocrisy. This man presented himself as a champion for ridding the country of illegal weapons to curb the rampant insecurity that had beleaguered the population throughout the years of Cedras and his puppets. Upon his return, his followers became encouraged to do as they pleased as they would threaten the opposition and even ordinary citizens who do not meddle in politics."

History tries hard not to say it. He had discussed with Morgan on whether the President had really placed guns in the hands of young children of a particular slum while he was saying "he wants, so, he can." Did he, and could he, ever? Regarding how the agronomist, still a staunch supporter of the President, fitted after the return.

"Did he fit in the second presidency?" one young foreigner inquires

History looks at his partner.

"No," Morgan Freeman starts. "The man, the agronomist, the journalist, Jeando, did not live to witness the second presidency of the man he supported vehemently throughout his first campaign. According to an interview his wife gave, we could gather that he may have been conveniently assassinated in April before the December presidential elections. The President at the time, Mr. Préval, a dear friend of Jeando's, did return the power to the former President, who, ultimately, would be ousted again in an uprising. President Aristide's camp would talk of his kidnapping by the United States, Canada, and France."

"Those Europeans," History interposes right in front of a young French soldier, "would have had 21, 685, 135, 571.48 good reasons to get rid of Aristide any way they could."

"After all the politicking during the post-Aristide transition," Morgan summarizes, "came the time for the next elections that the original 'Political Animal' seemed to cruise to win. Many think he won, but the blank votes and skinny dipping in some swimming pool got in the way. Remember, this political animal was that same Manigat whose election would complete the unwanted triangle with Castro and Hugo Chavez, this time. Think about them apples.

Then, he swam to get out, but like a damn snake, he slithered back in, and that time on his way out, he did not wish to close the door entirely on two terms or let it smack him on the ass. He tried to impose someone who, many agree, is not the brightest bulb on the Christmas tree. Well, before Y2K, it was rumored the

President seriously considered Jeando as his first version of a legacy-keeper. In the interview, Jeando's wife alleged that the "former" former President was pigheaded on being the unique candidate in these elections as one by one, potential opponents were being suspiciously and physically eliminated."

Hm! History does.

"Sit down, old man," Morgan Freeman says with a sneer as he continues.

Mrs. Jeando always referenced the interview between the President and her husband, the only journalist perhaps who would hold both Gibéa's and Aristide's feet to the fire. Jeando would not give these presidents a pass or cut them any slack. Despite his adherence to the party, Jeando hammered the President on the corruption and embezzlement transpiring right under his nose.

Long before Geffrard's "Eat 'em or be eaten" motto, there was, for a short period, since we are talking motto, slogan, and interviews, "Shut him up, or he'll shut us." According to another "interview," that and the assumption of his being a probable and worthy presidential contender, sealed the journalist's fate. The man was gunned down after he left the confines of his bulletproof vehicle to inspect a motorcycle that had provoked an accident. The dude could have even died in a skiing accident on a slope right in the middle of Port-au-Prince. This former associate had framed the President's frequent visits and interviews within a deliberate campaign of hypocrisy.

JEAN DOMINIQUE

Well, Mr. President, you come back. You declare reconciliation with the super-rich. You know. The twelve or fifteen wealthy families of the country… You shower those oligarchs with tremendous and sweet gifts… All sorts of donations to the left and the right… The oligarchs, what they give you in return? They have their protégées in all the institutions. They pay no tax. They don't pay their electric or water bills. That means, Mr. President, corruption is what they give you back. And that corruption is accepted by your administration and suffered by the members of the party…

PRESIDENT

Jeando, I agree with some of the things you said… I do not agree with most. One of the things…

JEAN DOMINIQUE

What? You don't agree with the notion of sweet gifts?

PRESIDENT

No. I don't agree.

JEAN DOMINIQUE

Yes, Mr. President. You gave them many gifts… Do you deny it?

PRESIDENT

Jean, ("Notice he stops calling him Jeando," History points out. "An indication Dominique had morphed into a blister under his fingernail.") yes, I do because democracy is like a bicycle. It has two wheels. One of the wheels is called reconciliation, and the other one is called justice… If one turns and the other does not, that means democracy is not functioning.

JEAN DOMINIQUE

President, ("Now," Morgan argues, "the journalist retaliates by dropping the suffix 'Mr.'") the TEVASA contract… is a gift… I can see the reconciliation but justice, President?

PRESIDENT

Now, you are talking about the TEVASA contract. So I am waiting for the people who had to answer first then I will put in my two cents.

"You see," History says as he stands up, "the son of a bitch was stalling. What did he mean in that last fucking answer?"

"Massenat, please," yells Morgan, "respect the President in front of those pee-on."

"Anyhow, History resists. "Mrs. Jeando thinks that was the interview that cooled off the relationship between the President and the man who campaigned for him. However, let me say in that same interview, the journalist referred to the President's enemies as also his enemies."

CHAPTER 13.

The Editorial

While in his second exile in the United States, Jeando spent a reasonable amount of time in Washington, DC with the McLintaughs, where young Leopold grew very attached to the journalist. The tot became thrilled after learning that he and this great and lovable man, as Jeando was reintroduced to him, shared the same name. As a matter of fact, within the first forty-eight hours, the child seemed to have forgotten that this was the same man on TV for whom he had called his parents' attention by the name he knew. As Dominique played hide-and-seek with him, he took to calling him Leopold as though the journalist and he were around the same age. Again, a few weeks before the talks at Governors Islands, the journalist spent time with the boy and his parents. Then Jeando was convinced that soon Aristide would go back, and so would he. During that stay, the boy's attraction to him reminded him to resume investigating when he returned home. Before the coup, Jeando was probing into the circumstances of his conception and birth. He had abandoned around the time of the coup, when he was close to finding out who the boy's biological father was.

When all was in place, and the radio station became operational, the Argentinian policewoman's story became evident when Dominique resumed what he did best and even seemed emboldened. That time, his weapon—his microphone—became an equal opportunity instrument to hold everybody's feet to the fire.

Perhaps, the officer adds, Jeando figured he had long fought for the freedom of the press and finally it had been achieved. With his friend Aristide in power, Jeando had a boulevard all to himself, and, by God, he used it!

Accrued wisdom. Morgan refrains from voicing what he holds against Dominique ever since his rant against the entire police force in the wake of the massacre at Rue Vaillant. On that occasion, the journalist took to naming all of the police officers on duty that day, suggesting that the population should not look the other way in dealing with them. If Dominique meant otherwise, it resounded differently for the police force. For a time, some officers even reminisced of the sinister role, according to them, a few people accused Jeando of in the post–Baby Doc mob reprisals.

Following through with his mental note, Jeando found the chance to investigate the conception of Leopold. At the same time, his involvement in bouts with laboratories pitched him in contention with none other than Tito Massim, who owns several of them. These labs, allegedly, were marketing low-grade ethanol or rubbing alcohol detrimental to the country's "kleren." And nobody can forget that the journalist was engrossed in a whistleblower's role of denouncing the efforts of the Clintons to destroy the country's agriculture. Speaking on the matter, Louis Farrakhan would bluntly expose the Clintons. They could not pretend, he'd say, to love Haitians and, at the same time, ruin their rice-producing capabilities to sell them rice produced in Arkansas.

History jumps from his seat and shouts, "If these are not apples, tell me what are."

"Sit your ass down."

"Other factors," Morgan Freeman continues, "or apples, as my partner calls them, that might have led to the assassination, were never looked at. Smokes in mirrors, I'd say or just rotten pears. Noises occurred around the polemic pitching the microphone of the journalist versus the influence and rank of a future senator. At the time, the journalist might have just reached his Eureka moment about the boy's biological father."

Despite Morgan's nonchalant attitude regarding the President's political party, the man, Dany Toussaint, may have done some favors on his behalf near the higher-ups in the government, including near Aristide himself and even near Gibéa, years before. He'd often told his partner that the senator was a man of his words. When all incriminated him, the policeman would talk of the unfairness and injustice in all of it. Dany, he'd say, was one of the easiest to accuse of wanting Jeando dead. Morgan argues that the man would not have much of a motive to assassinate Dominique. Though Morgan holds a grudge against Dominique since that macabre November of 1987, he loosely refrains from championing that the journalist actively played a part in his own demise. In that same vein, he would reprove anyone who implicates Dany, Aristide, but not Gibéa. Selective grudges or a suggestion that the former President is not man enough on his merit. The older officer feels more at ease to rather, place Michel Gibéa in meetings with another senator to plot the assassination. He would defend his friend while explicitly saying that he leans toward believing him over the journalist, although he questions his astonishing arrogance.

If History would point the finger even at Aristide, at Préval, Morgan prefers to say that his pal, the senator, is conveniently accused because of the freshness of his feud with Jeando. At the time, the journalist appeared to have been somewhere near the top on Gibéa's and Aristide's shit list since that famous interview. That interview was also mentioned in a conversation with the President of the Association of the country's journalists. It was nothing but a masking courtesy conceived by Gibéa, supposedly to make the journalist feel that nothing has changed and that no plot was being drafted against him. Rumors have that former President actively translating for his friend the exact meaning behind all of Dominique's questions. For instance, that question about whether the disbanding of the army was conceived in the English language. The other party in that discussion was subsequently gunned down in the street, like a dog, President Trump would say. Comedian Bill Maher rather would say that imitating the manner the President speaks as he calls him what he usually does. Morgan, however, maintains that the journalist had plenty of other powerful enemies. Folks who have lost a considerable amount of money and persona after the journalist made the ethanol and the tainted medications issue his own along with the rice dilemma. Morgan privately had wondered if the agronomist's issue with the Clinton administration concerning the destruction of Haiti's agriculture had ever really gone away. Some folks never set foot in the country, Morgan would argue, perhaps they could not find the face and the "huevos" or "balls" to do that while Dominique was still alive. Morgan believes the journalist would have swung his Samurai microphone at Bubba in the flesh.

Morgan equally believes that within all the names he included in his editorials, the killer, or all the assassins, can be found. Not on the Boulevard, for none would come that fatal morning. Folks, the officer privately thinks, have placed too much of a political connotation on the assassination while snubbing the underlying motive of few in the business sector. But he, a lowly cop, will never accuse anybody of the murder of Jeando.

"It's all there," he says. "Jeando had designated his killers. Like he would a weapon, Jeando swung his microphone at the people plotting his assassination. But justice is pretty far from being only blind in Haiti. The bitch is fucking stupid and a lazy slut too."

***

The two boys are both eleven years old and blond Haitians. Khalil and Kharim are the twin sons of Tito Massim. Whether they are play-fighting, the noises that they make in the drugstore (literally, store of drugs) disturb their mother, also Haitian of the same descent as her husband. Behind the counter, she seems impatient after she gives a white paper bag to a young dark-skinned woman who rummages in her purse for cash to give her in exchange. It is not that she does not have it, but it's something she has learned from her mother who has done this countless time when Papa Saddam happens to be at the drugstore. At the time, this nickname has not been attributed yet to Tito, who will adopt it later.

"Shh! Kharim! Khalil! Enough!" she yells as she turns up the volume and now the young woman seems rather be listening to the radio as she frantically looks through her purse. The young woman stalls. Her mother had instructed her on when to find Mr. Massim in the store and how to act. Until recently, Tito and his wife regarded Jeando as one of their own as long he did not meddle in their affairs. They had made a habit of listening to his radio since the ethanol and tainted medications story broke wide open in the media after some deaths had been reported. And personally, Jeando had taken ownership of it.

JEAN DOMINIQUE

Before our report regarding the expired and poisoned medications marketed by the laboratories MASSIM and others, I must denounce what took place in front of our station yesterday in the morning hours.

It pays. Faithful to the time he knows that Jeando would be on the air, Tito walks in behind his wife. He shuffles the boys' hair and greets her with a gentle kiss.

"You ate the breakfast I left on the table?" she asks.

"Huh! It was delicious," he replies while turning his attention to the young woman on the other side of the counter, looking at his wife as a wordless question.

"She's been rummaging in her purse for over five minutes," Mrs. Massim mutters before turning all her attention to Jeando on the radio.

"Hum! Wonder what he'll say this time."

The young woman finds a bill and places it on the counter just as Tito leans over.

"Ah!" Tito tells her. "It's okay, sweetheart. Go and say Hello to your mother."

The generic sound bites of the radio play on as Tito sits back near his wife, waiting to hear Jeando. He turns to the boys and sends them to play in the backyard.

RADIO

Does Dany Toussaint consider the children of the good Lord as wild ducks? Can a group of howlers pretend to take Radio Haiti hostage? Can they coercively use our microphones to disseminate their slanderous accusations against honest public officials and spew their racist anti-mulattos' rhetoric? These are the questions we asked ourselves yesterday morning when some forty hecklers blocked the Boulevard of Delmas, in front of our building for four hours. Howling sounds, shouts of profanities, rocks thrown against our façade. They violently shook our gratings. Faced with our resistance to their terrorism, they took on my person, apparently with their anti-Mulattos slogans, etc.

Our neighbors had tried in vain to call them to reason: "No, gentlemen, Jean Dominique has always been on our side since 1980, in '90, in '91." Take a look at the façade of his building, which stands as a witness. See the impact of the bullets from the coup d'état, and throughout it all, Radio Haiti silent, and Jean Dominique and his wife went into exile, etc.

The neighbors tried in vain to make them understand that those who attacked Jean Dominique are against Radio Haiti. Those who attack radio Haiti today are the Tonton Macoutes, the Duvaliers, the Bennetts, (three names withheld), Michel François, the spies of those bourgeois making and marketing poisonous medications. The Tito Massims, Serge Beaulieu, (name withheld), Isidor Pongnond, as in 1991, Namphy, Regala. And then, to this list, I must add Daniel Toumain, who, aided by a former president, killed Silvio Claude, perhaps on orders from on high. Those good people who wanted to tell the truth were beaten in front of Radio Haiti.

Beaten. Then, some other neighbors had identified the two vans which, coming from Pétionville, were unloading handfuls of new howlers from time to time. The neighbors and staff identified one of them as the H-5678. You see, we've kept our eyes open. Drivers and howlers, when confronted, naively admitted they had received a few dollars from the "major" to come in front of Radio Haiti.

The major? Dany Toussaint, of course. But why Radio Haiti, good God? During the campaign by Dany Toussaint against (names withheld) and against the higher staff of the police corps, he circulated in Tabarre the following formula: (names withheld) and Jean Dominique; they are two "little mulattos." I was then, for long enough, the target of the party of Dany Toussaint within "the political party of Aristide of which I am also a member."

On the other hand, in the aftermath of the police operation known as "Columbus," you remember, a campaign aimed at taking over the National Police was launched in all the media space of the capital sympathetic to the 1991 coup. One could have heard on some pro-Duvalierist radios: "One day, (name withheld) attacking the government." The next day, Dany Toussaint and (name withheld) would defame (name withheld). It was not difficult for these radios to change from one day to the next, drawing and shooting at each other.

Our enemies seize every opportunity to destabilize us. Here, at Radio Haiti, throughout this smear campaign, we have kept our composure. We've opposed to these breaches, of the Criminal

Code justiciable of a correctional court, and these racist attacks worthy of the best Macoutism, our line of strictly professional information. Our silence and our calm had annoyed Dany Toussaint and, maybe, his bosses.

Once fired (name withheld), Dany Toussaint, who had jumped with a certain lightness, it must be recognized, tried to molest (names withheld) at the cathedral and now, myself. So, what was a rumor at Tabarre is becoming a reality. Indulging in these reflections, I still kept my ear to what was happening in front of my building. Realizing that the graffiti against my person, the cries of hatred launched against me, the correction inflicted on the honest neighbors did not frighten me, they then wanted to negotiate. From the terrace, I told them that I would not accept their apology until they had erased all the graffiti about my person. This was done immediately. I agreed to listen to them to hear their justification, and I refused to give them the microphone, asking them instead to transmit, to whoever sent them, the following message:

The one who paid you, I told them, to come and try to terrorize me made three mistakes.

First. Saturday at the cathedral, he and his minions took advantage of a funeral. He tried to organize an accusatory and defamatory protest. Of course, they defamed (name withheld) and (name withheld). Of course, they physically attacked the Head of the National Police. Indeed, they desecrated, under the eyes of Father Jean-Bertrand Aristide, a place that should have been sacred to all, the Cathedral of Port-au-Prince. Sacred to believers and non-believers alike. But Dany Toussaint, despite these few progressions for him, was able to gather only a handful of people inside the cathedral. It was obvious. Despite previous attempts in the media by the backers of the coup before this funeral. Despite what is said about the widespread sympathy enjoyed by (name of the deceased), there were only a handful of demonstrators, parents, and officials at the funeral. Ah! This is a new proof of the tragic erosion of a particular popular convening power. That has been witnessed in Port-au-Prince for some time now. Don't you believe that our enemies do notice this erosion?

The first mistake made by Dany Toussaint. In military strategy, spreading in the eyes of the enemy the weaknesses in your warring capabilities is a capital blunder. The term "capital" taken in its literal sense. Is Dany Toussaint a good warrior? Was he? The answer doesn't get to me. But he is undoubtedly a terrible strategist.

Second mistake. He must have been intoxicated by the success of his elbowing with (name withheld) and (name withheld). Dany Toussaint is carried in triumph on the shoulders of some of his remunerated howlers under the enigmatic gazes of Jean-Bertrand Aristide and Michel Gibéa. Indeed, those howlers wanted him as chief of the police but, Titid, with piercing eyes, knows how to decode ambitions. And his smile, so naughty, says a lot. Tomorrow, this may be their business. Not mine. I did not fight for thirty years to today, decode the quarrels between the wannabe masters of the party.

Dany Toussaint's third mistake. He had just made it in front of Radio Haiti by taking it to me. Let's think about it. Since the end of Operation Columbus, he launched this attack for days throughout the media space to amplify his defamations, his anti-mulattos' stance. Traditionally, this is done by the Macoutes to hammer their slanders that could be brought to a correctional court. However, taking on Radio Haiti while all the media space supported him, applauded him and lauded his rise means what? Naturally, this media space claims to control the entire audience. Going after Radio Haiti and wanting to force the station to broadcast his words means only one thing is essential to Dany Toussaint. That is to be heard on Radio Haiti.

Ah! I've been thinking. "Calumny," Choderlos De la Clos tells us, "is a homage that vice renders to virtue." And the second consequence before our critics? To underline the independence of Radio Haiti from the party, our freedom from all the centers of power. Independence emphasized.

Let's go back to the cathedral. The mistake of Danny Toussaint is thinking that a little fearmongering of some "JPP Chimères" (howlers) could allow him to have access to our microphones. Oh, my God! It's underestimating two crucial things. Here we do not give our microphone to just anyone. Not to defamation. Especially not to libel against honest officials and to racism; be that racism anti-mulattos or anti-black as (names withheld) recently, held forth. But they get along.

Here, we respect the rules. We know that true justice cannot be exercised from howls of more or less well-paid oddballs. We know that when burglars flee the house they have just looted, they are the first to shout "Thieves!" How do you expect a respectable judge to take these "thieves shouts" into account when they investigate the looting? Let's be serious. And then I asked myself the question: During this whole campaign launched throughout the media space, Dany Toussaint never called me. Why? He never called Radio Haiti. Neither he nor (name withheld), to make any statement whatsoever or to expose some results of investigations he claims everywhere to have conducted into the death of (name withheld). Never. It's strange, this silence. And he unleashes a few howlers to force me to give him the microphone. The answer is this. Dany Toussaint knows better. Had he come to me with the results of his probe, the journalist that I am would have asked him, in private or publicly, the questions that would have pointed out the contradictions in his statements concerning his inquiry. Dany Toussaint knows that. That's why he prefers to go through the street to put pressure on me.

The murder of (name withheld), the aggression against Mario Andrésol, the recent assassination of dozens of policemen, the killing of Yvon Toussaint, the murderous attack against Marie-Claude Calvin Préval. All provoked and still provoke in us at Radio Haiti the indignation of the citizen and the anger from the party because we fought for justice, transparency, and participation. And we accompany, as everyone knows, concretely with professional, informative work of journalists, the preparation of the trial of Raboteau. We may be the only ones in this media space to accompany this preparation. But for us, there is only one feeling that animates us. An individual using his comrade's still fresh corpse in a campaign for his personal ambitions, as it was the case Saturday at the cathedral, is for us merely disgusting.

These are the elements of the messages that I asked my three interlocutors yesterday to pass on to Dany Toussaint. I will end with this last consideration. If he persists in this attempt to put a few howlers in front of Radio Haiti to block the Boulevard, he will break his teeth. Radio Haiti will remain closed for him.

But I know he's got guns. I know he has the money to pay and arm his minions.

Here, I have no other weapon than my job as a journalist, my microphone, and my steadfast faith of an activist for change, real change. And let it be evident to all. I will not leave any "freeloader" of the world the monopoly of the party. To nobody. If Dany Toussaint tries anything against me or against my radio, and if I am still alive, I will close the station after I denounce once again his maneuvers. I will go once again into exile with my wife and my children. Once again.

In 1991, Friends of Dany Toussaint tried desperately to take over Radio Haiti. I have resisted alone with my faith, my intelligence, and my professional experience. At the time, I had understood that behind a few politicians who were preparing the coup d'état, there was a stubborn will manifested by a certain Isidor Pongnond. Both of these dissidents frequented the salons of these great ladies, the lingerie of the party. I understood September 30, 1991. And later, Jean-Bertrand Aristide and René Préval would tell me: "You were right; they wanted to take over Radio Haiti to prepare the coup." Today, I ponder the same question. Isn't it the same exercise?

Last Sunday, the Bishop of Dessalines said in front of President Preval that there are old and new putschists who are trying to destabilize the government. In 1991, I had told Jean-Bertrand Aristide and René Prévlal: "Beware of Cédras." Titid replied, "Ah! Cédras and I are married."

Troubled marriage. With AIDS. Titid is stubborn. Yes, he's stubborn. He must understand that it is not only his persona and his sense of power that are at stake in this matter. If Radio Haiti is made silent again tomorrow, Ah! It will be a silence to wake the dead, the 5,000 from the coup, among others. This is the truth that must be gathered in this insignificant attempt to scare us yesterday. That's the truth, the right thing to say this morning. The fact of a free man.

Earlier, I quoted another free man, Choderlos de la Clos, now I end with Shakespeare: "The truth always makes the face of the devil blush." Thank you.

History's performance of Jeando's famous editorial stuns the foreigners. The older officers' memory capabilities and their knack for telling a story blow them away. About memory, one would wonder what the MIM at the FBI could achieve with such in an investigation. The young Frenchman who seems most interested in the country's history and who appears the most blown away by the old men would not let up. He asks the officers about how Dany reacted.

"These are," the UN soldier says, "severe accusations."

"Ah! Dany," exclaims Morgan for whom the man who grew extremely close to the President had pulled some strings and done many favors. He is not shy about touting the fact that he had, many times, been at the receiving end of Dany's favors. But he refrains from divulging the kind of these courtesies. Right out of the gate, he disclaims his being the right person to judge him, who had always respected him as a father figure. Only his partner knows how much Morgan had wished for the President to have taken a bite on the bait Jeando talked about six months before he was murdered. Never on Aristide's side, History has remained extremely cold and apathetic concerning the prospect of that close ally of the President leading the police force.

"I'd fucking walk away," he once told Morgan when it all became evident. "And I guess, you'd stay as his pet."

However, when briefly Toumain's power-angry cousin was placed in the position, the two partners went along well during his tenure. Officer Morgan is predisposed to let his partner accurately recite the words of Dany as he defended himself. He, however, thought he would tell the foreigners a bit about his benefactor without any bias. After a somewhat lengthy sugarcoating on the part of his partner, History grows angry and intolerant. He reprimands Morgan.

"Partner," he yells out as if no one else was present, "you must call it right. Indeed, I never liked the President. I have nothing to hide, but, at least, I believe I've always been in the interest of fairness. Those young folks need to know who the fuck Dany really was."

Turning to the younger policemen and foreign soldiers, he begs them to disregard his partner's sugarcoated malarkey. From the depth of his extraordinary memory, he pulls a news article that he's read while waiting for his turn in a Haitian barbershop on Eastern Parkway in Brooklyn, New York. In the piece, Ray Joseph was contrasting the real Toussaint to the somewhat charismatic man of whom some reporters have written.

"Well," History adds, "if it walks like a dog, barks like a dog, by God, I'm going to call it a dog. If you can control the thousands of powerful gun-carrying criminals of this slum in the capital, you need to be a thug. Dany, my young friends, just like his cousin who partners with Tito, is also capable of any of the things he's been accused of. I will not, however, accuse him of anything. I cannot help but think that his rupture with the man he previously bodyguarded seemed a bit too convenient. This, my young friends, after receiving the promotions onto Police Chief and another one that comes paper-bagged with the gift of immunity. His cousin wrapped that promotion with the favors of 'the ballots' of May 2000, only weeks after the assassination of Jeando for which one magistrate came hard onto him like a bitch."

"In fact," the old man continues, citing the article, "I could not make this shit up. It was public knowledge. His close ties to Tito Massim and his cousin were known to all. He was barred from entering the United States, where officials have always believed he was connected to drug trafficking and other criminal activities. Again, his separation from his former boss was but a front or a mask of some sort. In one form or another, perhaps in recognition, the party had shielded him from the charging judges/prosecutors who succeeded each other in the various chapters of that investigation. And the master Michel Gibéa and his acolytes manipulated their mobs each time a move was attempted on the case. For his being defensively active, those officials, either by intimidation, looked the other way. Or, by their incompetence, they failed to ask themselves whether he or former President Gibéa used their ATM card to purchase the bullets."

"Unlike my gratitude-ridden partner here," History continues, "I do not need to have received gifts and favors to defend him. His feud with the journalist was relatively fresh, and it became apparent and convenient to make him a person of interest. That is what he is. Dany is only a person of interest, just like Jeando's wife would be in any country of law. Not that she has anything else to see with the assassination of a person she's held dear to her heart. However," he looks at Morgan Freeman, "in the eyes of the law, the bitch could appear to have known some shit. And likewise, could fucking Préval, as Dany believed.

A peacekeeper from Chile of one Haitian parent presses the officers on the facts regarding the assassination.

"Before it occurred then, the young soldier says, the attack seemed to have gathered all the ducks and lined them up for it to be a perfect political crime.

"Yes, yes, it had," History replies. "Don't forget the rumors, at the time, had it that late president René Préval was considering the journalist to be his successor. The notion of President Préval prepping and pimping Jeando as his successor did not sit well with a faction of the party. That is according to what's his face, 'the guy who got whacked after spilling the beans.'"

Putting his two cents, Morgan tells the audience that to this day, in 2022, many are wondering why the heck that guy had not been charged with, at least, assistance to a crime. He had acknowledged that he received orders to contact a female senator who, he was told, had all the info about whacking the journalist in order to shut him up. That operation needed cars and money, and he was in charge of that type of logistics.

According to "the guy who gave the interview and died," a potential return to power necessarily goes through doing "something" about "The Little Mulatto of Delmas." You know, the guy said, to silence his microphone and see if that could raise the dead.

"That motherfucker could talk," Morgan Freeman quickly slides in, "clearly about the man formerly in charge of logistics at the party."

History hears otherwise. A different kind of wind was blowing that had Dominique thinking of what happened before the coup that overthrew Aristide the first time around. He deemed that perhaps, a few political hacks were trying to hijack his radio station to plan a somewhat similar putsch against Préval, feasibly, the journalist's "would be" predecessor.

"Folks, I agree with my partner," History adds. "Jean Dominique did talk a lot of shit, but he fucking made sense and had always taken the side of the country."

"Partner," he adds, "if you wish respect for big fucking lips, Aristide who should be prosecuted for a laundry list of shit, you do not call Jeando a motherfucker."

After he checks his watch, the Haitian-Chilean soldier tries to diffuse the pettiness. He asks them if any of the two would instead brief them about the man's reaction and what they thought of it as he points to the clock on the wall. The soldier's attempt succeeds in putting the partners back in agreement as they both turn at the same time to look at the clock.

"Gee!" exclaims History. "Where has the time gone?"

"You tell me, old man," replies Morgan.

As though the time on the clock pressed him, History declines to recite the exact words of Toussaint for his initial reaction. Morgan understands that History was only easing his way out and would ask him to take over. He feels volunteered and obligated to drop his partialities and paraphrase what Dany had said, knowing that his partner would not cut him any slack. For the first time tonight, the foreigners and the younger Haitians in the room witness Morgan's hesitation. Warned by History of the senior officer's predisposition in Toussaint's favor, the young

Haitians mentally formulate the questions they'd throw his way should he deviate. The foreigners also wonder if the whole thing is not all about showmanship. Many times, tonight, they had heard angry, and offensive words fly between the older men only for them to make up in their next breath. When he finally starts speaking after, he looked around the room to somehow palpate the weird and eerie silence amongst their guest and local recruits.

"Well folks," he starts, "Dany did not take the accusation sitting on his ass. In fact, he came out kicking and swinging as he incriminates even the late former President René Préval. The way he came out had Mrs. Jeando wonder what bad side of his bed he woke up on and he had up his ass in one editorial similar to that of her husband before his assassination."

"Before all this shit," Morgan continues making sure to employ his friend's words, "nothing has existed between the journalist and the senator until the event at the cathedral for the funerals of (name withheld). According to Dany, that was when it all started as Jeando, and a few of his friends wanted to pin (name withheld)'s death on him."

As his partner struggles, History takes over with his memory ability to recite Toussaint's reaction in light of the initial pursuit by one of the many magistrates assigned to the case.

"Dany had maintained he had been accused unjustly. He considered it a massive smear campaign against his character and his person. He had thought he could have contributed in his own way toward finding the closure they pretend to look for in favor of Dominique; he had wanted to come forth. However, he realized that it was not only about finding justice for the journalist but also to besmirch his personality and social standing."

"Dany said, it all started two months after the assassination, when then president René Préval asked (name withheld) to have him arrested. The first judge, given the case, may have asked for more proof or reason to charge and arrest Dany. President Préval entrusted the situation to judge (name withheld) who was hell-bent on implicating the guy from day one. DT reminded everyone that, at the time, he was not yet sworn in and did not have the parliamentary immunity. They could have arrested him at any time after the two warrants issued by the first judge but retained by the initial person who was to arrest him on the President's order. Perhaps in his effort to manipulate the press as pointed out by Mrs. Jeando, Dany reminded the media what their following steps should have been. He wanted the journalists to go out and investigate since he'd named a few people. It was clear the man was desperately sending out directives for the media to help him establish something. History wants the journalist's widow to have read right into the senator's reaction throughout the media space.

For him, President Préval only cared about implicating one person, and that one and only person was Dany. That was why, my partner's friend said that this particular judge, up to that time, only moved to arrest just a handful of guys whom he vainly tried to bribe hoping they would rat him out. That judge would have offered a host of sweet deals to (four names withheld). Many witnesses at the National Penitentiary could attest. That magistrate made many trips to the prison, expecting those guys to point the finger at me in the assassination of Dominique. By me, I meant Dany, the officer clarifies.

He even went to a hospital to put pressure on doctors and nurses. He wanted to know whether and what amount of money was offered them to kill one presumed accomplice in a suspicious malpractice during a routine intervention. A bullet had only scratched the surface of that man's buttocks before he went into that hospital to die of an all unrelated cause.

It is not that the media stood against Dany. But it was, at times, manipulated to feed the frenzy against him, Morgan alleges as he might have heard that complaint from the senator himself. Doctors and nurses were arrested. Some lawyers had had to negotiate their release. These maneuvers pushed Dany to declare that any judge could have arrested whomever he wished. It would not mean they would have found the killer/killers, and deliver justice for the journalist. Dany also accused the prosecutor of even pressuring the employees at the morgue. He wanted them to disclose whether and how much money was exchanged to have the corpse of a taxi driver's brother stolen."

In their regular storytelling practices, he had never heard of the existence of such a character in that particular story.

"I'll tell you later in private," Morgan promises his partner. "He lives. He was only a taxi driver nobody knew somewhat connected to Jeando's assassination on two fronts." History continues.

"Up to this moment," Dany would say, "neither from Adam nor from Eve do I know that cat."

"Dany talked of someone who was an essential person in the case who was on the site of the murder. He named one Markinton Philippe, a professional killer and an informant at the US embassy who had had to be contacted by a certain Daniel Wittman under some hierarchic authorization. *Who would have authorized such contact?* Dany wondered.

"For over twenty years," History says, "that shit has never ceased to sound so fucking incoherent. Does this shit make sense to you, Marcellus?"

"We are only reporting to those kids," his partner replies. It does not have to make sense to us. We're no judges."

"I guess they must also know that the deck has been stacked against Jeando even after his death. How would justice have been delivered?" History asked. "At the time, the new head of the justice department, before his appointment, was no less than Dany's own lawyer. Isn't that a bitch? We cannot tell these kids that the new government had ever displayed any willingness to see that case through. Shit!"

"Marcellus," History adds, "you of all people see what that President does when he wants shit done. This negro and fucking Gibéa, before him, would dance on one foot, bark like dogs, and kiss sick folks with all kinds of shit on their skin to promote their own agendas. For the amount of shit, Jean Dominique went through to support this bastard…."

"Massenat!" Morgan yells, trying to put the break on his partner's mouth. "Those kids are young, and most are guests in the country. Stop disrespecting the President in front of them."

"Fuck Aristide!" History explodes once more. "Fuck Gibéa too. Some folks came close to almost spit in Jeando's face when he supported the motherfucker in 1990. In 1991, the military wanted to kill him after the coup. Dominique went through fucking too much. And, Marcellus, you know what kills me? Many times, he would drag his ass up to that poor woman's radio station to sweet talk and bullshit her to death only to fucking do the other thing. That was badass."

"Young folks may not know it. That fucker was terrible."

"Massenat!" Morgan yells again, but History ignores him.

"Kids," the older officer continues. "In the '90s, he fled to Washington, thinking that cracker was his friend and ignoring that he was only saucing him for his own interests. He is said to have done in some of the close allies he thought could undermine his influence or run against him in the future. Such as… Aware of that list of people killed, Morgan tacitly implores History, who agrees, not to divulge any of their names in this setting.

"But, listen to this, kids. One associate of his might have suggested that he intervened to ease up the embargo that was crushing the most impoverished Haitians. That associate would be killed a short time after the suggestion. How about them fucking apples, Marcellus?"

History goes on and on until he finally names Oriel Jean, who had confessed a bunch of crap, including his love and admiration for Jeando. A load of shit, History always said of that confession. Initially, he did not want to actually name him for some reason. How in hell could this guy support his claim to love and admire Jeando, who has always been a straight-edge contrast to whatever activity his faction of the party engaged in? Hogwash. History thinks he was covering his ass, not knowing he would be whacked a short time later.

"The senator," he continues, "tried to hold a mirror to President Préval. He argued the President should also be heard in the case as he questioned the extent of the President's relationship to the journalist who has been his mouthpiece on various matters. He would ask that investigators look into why everyone else in the President's circle, but Jeando had security details surrounding them, and he got whacked just like a bum. Why is that, the Senator asked?

"The notions of my fleeing the country," Dany said," that I am guilty are false and groundless rumors because I am in no way implicated in the slaughter of the journalist. I extend a challenge, Dany went on, to anyone who could tell when it was that I had any problem with Dominique. The only time I had a problem with him was after the death of my friend (name withheld), to whom I said must be given justice. It is true I had named (name withheld) as part of the plot that killed him. That same night, I met with President Préval who took offense to my pointing fingers at his friend (name withheld). I told President Préval that I don't say he is part of any plot, but I have doubt, and his friend should remain in the country to answer a few questions. There were other things we talked about that night when (name withheld) mentioned that I am involved in drug trafficking. And that was when I found the courage and told him that he could not say that while his vehicles are used in that same traffic. I also told the President, right to his face, that his vehicles also are being used to haul drugs. So, he, the President, and his pals had better find some other stooge to pin that drug on."

"It was since that night, and after what took place at the cathedral for the funerals," Dany continued, "that everyone got angrily on my case. Then Jean Dominique thought he would defend his and the President's mutual friend in that editorial. I will say the same thing I have said before: '(Name withheld) must come back to answer the question as to why my friend got whacked shortly after being in his house?' I think that is where the plot to kill him originated."

Forty-three minutes after midnight, the clock says. The foreign soldiers and the younger policemen are already on their feet as the sign that they want to leave the headquarter. The young French soldier lingers a bit. He wants to thank the seniors for the time spent in their company and congratulate them on their storytelling. The others may already be halfway toward the UN trucks in the yard. Few of the locals walk toward their private vehicles and most toward the back of the black-and-white pickup trucks, which will perform as a taxicab for those who live relatively far.

The UN truck that was already idling starts rolling slowly behind the group commander, the young Frenchman who is now walking alongside Morgan toward his car. Not paying attention to the truck, he asks him again about Roger's death and why he thinks that the ousted President did not order his execution. Not because he somewhat cares about his country's would-be involvement in the assassination. That involvement has neither been proven nor materialized. Lafontant's killer, anyway it is sliced, is Haitian though his genetic constitution could otherwise suggest.

"That President," Morgan replies, "President Aristide, had no business with Tito Massim. Saddam financially backed the coup that ousted him in September of 1991 despite his close personal and business relationship with Dani Toumain, a steadfast Aristide supporter and the cousin of a close ally. Tito is a member of that mulatto elite who hated Aristide. They would lynch his supporters, be it one of their own, someone like Jeando, whom most of them viewed as a traitor. Now, had Daniel Toumain or his cousin shown up in that prison cell, then one would have been sure where that order would have come from."

"Roger Lafontant, like Jeando, in his own way had stockpiled a shitload of enemies. Likewise, folks would want to pin their assassination on their most recent feud. Contrary to Jeando's case, I am quite sure that President Aristide did not give any order. For me," Morgan continues, "Roger's was less of a political assassination than that of Sylvio Claude or Dominique. Toumain, who killed the pastor, is a certified criminal entrepreneur. He has no affiliation and would take any job from anyone who would fork the right amount, be it from the enemies of his friends. And I am almost sure that should the price be right, he'd even whack Aristide himself."

"Then again, I don't know," he adds, "but Tito also would. He'd do all three Préval, Gibéa, and Aristide. That son of a cow, Tito, is fucking badass too."

The truck pulls up beside Morgan's car, of which he is already behind the wheel. The soldier hops on, and by courtesy, they allow the older officer to drive out of the lot first.

PART TWO

The Investigation

"Jean L. Dominique was assassinated simply because his demeanor befitted a president."

Professor S. PIERRE-ETIENNE.

CHAPTER 14.

A Double Date In Washington, DC

Hypoxia. A young Mrs. Geffrard had had to suffer through a host of common illnesses. She was about twelve or thirteen years old when introduced to the pastime by a young American couple; her Haitian parents became somewhat skiing enthusiasts. For the first time, they took her with them for a week in Aspen, Colorado. After about an hour there, Claudine, the future First Lady, had presented with the symptoms. It is not that she has hypoxia on airplanes. She has made a mistake to condition her mind to develop some respiratory malaise whenever she boards an aircraft. Today, after having much-avoided air travels, she would not pass up this opportunity as her husband starts doing what presidents-elect do.

A few days have already passed, and the festive mood is still in the air throughout the country. Life or most of the things that it encompasses and as the people of the nation knew it has practically stopped. Lysius had gotten serious right on elections night. His old roommate at Yale himself, now the President of the United States, called to congratulate him on his victory. The same feeling that his Haitian friend is experiencing, David Sosa had also experienced.

"Two years earlier, he made an electoral mockery of a president nobody thought would last until the elections, O.J. Simpson, oops," the officer would add as he rectifies. "Of Donald Trump. Aided by a Republican-controlled senate, like the aforementioned, he beat the legal structure and got acquitted. In these last presidential elections, Sosa became the first Latino President of the United States. Like America fell in love with Barack Obama, the people poured out their hearts and their votes at David Sosa who has quite a story! Sosa's immediate older brother is a "Dreamer," who had lost his DACA protection due to Trump's racist aspiration to annihilate Barack Obama's presidency. With the Affordable Care Act, the Deferred Action for Childhood Arrivals policy became the icons for Donald Trump's demolition of Obama's legacy."

The invitation came from Mrs. Sosa to Claudine Geffrard, whom she has not seen in person for a significantly long time. It was worded in the form of a double-date plan as if they were still at Yale. Claudine, Mrs. First Lady, would not wish to pass up on that occasion. Though she does not feel too good, she has a lot to look forward to beyond this particular flight. Also onboard is a person the press, and most, deem a fish out of water. The president-elect considers his presence a strong statement to the world concerning the type of politics the country will experience. At least during his time in office. On elections night, right after the congratulations call from Sosa and his wife, Lysius convokes a meeting with his team. He stuns with the announcement that his former opponent should be part of the trip. He also wants to offer the post of Ambassador to the United Nations, where Duvalier enjoys the most privileged admiration.

Like good students and as instructed, the transition team put together a dossier on the assassination of Jean Dominique in the days leading up to this trip where the matter will come up. Many a time, Lysius had told them that he was along with Sosa in a dorm room when the assassination occurred. He had shared with them the ideas he and the President of the United States had entertained between them at the time. The two have talked a lot about what had happened. During the visit, Sosa and Lysius would recall about the girls who were visiting with them and who threw an unexpected pizza party in the dorm with absolute disregard for Lysius' grief over the slaughter of the journalist. They laughed as they also remembered how Sosa kicked them out and drove them off campus.

At the university, these two could goof off and waste time like animals. They wrote the books of party-throwing. But when came time for pressing matters, they would get all about them. For the two years, the President had been in office, Sosa had never displayed such lavishness in welcoming a guest head of state from any other part of the world. This is different. The Sosas parade the Geffrards along the Potomac. They take great pleasure in introducing their guests to their immediate circle. At times, the Sosas would herald the guest of their guests, Duvalier. On personal request from Sosa, the Yale alumni descended on DC. Their old-time pal had become the President of his country.

The Geffrards—father, president-elect, future First Lady, and daughter—all stay at the Sosas' private residence, not far from the home of former FBI Director Edward McLintaugh Sr., where still lives his son Ed McLintaugh Jr. with his wife, Dorothy. The same property where a journalist played hide-and-seek with Leopold, then a little boy.

President Sosa had become infuriated when he learned that the Trump Hotel was retained to house members of Lysius' entourage during their stay. He quickly felt relieved when he learned that all of them had declined to stay there. Even Nickesse Duvalier opted not to stay there. A few years prior, Duvalier had sided with then Senator Geffrard when he created an uproar in defending Haitians. The property owner had uttered some unpleasantness regarding their people a year into his chaotic and erratic presidency.

SENATOR LYSIUS GEFFRARD

"Such an individual is paralyzed from the neck up. That is why he thinks and speaks with a lower part of his anatomy. I will cut him some slack this time. I do not know for sure that he did say all of my people have AIDS. I know, however, that the words are those of an ignorant, arrogant jackass, and for anything else that individual may say about us, fuck him."

In a one on one meeting during the visit, it is President Sosa who first mentions the Jeando investigation. Not that Lysius would not have. That was the idea behind his asking for the complete and extensive dossier. Throughout the years since, they had often exchanged views on Jeando's murder and had kept each other up to date of all the happenings and not happenings about the case. Before also becoming a US senator, like his Haitian friend in his country, President Sosa had had a brief stint at the FBI as a newcomer agent during McLintaugh's tenure.

Today, the presence of Lysius Geffrard in the United States is creating a brouhaha. The Republicans who seem never to have recovered from the defeat David Sosa handed them criticized the lavish receptions the President gives the president-elect from a small and insignificant country. They consider Lysius as a man who insulted a sitting POTUS. They find it very unpatriotic of the young Democrat to welcome such a man in the United States, let alone these lavish receptions. Sosa's riposte is short and straightforward in a "man-on-the-street" lingo.

"At least," he posts on Twitter, "the only collusion with that insignificant country occurred to have a few Haitians fight for ours. Not to stick their noses in our s#!t [sic]."

Likewise, back in his own country, the timidly and gauchely shaping up opposition to Lysius finds itself at a loss of ammo. Detractors move to accuse him of not respecting the country's independence commemoration. Be it to meet with the POTUS, he should not have been outside the country on January 1 as president-elect. They ignore that Lysius would be back in ample time for the trip to the city of the independence alongside President Josaphat. And most say it is the presence of Nickesse Duvalier in Lysius' entourage that has toned down the criticism on the local front. The Haitian diaspora within the United States never felt so proud of and honored for the presence of both Geffrard and Duvalier. As for Aristide in 1991, they have descended on Washington from everywhere, but in a more significant number. Never before had an American president put so much of himself into the preparation for receiving a head of state.

"If you want to throw a wrecking ball," says President Sosa to his friend as they walk into the oval office, "at Dominique's conundrum, I will help you swing it."

The President and the president-elect both remember a double date with their now respective wives. That night, they had watched the movie *L.A. Confidential*, an oldie at the time already, from which they'd heard that line just spoken by Sosa as he enters.

"You remember these books, don't you?" Lysius replies.

"The author," Sosa replies, "lives down the street from us, and his son is one of the best agents at the FBI. I think you should meet him."

"Junior is slightly more technical. Whereas," Sosa continues, "the father swore by the science of the matter, Baby McClintaugh is more into gadgetry."

"Last I heard," the Haitian replies, "he has developed something that can light up brain stems and transform the hippocampus into a hub for his investigation method."

"Indeed," POTUS answers, "the McLintaugh is the prototype of American ingenuity."

Lysius and Sosa have both read the works of both the McLintaughs on criminal investigations extensively. Ever since the murder of Dominque, Lysius had given wholeheartedly into the legal and hypnotic aspects of the works. On his part, Sosa had only read the investigative facet. They both know what reopening the investigation would practically entail. Many long studying nights they had talked over and over about it. About politics, one could almost complete the other's thought, and that shows when they speak of Lysius' newfound friend, Duvalier.

"Tell me," says the American President, "you are going to appoint this cat, Nickesse, ambassador to the United Nations, aren't you?"

"How did you guess?"

"I did not guess," replies Sosa. "I only know I would."

"Still needs some political maturity," Lysius says, "I want him to become President one day.

He seems to be a quick learner."

Lysius seems less and less interested in talking about his former political opponent. He tells Sosa he will have Duvalier eat from the palm of his hand. That is former senator Geffrard's weapon of choice to "politically eat" his opponents and rivals. Not to kill them or as the journalist was preemptively murdered. If President Préval had had his way, the president-elect believes, Dominique would have been a redoubtable contender. "Jeando," Geffrard says, "would have thrown quite an amount of sand into the engines of some prominent power-thirsty folks. Enough sand to want him dead or why not, even assassinate him themselves. His murder was not free, although pusillanimous. It served a purpose 'to whom it may have concerned." The president-elect had learned from his father that Roger Lafontant had had to turncoat since he had no other choice but to become a born-again Duvalierist. Geffrard the younger seems to have perfected the practice, and ironically, the new President is making Nickesse drink his own grandfather's toxic Kool-Aid.

Lysius has already won Nickesse Duvalier over the notion of bringing back to the motherland the matured, skilled Haitian brain and muscles being exploited for peanuts everywhere around the globe. In less than a month, the two former political rivals have appeared to drink from that same cup, Geffrard's. The two agreed to see into the civic education of the people. A notion Duvalier championed during his campaign. Nickesse was not born when the instruction of civism was viewed as his grandfather's catechism. Well, that served a generation very well. But after 1986, there were plenty of morons to do away with it on the baseless ground that it had only been a brainwashing instrument that favored the old regimes. The present generation is entirely unaware of any civism. Even some members of the parliament ignore their roles and rights as citizens. Geffrard once challenged a colleague to recite part of the national anthem of the country. Sad, but this part is no fiction. The two have already agreed to prevent anyone of that former President's schools of thought from ever winning the presidency. They both reckon it would be detrimental and outright catastrophic not only to Josaphat's "legacy" but to the country as a whole. In years past, that movement had frequently demonstrated that they will destroy, mostly by fire, anything any president accomplishes and reset the country onto the path of regression. They are bent on destruction and revenge and have ramped up corruption and embezzlement to unprecedented levels. The former rivals jointly and vehemently condemned the "country-lock" tactic of the opposition to the outgoing President.

Lysius' number one priority now, as his inaugural approaches, is the investigation that he championed during the campaign. Not that the country's shaky and unstable economy, the education system, public safety, public health, and feeding the people do not concern him more. He had spoken extensively with some high-powered economists, entrepreneurs, and tech geeks that Sosa's staff had lined up for the circumstances. Lysius wants to make some military service mandatory. As he says, "This Ratpakaka generation will learn what it means to live with each other in a society" and serve the country in some capacity. In the Senate, he had manifested concerns for that generation. Of which generation, he says, each member is a separate little unit who does not give a rat's ass about the needs and rights of the others around him or her. Senator Geffrard called it "the one single worst ill that Bill Clinton had imposed on the country in the '90s." As a remedy, he floated the idea that a physically able but unwilling individual who did not serve must pay expensive fines. To have a passport, to get a driver's license issued, to occupy functions, and to run for an elective appointment. Geffrard's bill introduced the various social difficulties that the law would stipulate. Further, he tells Sosa, he intends to keep his promise to President Josaphat to be a worthy steward of his legacy. And he makes sure he adds at the end of his sentence: "contrary to your predecessor of his." Politicians.

"But, Dave," Lysius adds, "there is another ball you could help me swing. Two actually."

"Shoot that first ball," Sosa commands.

"It is a page in former president Aristide's playbook. Heedful of the Democrats' talking points on reparations during the elections, his buddy won. Lysius also wants to capitalize on some embarrassing admission to justify a vendetta. Around the early months of his second presidency, the former priest did that after France's admission that slavery was a crime. Aristide pressed that such, like all crimes, also calls for some restitution."

"You do remember Bill Clinton's admission, don't you?"

"Bubba," replies the giggling Sosa as the Haitian slides his hand to slightly part the curtain and catch a view of the garden, "has admitted to a lot of shit. But if it was at the UN or in front of Congress, I don't recall, but I remember that one about your country's agriculture. Right?"

"Bingo!" he says as he turns around. "I wish to use that as leverage to have your country restore my country's agriculture. Specifically, our rice production capability. Will you help me?"

Lysius spent a lot of time arguing in the senate in favor of the country's agrarian production. He reminds Sosa of that rice he tasted and had talked of so much when he spent time in the country with the Geffrards. This was the rice, he complains, that all Haitians used to eat from that particular region of the country until… The list of his complaints is long. He even tells his friend of chicken and turkey wings and legs. Lysius sorrows about the bloody franks shipped as fresh food to his country. "That shit," he tells Sosa, "would not reach the American consumers if it stays past twenty minutes outside a freezer." He tells Sosa of the taste of Haitian chicken as he compares them to what he calls "The Wet Ass Dead Chicken." He tells Sosa that it is in the United States that Haitians eat this shit that only takes thirty-six hours from egg to whatever it becomes that they put in their bodies. Lysius wants to stop a lot of things.

"Dave, you ought to work with me to stop the bloody importation of second-hand shit to my country. That is not worthy of the glorious history of my people. The crap comes not only from your country but from all over." An earful for the US President who is very aware of whom he deals with. Someone with whom he spent many long nights, if not partying, studying and molding their similar political fitness. The president-elect wants to end the migration of the country's youth to South America, to Chile and Brazil in particular. As he promised to President Josaphat, he wishes to build on his decentralization politics to curtail the internal migration instigated by Aristide and Gibéa before him.

"For Christ's sake, Lysius. With those bloody republicans out there, that will require some substantial lifting."

"Then," replies Lysius, "lift heavier, you goofball. And, slit their fucking throats if the shit comes to that."

"I am already growing impatient to hear your other wrecking ball," says Sosa, who had gotten up to look through the window like Lysius did a minute ago.

Lysius postpones the asking for after they meet with Ed McLintaugh later tonight. He reminds the US President it is something that they both had agreed on when they were together at Yale. They had made up their minds as students about Jeando's assassination. Likewise, they had determined that the US occupation of Haiti was more of a cover-up, a front. As students, they had agreed it was a well-orchestrated bank heist with a racist undertone, which saw the country's gold reserve end up in a vault in New York. The narrative was that Haiti's National Bank had requested the move for safekeeping from the Germans whose influence in the region worried the shit out of the Americans. Before that, Haitian currency stood toe to toe with the US gold standard dollar because gold also backed it although the nation was crippled by France's extortion. And once the Yankees had paws on the country's metal, it became more comfortable for them to declare in 1919 that the Haitian money was worth only twenty cents of their dollar. Talking about injustice to a shithole country? At Yale, the two had agreed on what could be done, and today, destiny has placed them at the junction where one is determined and ready to stake a claim and the other to put up and help or shut the hell up.

With only a day left in the trip, Lysius wants to make sure he gets a firm answer on when he and the US President will pay that visit to Ed McLintaugh. He wants to have a clear idea of the possibilities of which he has read about since he was at Yale.

"Davy Boy," Lysius will tell Sosa coming back from the McLintaugh's to rejoin their wives, did you know those robbers also took the crown of the Emperor Soulouque from the bank? They fucking stole every shit of value that guaranteed our currency's strength."

He had continued to brush up on the subject as a senator witnessing, at the same time, the cowardly behavior of the folks in power vis-à-vis Jeando's assassination and the many incomplete, messed-up, or torpedoed investigations. Nonetheless, and knowing Sosa's impulsive mannerism, he would not like to go right away to that meeting. He would wish first to consult the dossier once more for small details. At least, talk to his advisors since the encounter would only involve McLintaugh, himself, and the President of the United States. At a significant distance, of course, will be the Secret Service for Sosa and Jacques Cyprien, who has been in charge of Lysius' security for a while. But this man, from day one, has sent bad vibes to Claudine Geffrard. She never could explain it to her husband, but she has told the president-elect that she does not trust the obese man too much. Perhaps it is the type of relationship Michelle would have had with some folks in the entourage of Nickesse's father back in the day.

Jacques Cyprien really had come late to the party. He was not in Geffrard's camp until it was time for President Josaphat to assign the prescribed security detail to the top presidential candidates. When it became clear that Lysius and Nickesse were the two who would remain in the race, Dani Toumain decided to play his hand. He managed to convince the President to assign one of his protégés to each of the candidates. He presented himself as a Geffrard's fan. He easily persuaded the President for one more man to his horse in the race, Lysius, thus, Jacques Cyprien.

CHAPTER 15.

Quantico

The blond little girl elegantly wears her pink jacket with an angel drawing at the back. Yesterday, she had pressured her mother into purchasing it for the occasion. The girl is unpretentiously adorable. She has heard that compliment quite a few times in the span of the morning. She hears it again as she and her mother walk out of the elevator in the lobby of the luxurious high-rise. When the door slides open, four-year-old Maddie runs off paying no attention to the older gentlemen caretaker of the property. The little girl plows right into the man, causing him to spill his morning coffee and donuts on the lobby's floor he had cleaned a minute ago. Her mother spends a few minutes apologizing, and she even attempts to wipe the floor with the roll of paper towel that had also fallen from the caretaker's hand. Maddie only stands watching her clean the floor without saying a word.

"No, ma'am, you don't have to," says the gentleman. "It's my job. Every time such an adorable young lady will bump into me, I'll clean what she spills."

He takes the roll away from her hand.

"Sweetie, say sorry to the nice man."

She runs off. It seems that everyone they meet today would notice how charming Maddie is. Everyone, but that vicious dog who scares her from inside its master's vehicle in the parking lot. However, the master finds that a golden occasion to strike a conversation. He had observed her from afar for quite a few times.

"Good dog"! He would praise the canine a tad later as he drives away. For days, he had wanted to speak to her, who blushed when he complimented them both on how beautiful she was and how lovable the little girl is. The stunning blond woman with her daughter that he looks at in his rearview mirror is twenty-nine-year-old Teresa McLintaugh. The estranged wife of Leopold thinks her husband had given more importance to the FBI than to their marriage.

Leopold McLintaugh, because of his father's and grandfather's standing and influences at the bureau, did not have much trouble transitioning from school to the field. He and Teresa had married during their senior year in college. Once at the FBI, he would not take long to establish himself as a promising agent in the forensics division. As a rookie, he had to travel extensively on international cases, and the ones where he made a name for himself took him to Holland five years ago and to Italy just recently. At thirty-four years old, Leopold had already accumulated a wealth of field accomplishments and recognition that would make many older farts at the bureau jealous. Indeed, Leopold had not been home much since he had started his FBI career the year of his marriage to Teresa.

It is not that she and Leopold are incompatible. Nevertheless, besides having known each other through all their college years, they have not had the privilege of really experiencing marriage life together. The last year in school, after they had wed, they both agreed to enter the attitude of "let's get it done with." Leopold McLintaugh and Teresa Stone, husband and wife, indeed graduated. The husband also became an agent the same year with no roadblocks. Before starting his sophomore year in college, he had taken the Quantico journey on advice from a friend of his father's, the laboratory director. And in the summer right after the laboratory moved into the newly constructed 500,000-square-foot facility in 2003, Leopold started the NAT or New Agents Training. After considerations, along with his excellent references, he will have entered the bureau as a third generation whose grandfather was the director just a few years back. Around the time Maddie was being born, a wave of terrorist attacks had him traveling throughout the Mediterranean and Northern Africa. They only had what he called "short layovers" at Dulles where Teresa would check into a nearby hotel to meet with him. She even believes that they had conceived of the little girl on one such brief rendezvous. It is said that with a lack of wood, the fire goes out. For this marriage, it has perhaps proven right. Teresa did credit him for, at least, trying to be there for the occasion of her birth but could not make it all the way at the last minute.

She had agreed to drive Maddie, who had asked many times these last days to see daddy. Teresa had made the call to Leopold after the little girl kept her end of the bargain with mommy to eat everything that was on her plate before she could see her daddy. Yesterday, Sunday, Maddie ate her whole plate and, a bonus, her entire breakfast this morning. The anticipation has built. It is easy for Maddie, who has been there on other occasions, either with Teresa or with her grandparents. She had started seeing in her young mind the image of the massive granite stone near the entrance. That fixture stands as a reminder to employees and visitors alike that the laboratory is dedicated to crime victims and their families. For Teresa, it was time to render unto Caesar and honor her end.

In her new black and pink coat jacket, Maddie runs into Leopold's open arms. Her little face glows with happiness on Leopold's shoulder. She blushes as he murmurs in her ears how beautiful she has gotten and that she has to take good care of mommy. Her little angelic face on his broad shoulder literally lights up. The ever-elusive picture of perfect happiness was right there at that instant between Leopold, his daughter, and Teresa. Though she would not have appeared in it, Teresa would undeniably be a part of the complete picture. At that exact moment, that little feeling, that chemical reaction, or that same particle transferred a transcending emotion. The three of them, during that ephemeral "blink of an eye" through their hearts' wavelength, have interconnected.

After she lets Maddie run into her father's open arms from halfway across the lot, Teresa returns to the passenger side of her car to close the rear door. All the while, with Maddie in his arms, Leopold never took his eyes off her. Teresa walks around her vehicle's rear end to lean on the car. She looks on and chews on her thumb when Leopold diffidently waves to her. In fact, even Dorothy and Ed don't hold anything against her for leaving. They understand. And they have spoken to their son many times on the matter. Everyone remained cordial. In their separation, civility has prevailed, and this explains why Dorothy still hopes things will turn out great for her son, Teresa, and Maddie. Neither Leopold nor Teresa has ever uttered the "D" word.

"Hello, Teresa," says Leopold when he waves to her. He releases Maddie from the hug in which he held her so tenderly while looking at and noticing that his wife had lost a few pounds but not one iota of her beauty.

"Hi, Leo," she merely replies. Very quickly, the image of the face of the man whose dog had scared Maddie earlier in the parking lot flashes in her mind as to force a casual comparison with Leopold. Equally as quickly, she dissuades herself from such an absurd association. All the time she had stayed away, she had never thought in such a way of being with another man. Teresa does not allow her mind to wander. She decides right that minute that Leopold is her man and the father of her little princess.

With no emotion, she waves back, gets in the car, and looks away, biting her lips, grumbling while he stands erect to walk Maddie to the vehicle. Leopold opens the door and kneels again to hug his daughter. Teresa tries to look straight frontward and not to turn her head.

"We miss you, daddy," Maddie says.

Leopold squeezes her against him, shuffles her hair. Teresa starts the car, still looking ahead as she fights the tears.

"I know," he says loud enough. "Daddy misses you guys too."

He sits the girl in the car, closes the door, and crosses toward the entrance. There, Heather, that hot and sexy young blond intern, had been pacing to catch him and let him know about the many visits he had gotten from the director. Leopold had arrived sooner but stayed in his vehicle to spot Teresa and Maddie as they pull up. She had seen him near the car across but could not see the driver who was looking straight onward. Heather knew he had a child, but he had never talked to her about being married. To her close girlfriends, she has admitted having fantasies about Leopold. In her mind, Heather mounted quite a few scenarios to determine why the FBI director wanted to see Leopold lately. She even ran the strange idea that Peter Ekstroem perhaps was thinking of a Ping-Pong game with the son of his rival with her being the ball. After her romantic getaway to Labadee with Ekstroem before Christmas, the blond remained confident that the director would want to date her again. By his kinky, freaky nature, she thinks the director would welcome the suggestion of a threesome with her and such a hunk, Leopold. However, the FBI director and the third-generation McLintaugh are in no way ready to forget the year 2017.

Leopold could not see his head in the reflection in the glass door. Either because the bold silver letters making up the words "FORENSICS DIVISION" cover it at that level. His image appears to flee horizontally as the glass door swiveled when Heather pushed it open for him. A field agent, Leopold, no longer has a job in this division. Walking into this office has become a product of habit. As a toddler, a lad, a young man, he had many times accompanied either grandfather or father at the bureau on "Bring your child to work day" and on many other occasions. He had become a fixture at the bureau where the most senior employees had gotten familiar with him long before he had joined. Reasonably, it would be considered "genetics" or even hereditary. Leopold now helps the federal laboratories all over the country and, at times, abroad.

"What have I done?" Leopold asks the young blond woman.

"To deserve such as I opening doors for you?" Heather completes, more to emphasize her physique instead of the act.

"Good morning, Heather."

"Or maybe," replies Heather, "your intended question is why, the heck, the boss took the ride twice from HQ only to see you instead of a simple phone call."

The day before, what Lysius had wished not to happen due to the impulsive nature of his friend, President Sosa, did occur. Last night, the President did drag him to the residence of Ed McLintaugh. Lysius, however, only managed to delay the meeting for only three hours to consult with his advisors. The tension in all of this is the fact that Sosa knew of the rift between Ed Jr. and the FBI Director but was unaware of its spilling into office and political rivalry. He wisely chose not to include Ekstroem in that gathering. However, he did call him for advice on the matter, thus handing him a superb leg up. This explains why he wants to see Leopold with, of course, something off his sleeve and on his mind. As they walk and talk, the reflection of Leopold and the FBI Director appears in the window behind which the voluptuous blond observes the two objects of her wild and kinky fantasies. The look on Leopold's face divulges his puzzlement. He carries a crate and wishes he could also cram his emotions in it.

"We are sending you there to lead that investigation."

"Why me?" Leopold asks. "Sir, Mullins did most of the work in Italy. This one is his job. He deserves it."

"You're a McLintaugh, are you not?" Ekstroem asks as though he were a father figure to Leopold. "Be like one."

"That name, son," he adds, "precedes you by two generations of great agents. Some of your ancestors' works would amaze Hoover himself. Last night, I recommended their grandson, nephew, and why not (hesitation) their son to the President of the

United States. Sosa wants to help his friend down in Haiti solve the assassination of a journalist. The new president there was Sosa's college buddy. He and the President "really" want that investigation to succeed this time."

They briefly stop and stand face to face. Leopold did not see that one coming, but because of his secret and genotypic ties to the country, he knew very well of the assassination that had hit his home hard when he was just fourteen years old. There was probably no way even J. Edgar Hoover could have known of this. When they had stopped walking to be face to face, Ekstroem could have read and detected any slight facial nerve movement, which could lead him to think that there is something there. And his little hesitation has the younger McLintaugh conjure in his mind a multitude of things. Leopold is aware of the mysteries of body language as he finds himself face to face with this super cop. That fraction of a second, he stood tall with complete control over the minutest details of his facial expressions.

"This Dominique," the FBI Director asks, "you heard of him?"

Leopold answers very fast. Haitian – agronomist-turned-journalist – political commentator – activist – radio station owner – assassinated on April 3rd of 2000.

Amazed, with an avoirdupois-ounce of force more, Ekstroem would damage the agent's acromioclavicular joint capsule as he taps on Leopold's shoulders.

"Impressive!" he exclaims. "And like your mother, you are fluent in French. Ask yourself "why not you"?"

Leopold quickly recalls a little story Dorothy had told him about her past romances. Politely, with a small smile, he reminds his boss that his mother is not the only one who is fluent in the family.

"My father also is fluent, and so was grandpa," he says. Leopold may not be too aware that it was Edward Sr. who had first befriended Jeando in Paris.

"Now, McLintaugh," Ekstroem continues as they resume walking. "Let me emphasize quietly. This Dominique business is very touchy. It can quickly raise a shitstorm, and there's no telling who will get up to their neck if it blows."

"This job's cut for Mullins, sir. He deserves to lead his assignment now."

They have reached the room where Leopold was headed to help another forensic scientist. As a courtesy, Peter helps Leopold, who carries the crate with both of his hands. The director pulls the door open and stands there. Leopold gets in, places the container on a desk, and puts on a blouse.

"We'll talk kiddo," Ekstroem says. "The President seems to believe in the McLintaugh brand."

Leopold puts on his protective gear as Ekstroem turns around and leaves with a mischievous smirk on his face. Inside the lab, Leopold's mind turns and turns around the idea. He did not know what to make of some of the crap he has just heard from the Director. Leopold knows, however, that saying well of the McLintaughs was never a characteristic of Ekstroem's. As he juggles with the investigative elements he has in the crate, Leopold wonders how he can make sense of it all. Then he remembers the date recalling that he was not in the United States for Christmas and thinking that New Year's presents are just as good.

CHAPTER 16.

The Ball Drop

Numbing cold night. 2022 did not want to go out without giving a dusting to Washington, DC. Leopold was still in Quantico when it started to snow, but he had no choice but to brave the elements and take care of his holidays shopping. He regrets many times at the lab today that he had not gotten any present for his folks while in Rome. The case that took him to Italy has indeed required a lot of his time and attention. He knows anyway that his late grandfather would bluntly call any excuse of a load of crap for not remembering to buy gifts in Italy. He "LoLed" (laughed aloud) alone in the lab as he reminisced the elder McLintaugh's sarcasm.

"Ha! Ha! That old man," he laughs to himself.

When he hits the shopping center, in his cop mind, it was still pre-holidays. As he enters one of the few stores still open, he silently enumerates the people on his virtual list. He tries to remember what he last gave his daughter but cannot get around the wax covering of his recollection as to what and when he gave a Christmas gift to his wife. For Ed and Dorothy, he sees no big deal in offering them holiday presents, but he still tries to remember what he gave them the last year. When he left for work in the morning, it was not as brutally cold, but it has gotten almost unbearable throughout the day. With two shopping bags in his hands when he showed up at the residence, he wears only a suit jacket. Suddenly, as he reaches the front door, he gets the feeling that the holidays are still here and that he is not after all very late. From the first trees to the door, decorative lights still hang. Dorothy McLintaugh, who wears her sixty-four better than most fifty-five-year-olds, welcomes Leopold with rapid-fire questions right from the doorstep.

"My son!" she cries. "Aren't you cold? Why have you not called since you got back? Are you and Teresa getting back? You know, she was here a minute ago to pick up your little girl. Huh! Isn't she lovely, that little girl?"

"Gee! Dorothy! Let the kid in," Ed complains from inside the living room.

He gives the shopping bags to her as he apologizes for being late on his holidays' gifts.

"I'm late," he tells her, "but Happy Holidays, mom!"

Dorothy kisses him as she takes the bags. Now she whispers some of the same questions as they walk toward the living room. Ed McLintaugh follows the broadcast of what is "Times Squares' wildest and biggest ever ball drop celebration." Ed McLintaugh silently expected Leopold's visit because he had called him at work but without telling him anything of the visit to his residence by the two presidents. He had not told him of it over the phone by professional instinct. At this point, Ed is split between the broadcast and what he assumes Ekstroem might have already told Leopold in Quantico earlier today. The President, last night, told him that his son comes highly recommended. Ed chews on the idea of heaving his son down in the jungle that Haiti has represented to the outside world. He weighs the pros and cons of Leopold's decision that he had managed to send Sosa back to the White House and Lysius back to Haiti anticipating.

On the TV screen, the crowd celebrates in Times Square as the ball drops.

The 2023 wish message blinks on the TV screen when Leopold and Dorothy arrive in the living room.

Ed pops and pours a bottle of champagne into two glasses. One for each of the men. Dorothy would not touch that beverage on any occasion or for any reason.

"Happy New Year, agent McLintaugh," Ed proudly says.

"Happy New Year, agent McLintaugh," Leopold replies as the men do in the family.

Ed puts down the bottle and glasses. They hug. He gives a drink to Leopold, and they sit down across each other as Dorothy looks on, wondering what they will talk about this year. At the McLintaughs, the tradition had always called for some philosophical discussion right after the New York City New Year ball drop. This year, the debate is usurped by an unexpected topic though quite familiar factually. And Ed will not waste any time to announce the colors. He lifts his glass.

"To your new mission, son!"

"You know about it, Father?"

"What do you think, son?" Ed asks at first sip after gulping. "Sosa himself and his friend came here last night."

Leopold sips and gulps as well, unable to hide his surprise.

"To have you persuade me?" he asks as a complaint.

However, the Jeando factor in the mission is more than tempting Leopold. Deep down, he will have loved to take a bite at it. Forget Sosa, Lysius, with their political ambitions. If he decides on the affirmative, he knows that it will neither be because of the President's power nor Lysius' persona and charm that have taken America over the past days.

"I lead in Italy," he adds, "but that was all Mullins. Why not him? And again, twenty-three years later… Why now?"

Ed takes sips, puts down the glass, and leans toward Leopold to whisper.

"The President of the United States and Haiti's president-elect who sat right where you are now… were college buddies at the time they assassinated Jeando. Some people who were at Yale at the time say they were having some sort of threesome, well, a foursome over pizza when the news broke. The word is Sosa became furious when the girls showed absolute disrespect toward his friend's grief over the loss."

"What did he do?" asks Leopold.

"He kicked the chicks out," Ed replies. "And he drove them off-campus. 'T seems like they had made up their minds about the whole thing since that day, in that dorm room. And Lysius, yes, that's his name, has read all of my books."

"Ah!" Leopold reflects. *"That explains their double dates over the past three days."*

"And why the President paraded him all over…," the father adds. "Some folks even say Lysius' father supported Sosa financially when he had but the skin on his butt. Now, he wants to help the son to return favors."

Leopold picks up his glass, walks around, and goes on the couch next to Ed to whisper in his turn.

"But father, what about my ties to Jeando… and with the country?"

Ed wiggles his finger to reassure Leopold.

"Only your late aunt, her husband—who just passed—and Jeando knew the circumstances of your birth."

"How about in the country itself?" Leopold asks. "My biological mother did have a family, didn't she?"

Ed doesn't find the time to answer that question. Dorothy had stayed in the kitchen, checking out the presents that Leopold brought earlier during the past minutes of the previous year or hoping the men would call her for the discussion. In the bags, there were gifts for Maddie and her mother. Indeed, this is the reason she gets all that excited. She had not given her blessings to the fact that Leopold and Teresa are separated. She had begged both of them and each separately to reconsider and to always focus on Maddie's happiness.

"You were never too young, she once argued to them, to have gotten married when you did, but, Lordy, in my mind, you two will always be too darn young to go through this."

Dorothy was in the hallway when she started calling her son's name. Neither man heard nor even paid attention due to the intense whispering going on in the living room.

"Leopold!" she calls more than twice before she appears in the living room. "Don't forget the gifts we got for you."

Leopold gets up and goes to her. Ed follows Leopold with a pressing question on the tip of his tongue. An enigma he had thought of at the onset of the conversation. To confirm his wariness of Ekstroem, Ed had wanted to ask how, in the blue hell, Leopold had learned about the mission before his father had told him. Ed only called Leopold at the lab to make sure he was coming to the residence to watch the ball drop and uphold the family tradition. Heather had told him that Ekstroem had looked all morning for him at Quantico. The boss himself walked the long hall by his side as they talked of the matter. Then, Leopold had pretty much guessed in advance what the topic would be at his parents' residence. Nonetheless, Ed had no idea that the President had consulted with the FBI Director before coming to his house.

"The Director," Leopold replies, "Ekstroem came once or twice, looking for me before I got to the lab today."

"That son of a bitch!" Ed instinctively exclaims.

Dorothy arrives first near the gifts in the hallway, and Ed pats Leopold on the back as he follows them into the hall.

"What you got this time?" Leopold asks Dorothy as though he does not hear his father's remark about his boss at the FBI. Ed wonders if this is the occasion Ekstroem was waiting for to get even since the bureau initially adopted the McLintaugh Investigation Method.

Dorothy pushes a door open and shows him a set of luggage.

"Well," Leopold says, "looks like—" For some reason, he cuts the sentence short and does not finish it. Leopold hugs his parents kissing Dorothy's forehead and Ed on the cheek.

"Thanks, you two."

CHAPTER 17.

A Chance Encounter

All the renovation work at the airport in Loudoun and Fairfax counties, Virginia, have been completed. The futuristic design envisioned years ago has indeed come to life. As he walks past the massage parlor in the terminal toward his departure gate, the beautifully shaped long legs of a young woman get his attention. When he and his wife, Teresa, first separated, he had tried to teach his macho mind to remain faithful to her. At Quantico, Heather always presented a constant temptation. The young blond woman has everything in her favor. She is splendid, intelligent, stunning with the physique of a goddess. A solemn DNA test should be able to retrace her lineage straight back to her grandmother Aphrodite, the mother of Eros. A long list of distinguished men at the bureau succumbed to her charm and gave in. She has seen quite a world out there by courtesy of her physical assets.

Up to Heather and Ekstroem's adventure in the Caribbean, Leopold stayed on his guards when it comes to sexual encounters with any of the females at Quantico. He seems to, however, have a different set of attitudes as it regards downtown DC. Leopold taxes them by selective faithfulness to his wife. He was on his last trip to Italy two or three weeks ago when the young blond called him to let him know in detail about her journey to Labadee with Ekstroem. Americans are very open about their sexuality. They may first tell of their sexual exploits with their husbands, wives, significant other before revealing whom they voted for in an election. The marital situation with Teresa was at the time a bit uncertain, but she as well as he still hopes it will resolve. The self-imposed condition was, at first, to hold off extramarital sex for Providence to be merciful and fix what needs fixing in his marriage. The young woman was candid when she called him in Italy about her trip to Labadee. It was after the call that he had made up his mind and decided he would indulge with her for a nightstand or two whenever he and she are back in the United States. Just a little bit will not hurt, he coerced his mind into believing. The next time she makes an advance or throws a bait at him, he decided then, he will bite. Leopold is mindful of the rift between his father and his boss. The young McLintaugh smiled as he welcomed the pleasant prospect of fucking the same girl as "dick head" and "fuck face" Peter Ekstroem.[sic]

Lately, he had given in and let his mind drift about when he would notice one well-endowed female. With just that quick gaze, his mind finds the time to process a myriad of thoughts. He thinks of a Puerto Rican friend of his who had explained to him what a *Carajo Coño* is. That friend may have also told him why it is probably an absolute truth when a Latina woman says that she "was with Jesus the previous night."

Hmm! For sure, Leopold hopes and mentally tells himself as he pulls his carry-on, *those legs don't belong to a* Carajo Coño.

He had heard his workout buddy many times talk about it with other Spanish-speaking guys like him. Once, they both took their families to the beach. He and Teresa were not yet separated. Teresa and the "Boricua" friend's wife walked Maddie and the other child to the water. The two men engaged in an ordinary conversation as they seemed lost by the look of a physically attractive woman from afar walking toward them. Leopold was consumed and the friend could not help but utter his feelings out loud.

"*Carajo*!" he exclaimed.

They say that beauty is in the eyes of the beholder. But this beholder makes his living judging beauty exhibitions on the world stage, and that alone disqualifies the beholder in him. As the woman got closer, the level of his interest dropped. But when she walked near them, Leopold heard him sound his disappointment of his having wasted that time he could have spent in essential conversation.

"*Coño*!" the friend complained as loud as previously.

This was when he learned about *Carajo Coño*. That day at the beach with Teresa and his little girl comes vividly in his mind as he lingers his eyes a bit on these sexy legs. In the first weeks or months into his separation from his wife, he tried a lot to keep clear of entertaining sexually explicit thoughts about other women in his mind. These legs are now added to the sins Jesus warned about in Matthew 5:28. However, considering he has not seen the whole but just part of the woman, one could debate whether it is what he, that Jesus, referred to as "lust."

A Spanish-speaking Latin man would say that she has *pechonalidad*, referring to her chest. Her gluteus maximus mesmerizes. Tall, elegant, brown-skinned, the long-haired young woman is twenty-five-year-old Christiane on her way to MIA, Florida. There she will connect on the 11:45 flight to Haiti. She flies to visit her father, her nineteen-year-old younger brother, and perhaps, by obligation, one other person of whom she had grown sick and tired. When she walks out of the kiosk with a magazine and a bottle of juice, Leopold gets a good look. He decides he will get to know her and probably have, why not, a traveling companion. He has no idea that this beautiful ebony face was at the other end of these sexy pair of legs he's seen on his way to the boarding area. Leopold is probably not the only one savoring in the woman's ambulatory manner, which brings a thousand and one suggestions to every gazing fellow out there. She is very conscious of that. She pulls her small luggage, and a designer purse hangs from her shoulder. She senses or smells at a distance the contemplating opposite sex.

Mesmerized, a cart operator slows down as she steps fearlessly through across his path. The FBI agent anticipates that Christiane will walk straight toward him and possibly take the empty seat beside him. Or, as he already makes up his mind, he is going to invite her to sit next to him. But two things that occur at the same time derail Casanova's plan. The airport P.A. announcement, for one, and the other, he must pick up a call from the hot blond at the lab who wanted to wish him a nice trip. He had missed a lot. Christiane walks past and haphazardly notices him only to find a seat far behind him on the same block of chairs. When he finishes talking on the phone, the girl with the legs and the hips had disappeared. He, of course, was poised to hit hard.

"Where has she gone?" he asks himself. *Maybe she went into a different gate boarding a different flight*, he consoles himself, understanding that he may never have the chance to meet her again. That same thing happened to him in Belarus last fall when he miserably failed to ask Gregoriya for her digits or any means of contact with her. Since he had seen her a few times before, at that small-town station, he may have thought that he stood the chance of meeting her again. That never happened. Each time he fails like this, he tends to brush it off with the thought that he would not cheat on Teresa anyway. In fact, for Christiane, had not it been for a physiological urgency that pulled Leopold into the first restroom he found in the hangar, they would have appropriately met. Before she had decided to walk to the duty-free shop, Christiane briefly sat in that very seat next to Leopold. Hypothetical.

Currently, neither is aware of the presence of the other at MIA. Either may think that the other's face was just another one passing in the crowd at Dulles. She respects her airport ritual. She has already done massage in the first leg at Dulles. Now is time for the duty-free kiosk for another magazine and bottle of juice or water.

Christiane checks her lip then closes the small mirror that she puts in her Louis Vuitton purse. She is confident and knows that she is stunning. This, however, does not keep her from compulsively pulling the little mirror and fixing something, anything. She sits comfortably and opens the magazine. She takes a sip from the bottle of juice. She has not even swallowed yet that a flight attendant leans toward her and silently talks into her ears.

She nods her head with her priceless smile in agreement. As she readies herself to leave her seat, the flight attendant waves toward an elderly Caucasian couple, who arrives all smiles and full of gratitude. Christiane also gets emotional as she gets up with her face still radiating. She had the privilege of knowing her great-grandparents, and that older couple sitting down in these two seats have her recall Meme and Pepe. They both have lived physically able to one hundred two and three, respectively. Pepe outlived his sweetheart for about a year. Though she does not get very far in that quick little chat with the couple as they express gratitude to her for giving her seat to them, she has guessed their age. She is thinking that perhaps no one else in her family would get to be that old. Not her father, for sure. She believes with the types of activities he leads he could get whacked anytime.

"Thank you very much. You are very kind," says the couple again as they get themselves installed in their seats while they continue talking.

Walking toward the front of the cabin following the flight attendant, Christiane is still within hearing distance as the couple keeps on talking out loud about her. Anyway, all can hear.

"Herb," she says as the most talkative of the two, "did you see how gorgeous she is?"

"I saw," replies the more discreet older fellow.

"If you were still young and able," she adds loudly, "I sure wouldn't mind her too much as a rival instead of those ugly witches you had."

"For Christ's sake, Susan," the old man exclaims.

Herb and Susan are longtime senior citizens, retirees living out their bucket list. Die-hard Donald Trump supporters, they had grown extremely tired of his shit. Their words. What had finally blown up the kettle had also led to their being on this flight to Haiti today. Although they supported him, they never went along with the idea it was heresy to watch any other network but Fox. That January night was their "cheating night" when Anderson Cooper poured out his heart in response to Donald Trump calling Haiti, among others, "shithole country." Anderson had visited the "former" Caribbean pearl on many occasions, including for his line of work, reporting on that devastating earthquake of 2010. He had, therefore, developed ties in the country. He had even recounted that one math teacher of his who had helped him a lot was a well-known figure from the country. Later that month, it was time for the comedian, show host Conan O'Brien to air a piece on Haiti after a visit advised by Anderson Cooper. The older couple watched the show and decided that same night they should add a trip to Haiti to their bucket list. Two years before they could materialize this trip, they would have voted for the young Democrat David Sosa.

"Calling that country a shithole," Herb hurriedly says to keep his womanizer's past buried, "I bet Donald Trump never saw such a marvelous person like her. That young lady is much more beautiful than that stiff plastic-face daughter of his."

"And Marion, who worked at Yale," Suzan adds, "told me the young kid the Haitians just elected as their president is just incredible."

"He was just in Washington with Sosa the other day," Herb reminds his wife.

The attendant parts the curtain with the new passenger behind her. Christiane notices that there is but one empty seat between a bald older gentleman and the blond person who appears to be the tallest in the cabin. In fact, it is FBI agent Leopold McLintaugh. It does not cross Christiane's mind that this is the man she had noticed earlier at Dulles. To this point, neither has any knowledge that they have both noticed each other. This, Leopold, is the rightful titleholder of these pair of legs and hips.

The attendant must have previously informed Leopold that she was to bring a passenger into the seat next to him. Before she reaches the row, she does not tell him anything, and he'd started to arrange himself and make way for the passenger to get in her new seat. As she does, the bottle of juice falls in Leopold's lap, staining his light-khaki pants. They are nevertheless honest in their behavior. They take it as two people who have never laid eyes on each other when the litany of excuses on her part begins. They are right, for they have not recollected having seen each other. Christiane slides her eyes down his crotch where the stain looks pretty objective, and perhaps, she thinks of these other things that cannot be written of here. It may be true that a woman already decides what she will make of an encounter within the first minutes thereof.

Wow! she thinks to herself. *That is some big deal.*

Leopold covers his pants with the small pillow that he found on his seat. He could swear he just heard the voice of Sandra Bullock. He had convinced Teresa she would have looked like her had she been a brunette. He has connected with the young woman in the next seat mentally for the two were a second ago thinking of the same thing. Christiane knows how she likes her meat, and Leopold mentally made a detour to reminisce the film *A Time to Kill*, in which the actress took a quick peek at the young lawyer's (Matthew McConaughey) buttocks that she had to dress after a minor accident.

"Good butt," Ellen Roark said after a little tap on his butt.

Leopold felt she looked at his package because the shape of the stain is pretty revealing of whatever lies beneath. He then thought that the small pillow would quiet and cool things a bit.

And it did. They spend the whole flight getting to know each other, and she would think that she taught Leopold more about the country than he had led her to believe. However, Christiane will be a tremendous asset during the time he will be in down there.

She usually travels light with only a carry-on, but she wanted to help him claim his luggage. She insisted on not noticing the two young marine officers already there, at the end of the carousel. She fails to sequence why the marines are claiming luggage for this tourist. She chats on the telephone as she turns around. Leopold walks carelessly toward her with the dry reddish stain on his pants. Christiane finds that both embarrassing and humorous.

Mon Dieu! she says to herself and turns around as she covers her mouth to hide her chuckle.

Perhaps at the same time, Leopold realizes the grossness of his red-stained hunker. Notably, the revealing shape the stain has now taken. He realizes that the small pillow he covered his lap with had made things worse. When Christiane turns around again, he has disappeared. He thinks he'd better change pants and had detour straight into the nearest restroom.

Where did he go? she wonders.

Instead of providing herself an answer, she allows her female mind to go about an errand that she has already decided she will soon walk herself. The same one she ran mentally after "her juice" stained his crotch on board the aircraft. Leopold comes out of the restroom wearing another pair of pants. A plastic bag hangs atop the handle of his carry-on. Exiting the terminal, he and Christiane walk together as though neither wants to part ways. She comes up with a brilliant idea.

"You really want to do this?" Leopold asks her.

"Hmm…" she says. "Not a hot-blooded American. Huh!"

"Umm… Could say that… and be entirely right."

"Take it, mister, as a thoughtful excuse to see you again." Soon, she boldly adds with a sexy wink and smile.

"Here, then," he says, smiling as he tends the bag to her.

She takes the bag, turns around, and walks away.

Leopold stands to look at her as she walks away. Her hips convey the message that she knows he is watching. A group of happy friends greet her as Leopold walks on; maybe, for the last time, he would move around that freely in this slippery country.

CHAPTER 18.

A Kinky Welcome

On the top back rail of the chair, Leopold's pants are crispy clean in the hanger inside the clear dry-cleaning plastic bag. Christiane's expensive purse is also on the chair with a pack of Kit Kat sticking out of it. Leopold was just wondering how the candy bar manages to retain its shape in this kind of temperature. Then he thought that probably, this bar did not spend any time in natural warmth since it was made. Perhaps, as they say in the country about rocks, "A candy bar in the cooler will ignore the plight of the one melting on sidewalks or atop a street vendor's head." The young woman drove to the hotel in her newest reinforced bulletproof SUV from Lexus. From the supermarket's shelf to that chair, the candy bar has undergone no break in the cold chain. Leopold is on the balcony with her on the phone. He is looking at the city down in the distance when she gets inside the suite.

"I'm helping myself alright," Christiane says in response to the agent still scrutinizing the country from the terrace.

"How about you, she asks?"

"I'll take anything," his voice reverberates throughout from outside.

Christiane places the bottle on the counter. She walks out with the two glasses in her hands, each with a slice of lemon.

"Wo! Wo! Wo! Aren't we too young for that?"

Christiane taps her glass with her fingernails. She does not exactly know why, but she recalls she had heard from a group of girls in her circle that doing so sends signals to a man that the girl means business and would feel more confident about making his move. Trick or not, Leopold was going to score. The Haitian bombshell recreates the first time that she was told this shit. She had wondered if pheromone had ceased to work. Has it been demoted to only signaling when the species want to defecate? Yet, ever since, each of the times she has done that she has entertained the same thought.

"To my health," she says, "and to yours, if you care."

She chugs her drink. Leopold wants to look amazed but comes around rather awkwardly. The young woman who was not born yesterday reads well into somebody who is, himself, not at his first trial.

"Okay!" says Leopold. "You know what happens afterward?"

"Do tell. A girl could be adventurous."

Leopold does not tell. Instead, he takes a sip and places his glass on the small mahogany table. Christiane chugs what is left in it. She does not put the empty glass on the table, but instead, she goes inside to pour more drinks into the glasses. However, a bottle of wine gets her attention. Leopold follows and comes inside behind her. He opens the fridge and gets a bottle.

"Have you had this before?" he asks.

"No, but I am game," she says with a sexy vibration in her voice that could befuddle any untrained mind. Leopold reads it's time to make his move and score. He walks up behind her, and at his slightest touch, she turns around and locks in a passionate kiss. She pours into the second glass and gives it to Leopold, who leads her into the bedroom, but it seems instead that they are inducing each other. Christiane's empty glass crashes on the floor. She starts to moan. The pieces of broken glass are not the only things on the floor. One by one, articles of clothing fall to the floor here and there, creating a trail toward the bed.

"Are you sure you are cool with where this may lead?" he asks.

"Why do you think I begged to launder your pants? I will be the coolest if you give it to me good."

She gently bites his ear as she whispers into it, something he could not hear as she unbuttons his shirt.

"Let me do," she repeats a little louder as she pushes the shirt off of his shoulders. With an extraordinary ability, she unzips his pants, takes them and his underwear off. Christiane takes half of a step back as though she wanted to be sure that Leopold is entirely naked. She kneels in front of him and takes his cock into her warm mouth that she slides up and down his thick, long Caucasian meat and little does she know she is consuming locally.

"You smell lovely," he says.

"You sure can already smell me," she replies. "That is because I am so fucking wet. I have wanted to do this ever since I first laid eyes on you. Oh! Fuck me, will you?"

The FBI agent thinks that this young woman's erotic aggression could be the result of some score she is out to settle, some issues she needs to get even on with somebody. He will learn all of that soon. But for now, he is on the clock and has a job to do. He pulls her up, turns her around, and bends her over. He tries to line up his Mr. with her Mrs.

"Huh! Wait, wait, wait," she says as though she is competing for dominance over this blond monster of a hunk. She lays down on the floor right in front of Leopold, spreading her legs and pulling open her lips as she issues an order to him.

"Eat me a little first."

"Uh!" she screams. "Come on, you are just teasing me. Fuck me good and hard. Please. Please. Please! Ahh!"

She looks up, and their eyes click.

"Uh!" She knows now she is going to get a romp, the mother of all pounding as they can see how turned on they both are as he gets in her harder now, harder and faster. Harder and faster. Harder and faster. Harder and faster.

"Oh! It feels so good," she screams. "Fuck me! Fuck me! Fuck me! Oh, my God! Shit!"

"Oh God! oh God!" she screams as she gives him what they know in the country as "gouyad" but, at that instant, ignores the English equivalent to teach the word to him. His hands reach out and squeeze her nipples as she intensifies the screaming and continues her hips rolls on his dick.

"Oh, my God!" she screams. "Oh, Leo," she adds. "I can feel my pussy being stretched out. Oh! Oh! It is about to explode all over the place."

"Oh! Oh!" Christiane continues to fill up the room. "Oh God! Oh God! Leo, come with me, please. I can't oh I can't. I can't stop. I can feel you come inside me, oh God! The whole room smells like my pussy."

Like Chloe Nicole's, her eyes seem to roll to the back of her head, and she trembles as she orgasms.

"Uh! Uh!" She moans as Leopold breathes faster and yells, "Yeah! Oh shit!"

Christiane is glad and feels exhausted but satisfied. For sure, she has gotten what she expected. She wanted him to come at the same time as her. She slides herself off that monster that appears not to know the first thing about limpness. Leopold seems to be up for another round, and so does Christiane.

"I am so glad, Leopold."

That afternoon, they will give it another round, but now, they seem to be thinking again about the same thing. Leopold and Christiane think about comedian Chris Rock who said that women could never go backward socially, whereas men can never downgrade sexually. And they seem to be on the same page because they are mentally making the same resolution that from this day forward, that will be how they fuck. Christiane, for one, knows how tired she has gotten lately with the crap she has been having. She calls it "A Blasphemy of the Sacred Name and Pleasure of Fucking."

Their conversation during the flight got far enough for Leopold to get somewhat inquisitive of her sex life.

"Blasphemy," she answered. "What I get lately, I call it a curse, a far cry."

Leopold lays on his side, looking at her beautiful and well-kept Queen of Sheba–like brown body.

"Uh!" she says. "Leo, this room smells like pussy."

"Yours," he instinctively replies. "I hope this is 'Welcome to Haiti for me,'" he whispers into her ear.

"And I, Christiane Toumain, on behalf of the committee… Want to meet the rest of us?"

He has not told her of the nature of his presence in the country. Until now, he did not ask her for her last name that now rings a bell in his mind.

"Is all Haiti as welcoming as you are, my dear?"

"My folks are," she answers. "You'll meet my fam," she adds.

***

Daniel Toumain has traveled and seen a lot of the world's beautiful things and architectural wonders. He has consequently developed a refined taste for exterior as well as interior decoration. It was on a trip to Europe that the idea was born in his mind. He knew that he could fork the money necessary to throw a replica of a portion of Tulips Island on his front lawn at Vivy Mitchel, in Port-au-Prince. The environment into which Christiane brings Leopold cries out loud. And, anyone who steps on these grounds can undoubtedly palpate the owner's magnificent opulence. A stream of water sprays softly on the beautiful tulips. The old gardener had received specific orders to favor much more the yellow ones. Dani has an affinity for the color, not that his orders gave the old man carte blanche to neglect the various other colors and varieties. On both sides of the long red brick-paved entrance, there are rows of tulips of many colors such as red, yellow, lavender, etc. The look, the feel, is just excellent. An awesome treat for the eyes. To top it all and add a reminder, a touch of Amsterdam, Dani had ordered a beautiful wooden windmill installed on the lawn.

About the old gardener. According to neighborhood's talking heads, this is a true story. Toumain rescued the middle-aged fellow in Saint-Louis du Nord in the Northwestern part of the country. The crime boss did not wear or use any equipment, any hero cape, or paraphernalia to save the man from drowning or anything of that sort. He kept him from being slaughtered as a bull. It was Christiane at around five years old who had asked her father to stop and back up to the animals in line that morning to be slaughtered at the marketplace. As the vehicle slowly passed by, she claimed that she had heard the bull's plea to her in particular. To this day, daddy has always done anything to please his little girl. Now? Well, a far cry from the Christiane who was just in the hotel room.

As the vehicle backed up, four or five animals approached the windows, and the whole family actually heard and witnessed the cows and the bulls cry like humans, pleading to have their lives spared. Dani Toumain—the man who, a few years earlier, in 1991, aloofly killed that pastor/politician—had gotten off and bought all the "animals." Toumain then took them to the family's property in the North. The story goes that Mr. Toumain himself knows a thing or two. He knew where to go in order to have his daughter's preferred animal transformed into the gardener who has been in their yard ever since. Quite a story, isn't it?

The old man, who does not talk much except a smile here and there only to Christiane, places the watering can on the floor and goes to open the gate after he hears the cars on the other side thereof. He wonders if the previous guest had forgotten something and come back for it. In fact, the last guest whom Christiane and Leopold have just crossed paths with was none other than Uncle Dany. Christiane and her brother call the former senator uncle, though, in reality, he is a cousin of their father's.

Christiane's car enters first and is followed by a white custom-made bulletproof Suburban.

The two cars are parked in the shadow of a tree. Leopold and Christiane meet behind hers. The gardener perhaps smells something unusual about Christiane and her guest; more so about her, because he is seeing this blond fellow for the first time. The old man's subtle and instinctive sniff could tell that the fellow also smells like what Christiane said of that specific odor in the hotel room. The gardener, in a prior life, might have had some special powers to discern things of the sort. There is no way anyone could detect the slightest rare odor. The two have showered after their session of legs-in-the-air right before heading out to Vivy Mitchel.

"Well, mister," Christiane says as she returns the gardener's rare smile, "welcome to my crib."

With trained eyes, Leopold pans the beautiful and colossal house. He looks at the old man watering the flowers as he reconciles his mind with the component of being in a "poor country."

"Hmm! Impressive. This is Vondelpark," says the agent, whose work has brought him to Amsterdam on quite a few occasions. "I take it somebody does have a thing for tulips."

"My father," Christiane answers. "And, what's not to love? They're beautiful."

A luxury car seems to rather rise slowly from the lower level on the side and stop near the front of the beautiful house. When the father goes out, the son has the assigned task to check the vehicle thoroughly. Toumain has grown paranoid as he ages.

The man dreads the families of folks he had silenced for good as part of his routine business might, one day, blow him up.

A tall young man gets out, leaving the engine running. Christiane calls him.

"Junior!" she yells out.

As the nineteen-year-old crosses the courtyard, Leopold notices the uncanny resemblance to the young woman in front of him. Because early that morning, he and his sister had a small and predictable siblings' dispute, he is not too eager to go to her. The stranger, however, commands his curiosity. He takes his sweet time. Dani Jr. is like any teenager, but because of his father's past, he has missed many things young folks his age enjoy. He only spends time together with the two sons of Tito who are much older than he is and who take him everywhere, and whatever the youngster knows he's learned a great deal of it from them. The Massim twins themselves relate because when they were growing up, Tito's past wrongful activities have also prevented them from being out in the open. Dani yearns to get out and see and learn about the world that he only sees on television and in movies.

He is in love with cars and their mechanism. As Dani Jr. develops his fondness for mechanics and teaches himself all he can about his passion, Uday and Qusay grow closer and closer to him. The twins come to him for guidance on all of the hot new cars coming out on the market. They have the money to throw at them, and most often, he is the first person who gets to try out their new acquisitions. In all, they live richly in a poor country. They would instead purchase 4 × 4 vehicles rather than fix the roads that lead to their houses. They would live in castles out in nowhere and not invest in establishing a hospital nearby just in case. Heavy traffic would claim their miserable lives on the way to the airport to catch a quick flight to Florida. The motherfuckers, as Lysius once referred to the elite and some wealthy authentic Haitians, never think of that shit. “Shame on them! Shame on these wacko politicians,” the former senator and now president-elect would say, “who let this stinking elite buy them to do its dirty jobs.” Senators and former senators receive money from those folks to manipulate the population into toppling legally established governments without an alternative of their own. They do actually. Those hacks called it transition. A thing they champion at every president's midterm in function for it is when they can pillage the country's treasury without any control. The example of that flagrant lackluster was the years they beleaguered the country in vain to overthrow Josaphat's administration.

When he was a senator, president-elect Geffrard would get under that elite's skin. He denounced their unwillingness to help turn the country around for good instead of only catering to their own interests. He would accuse the descendants of the Arabs who arrived on Haiti's shores at the turn of the last century. Not that he harbors a particular hatred toward anyone of that origin, the senator was, instead, motivated by the Massims' attitude vis-à-vis his family. He would go off saying that wherever they arrive around the world to do business, they change the environment into a “shithole.” He has said that. Either Morgan or History will confirm. When sometime, in 2018, that Haitian senator gave the American President a piece of his mind, his detractors back in the country accused him of only fighting Donald Trump for infringement rights. Until then, Senator Lysius Geffrard was the first and only politician in the Americas to ever have uttered the words “shit” and “hole” that close together while talking of Haitians and of their country. Defending himself later in a radio interview, the senator did not mitigate his words. He would go completely off as he put to shame the country’s elite.

“They operate their businesses,” he would hammer, “right in the stinking mud, in the pestilence. They would not even clean the very entrance of their places of business where patrons walk in to buy their shit.”

“Compare them to Jews, Hindus, and many others, and their beautiful places of business,” he would add. “This “f” country is our hole and all we have. Those folks are not authentic Haitians. They are here only to shit in our pit. But because they feel good about eating where they shit, they’d even care less about the environment in the hole. They are what you may call ‘Convenience Haitians.’ They are Haitians when all is hunky-dory but something else at the slight sign of hardship in the hole. They don’t invest in the country’s future. Look at our kids. I am talking about the lost ‘Ratpakaka’ generation. What will they inherit? The establishment is paid or bribed, preferably to have our children assume that all the shit they are witnessing in our society is natural. No kids.”

“As a senator, take my words for it. It is not fucking normal,” he said, audibly pounding the station’s table. “But first, we must stop accepting crap from other people. Kids, we cannot call this country an agricultural land. At the same time, we drink some powdered shit for juice from the Dominican Republic. Two of the most significant wounds we need to nurse as a people are the good-for-nothings of our elite and the Parliament that sadly I am a part of. Because I love this country very much, if I need to get down in the mud to fight with pigs for Haiti, by God, I will roll up my sleeves and get dirty among thieves, thugs, and pigs every fucking time. Some of you have seen me on the field and in the Senate. The bar, the standard to enter that body needs to be raised. And with every new election, the republic needs to send in their best as Nickesse's grandfather and father were accustomed to choosing them. The Duvaliers never elected traffickers who had no interest in the education of our children and the welfare of the country."

"Today," he continued, "I want the republic to know something. All of the colleagues who criticized me for the way I handled Donald Trump in defending my country's pride and honor did so only after they received orders from the Park. Those 'would be elected' hacks, every one of them, use the Park as a fucking ATM. They have never voted their conscience down there but to line their pockets. That is why you see a lot of those guys sell their souls to this stinking elite to impede the progress of all legally established administrations. President Josaphat is not the only victim. They came after Martelly, they certainly got Aristide, and they tried Préval."

"See," Geffrard continued, "the presidents were different, but the same 'fucking' bulls have charged against them. Just like the members of the elite, these losers don't have the country's and its people's best interests at heart. Most have their wives and kids in foreign countries; they don't give a shit if our Haitians kids miss days, weeks, and months out of the school year. Some receive big money to oppose everything that President Josaphat or any president undertakes. Some in that stinking elite are angry because of this president's willingness to close loopholes that had allowed them to overcharge the treasury for their mediocre and poor works. This is the country we have now, a state in which the elite criminally use lawmakers to undermine the accomplishment of legitimately established administrations. Then, you hear folks on the radio talking shit about how dirty, how this and that the country is."

"No, ma'am,"he hammered, "you should not talk about the state of our roads. It is you who order your stupid, illiterate, and bribe-angry followers to burn car tires on the pavements for one shit or another. Last I checked, asphalt and fire do not go together although you need both to build and repair the roads. It is like electricity that can both fry food and shit for a man and also cook the motherfucker." [sic]

From the time Christiane innocently spat out her last name to her brother crossing the yard toward them, Leopold had kept his mind running around one probability. That of a relationship with one of the men about whom he's been briefed and the young woman he had just "Fornication Under Charles the King–ed." A polite way to tell what happened in the room. He had already perceived a Maybelline-covered likeness between Christiane and one of the photographs. Around the same time the young man arrives near his sister and her guest, his father, dressed in an elegant suit, steps out of the house toward the idling car. Noticing a strange and new face on his lot, he stops a bit to take a look at his daughter standing near the white man in his yard as his son is walking toward them.

"Who the fuck is this?" he instinctively asks in his mind.

Leopold becomes fixated for a few seconds. Up to that moment, he was looking at the young man walking across. But when the father came out of the house, he becomes sure that he was on to something shifting his gaze beyond the approaching young man. What is at work here? It is, perhaps, the ash particle from Jeando's cremated remains that he sniffed from Dorothy's collar when she had returned to DC from the funeral service. That has, perhaps, started to put the pieces of the puzzle together. *Yes*, he mentally acquiesces, *this is one of the men.*

Just this week, in Washington, after Sosa and Lysius visited his father, he has learned that nobody meets this man this easily. Looking into Christiane's eyes, he thinks of his daughter wondering if one day, Maddie would lead the heat to him as had unknowingly done this beautiful Haitian woman. Leopold decides then that he was going to have her lead him to most of the men on his radar.

Junior arrives under the tree near the cars and shakes hands with Leopold.

"My brother, Dani," Christiane introduces him.

"Good to meet you, Dani," he says as the young man sends signals he will not linger much.

"You too," the youngster replies. "Welcome to Haiti, sir."

"Father!" Christiane calls out aloud.

"Ah! Sweetheart," he answers as he pushes shut the car door he had already opened. Typically, he would not walk across the lawn, but he had to check out this blond fellow he had never seen before. He crosses the court toward them.

"Who do you have with you there?" he asks as he approaches.

The two men shake hands.

"Daddy, this is Leopold," she says. "He's a friend from DC."

If the father had half the extra sense of the gardener, he would query his daughter about how close of a friend this cracker is. If both could show up in his lot wearing that subtle and latent odor… He may never find out. For that particular odor that the gardener easily detected, the man in the elegant suit will forever present with a serious case of anosmia.

"*Bonjour, monsieur*," says Leopold in an impressive and perfect French that grabs the attention of the new man he just met and who seems determined to withhold his name.

"Welcome to our land," he says. "I am sorry. Some pressing matter calls me in town."

"See you later," Leopold says as he retains the man's hand in his firm grip, "*Monsieur*?"

"Oh! Toumain," he says with a bit of embarrassment. "Mr. Toumain."

Toumain's car leaves through the wide gate that the gardener had already opened standing guard nearby as though this zombie could prevent anybody from trespassing. Dani comes back in front of the house to make sure the old man quickly closes the gate after his father leaves. What urgent business calls Toumain this late in the afternoon in January?

Leopold returns to his hotel, where he establishes a last-minute communication with his team that is to arrive the next day. With not a lot of time, he has opted to bring with him everyone who was in Italy the previous month.

In one of his business's establishments downtown awaits none other than "Fat Jacques" with the info he was paid for.

Jacques Cyprien was introduced to President Josaphat by Toumain posing as a jubilant Geffrard's supporter, as the perfect guy to be in charge of Lysius' security details. Unusually unwise but stubborn, Josaphat bought in and picked Fat Jacques for the job. Back from the trip to Washington with Lysius and taking a detour from Geffrard and Duvalier touring the nation, he comes to deliver and collect before rejoining the young former rival politicians.

A canary envelope is on the desk, but Toumain is not too eager to open it. He is well aware of the president-elect's ability to rally opponents and foes to his cause. He takes advantage of the yellow tulip's arrangement in the vase on his desk he had previously positioned to read into the fat man's facial expressions while speaking to him. Cyprien, of course, cannot claim that he was aware of everything that was said or talked about during Geffrard's trip. He has gathered a wealth of information in and out of the scoop of his duty near the president-elect.

Maybe he puts too much mustard behind it. Toumain slides an envelope on the desk toward Cyprien. The man behind the flowers feels he needs to let the man in front of him know from where the money comes. Pocketing that money for useless information Tito cannot trust means that his fat ass would belong to the Syrians. But Toumain knows he could count on Fat Jacques, who would report everything to him, be it insignificant or boring. The security chief claims the man's attention with this report from one of his men who sat near Duvalier during the flight to the United States. The president-elect supposedly left Claudine alone and walked back to the empty seat by Nickesse Duvalier. There they yakked for about an hour before he rejoins his wife and daughter. The tale reported to Cyprien conveys how the president-elect feels about Duvalier's mother. During the campaign, and long before, she had been extremely vocal and had had more than plenty of shit to say.

"Tell me, Nico," the former senator reportedly asked his new friend, "during the campaign, did you ever wish that bitch would shut the hell up?"

"You bet. Of course, I did," Duvalier replied as he returned the question to Geffrard.

"Fuck no" Lysius convincingly replied. "I love the bitch, and I think I'll meet her. She was my favorite surrogate. I was beating your ass," he added, "each time she opened her pie hole."

Cyprien tells Toumain he remembers Lysius indeed, and Nickesse exploded in a burst of loud laughter at that precise moment, and the report from his man confirms the reason behind it.

"From Tito," Toumain says, signaling he wants to "cut to" when the fat man catches and glances at the crisp Bens before he pockets the pouch.

"Gee!" he says. "This envelope is fat like Fat Jacques."

"And the trip?" Toumain asks, dismissing Cyprien's self-shaming wisecrack.

"It was a success for Lysius. All of America seems to be in love with him. The Haitians over there think he is some messiah. After all, he was the only Haitian official who handled Donald fucking Trump."

A Dessalines' nationalist, Cyprien enjoyed the way Lysius went head to head with the POTUS in 2018. For one, Fat Jacques believes that only Hugo Chavez could have. For the past five years since it happened, he has never missed an occasion to talk about the way the former senator insulted Trump's mother. Like Michel Martelly, Lysius told the US President that when he learns the Haitian Creole language, he'll understand. Both Toumain and Tito, who are not fond of Lysius, have had to hear that story from Cyprien before. Toumain is not in that mood now, so he slants his head clear of the flowers to send one of these looks his guest's way, who quickly understands.

"It turns out," Cyprien continues, "there's more than just a relation between presidents for him and President Sosa."

"What you saying?" Toumain asks. "Are they fagots?"

"The two were buddies in school and have had the same ideas on everything that got them both elected."

Toumain slides another envelope on the desk that Cyprien quickly catches at the edge thereof.

"From the rest of us," Toumain says.

"And this agent? Already here, you said?"

"Perhaps, even before we had arrived in Gonaïves with Josaphat."

"He has a name?" Toumain inquires.

Jacques Cyprien knows nothing about the agent. He remembers vaguely that along with the American President and Lysius, the last person they visited had briefly been a director of the FBI. Or maybe it was the father and who has written many books that both Sosa and Lysius have intensively read. He does not command the details of the visit. The atmosphere, supposedly the most relaxed of the entire trip, has practically offered him the night off. The champagne had not cleared from his system when he picked up scraps from the conversation between the two presidents. From the English, they spoke most of the words flew right over Fat Jacques' head. Initially, he also thought that Ed was supposedly the one to come to Haiti. And he also thought he has heard Lysius tell Sosa that some agent is just a little younger than they are. A light quickly goes on in Toumain's head, but Cyprien remembers some name, thus turning off that activity within Toumain's noodle.

"McDonald," Cyprien guesses in a low voice. "McDougal. No McIntosh. That's it… McIntosh."

Toumain taps a tune with his fingers on the desk, wondering whether the blond man his daughter presented him had told him his name.

CHAPTER 19.

The Other Welcoming Committee

The larger red SUV pulls up behind a smaller one already parked and waiting. Like his boss, Chapo has taken up in age and has remained loyal to the enterprise. Now sixty-two years old, he's not lost an iota of his physical ability. Throughout the years, he had stayed in shape, had taken up martial arts, and that cat is tough as nails. He will fight you like a pit bull on steroids. It is he who emerges first from the smaller vehicle and takes off his hat as he meets the three mulatto men with dark sunglasses from the other automobile.

The twin sons of Tito Massim, Kharim and Khalil, or Uday and Qusay, are with their younger cousin, Jimmy Massim. Jimmy is a twenty-four-year-old deportee from the US who's served time for theft and drug trafficking. Jimmy has had the glorious privilege of being among the first fifty deportees the day after Donald Trump took the oath of office. At his arrival, Tito knew how to give him a clean slate bypassing all the legalities. Thus, the country's judicial system has no record of a deportee with the name Massim, and not even a single fingerprint was taken of the young man. Bribery.

Uday carries a black case probably snipers' shit, and Qusay has a briefcase. Chapo opens the back of his vehicle. The case and briefcase are placed in and opened by each of the twins. Chapo glances at Jimmy, who already stands by the rear door behind the driver's seat of Capo's car. Jimmy executes precisely how his cousins have told him to mess with Chapo whom they have known ever since they were born.

"He's on the border," says Qusay. "Here are the money and the weapon he precisely asked."

It worked because the one thing in Chapo's mind is not the drive to the border. He gets paranoid thinking of Jimmy as someone Tito sent to spy on his dealings or perhaps even to whack him. However, he is sure that Tito is aware that not anyone could that easily take him out and indeed not a pencil-neck like Jimmy.

"Who's the kid?" Chapo asks after a lick of his teeth.

"Oh, he's coming with you," Uday replies.

"What!" he asks in a controlled rage. "Tito don't trust me no more?"

"This is Jimmy, Chapo," an amused Qusay replies to calm down his paranoia. "It's the kid from New York Father said you'd work with now."

"Like you worked with us," Uday, the other twin, soothes him.

Chapo looks at the young man with disgust.

"Hop in! Motherfucker. I am no babysitter."

The men get in the cars, and Chapo and Jimmy drive straight. The twins make a U-turn as they laugh.

"Damn! That old fart is mad," Qusay says.

"They'll get along," his brother replies.

When they make it to the main road, the brothers decide to part ways. Kharim remembers he needs to meet with Junior Toumain, or that is what he tells his brother. In fact, he thinks he would try to go and save face near Christiane, who had for months now attempted to end all relations with him, for she understands that she was a hostage in the deal. In daddy's mind, the twins are the only men she had known all her life. Toumain welcomed the relationship but agreed to allow her to go and see what's out there on her own. She had chosen to study in DC with frequent visits back home.

When the other twin, Khalil, or Uday, arrives in the lobby of the hotel, a handful of guests, mostly foreigners, file in or await some service from the concierge. With much arrogance, he walks up to the counter. He slides an envelope toward the skinny old man whom naturally, Toumain has helped in that position as he did for many others at that hotel. To the guests in line, Khalil is probably part of the staff and a superior to the concierge. No offense.

"Yes boss," says the concierge as he puts the envelope in his pocket as the guests look on. "The battle of Vertières will have to wait. It's a hotel policy."

Uday turns around and walks away, thinking of November 18.

"Hotel policy, my ass," he says as he passes by the guests in the line.

Massim turns into the hallway and disappears. As he does in all the countries he goes, temporarily, the agent stays in a hotel until the rest of his team arrives unless he should stay separated. He plans to be 24/7 at the American base. He is relaxed, in the projection room with his fingers interlocked as a net in support of his head. Leopold sits with his feet on the chair in front of him. The officers had already introduced him to "Prestige," hence the empty bottles near him. A while ago, he looked at maps of the city. Now, two Marines officers, an African American, and a blond officer instruct him when his telephone vibrates on the table next to him.

Leopold slides a finger on the phone, and a life-size 3D holographic image of an Apple iPhone screen appears in front between him and the marines. Christiane shows up in her bikini by the swimming pool at her father's estates.

"McLintaugh!" he answers.

Christiane and Leopold have briefly talked about doing some sightseeing around the country. To this point, she thinks he is only a visitor taking a tropical break from these winter storms that are becoming more and more horrible and dangerous every year. Leopold reminds her that he is still in the room and cannot stay too long.

"Well," she says, "I mean if you still want to discover the country, I have gotten an idea to make Columbus turn in his grave."

As though he was asking for their permission, Leopold holds his finger up to the marine officers who look impatient and intolerant. For sure, they are much older than he is, and they seem to command strict regards to the rules. They presume, perhaps, the agent had not gone through this at the bureau already. They are aware though.

"I'll buzz you," he tells her hurriedly, in a whisper.

Leopold touches the phone on the table, and the hologram eclipses.

"Forgive me… Go on, please," he tells the marines.

A picture of Tito Massim with his sons appears on the screen.

MARINE OFFICER

Tito Massim and his twin sons. Businessmen of Lebanese and European origin, but here, people call him "Saddam." Subsequently, for their excesses, his sons next to him are called "Uday and Qusay." They are twins. They themselves adopted these names that they use to send out threats and ransom notes. They even conduct business using such names.

The blond officer walks to Leopold and bends to his ear.

"These images are not for kindergarten children," he tells him. "They are accused of these crimes they committed before and after the assassination of the journalist." Leopold rests his chin in his hands as the images reflect in the sunglasses atop his forehead. He sighs as the African American continues.

"Agent McLintaugh," he says, "as you are aware, your father himself looked into the assassination of this man back in the nineties. This is Roger Lafontant, a former strongman from the Duvalier regimes. The photograph, on the right, was taken a few hours after the man seen previously with his sons executed him in a prison cell. Still, there is an unofficial version of his death. That is actually in the prison courtyard."

As the photographs continue to show up on the screen, Leopold seems eager to revisit what he heard of Toumain. He wonders if he had indeed met one of those men. The agent wants to be sure for a third time. He has seen him in photograph at the downtown office in DC, his daughter might have innocently led him to his home and has even shaken hands with and talked to him. The officer continues. Something he did not expect occurs as the officer goes through the list of the scot-free crimes of the Massims. The marine talks of the massacre that Tito orchestrated and coordinated with and for the military. He feels something hit home as he recalls Ed and Dorothy recounting the story of his miraculous birth there. He envisions the visit he took with Dorothy and Dr. Pierre, in that very yard shown in the photograph of the school Argentine Bellegarde, a year after the murder of Jean Dominique.

"My son," he recalls the doctor saying, "you were born right under that tree in the middle. You are a miracle."

For twenty-one years, he has kept his mother's response to the Haitian disciple of Hippocrates of Kos securely guarded in his heart and mind.

"Thank you, doctor. If he's a miracle, you made him possible."

He manages to keep his emotions in check but makes a mental note to look around for this doctor who, he thinks, should be pretty old by now if he is still alive.

"Sir, Agent McLin…," the African American says looking closely at him, "are you 'right? Is everything okay?"

"You looked removed over there for a minute or two," the other instructor says.

"Pardon me," he says. "Go on."

"This is the Reverend Pastor Sylvio C. Claude," the blond instructor says as the Reverend's photograph comes on. "Assassinated the same day as Dr. Lafontant by this man, Daniel Toumain, in the city of Les Cayes in the south of the country alongside his would-be accomplice, this man, a former president of the country. Just like his cousin whom you'll see soon, he is a person of interest in Dominque's murder. About him, folks over here say, it's by the favors of the journalist's last feud."

"That's some shit," Leopold mumbles to himself.

"Say what now sir?" inquires the African American officer as a photograph of former president Michel Gibéa comes on the screen.

"Oh! Go on, sir. Just making a mental note. Just making a mental note."

The photograph he was waiting for finally shows up on the screen. However, it does not have the anticipated impact on him. Seemingly, he had somewhat become anesthetized courtesy of the extent of his previous emotional straining viewing the photographs of the place of his birth with, in one of the shots, the image of people standing in line that election Sunday. He envisioned the heedless fortune that maybe some of the people in that line had in the ability bestowed upon them to lay their eyes on his mother. He had never had that chance. Not even in a photograph.

Back at the hotel. When he turns into the last hallway, Leopold pulls his mag-card. He makes sure his gun is accessible enough as he sees something protruding from underneath the door. The agent slides the magnetic card and picks the paper up from the floor, mentally reconciling that he does not have such a service at the hotel. A note fell. Up to when Leopold unfolds the paper, he has been remarkably silent. So quiet, one would guess that he was still on the phone with the young woman of whom he now wonders if she will side with the investigation. Will she withhold information and withdraw altogether once she learns the motive of his being in the country? He reads the note and pauses to reflect on who probably would write this note to welcome him in the "Slippery Land" as the memo reads. Then, one would be correct. Leopold was listening to Christiane.

"Saturday then," the agent says when he opens the door, "if you think it's better."

She displays a real eagerness to be with him again for. At least, for a quickie.

"Today? No, not a good day," he adds.

For several minutes after they had hung up, Leopold remains flabbergasted and bamboozled. He folds the note and inserts it into his pocket. Today, he has to receive the other agents who will help him. His father did not mention that President Sosa and Lysius were single-mindedly interested in the method that they have, since their Yale days, read about. Lysius would swear by it since his extensive library includes an entire McLintaugh section.

In preparation for her first outing with this hunk of a catch, Christiane drives Toumain's luxury car to a few stores around the city. She can usually plan that sort of thing without flaw, but a small detail has added itself to her to-do list. The young woman wants her mind to believe that it is Qusay who invited himself to a restaurant with her to talk things over. When she arrives outside the restaurant and is ready to get off the vehicle, she must send Leopold away and psych herself up for what may come.

"Leo dear, I gotta go."

Christiane hangs up and gets out of the car. She crosses the street and enters a restaurant where Qusay sits facing the entrance but is caught off guard when Christiane walks up to his table and towers over him. For someone who was waiting for his date to arrive, he is genuinely surprised to see her somewhat unexpectedly. He suddenly loses his words, but of what he has no idea yet is that he should start missing her who had already made up her mind even before the first time she had sex with the agent.

Leopold is forthcoming with her about his situation and his actual feelings. She is aware that he is a married man who prompted her to literally feel all the way deep within her walls, all of "what" poor Teresa must be missing and yearning for.

"Huh! Oh! I… I…," he mumbles and takes a sip as he fixes himself up.

"I was not expecting you to get here so fast."

"Well, I'm here," she says.

"Babe, I want to have things as they were."

"What things?" she asks. "How were they?"

"Well, you know…"

"All I know you can't treat a woman right. You can't just flash your money in a woman's face and get into her pants… The times we spent together, you jerk…"

"Qusay cuts her short."

"Look. All I'm saying is our fathers are the best of friends. Don't you think it's fitting if…?"

Qusay gets near, and under the table, he runs his hand in between her thighs.

"Yeah," she calmly says with a misleading smile, "Kharim, Qusay, or whatever the fuck you call yourself…"

She gets up with the water pitcher in her hand and slowly pours the water on his head.

"Sweetheart," she says as she pours, "it's fitting if you start to respect women. We're not all pieces of meat." She leaves.

Qusay's facial expression shamefully turns to sorrow as the patrons observe in awe but with the fear of him seeing them. *Who is that brave woman*, they quietly wonder, *to dare treat Qusay in such fashion?*

CHAPTER 20

Sex On The Beach?

For the first time, Leopold is alone in the land of his birth. The last time he visited was twenty-two years ago when he was only thirteen years old. Then, an already aging Dr. Pierre took him and Dorothy to the Argentine Bellegarde's schoolyard. To the present day, he still remembers the answer he got from the doctor about the song he heard the students from the nearest classroom sing.

"Mommy," he asked in French, seemingly interested in the rhythm, "what are they singing?"

Dorothy had redirected her son's query to the local. Dr. Pierre responded that the song was about what all-girls schools have for dinner compared to what their boys equivalents resort to eating. Leopold found the song to be very amusing. After his first full day working with the team, he feels ready to let Christiane lead him to the discovery adventure she talked about. Rare are outings that do not involve the beach in this country. With that in mind, he deems it a good idea to visit Commerce Park. He wears Bermuda shorts and a University of Michigan football jersey. He drinks from a bottle of Prestige under an umbrella. He hopes to keep it as low key as possible or so he thinks. Could such a blond man be low key in that town?

As he sips his beer, Leopold observes an old man dressed in white, stirring his coffee with his bag on the table in front of him. *He must be a medical doctor*, the agent judges from the

Tuscany Leather briefcase the old man has just received as a birthday gift from one of his grandchildren. Leopold's phone rings.

"McLintaugh."

In Washington, DC, all the noises that Ed McLintaugh hears around his son in Port-au-Prince have him lower the volume of his TV set at his end. The Capital had become for the past decade the noisiest place in the Caribbean. Every rat makes its own collection of noises with no regard for its surroundings. Probably it is "Fake News," but it is reported that Cubans hear the noises that Haitians make at home.

"Father!" Finally, a voice that sounds familiar and reassuring.

Leopold listens to Ed as he keeps checks on Chapo and Jimmy, each with a bottle of beer as they walk by unaware that Leopold had already spotted them. By the note left under his hotel door, the agent is free to believe that these two could be on to him. He is right. After Cyprien's report, Tito had indeed assigned them to follow Leopold around town. However, he was not yet sure he was that Agent "McIntosh." Words from Toumain warrant Tito's decision.

"Son," Leopold hears through the receptor, "I respect your feelings, but it is also my father and your grandfather's name with you down there. Jeando and I were too close. I can't be part of it. There's more to your leading this investigation. And I'm not about to take it sitting on my ass… Or you may as well do police work over there running after thieves."

As he listens to his father, Leopold looks at the old man's table as Jimmy walks away with his bag. In DC, Ed announces to

Leopold that he had gotten in touch with James Madigan, who agreed to travel for a few hours to give him a hand.

“Okay, Father, I’ll expect his call.”

Suddenly, Leopold gets up and runs. Not directly after Jimmy but toward his own vehicle so he could follow Chapo’s car in which he had previously seen them.

“That’s why Trump deported you,” Chapo says. “Make up your mind, kid. You’re either a thief or a paid assassin.”

“Did you see that shit?” the remorseless young man asks after he gets in the car. “Nobody saw shit. I’m good.”

“’Got no idea who the old man is. You just stole the bag of the country’s oldest doctor,” Chapo says.

“Oh, shit!” Jimmy says sarcastically. “I should return it, then. Nah! He follows through, I owe people money and shit.”

Leopold’s Suburban pulls up suddenly and parks diagonally in front of them. He runs around the red vehicle and appears beside Jimmy.

“Hey man!” the agent says. “Bring the bag back.”

“What bag, dude?”

Jimmy gets out and pulls his gun. He ignores that he deals with a trained FBI agent who might have routinely had guns in his face. Chapo just sits calmly behind the wheel and watches as Jimmy gets in Leopold’s face.

“Kiss my ass, man. Are some kinda—”

Before he finishes the sentence, Jimmy is disarmed as Leopold reaches and grabs Jimmy’s scrotum and gradually applies pressure.

“You call it, tough guy,” Leopold tells him as he grips firmer and firmer. “The old man’s sack or your balls’ sack.”

Jimmy starts sweating and screaming. Chapo, who had already gotten tired of Jimmy's attitude and who wanted to teach him a lesson is quietly happy to see the agent do it for free. Chapo would straighten out his ass, but because of Tito, he has refrained from harming his nephew.

"I don't want to do this. Give me the bag, kid."

"Fuck!" Jimmy yells. "Let go of me, motherfucker."

As Jimmy screams, sweats, and pees on himself, Chapo grabs the bag from behind the seat and hands it across to Leopold, who empties the bullets from Jimmy's gun onto the floor.

"Okay, okay," Chapo says. "That's enough. Now give him his fucking balls back… Shit!"

Jimmy continues to sweat profusely, holding his balls as he gauchely gets inside the vehicle while a policeman slowly approaches.

"Now, go on," Leopold orders them. "Go on!"

Chapo backs up and drives away very fast. On the passenger's seat, Jimmy still agonizes in pain, holding his crotch inducing his companion's mockery.

"Shoulda seen your ass back there," he lightheartedly tells him.

"That jackass coulda pop my balls, and you sat there n' watched, you old fuck."

"Wouda do da same, kid… I no like fucking thieves." [sic]

When Leopold arrives with the bag at the old man's table under the umbrella, he seems spellbound and confused with his chin resting on the back of his hands atop his cane. He places the bag on the table and pulls the chair to sit across in front of the old man. He crosses his legs, joining his hands at the fingertips.

"Your bag, old man," he says in French.

"Ah! My bag! It was there. Then, it was no more… But I knew it would not be lost."

"I caught the boy who took it from the table," he says as he switch-crosses his legs, allowing the old man to notice the missing finger on the left hand. At that instant, his mind takes him back to the single corner in the limbic system where such a memory particle might have been dropped. A beautiful smile radiates his old face, and Leopold cannot register whatever it is that begets the smile. When this lightning flashback occurs, the old man briefly revisits his fifty-something year younger self. Inside a type of a photographic vignette, he lifts a white newborn infant as he inspects it. Blood drips from the infant's left hand. The old man still looks distant, lost, and baffled. He only sighs.

"Well, gotta go, old man."

"Son," he tells Leopold. "Don't trust this country's calm. Here's my clinic's. Visit me, and we'll talk."

He takes the card, taps on the old man's shoulder, and walks away as he puts the card in his pocket without even looking at it. The old man watches him go and shrugs.

"Hmm!" the old man does.

In the distance down the street, Leopold stops. A woman vendor lays a blue beach shirt on his jersey. He is not the only one out shopping for his date. Christiane also is when she pulls her father's car over and runs to a store across the street. A sudden commotion. A man running, perhaps from the police, pushes from behind a street vendor with a tray on her head. The content of the woman's tray falls. A pack of the laxative, Ex-Lax, drops inside Christiane's open purse without her noticing it as she holds the woman to prevent her from falling in the middle of the busy street. She helps the woman pick her things up and gets in the store. Because of her previous encounter in the afternoon, she completely forgets what she had come to town for. Anyhow, she recovered just in time. And her new beach outfit will match Leopold's blue shirt that he bought from that skilled and persistent vendor.

This beautiful environment, where Christiane takes Leopold, formerly belonged, somewhat rightfully, to the father of Nickesse. Agent McLintaugh, who sits on the long chair beside her, massages her back. One could only guess how the keys to that villa by the sea had gotten to change hands and be today at Christiane's disposal and not at that of the luckless presidential candidate. After the fall and exit of Jean-Claude Duvalier in 1986, many high-profile real estate professionals entrusted with his various properties gambled on the prospect of that family ever returning to Haiti. They supposedly sold off their luxury automobiles, houses, lands, and other precious shit. Many of those professionals would later find themselves enticing "victims" of the regimes to press charges long before Jean-Claude came back to the country. That move of desperation apparently was designed to keep Duvalier at bay. When he did finally come back home, none of the plaintiffs really had a well-constructed claim against him. History would maintain that a lot of folks complain the Duvaliers did this and that to them and their relatives. However, not all would divulge what shit they had done for the motherfuckers to cite National Security to validate their retaliation. Among the very few who ran across him in restaurants or other places would even notice Baby Doc's dirty fingernails.

Although not in the best of his health, Jean-Claude Duvalier had put his ass to work. He tried to put in order what was left of his shit. Toumain had gotten that steal of a deal. He bought the entire thing for peanuts before the young woman on the beach was even born.

"Hmm!" she moans. "Lower… Lower… Hmm! Expert hands," she adds, thinking they were all alone at Carriès.

But, unbeknownst to either of them, behind a relatively distant bush, dressed in a white and light pants, Chapo and Jimmy spy on the couple who is making out on the deserted secluded beach. As they hide behind the trees, dry leaves, and sticks of wood break under their feet and while kissing Christiane, Leopold thinks he heard a subtle noise. His eyes open suddenly. Between the bars of the chair, Leopold looks at the movement behind the bush without alarming the young woman. He kisses her on the forehead, and very slowly gets up.

"Stay here," he whispers. "We've got some company."

Christiane wonders how anybody knew she and Leopold are here on this secluded beach. She has no idea that even her father is on to her. He now thinks the man whom his own daughter introduced him to might be the one agent "McIntosh" about whom Cyprien told him. It turned out that Fat Jacques had earned his pay though he could not remember Leopold's real last name. Almost all the information he provided was accurate, and, at least, he got his first name right: "Agent" and has gotten the "Mc" part of his last name.

Meanwhile, Qusay, assigned to shadowing Leopold's every move, sits in his car with a headset and mouthpiece. He monitors the images sent by the drone flying over Carriès while communicating with his deputies on the ground. The photos from the beach could have added other elements to the mix, jealousy, and rage. However, he'd never learned how to set the camera on the drone for an optimal resolution that would allow him to have face recognition close-ups from the air. If he had not learned, his more tech-savvy twin brother had, but he is not answering his telephone just now. Leopold may have progressed undetected toward Jimmy and Chapo during the time Qusay is blind, for he has recalled the drone while trying to get through to his twin.

Through their earpiece, however, Chapo and Jimmy receive the last info from Qusay that the white man was on the move possibly toward them. Indeed, he had gone around unnoticed to surprise the two men. As Leopold moves from behind one tree to the next, a telephone buzzes. It is Jimmy's, whom Kharim calls to inform that he has wholly disabled the drone's camera rendering them spatially blind or crippled.

"Yeah," Jimmy whispers into the phone. "We did."

"Who's the chick with him?" Kharim asks.

Jimmy motions Chapo to follow Leopold, who jumps from behind a tree to another.

"Kharim!" Jimmy says. "Okay! Qusay. It's your fucking girl, man. She's making' out with him. Yeah, on the fucking beach, man."

"She knows you," he replies, but she does not know if you know her.

As Jimmy watches Christiane on the beach, perhaps yearning for Leopold, the tip of the agent's gun kisses the back of his head. He had managed to outsmart Chapo to get to Jimmy, however not for long because Jimmy will soon have something he had wanted and coveted for a while. Chapo comes back, not empty-handed. He now carries a two-by-four piece of timber with which he'll send Leopold dropping hard like a domino piece at Jimmy's feet. The younger Massim pounces on Leopold's gun and repeatedly kicks him in the guts as he insults him.

"Messing' around with Qusay's bitch?" he asks. "He's gonna fuck you up now."

Like a child with his new toy on Christmas morning, he is amazed as he carefully examines the gun.

"Wow!" he exclaims quietly. "Now, that's a fucking piece! Kiss it fucking goodbye, motherfucker," he adds as he puts the gun in his belt behind his back while Chapo looks on and whispers.

"Fucking thief..."

Jimmy takes the stick from Chapo and bends over Leopold, who is in pain and wiggles a finger in his face spewing trash.

"Fucking fagot!" he says. "Squeezin' ma balls... Squeeze that, bitch." He kicks him again in the guts.

He kicks him again knocking him out as he violently hits him on the head with the wooden stick.

On the chair, feeling impatient that her companion has not yet returned, Christiane decides to get up.

CHAPTER 21.

The Platform

The all-terrain vehicle speeds away on the long stretch of road with no other cars in sight. With the sunglasses over the white straw hat, Christiane searches nervously in her purse. She is mad that the two have tied Leopold's hands and forced her into the vehicle with only her beach robe and what she did not have on and underneath. Her pants and shirt, they only allowed her to put on inside the car. Daddy's girl is pissed and is thinking of a million ways to make these men pay. She knows Chapo, all right, but she has no idea who the heck the other younger man disguised with a bandana over his face and dark sunglasses is. Her father, she thinks, could have Chapo's ass, but that is her only assurance now. At least, she hopes she could bargain her way out of trouble with Chapo, who, she knows, has a weak spot for liquor and cash. But she is still disgusted. Everything in the car annoys her.

"Yuck!" she complains. Coulda left me on the beach, not knowing it would have been a disaster since Qusay later drove to the beach looking for her, Leopold, and for trouble. His girl, his cousin had told him, was making out there with the white dude.

Seated on the right side in the back, Jimmy plays with Leopold's gun, then places it behind his back, and muffling his voice, he answers her complaint.

"It's not up to us. We got orders."

"Right, ma'am," Chapo adds in support. "Not up to us."

"My father," she asks, "put you up to this shit?"

Hands tied at the wrists, Leopold makes a complaining sound from the depth of the car and is stomped on by Jimmy. That prompts Christiane to devise some shit. Perhaps, at that moment, she had discovered something in the purse that she could use.

"How about your breath? Chewing gum anyone?"

"Give, then," Jimmy says, "forgetting to disguise his real voice, which gets her thinking."

"Want some too, ma'am," Chapo says, looking into the rearview mirror.

Christiane dives into her purse. She gives to Jimmy and unwraps one for Chapo as she deliberately lets the gum fall.

She picks up the gum as she puts an ingrown toenail clipper in Leopold's hands. She has bought the instrument at the store after she had helped that street vendor with her stuff. As she looks through her purse now, Christiane makes sense of that other box of "candy" that she did not purchase and that she knows isn't chocolate. She thinks up evil shit.

"I also got chocolate…Want some?" she asks.

Jimmy takes the gum from his mouth and sticks it on the back of his hand.

"Yeah! Chocolate first."

As Christiane dives in her open purse through candy bars and empty wrappings of Kit Kat, Reise's pieces, she finds other brands of chocolate candy. She establishes eye contact with Leopold on the floor below, struggling with the nail clipper that falls time and again from his understandably now clumsy fingers. After some more driving and chocolate/Ex-Lax eating, the time has come to render when suddenly, the car stops. Chapo takes the keys off the ignition and gets out running.

"Keep an eye on 'em," he tells Jimmy as he runs toward the bushes while unbuckling his belt. Chapo disappears behind a low trees' alignment. The sound they could hear all the way back in the car brings the news of his relief that he confirms.

"Ahhhh!" Unseen, Chapo lets escape the breath that he has been holding for quite some time now. But, back in the car, Jimmy is not in the OK column as he sweats and fidgets holding his stomach. Christiane fed the motherfuckers quite an amount of laxative. He sweats a little more, wishing Chapo would come out of the woods fast enough. He does not. Desperate, Jimmy opens the door and stands a bit outside the vehicle as Christiane, who knows what is happening, keeps her composure.

"Go ahead," she tells him. "Where could we go? He took the keys anyway."

Jimmy quickly looks at the ignition.

"Oh! Right," he happily says in a pre-relief feeling… "Thank you, Miss," he adds as he takes off toward the woods showing the seat of his white pants already with a brown stain, which amuses her. When both the driver and Jimmy are out of sight, Christiane goes to work and remains as she was as the men return from the bushes, with Leopold still on the floor. His wrists are untied when Chapo comes back first to the vehicle. A few minutes later, Jimmy does.

With intestinal relief had, comes the calm. It is tranquil in the vehicle, and suddenly, Jimmy screams as though he has been bitten by a croc. Christiane quickly sticks the tip of a hairbrush to Chapo's neck.

"Stop the car," she orders him. "Stop the car. Now!"

Leopold sits up from the depth of the car with a firm hand grip squeezing Jimmy's marbles. He punches him in the nose and sits in the middle next to Christiane. Jimmy bleeds and bends on his knees, exposing the gun in the back of his pants. Leopold quickly grabs his weapon as Chapo brings the car to a complete stop with Christiane at his neck.

"Now! Down, both of you."

Through the rearview mirror, Leopold reads the look of great disenchantment on Chapo's face as he, at about the same time, realizes that Christiane only has a hairbrush to his neck. Leopold quickly points his gun at him since he is trying to reach for something below the level of the steering wheel.

"No, no, no!" says Leopold. "Do not push your luck."

The table has turned. Leopold has now tied Jimmy up and put him in the back of the car. He suspects it was either that stain in the seat of his pants or Jimmy had been passing gas in the vehicle. He ordered Chapo to drive back to Carriès to retrieve Christiane's car. She would find a nasty note from Qusay promising to deal with whomever was on the beach with her. Christiane does not readily tell Leopold of that memo, as he busies himself tying the hands and legs of Chapo before locking them up in the back of their SUV. He and Christiane leave them on the beach, all tied up until late in the afternoon when Qusay comes back. There, they argue about how the heck they get out and about who passed the last gas. And the smell of the stain in the seat of Jimmy's pants keeps them company. In the meantime, Leopold and Christiane enjoy the quietest ride toward the city during which an international call comes into Leopold's phone.

Ed McLintaugh had promised his son that he would intervene to save the investigation and his name. But it is after the call that it starts to sound reasonable to Leopold.

He has been in various other parts of the world, and his father never worried to the extent of even advising him, let alone intervening in his investigations. The current FBI Director has always considered Leopold's adopted father as his possible replacement had he to lose his job. Since he was promoted, he discontinued the use of the McLintaugh method telling everyone he was ready to go to war to defend his decision. The recent visit by Sosa regarding Jeando's case lit a Machiavelli's bulb inside his head. He considered the many botched investigations into the journalist's assassination. Ekstroem remembered the agents, commissioners who have been threatened either indirectly or directly by the higher authorities of the country. The director recalled one particular instance in which they obstructed by neglecting to renew one judge's mandate. He now thinks he can get even with Ed about his marriage to Dorothy. And above all, once and for all, he will discredit the MIM. That opportunity has finally arrived. The politically slippery Caribbean nation seems to be the perfect venue so to do. A day only after Leopold had left for the Caribbean, FBI Director Ekstroem lifted all restrictions on the method. Ed smelled a rat or a bait and has decided to deal with it and cautiously bite; thus, the quick trip of James Madigan in the country. The investigation into Jeando's assassination, as wished by Sosa and Lysius, should not and will not be conventional.

Like Ed, the sixty-seven-year-old Madigan is a recently retired FBI special agent and a longtime friend of the

McLintaughs'. An expert in forensics and hypnosis, he swears by the various gadgets involved in the method's arsenal. James knows them inside out and all of what they can accomplish. He believes the MIM is as much versatile and elastic as the human memory and minds it deals with are malleable. And, as per Leopold's father, he comes to Haiti bearing quite a few toys with which the son is no dummy either. Field agents who all had gotten to appreciate the gadgets within the MIM not touched by the restrictions had made it a habit of taking them wherever on the job.

"Welcome to Haiti," Leopold greets Madigan with a lot of excitement. He also understands that Ed is not taking things lightly if he sends the most proficient non-McLintaugh MIM expert there is. He recalls that Ed had told him he was not about to take it seating down on his ass. But what is it that his father will not take sitting down? He will ask Madigan, but he decides to allow him first to settle.

"Only a local can welcome someone as you do, McLintaugh," Madigan says as they shake hands and start walking.

"Not everyone knows it," Leopold replies "but I am indeed a local."

"Hmm!" replies Madigan. "Undoubtedly, by the favors of some pretty girl who has ventured into your room."

Leopold smiles. "Well, I won't deny any of that."

As the Suburban makes the roundabout to exit the airport area, Madigan observes the dynamism in the streets. This is the first Caribbean country he ever set foot in. James Madigan had mostly traveled to Africa and Asia in his career. He knows that he could have at least taken a cruise like Ekstroem just did on the very day of the country's presidential elections. Madigan jokes in his mind that maybe he really would have had he had a hot date like Heather. He then turns around.

"So," he asks, "Ekstroem really came here?"

"No, he was up North, at Labadee for half a day in a room."

"He must have had a hot date," Madigan says, aware of the Director's ways with the ladies, but Leopold tries to avoid the gossiping.

He finds the perfect topic. A moto-taxi, seemingly carrying a family, suddenly stops at the intersection. As he was about to speed through, he slams the break.

"Jesus-Christ!" he yells.

"Is that legal here too?" Madigan asks.

"You've seen worse in Africa, I'm sure."

Even here, a moto-taxi shows its usefulness. It had just helped Leopold escape some mindless blather. Madigan indeed resorts to asking about moto-taxi and where the new president stands since he heard that many high profiles are involved in the business. In fact, many people here in the country use this phenomenon as a side business. At the same time, the government and those who flocked from the backcountry to the suburbs and cities consider it a tremendous employment source.

"Oh!" Leopold answers, "Lysius does not like it. But he says that after that president had encouraged folks to come to the capital, and later with the earthquake, they had no way to earn a living. Now, they found this shit, taking it away would be criminal and worse than telling them to leave their homes and come to the capital. As a senator, Lysius advocated for the idea of emptying this city for a significant refurbishment. To do that, he thinks that the work should start everywhere outside Port-au-Prince, where the internal displacements originated. He wants to create jobs outside of Port-au-Prince."

"Madigan," he continues, "you've heard him talk. The president-elect says, 'Fuck – Shit – Pussy – Ass,' and this guy will not be shy to call his political foes 'motherfuckers' when he has to. In fact, Madigan, during his campaign, he said his opponent Nickesse Duvalier, who is now his pal, has a motherfucking last name."

After a burst of good laughter, Leopold continues…

"But everyone agrees that he is an awesome cat. One heck of a guy. He tells the people these are just words and not to be afraid of using them, and if folks think President Geffrard is a fucking moron or is full of shit, they should feel free to say so."

"You met him?" Madigan asks. "Heard Sosa took him to meet with Ed."

"No, he does not want to till I am ready to report to him twenty-five hours after he takes the oath of office."

"Wow!" Madigan exclaims. "Some fucking deadline. Why does he want to do this?" he adds. "I heard Lysius' father and Jeando did not agree completely."

"And you believe this crap?" Leopold replies. "Dominique and Geffrard Sr. never got out of character. That's what it was."

"What do you mean?"

"Publicly, they were worst enemies," Leopold says. "In private, best of buddies. They once visited us in DC together. Lysius' father was one of Duvalier's most trusted men the whole time Jeando was hammering the father and son's dictatorships.

Jeando knew everything that was said and done deep within. Geffrard may have been the one who saved Jeando in that November raid. Word is he drove him to the airport personally when the smoke finally cleared around the first days of 1981."

"What does he think about the wealthy folks most opposed to this investigation?"

"He thinks he's ready to take them on," replies Leopold as he looks in the rearview mirror. "He knows they can whack him, but he says he has no fear. He told my father an NSA-modified drone was delivered somewhere here."

Madigan gets more interested and inquisitive. "Any idea who delivered and who received it?"

"He said one man who has more than enough money for that received it."

"Wish that guy was your daddy, don't you?" Madigan asks jokingly. "Umm, well, my kids would."

"I knew a man at the NSA who does these things," Madigan adds.

As he drives on, he recalls what his father had told him of the folks he will be up against. He decides to here and now let Madigan be aware that the people who are opposed to the reopening of that investigation are merciless. They are the untouchables of the Caribbean, they could be anybody, and they have remained somewhat faceless throughout the years. The only two who operate in the open do so as though they had declared it what they do as their legit business for which they pay the country's tariffs.

"Lysius is a very loved man down here," Leopold tells Madigan. "They say that the majority of those who voted against him did so to protect him after he promised to go after Dominique's real killers. They knew he does not bluff."

"I think Americans love him a lot," he adds. "They do Sosa only by default… 'son of a bitch seems determined though."

"To go to the end…?" Madigan inquires.

As a sort of omen, the vehicle stops suddenly and abruptly facing a wall with a "Dead End" sign.

"Gosh!" He gets upset. "I always get lost here."

"The Base is on the other side of that wall," he tells Madigan as he backs up.

Amid the chatter, Leopold had also given the retired agent a report on the progress of his team. The assemblage of agents arrived in the country a little after Leopold had hit the ground. Mullins had already driven up to Delmas to survey the area of what used to be the station where Jeando's murder actually occurred with his "Recog crew." The Forensics Recog uses a unique and special lens Ed had developed after the MIM was approved and that Mullins had taken a liking to. Ekstroem had always been kept aloof about that aspect as a late addition to the MIM. Mounted on a now older IMAX 3D camera, this lens sends to the sensor a range of data that the human mind would consider forever lost throughout time and after natural events. In other words, the lens captures the living memory of an environment or the site of a crime. In this case, Delmas Blvd. around Jeando's old radio station's building or what is left of it. The team shot various angles from the street to the exact spot where Jeando was killed to be included in the platform or the canvas for the MIM to operate. For this investigation, that canvas will transform the participant's brain. The hippocampus becomes an exact replica of the crime site, of the boulevard at Delmas, which the agents call “realm.” Mullins would direct the crew to repeat the shoot in reverse from the spot toward all angles toward the boulevard. From that angle, a plethora of witnesses are identified.

Despite all the transformations that the periphery has undergone, the wealth of information Mullins’ crew brings to the Base is staggering. No wonder Ed calls this last gadget of his “Carbon 14 on steroids.” Since its introduction, Mullins has never left home without it. The symbols on the monitor baffle the agents. They did not expect such at their first viewing of the footage.

“What the fuck is that?” Leopold asks.

In subsequent replays, one younger agent suggests they look at the date in question within the image clip itself. In most organizations, the military for example, the person who gives a suggestion is usually the one everybody volunteers to see it through. The rookie is assigned. As he reviews the specific clips in the other room all alone, he gets completely sold to the idea of what the “Recog” system does. He marvels at how the device will bring to life the memory of a physical environment or structure. A slick idea also slithers up into his mind. He thinks he could rent the RED WEAPON camera and borrow this gadget to film his conjugal bedroom after each of his trips outside the United States. A few minutes later, the younger agent barges in and announces that the date was the 12th of January 2010. He also declares that much of the structures in concrete or part of them yielded no memories after that date.

“What’s that date?” asks Mullins.

“It’s that fucking earthquake,” Leopold answers.

"Oh right!" agrees Mullins looking closer at the erratic symbols that populate the screen. When they play back to the date the journalist was killed, they identify all the symbols representing humans in the footage. A considerable number of the folks represented by the characters on the screens are already dead. They were either assassinated in the frequent political killings around the early Y2K years or a decade later, decimated by that earthquake, which, in the country, folks call "gudu-gudu." With the data gathered and with excellent investigative footwork, they have been able to rapidly locate and make arrangements to meet with the ones who have survived. From that pool, the agents found a few willing to come forward and help with their testimony or so they think. This effort, Leopold reminds Madigan, explains the detailed list he had sent to Kansas right before he left the US for this trip.

The toilet flushes. The door opens, and Madigan comes out, fixing his zipper. With his legs on the desk, Leopold flips through the pages of *Time* magazine with Lysius' face on the cover page under the headline "Americans' Other President."

"And those people, McLintaugh?"

"Where are they?" Madigan asks as he looks at a US map on the wall. "I fly back in four hours…Tomorrow by noontime, I must be in Topeka."

"I sent for them…Tell me," he adds. "Why didn't you choose to work with the woman? She actually eyeballed Dominique's killers, all three of them."

"Horse shit! She did not," Madigan replies. "I am not here to find the worthless pieces of shit that pulled triggers on the boulevard. The McLintaugh will give us the scaredy-cat motherfucker who did not come."

Madigan is already all business as he starts setting things up around the place. He walks behind Leopold while he speaks. He places his case on the desk and plugs devices into the computer and printer. Shortly after his father's death, Ed McLintaugh had entered a contract with Apple Computers to have all the MIM gadgets and devices made. All of Madigan's business around the office lead Leopold to almost feel the older man had dismissed or not heard the question.

"Yeah, Madigan, tell me," he asks the same question again.

"That taxi driver did not see or hear anything," Madigan answered after a long minute. "And that's where I come in. Her panicked mind just flew through the scene while his relaxed mind was at rest across from the radio station for a very long time. Ten minutes," he adds after he pauses. "It saw it all, and there is no telling what we could do with such a memory. Tell me more about him."

"He comes in with a condition, though," Leopold says. "But it's nothing we cannot pull."

"What's that?" asks Madigan as he flickers on and off the lighting umbrella towering a soft pillow on the red couch that he had a minute prior pulled into that corner of the room.

Leopold's answer comes as Madigan projects the laser-like beam incorporated within each of the lighting sources in the room except for the leading overhead light, which will be off. Madigan needs to have the correct distances from all the lighting sources to the witness's hypothalamospinal tract. Madigan knows these measurements by heart. Though the individual will physically be immobilized on the couch, during the whole process, the organism will undergo all the experiences that the mind does. A lot of internal movement will occur. The slightest mistake is not allowed, for it leads to severe lesions of the connecting track from T1 to L2. A rookie cannot afford any other task while setting up. Madigan masters his craft. He still listens to Leopold, who knows he would not have been talking had it been some rookie.

"Mr. Domersant speaks perfect English," Leopold says. "As a younger man, he had lived many years in New York on a B-2 visa.

The guy came back after his parents were murdered by thugs, and since he has had difficulty in obtaining a US visa. He found himself on the scene as Dominique got whacked but didn't see a thing."

"The whole bureau knows how you feel about memory distortion, which is a brainchild of your grandfather's," Madigan explains. "Well, that's what I do, kid. After I'm done, you'll see it's a waste to send you, Mullins, and the others down here. It would be cheaper to fly those folks to DC."

"Maybe this case screams for it," Leopold agrees. "Still afraid of one thing, though."

"What's that?"

Leopold gets up, picks up a microphone, and follows Madigan, who carries the case into the hallway. They will be setting up a control room far enough from where the subject will lay on the couch. Madigan, seating nearby, will guide the events that will unfold. He will invade, take control of the witness's memory that gets picked, stretched, and even gets wittingly distorted.

"Legally," he clarifies, "it's not substantial evidence."

"Horse shit, Ed would say. It gives you people and shit to look into. Tell me again," Madigan asks, "why do these people want to do this? To prove their love for Lysius?"

They come back to the front office as the sound of an old vehicle is heard. Not to lose track of his line of thoughts, Leopold continues his response.

"On the contrary, two of them, including Mr. Domersant, voted against him for Duvalier… They do it maybe for Dominique, whom they called their voice and the poor guy who was killed with him."

"They're here… Let's go meet them," he tells Madigan after a peek through the window.

The FBI could have rented any top-notch new vehicle or just use one car in the lot to fetch those poor volunteers. They are taking the risk to come at the Base that is being watched by thugs. An old beat-up white automobile that resembles the one used by Haitian comedian Languichatte in his weekly TV show pulls up in the lot. The idea was that nobody would have conceived that the bureau would use this type of automobile. Two women and a man get out. The car is parked, and the driver stays inside.

"McLintaugh," Madigan says as they walk to meet the people, "just as memory distortion has no importance for some, voting for or against a politician is horse shit for others."

Sensing that spear was intended for him, who is not a proponent of Madigan's expertise, he chooses to diffuse the situation. He knows he is dealing with a straight shooter, and there is absolutely no time for that shit.

“Like Sosa and Lysius told my father, the pieces of evidence will come by themselves.”

“Let’s hope and see, McLintaugh,” he whispers. “Let’s hope and see.”

CHAPTER 22.

On The Sofa

She comes out of the room where she was on that sofa for the past twenty-four minutes. About the same time that she takes her first steps outside of the door and back onto solid ground, into the real world, Leopold emerges in the hallway from the control room. There, he monitors the many screens showing the living images of what is happening within the hypnotized subjects' mind or "the realm." This feature has practically been the one that differentiated the MIM from the system that Peter Ekstroem, the current FBI director, had developed. Had it been that system in place, and perhaps with somebody else leading the investigation, it would have necessitated a whole army of sketch artists to render their impressions of what the person monitoring the screens would communicate to them. No wonder Ekstroem had to shy away and discontinue.

Leopold meets her right out of the door. Inside, Madigan, probably reviews what he has gathered from her latent memory for later comparison with the data on the central system that Leopold controls. It is there in the monitors' room that the agent realized he has been mistaking Mrs. Louis for the widow of Jean-Claude, the station's superintendent, who was murdered alongside the director and owner. She may very well be just a close female acquaintance.

The woman that Leopold has in front of him at the Base was at the time of the assassinations setting shop in the morning as she usually did. She lived deep inside the small corridor located across the station's building, where she had witnessed a lot of the horrific things perpetrated against Jeando and his radio station. Mrs. Louis, according to the symbols from the Recog, is that neighbor handing Jeando the piece of paper with the license plate number of one vehicle hauling jeerers in front of the station. The journalist had mentioned that in an editorial. On that ill-fated and frightful Monday morning in September of 1991, she had braved it out onto the curbside and set up her little commerce selling coffee and stuffs passersby would need for a quick breakfast.

Every morning, she would gather if Jeando's car is already parked across that she has stayed a bit too long on what she had no choice but to call a bed. She had witnessed first-hand what Jeando told his interviewer in Demme's documentary, *The Agronomist*, and told his friend Ed in that call to Washington.

The army truck came racing up the boulevard and pulled over by the curb for two to four minutes, during which time, the men onboard shot extensively at the building while Jeando and his wife broadcasted live news about the events of the night and carly morning that had toppled Aristide.

"Thanks for your help, ma'am," Leopold tells her in French as he presents her with an envelope. "I know you do not want to. Please accept this."

"*Merci monsieur*," she says as Leopold escorts her to a seat next to the other woman. Mindful of the constraint on Madigan's time budget, he invites the man to come in with him when he turns around.

"Well," he says, "Mr. Domersant, ready to meet the man we talked about?"

As Mrs. Louis sits down, Madigan appears in the waiting area. On his way from the door, after pushing it shut, the older American may have heard the mention of a name he has been told of through a previous conversation with Leopold. He may have also recalled the name of one of the men who are to come today. When he arrives near the people in the area, the police pickup truck pulls into the lot. Leopold hurries to introduce Domersant to Madigan as the police truck parks alongside the old beaten-up white Peugeot 304.

Madigan needed to query Leopold regarding the older gentlemen, not physical witnesses, they agreed he was to see just after Mrs. Louis. He remembers the young agent telling him they were older and reasons that the only fifty-four-year-young Domersant could not be one of them. When Madigan instead asks who it was that had just pulled up, Leopold, who did not believe the older men could still drive, looks through the window and goes at the security screens. He touches a screen and gets the entire image on one monitor of the older men getting out of the truck with much agility for their ages. They walk steadily and a little fast since they know they are running late.

"Ah!" says Madigan, who had also peeked quickly through the window. "'T must be the old officers."

"Affirmative," replies Leopold, who walks with Madigan away from the others. "The driver's real name is Maurice Massenat but goes by the nickname 'History Channel.' They say around here that he is a walking, talking history book. He's been in the police force since he was nineteen. For short, everyone drops the word "Channel.'"

"Gee!" Madigan says. "Is that the actor," he asks, "struck by the striking resemblance?"

"No," Leopold answers, "but that's how they call him here. Real name is Marcellus, Gustave Marcellus. And like his partner, serving since age nineteen. Together, they have seen plenty of shit in this country."

Having already met with Leopold, it is casually that they see each other again. When introduced to Madigan, it becomes a little ceremonial, and they start liking each other on the spot, which is to render Madigan's task much more comfortable as the bond of trust is rapidly established. Without stepping into the waiting area, History goes straight into the room following Madigan, who had wordlessly suggested that he follow him. And for the next twenty-seven minutes, the McLintaugh may never again have such vast and vivid a memory to toy with. Leopold returns to the waiting area to explain the change and little delay to the others.

It is as though no other preliminary steps were necessary as History was "gone" the second his body hit the couch and his head, the small pillow. But the well-advised expert will never omit these steps as required by customary laws to inform the subject of all of what he or she is to undergo. Perhaps it was more relaxed with the older policeman who still wears the uniform and actively cooperates, along with his partner, in the formation of younger recruits.

In subsequent short visits to Dr. Pierre's pediatric clinic, Leopold had gotten the incredible feeling that he could entrust the old physician with the purpose and nature of his presence in the country. The doctor has then tried to lecture him a bit about the risks associated with that Dominique's case. Leopold, who had dealt with dangerous and merciless terrorists around the Mediterranean region and in Europe, stayed confident he could take on whom or what it may come to. When he explained to him a bit of the method that is used in the investigation, the old man actually pulled his prescription pad and wrote the names of Gustave Marcellus and Maurice Massenat from the police force.

"You could talk to them both," Dr. Pierre said as if he were writing a prescription to the agent, or either one for that end.

Leopold gathered enough information from the bureau to determine that he could really work with Morgan Freeman and History Channel. He managed to have them both to agree. However, Morgan withdrew at first after a little health scare the day before the session but is here, at the Base anyway. His course on the couch, for that reason, will be quick and short.

The data gathered from Morgan's memory is similar to History's except on the issues about which they continuously argue; respect or non-respect for those former Presidents being one of these. The most significant thing that Madigan uncovered as he stretched and distorted the old officers' memories has to do with one of the issues that had retained the public's judgment for a very long time.

"What's Carib Patrol?" Madigan would ask Leopold through the intercom. "Is that the equivalent of The Canadian Mounties?" he would try to guess with sarcasm.

Madigan is probably bluffing at this point. Definitely more nationalist than McLintaugh, he reads differently into how the symbols emanating from within the old man's latent recollection noodles convey his ulterior belief in respect to the behavior of "his country" when it comes to the funds of the Petro-Caribe accord. Well informed in world affairs, James Madigan had heard a great deal about Petro-Caribe in meetings and briefings that he's taken part over the years. The elderly Haitian police officer holds deep in his mnemonics the belief that these funds were not loosely squandered by Haitians alone on their own dishonest merit and genetic makeup. In his own words and his filthiness of the mouth, History, on his part, argues that some folks elected to calculatingly "rat-fuck" the program. The sole basis is that it was the legitimate brainchild of the late Hugo Chavez who had no ill will toward the people of Haiti and of other countries of the region.

"Any difference between the memories?" Leopold would ask after he told Madigan about the dilapidated funds' original designation.

"Ah! Not much," Madigan replied.

Morgan's memory, even before the scientist does anything, presents as a fertile ground for these thick hearsay symbols suggesting his firm belief in the truth of the information that generated them. In his mnemonic receptacles, Morgan keeps a laundry list of folks who were beneficiaries of the funds as hand exchanges occurred. Hush payments were made, according to his hearsays, to people nobody would think. Among them besides elected officials, some of the loudest pie holes behind the radio stations' microphones and "reputable" columnists in the country.

When Leopold asks Madigan to isolate and distort a tiny fiber cautiously, the information is stunning. "The Caracas' man," as Madigan translates the symbols, "would have confided to President Josaphat that the names of none of the folks who assuredly dilapidated the funds were on that shoddy investigation report. However, some companies, dubious or whatever, still find themselves hard at work on sham contracts here and there but nowhere in between."

Right before Morgan Freeman, as History involuntarily spills his large memory to Madigan, who only sees the passing codes on the monitors, Leopold, in the room at the end of the hall, was in for a treat, and he had had no idea yet of what it really would be. Otherwise, he would not have interrupted the session at the moment he does. Indeed, after a series of bits to Madigan which are vivid images to Leopold of the time when he and Morgan enrolled to help Papa Doc combat his detractors whom he called "Kamoken." Leopold contacted Madigan through his mouthpiece as he recalled the advice the police chief gave him.

"Madigan," he said, "we ought not to read too much into what you find in the officers' memory from this point forward."

"May I ask why that is?" Madigan inquired.

"Up to that point," Leopold answered, "the journalist is an idol to the young police officers. The events that his noodles will yield next mark the beginning of their prejudices concerning Jeando for his coverage and his explicitly naming him and his partner as the officers on duty at that specific time and location in 1987."

While Madigan listened, the uneven movements of the symbols on the monitors reached higher and higher levels.

Meanwhile, in the other location where Leopold is, something outlandish unfolded.

On Leopold's main screen, the two younger police officers were crossing from the North toward the South corner of the intersection of John Brown Blvd and Vaillant street (this is the left-hand side of the boulevard from downtown Port-au-Prince) with people mostly dressed in white standing in a line. Leopold does not look at the screen, since he had turned sideways, explaining to Madigan why they will not buy too much into the assertions of Morgan's and History's raw memories. The back of his head and his right ear remained exposed to the monitors.

The two officers approach the end of the line, where a young pregnant woman arrives as the last person. She runs her hand on her belly, turns around, and smiles as the policemen get near to engage in a casual conversation. History stares at her as his partner speaks with her. She smiles, looking straight into History's eyes as though she were in front of a camera lens, sending a special message with her eyes and smile, deliberately pointing to her belly. To anybody watching the scene beyond the officer's point of view, her hand gesture with her fingers on her stomach translates as her talking to her budding baby in a very distant future.

"Be aware," Leopold continues, "that you might find out that their minds and memory systems work together to incriminate the people they do not like or folks they had a biff with. The police chief told me their mind could be set to convict former presidents Gibéa and Aristide. The old men had never been fond of either one. And, they would attribute to them personally all the crimes that happened on their watch. History would throw buckets of the people's blood on them. In the mind of the guy you have now on the couch, Aristide is a monster, a freak, a bloody assassin. He may not come short," Leopold adds, "of telling you that indeed 'fucking Aristide' paid for the bullets that whacked Dominique to easily win the elections. Don't buy into it," he urges Madigan.

Leopold may not have recalled the exact name. It is, however, clear that he refers to the assassination of young attorney Bertin as an example of how cruel History's bias can be. McLintaugh tells Madigan that in the officer's mind, former president Michel Gibéa, not Tito Massim, can add that crime to the shortlist of his life's achievements. "For the record," Leopold adds, "Gibéa was not even in the country at the time. But he still wants to place the former president that day, on that criminal errand for his boss or buddy. When the young and beautiful attorney got whacked, in his defense, Gibéa was in Cuba with his sick young daughter for three to four months."

"I will tell you," Madigan, he adds. "His noodles may display many of those ordered crimes during some specific period."

Madigan laughs audibly upon discovering another cluster of codes suggesting one of History's strong beliefs that he discloses to Leopold. The elderly officer vehemently believes that, at times, the governments of the three countries can be insincere with each other. The people thereof, however, have always engaged in a genuine mutual love-and-respect affair. What got the laugh out of the American are the visuals History's memory associates with his arguments. If countries, Madigan translates, could have orgies or threesomes, the officer believes that Cuba,

Haiti, and Venezuela would always be the guilty, kinky bad boys and/or girls. On this earth, only those three societies, not countries, categorically love and value each other.

As Madigan starts to formulate his next question, he stops and instead asks Leopold what it was that made him react as imperceptibly as he did. It is not clear to Leopold as to what precisely the retired agent refers to. When the representation of the young woman came on the screen for the first time, a virtual hand appeared to reach out from within the monitor and poke his shoulder and gently blow his blond hair. Although he felt the little breeze and the poke, he does not know how and what to answer, for he is unaware that he reacted any distinct way. In fact, as he warns Madigan about History's preconceptions, he turns around momentarily to look at the screen on his left to check out what was occurring with the symbols instead of the vivid images in front of him. He turns back to make sense of who or what had poked him. This is the instant when the young woman looked straight and deep into the officer's eyes and when she shot that smile from the depths of her guts. Leopold feels the heebie-jeebies and trembles like a tree branch with goosebumps all over.

The agent is shaken; he feels warm and cold. He does not understand. He is dumbfounded and speechless. It will take five or six visits to Dr. Pierre's to, at least, make sense of it all. As a pediatrician, the agent assumed he could remember such a person. In this country, not all women are entitled to such practice throughout or post-gravidness. Leopold will have understood the no help from the old doctor, but he keeps showing up. And finally, on one such visit, he resorts to showing the doctor the young woman's photograph that he had printed from the distortion of

History's memory the afternoon after he drove Madigan back to the airport. At the time, he did not know why he made that extra print, but it will have gotten Dr. Pierre thinking.

"McLintaugh!" Madigan calls out twice. "Are you all right in there?" he asks Leopold who has been eerily silent for the last few minutes.

Leopold sighs. "Yeah. I'm 'right."

"Check these symbols with the vivids for me, will you?" Madigan inquires.

"Huh!" Leopold responds. "Temporarily, I don't have symbols in here."

Leopold had stopped the other screens. Madigan resorts to having him leave his remote station and come into the room where he is with the deeply hypnotized older man.

"What you got?" Leopold whispers when he arrives.

Madigan had inadvertently gotten somewhat adrift inside a dark alley deep within History's memory, and the behavior of the symbols on his monitors screams for particular attention, and that is why he called Leopold in.

"This is probably what you were talking about," Madigan tells him, pointing to the fitfully moving symbols on the monitors.

"Gee! What's all this shit?" Leopold asks.

"Your grandfather, I recall, had determined this to be how 'hearsays' behave. You know, things that are probably not true at all, but the host believes the reinforcement suggesting that other people thinking or saying the same will ultimately make them accurate. Former President Donald Trump certainly has had a lot of these hearsays. Most of the time, they can't even name one person among those 'many' others they say are saying the same thing."

"But wait," says Leopold after he approaches and runs the tip of a pencil on one of the screens, "there's a name in this segment."

"They always do remember," Madigan replies, "if there is at least one, that is. Here," he points to the screen, "this Aiel Jean. Can we meet him? I would postpone my flight if you can get him on that couch this afternoon."

Madigan gets up and goes to a far-off monitor circling portions of the symbols within a grayer and denser area.

"You were right, McLintaugh. All these clusters are grudges and resentments that the old man already has toward the former Presidents before the journalist's assassination. You see," he continues as he runs his finger on the screen, "from here to here, 'flimsy symbols' the old man only 'thinks' Aristide and Gibéa ordered Dominique's death. But, look here," as he pulls his telephone and turns it on to view his calendar, "that is a firm fucking belief, McLintaugh."

"Get this character on that couch, and I'll hop on a later flight," he adds as he turns around.

On a computer in the corner of the room, Leopold pulls the FBI's dirt on the man Madigan wishes to see on the couch. He brings the monitor in front of his temporary partner.

"Oriel Jean," Leopold pronounces clearly with his fluency in the French language, "savagely whacked shortly after he went on a "spill-the-bean' rampage in the media."

"Too bad," Madigan says. "Then you, the old man, and anyone else have got nothing on neither Aristide nor Gibéa. Up to this point, those two presidents have nothing to do with the journalist's murder."

And turning around to face Leopold, he adds practically in the same breath, with a detective smirk "unless, of course, they are men enough to switch place with History and bring their asses on this couch."

The symbols on the monitors have entered a new phase while the two men were whispering. As he reads and deciphers the erratic symbols, he is jotting on a notepad people's names and events popping up everywhere on the screen. Once back in the control booth at the end of the hallway, Leopold will input and run this data through the mainframe. As a result, he will get mentions of cocaine, tainted medications, and alcohol. Further, He would get exposed to a salad of names and dates. Names like Tito Massim, that senator, and his cousin Dani Toumain, Berlanger, Aristide, Préval, Duvalier, Clinton, Gibéa, Jean Valme, Wittman, Markington, Lalanne, Martelly, etc. As events, a plethora of dates would pop up as well. Times such as 1950, December 5, September 29, and November 30, 1980, and of course, April 3, 2000, and January 12, 2010: with a special emphasis on the date of May 14, 2011.

"Do you also think that is hearsay?" Leopold asks as he points to another screen.

"No," Madigan replies, "this is a big fat truth. He knows it, thinks, and believes it without the assistance of any stimulus or reinforcement. That, over there in the bottom," circling it with his laser pointer, "seems interesting." Leopold looks closer at what is going to hit a nerve inside him because the Jeando whom he and his parents knew all these years was much better than that. The friend, the agronomist, the journalist, and the man, the human who ran around his childhood home playing hide-and-seek with him as a kid, was a class. His parents have always talked of him as a man of integrity, character, and high moral standards. He recalls his grandfather saying that a man of such caliber had no other destination but to ultimately reach the presidency. That man would not stoop down to molesting his own daughters. No, he thinks, not Jeando. He wishes his grandfather had thought of a way to obliterate hearsays. Then, his following thought, the McLintaughs would centuple their fortune by erasing them from that of a certain stable genius' "tremendous" memory. As a downfall of such, they would never get to know that it is not hearsay but a firm belief or an outright accusation. Madigan deciphers that History accuses the leaders of the country of taking decisions that frequently, have absolutely nothing to see with administrative or even diplomatic purposes. Stretching and pressing more in-depth into the old man's mnemonic fibers, the scientist learns it is always about covering some asses. They practice cover-ups for either corruption or for their involvement with narcotics as a powerful entity breathes down their necks while threatening to drop its most lethal joker card: blackmail. Of late, the older officer believes, the country's leaders have all had somewhat a Damocles' sword hanging over them. Lysius is the only one who comes on his shift with a clean slate, and History wants the Americans who always foster corrupted officials for leverage, to be shaking in their pants even though Lyzou and their president have been in a womanizing bromance for years.

While Leopold seems to be drawn-out into his past cozy experience with the journalist, History's memory does not stop to gratify Madigan's expertise. Like a professional thief inside a well-guarded and secure environment, the scientist performs a detour inside the old police officer's memory.

"Hmm!" he says. "There go two others."

"Who? What about?" Leopold asks.

"One 'bout Duvalier. The granddaddy, that is."

"The other?" Leopold asks.

Showing a strange curiosity, Leopold moves to sit near Madigan's chair and starts connecting some audio gadgets that Madigan has not been using yet in this session with History.

"Hmm, Aristide!" he says as he tries to decipher what he is reading on the monitor.

"What the…?" he questions. "He'd threaten to kill daughters if the wife leaves?"

"Yup," answers Madigan. "That's what you read. Good news for Mr. Aristide, these are weak symbols. Not true. But shit's out there possibly on YouTube and other shit like that also."

"Gee!" Madigan exclaims. "McLintaugh, take a look at this. The old man's noodles seem to place that President in a room with some other folks conducting some creepy ceremony involving a baby."

"So, what are those?" Leopold asks. "Do these codes mean they crushed the infant?"

"We don't know yet," Madigan replies.

"Make him talk," Leopold suggests.

Madigan comes back to his chair and sits, with a smile on his face, near History's head. He knows the old man will not be uttering the words. Madigan must voice out what the old man wishes to say. The inventor and Madigan had broken their teeth and bled their noses studying and researching to come up with the reason why the system renders the subject's vocal cord entirely inoperative, once connected to both the subject's Broca and Wernicke's areas. A fix had never been found till the passing of the elder McLintaugh to remedy this aphasia. However, Madigan had developed a way to prevent it from becoming total. The scientist would not find the time now to explain these intricacies to Leopold. So, he just complies. After all, for someone who did not really like the invasion, Leopold is in charge here and is pushing the envelope. Madigan sits, and as though he talks to the former president, it is amusing to hear.

"Well, Donald, talk to us," he tells hypnotized History. "Tell me what you've heard people say." Leopold readies himself to listen.

The period is late 1940s, very close to the fifties, Madigan deciphers. The doctor who had already served in other administrations, is now ready to take on higher responsibilities, and why not the presidency?

Madigan stops and turns to whisper into Leopold's ear.

"See here," he says, "that old man is very selective as to what he believes to be the truth. Look here," he guides Leopold's attention. "The old fart does not assume any bit of that shit, over here, he tells us that he heard people say. Look down here, he knows, he thinks, and firmly believes that François Duvalier and Mangate have been the best ever prepared politicians for the presidency. This belief, McLintaugh," he adds, "is as strong as steel with the symbols more prominent about what he believes of the latter."

"The debate is a fair one," Leopold says. "Anyhow, that other guy's name is Manigat, Leslie Manigat. Not Mangate."

"Now, look. Look how flimsy they are up here for what's coming next."

Leopold signals Madigan to wait for a second as he pushes the intercom's button and asks Mullins to man the booth for an instant.

Madigan checks his watch.

"He made up the story that sounds good to him," he adds, "knowing it may never turn out to be the truth and stored that shit inside a folder-like apparatus deep within a secluded corner of the limbic system which ultimately sticks a 'hearsay label' onto it."

"This has got to be sensational," Leopold says excitedly.

"In short, what is filed in his memory vault is practically this," continues Madigan. "The old man thinks he's heard that perhaps the Haitian cardinal had fathered a child when he was in some parish in the city of Jacmel. Down here, according to these fidgeting symbols, there is a good chance, Jean-Claude, you know, 'Baby Doc,' was not the child of Simone Duvalier."

"Make him speak," presses Leopold. "Make him speak."

"People around him (Papa Doc)," Madigan continues as he deciphers what the old man is yielding as beliefs, "knew it. The folks who undoubtedly would have to reckon with him on the way rapidly took notice of François Duvalier's uncanny political fitness, and they would plot to physically eliminate him. Traditionally in a way, just like Jeando was assassinated because, apparently, he would have had nowhere to end up but in the presidential palace or six feet under."

Madigan momentarily stops his reading and translating of the symbols and looks at Leopold.

"That is why," he says, "my friend, we are here today trying to find out who is still holding that measuring tape and who paid for the bullets that killed the journalist. For sure," he adds, "neither Gibéa nor that other former president physically came on the boulevard, that bloody morning."

"Whereas," returning to the screen, Madigan continues, "the journalist used his fight disposition, the future dictator chose the flight response to the same ordeal. Jeando or Papa Doc? It is not a question of who the bravest has been. To his credit, Papa Doc had no other choice. His detractors had been, for the most part, faceless and could have been anybody. They could have even been made-up boogeymen of his own psyche, according to some who had studied the man." Madigan suggests that Leopold take note of the relationship between that last revelation from the old officer's hippocampus and the actual creation of the Tonton Macoute militia. So, once he had the power all to himself, he handed his enemies their worst defeat by their own courtesy, actually. They had given him on a silver platter the privilege of defining, describing, and putting faces on them. François Duvalier's definition of a "kamoken" is of the utmost political braininess.

Leopold is baffled by History's argumentative abilities, though too often in support of false notions such as the shit he had stored in his brain about the cardinal. Or, another falsehood, his accusations of whom he says played substantial roles in the assassination of Jeando who, on the flip side of the coin, knew very well all of whom he was up against. Jeando stayed in the middle of his enemies and fought. With his only weapon, the journalist had designated or pointed fingers at all who could wish him ill. Like a samurai, Jeando swung his microphone mercilessly. He had bouts with all of them and often picked the fights himself. One might say that he chose his battles sometimes, most would agree, as the aggressor in his editorials. Dominique is not in the old man's mind as a saint waiting to get victimized. He preempted sometimes. The commentaries closest to his murder had earned the folks he was pitched against some severe allegations. The accusations leveled against the former presidents and the senators throughout the media and, ultimately, in the collectivity's limbic system. All these are accusations that the American scientist and the FBI agent decode deep beyond the neocortex of History, the never-retired police officer, and of course, along with that other hearsay regarding former senator Toussaint.

The next clusters of flimsy symbols inform the Americans that during these days, François Duvalier was in hiding gratifying the conservation instinct that we all have. The material makeup of most of the symbols emanating from deep inside History's medial temporal lobe also suggests that the man, François Duvalier, had a terrible case of paranoia. As a youth, he was always afraid of the next person, of the next thing, ever fearful of something. His psychotic mind might have created the monster he feared himself before using it on the whole country. During that period, he would have to be away for an extended period without seeing his family consisting of the future First Lady and the girls. The weaker symbols would place the future dictator inside some secluded little room in a basement, at times, even hiding under a bed. François Duvalier would have retreated in some kind of crypt with some female, possibly even the wife of the trusted friend sheltering him, continually bringing him food and news of the outside or, if you will, from the heat zone. There, subsequently, like they say, "the flesh is weak." Shit happened. When the smokes would clear, and the roaches would be coming out, and contrary to typical Haitian men who would leave the infant behind, Papa Doc would bring a chubby baby boy to his wife and daughters.

"Gee, Madigan!" Leopold says, circling the light from the laser pointer around that area of the screen. "What is this old man? Look at his supporting argument."

"The girls, predictably the younger one, instantly and naturally took a liking to the infant who does not really look like their mother, Simone, who could only accept it. In those days, women, 'the symbols' indicate, did not really have a say. And throughout the years, according to the older officer's latent argument regarding the matter, the First Lady never spoke publicly."

Having cleared the snag of the biases of History, Leopold, Madigan, and Mullins resume the unorthodox investigation. This small space is probably more significant than a tiny hole familiar to the journalist, who also lived in hiding for a considerable amount of time with some friends or relatives. That was, of course, during the dictatorship and probably tipped off by none other than his protector inside the regimes, possibly the father of the president-elect not born at the time. They all return to the point where they left off. For the following twelve minutes, Madigan would have thoroughly surveyed all of History's mnemonic apparatus to gather the data he deems credible. There is no telling that many names have surfaced again and again as the purported killers of Jeando. Unaware of the many "hearsays," the misconstrued auto-instilled beliefs and the biases of History, an ill-advised plainclothesman would perhaps unlawfully indict Gibéa, Aristide, Dany Toussaint, Daniel Toumain, or Tito Massim. This has already been achieved. That indictment is enjoying an inherent existence as an ineffable perception within the collective psyche of a specific population of which the older officers could be worthy samples. Based on the data provided by History, the former would be indicted due to his criminal profession and associations. The latter for his arrogance during his feud with Jeando and after the assassination. The former presidents would be looked at for their behaviors since and after that interview when Jeando really took somebody to school. Something no journalist has ever attempted with any president before or after Aristide. To her credit, though, another radio journalist who worked with Jeando did bait President Manigat but "The Beast" stood his ground, kept his cool, and chewed her. How one other president, or even Micky for that matter, would handle such bait should be anybody's guess.

Mrs. Jeando thinks this particular interview had drastically morphed her husband's relationship with the man he so vehemently supported to the extent some folks of his same genotype would label him a traitor. He would be looked at before, during, and after, along with most of the people in his second botched administration concerning the sickening crimes which appeared to have been coldly calculated, why not sponsored. After fancying the heat he would have leveled on most of these would-be untouchables, Madigan turns around and fires this pre-meditated question at Leopold.

"Kiddo, you think Sosa and Lysius have enough balls to put Gibéa and Aristide's fucking asses on this couch?"

Sensing where the scientist wishes to drive the matter because he recalls that less than two hours ago, looking at President Josaphat's photograph at the airport, Madigan had bluntly said that there is a pattern to Jeando's murder typical to all political assassinations. He argued in the SUV that the masterminds sponsoring such crimes usually expect to share some sizeable political jackpot while the little fingers that pull the triggers or the hands that thrust the blades are often left to be considered as simple, cheap accessories and props. Leopold also recalls reading about that professor who had declared under oath that Dominique died in a politically motivated and sponsored assassination because alive and breathing, his candidacy would have shut down even the campaign slogan of whoever would win the immediately following elections. The other thing occurred on the condition that the journalist was made "silenced." No one else could have said this, but that professor who claims to have grapefruit-size balls.

In that short second, the young agent's intuitive mind had processed all of the information he had gotten on the case, including the fact that more than one person or accessory claimed under oath they indeed killed Jeando for different amounts of cash money. Then, one by one, like rotten teeth, they would fall, disappear, or flee the country. So, these power-angry sponsors have enlisted many for that one dirty job. A trademark that inspired one lawmaker at the time to declare on a favorite

Saturday morning radio show that Jeando's assassination will never be solved even after fifty years. Clarifying later under oath, he equated the journalist's murder to these of quite a few individuals who were assassinated following the pattern that Madigan talked about upon his arrival at the airport in Port-au-Prince.

"I don't know for Sosa besides his cutthroat style in dealings with the Republicans," Leopold replies. "Lysius is a fucking monster. If push comes to shove, he won't need Sosa for that. That son of a bitch could personally grab both Aristide and his pal Gibéa by their fucking throat and drag their asses here to this couch."

"Gee!" Madigan excitedly exclaims. I'd stay here longer or come back for that."

CHAPTER 23.

A Political Calm

The country enjoys a relative calm at the approach of the presidential inauguration. Dr. Pierre would caution that it is usually then it becomes the most slippery and dangerous a place to find oneself at certain hours and in specific locations. Anywhere else in the capital, life itself carries a monotonous feel to it after the overexcited elections season. However, near and above the periphery of the national palace, Tito's drone sends to his control screens the images of a beehive-like business around the partially white formerly destroyed edifice. By courtesy, the Massims freely let the foreign press, in the country for the last months, use their aerial shots of the activities around the capital. They had done this on the day of the elections allowing Peter Ekstroem and Heather to briefly watch that news broadcast on CNN at Labadee.

After he got back from celebrating his victory with President Sosa in Washington, DC, Lysius went straight from the airport to join President Josaphat's motorcade to the city of Gonaives to commemorate the nation's independence. Leaving his team to carry out the business of the transition and inaugural. To this day, he had not set foot in Port-au-Prince, and neither had Nickesse Duvalier accompanying him on what they call "The End of Traditional Haitian Politics Tour." On foot, by small boats, by car, and on the backs of taxi-moto and donkeys, the former sworn political rivals have embarked on this journey to meet the people in the furthest and unknown regions throughout the country. Nickesse, who had lived the better part of his life outside the nation, welcomes the experience. He grows even closer to his former opponent who whooped his ass in the last presidential elections.

The motive is far from being to capture areal views to sell to the international press. Indeed, Jacques Cyprien has given useful information minus the real name of the FBI agent in the country to investigate Jeando's assassination. They have followed the American's every move, and just like the rest of the country, the politicians are puzzled by the lessons Duvalier and Geffrard are teaching them. Tito, Toumain, and all the wheeler-dealers of Jeando's slaying are baffled, wondering about the investigation that, in their opinion, seems not to be taking place. The drone, Chapo, and Jimmy report few automobile movements to and from the Base, and that is all with no significant noticeable development. The white, apparently, had disappeared.

The police pickup truck is followed from above directly to the police headquarters' parking lot where the driver and passenger; the older officers join a large group of policemen in uniform. It is the first rodeo for these novices. The officers must prepare them for the presidential inauguration events as they did before elections day. They know that they still have the assistance of the peacekeeping soldiers from the United Nations.

Meanwhile, as the recently graduated officers, History Channel and Morgan Freeman congregate in the police lot, the other woman, the widow of Radio Haiti's building caretaker, has just been escorted back from the sofa by Madigan. Leopold comes out to thank her for her presence and participation as he did the others. Domersant is knowingly the only one left to go through the experience. However, he now has an idea of what to expect, but does he? When he was left alone with the women as Morgan and History spilled whatever beans they had in their large memory, Domersant eavesdropped on the females' conversation. The anxious widow was inquiring how the experience was from Mrs. Louis. Still later, when it was Mrs. Louissaint's turn on the couch once the old men had left, he had Mrs. Louis for a whole half hour.

During the session with Jean-Claude's companion, the one significant hearsay that Madigan comes out with is that Jeando's employee, who died with him, was bathing in sexual infidelity. Just as in the case of History, whose biases toward Aristide are the stimuli that create the hearsays in his mnemonic apparatus, jealousy and insecurity fertilize her neocortex turning it into that ground rich and fertile enough for gossip that had often contaminated her judgment. Nevertheless, the distortion Madigan exerted on her memory substantiates the testimony of some neighbors of the station's building, among them, the breakfast lady, Mrs. Louis.

After Madigan had flown back to the United States, Leopold would put the pieces together while keying data into the MIM's mainframe. At that time, he will have discovered that, to no small extent, the testimonies of most in official courtroom examinations check with most of what raw memory had supplied to the MIM. Madigan extracted from Mrs. Louis' distorted recollection the actual color of the clothes that a witness has affirmed a would-be assassin was wearing as he hid behind a wall until a white vehicle stopped to scoop him up. The scientist pushed the envelope to extract that vehicle's license plate from the witness's memory. And further still, the witness had subconsciously registered the color of that different thread, attaching the third button from the top on the shirt of the assassin who shot Jean-Claude.

When the woman returns to her seat, neither Madigan nor Leopold comes out. Perhaps they assume that Domersant would get with the program and would wait for a few minutes, allowing them the time to fine-tune and set up in preparation for the next session—his.

Assumption checked. He waits. And without being called, Domersant presents at the door and knocks. From the women, he feels he had gathered enough information about the procedure and assumes, in turn, that he could exhibit this type of confidence or cockiness. He enters even without Madigan answering his knocking at the door as the scientist seems to be setting the microphone to accommodate the height of the next person on the couch, namely, Domersant, whom the American greets by name without even turning around to look at him. Knowing that the following subject has lived in the United States and speaks perfect English, he welcomes the idea of saving his bad French.

"Come in, Mr. Domersant. Come right in and have a seat." Madigan says after the fact.

The setting differs entirely from what the women had described. He looks around and wishes one of the police officers had only come for one minute in the waiting area. He thinks he would have given him a much faithful description by courtesy of their profession alone. Little does he know that the décor is mutated to suit each subject relative to the circumstances, gender, age, the witness's health, and the needs of the investigation. The first instinctive reaction is to shake in his pants as he reminds himself that he did not see shit, although he was physically on the scene of the assassination as it was taking place. He wonders how the heck he fits into it all. For the time being, the Haitian can't see it. But when Madigan dims the overhead lights, which he will not even realize, he will think he is standing right in front of the building of Radio Haiti, on Delmas Boulevard, as it was in the year 2000. This is one key usage of Mullins' footage with the C14 lens on that particular camera. Domersant sits down on the plush chair near the door facing the red couch and the other chair where Madigan will sit. Now, he turns around as he reaches for the legal papers with the repetition US legislation had mandated along with the consent form Domersant will gladly sign for in two days, Leopold assured him, the US consulate would conclude in his favor. Finally, Madigan orders him in the supine position on the couch. As a docile student, he obeys and executes.

With a touchscreen stylus that also serves as a needleless syringe, Madigan applies wireless electrodes leads that are in the form of fluorescent dots on various points of Domersant's head, forehead, and different strategic locations of his anatomy. On contact with the skin, the mercury-like liquid crystallizes to become these dots, each one radiating a little purple light toward each other. On 3D images of a mannequin's head, torso, and limbs that appear on a neon-like screen in front of him right over the couch, he digitally places corresponding dots. He repeats the same process as though he was to perform an electrocardiogram or other similar procedures.

"Did you do the same thing for the others?" asks a baffled Domersant.

"No, Mr. Domersant," he replies, looking at his watch, realizing he must be at Maïs-Gaté in under two hours. However, in his mind still, should the son of a bitch President-elect, as Leopold calls him, work that feat and place either Aristide or his pal exactly where Domersant is, on that godawful sofa, he'd be game. Madigan has no reservation. He'd forgo the trip back. He is confident that he would find plenty of shit, weird crap too, within those guys' limbic structure, but he refrains from forestalling any further. He'd better reassure his subject now on the couch.

"I hear you are passionate about birds."

"Yes, sir. I always loved pigeons."

"Me too, Mr. Domersant."

Near the couch, Madigan adjusts his headset and puts earbuds for Domersant. The sessions are each saved entirely into a five billion terabyte portable drive for each of the participants. The sequence for the old officer has left two-and-a-half-million gigabytes of empty but not usable space due to the nature of memory. At the end of all sessions, the data will be consolidated, and Leopold will compile it all into readable and understandable files, which Lysius expects to have one day and one hour after he takes office. Meanwhile, in his booth, Leopold gets the gadgets under his control ready as the data transition from sketch-like drawings into standard, vivid images of the scene around the periphery of the station's building in Delmas.

During his extended stay in New York City, Domersant had gotten a Social Security Number and landed a job at La Guardia as a Ramp Agent. Occasionally in the scope of his duties, he would go up and clean the interior of the aircraft cabins. Many times, he had the opportunity to glance into the cockpits. One thing the two women who came in the room before him failed to mention is the panel beyond the couch, accessible to the right hand of Madigan, who manipulates the knobs to make late and final adjustments to the system both on the panel itself and on an iPad-like handheld console. That corner of the room reminds him of the board of an airplane. The large screen towering over the couch in front of Madigan comes alive with black and white lines and dots running, circling and turning in all directions on the screen. He thinks of that screen he saw at the clinic he went for a colonoscopy. Ouch! Perhaps, he thinks, the doctors could also do what Madigan does with the patients. All system is ready, and so is Madigan. However, nothing has occurred as Madigan dims the lights, but Domersant realizes that his perspective of the room in the standing position has not changed although he is now in the supine. The Haitian sees and feels himself on the boulevard of Delmas near Radio Haiti's building. Still the master of his faculties, he slowly pans his eyes on the scene depicted in the room and wonders how the Americans did that. And just a little further, he sees the car he was using at the time. It was a little dark four-door Daihatsu sedan he had rented to work as an occasional taxi driver.

The scenery makes absolutely no sense at all to him. He thinks, and he knows, that he had just entered the room on a January afternoon in 2023, and he is not asleep. The three-dimensional scene all around him places him twenty-three years earlier. Since his mind is still unscathed and he knows why he is in this room, he quickly recalls the year, the morning, and the exact date and time. However, he is not able to notice the little line at the lower right corner of the recog footage the system has generated as the date/time stamp of the shots.

Madigan, who already knows what he is looking at, takes to guiding Domersant's eyes to a specific item in the scenery: his own image. On the right side of the dark-blue car, a figure is bent near the open rear passenger door as if to enter and grab something in the back seat of the vehicle. That still photograph supposedly represents an image, a memory that one of the concrete façades or surrounding fixtures in the neighborhood had captured at that exact time in the past, Thus, April 03, 2000, 05:44 AM, according to the C14 lens and the MIM. In other words, this three-dimensional rendering in the room where the former cabbie now finds himself is actually the inanimate memory of the structures and objects in the vicinity of Radio Haiti's building.

"You feel ready, Mr. Domersant?" he asks as he circles the figure near the car.

"Yes, sir… I'm ready."

After the Haitian lays comfortably on the sofa, the American pushes a button on his watch, and the 3D image of a little five-year-old blond girl waving the American flag appears in front of Domersant's face. Madigan tells him that the little girl is his granddaughter, Samantha, and asks him to listen to her beautiful voice. In fact, it is Madigan who gives the direction, and Domersant hears the little girl's voice through suggestion.

"With your eyes," he instructs him, "follow the waves of the first two stripes under the stars. Imagine you are under these stars at the top of a beautiful staircase. Each stripe is a stair and you are coming down. Each step you take down these stairs, you feel lighter on your feet and more relaxed. And your eyes become heavier and heavier."

Submission. Domersant starts to execute Madigan's commands so quickly that even the American is in awe. The Haitian rapidly sees himself, as suggested, at the top of that staircase. Everything he sees, he becomes. He starts by morphing into the waving stripes under the stars that dissolve into a dark sky and bright stars behind him obeying the commands or suggestions of Madigan, who leans over the physical frame of Domersant on the couch.

"Very good," Madigan compliments and suggests the Haitian keep going down the stairs. "That's it. Keep coming down. Three more stairs, and you'll fall completely asleep, and you will tell me everything that you see until you can't speak anymore."

"I will speak for you," Madigan adds, cognizant of the aphasia that will ensue once the system kicks into action.

In his near-hypnosis state, as he takes the last step down the stairs, Domersant becomes deliquesced as he walks through the white clouds toward the entrance of a bright white room. Madigan can now have a visual of him on the monitor, at first as symbols on some monitors, then progressively as the vivid images of his human form on other screens in the room. A feature that Madigan deemed not necessary for the previous sessions. In his booth, Leopold silently follows as he stands ready to record the session. As the entire room becomes alive like the boulevard, Madigan starts to navigate his memory toward the car he was driving around that fatal morning in the year 2000.

The printer near Leopold's desk already spits out thousands of sketches that illustrate Domersant's state since he began the immaterial journey from the top of the stairs. The scientist considers unimportant the drawings aspect, now that modern visual technology compensates. He nods, looking satisfied when he pulls from the pile, that image depicting Domersant entering the bright and spacious white room where he meets Madigan dressed all in white guarding a gray file cabinet. The scientist's representation waves to invite Domersant to come to him. Surprised at first, and midpoint to being freaked out at seeing him dressed differently from how he knows him to be at the Base, Domersant slowly and reticently walks toward Madigan.

"What is wanted" inquires the figure near the filing cabinet.

"Talk to me now," he softly tells him in his physical state by the couch at the Base.

"Sir," the hypnotized man, replies to the figure, "We want to open this cabinet."

"Let us open the cabinet," the real Madigan whispers in his ear. "Open it now." The figure in the image on the screen steps aside to allow Domersant to approach the cabinet.

Domersant pulls and holds on to the handle. The case of the cabinet travels backward in time and space, as would Apple's Time Machine. They start to walk by the side of the elongated assembly, in the direction the case moves along the sliding drawer that contains many folders. As they walk, each step makes Domersant appear younger and younger. At one point, the American reaches into the drawer and pulls out a folder that he opens. A scene of debauchery briefly comes on the screens, and he rapidly closes that one folder. That was entirely unexpected, and Leopold instinctively calls Madigan over the intercom.

"What the heck was that?" he asks.

"Our guy must have opened an old folder by mistake. I think he's trying to tell me something."

"Oh!" Madigan continues, "That was him wearing the green shirt with no pants on. He had just turned seventeen that day. And it was when he lost his virginity."

That was not a mistake. Domersant's curiosity was somewhat deliberately tampered with and stimulated by Madigan. In fact, he does that quite often. Per congressional dispositions, Madigan must not exert any control over his own figure, during the subject or witness's transitioning away from consciousness. However, there is never a congressperson or a whistleblower chaperoning him. With his ever-increasing abilities and growing know-how, he has, over the years, found ways to recapture that control. That is one aspect that Leopold does not like about what the invention has become with Madigan's extraordinary expertise. At this level, where the subject travels away from consciousness, he still has enough control over what he or she wants to divulge. He is of the type who think that laws are made to be broken. Madigan knows that his figure and that of Domersant had just started walking toward the moving cabinet casing. He is aware that any folder within these first steps could only contain either recollection from early childhood or late-adolescence memories recently revisited and relabeled as "short-term or temporary." He had then programmed his figure to do just that within the subject's mind as he has in that famous DC assassinations' case. In this instance, it was easy since the real Madigan near the witness on the couch had already identified through reading the first symbols the Haitian's desire to revisit that particular event. There is no telling what he has seen over the years concerning female participants and their most secret, intimate, and far-fetched recollections or fantasies. Oh boy!

One congressman, during these crucial hearings with the inventors, Madigan included, had read precisely through this particular concern. The patriarch Edward McLintaugh knew how to circumvent the politicians in defense of his patent. Earlier in the afternoon, he learned of Mrs. Louis' overpowering crush on the station superintendent, who each morning, before Jeando arrives at the station, would cross the boulevard to have a quick breakfast usually buttered bread and a cup of coffee. At night with her husband who will have died in the wave of vengeance killings between 2001 and 2004, next to her, the symbols had told Madigan of quite a few X-rated scenes with Dominique's employee, fantasies that her mind had created at her directives.

They have finally arrived near the point marker for the year 2000, and Madigan, at the Base, leans over the couch and whispers. On the screen, his likeness appears to invite Domersant to pull one folder out.

"Now," he whispers calmly, "you want to know what's in the folder."

"Yes, sir… What's in it?"

Within the realm, there is nothing written on the folder. McLintaugh, the inventor, had equated that fact to our mind not being trained, although equipped, to capture everything. This extraordinary feat is part of our innate disposition. Our brain does this for us anyway. At first glance, we encompass all the data available at any time. It is our consciousness that is limited, for our good, to the number of facts and things it can handle and process at the least amount of time. That point would be part of Madigan's answer to the question as to why he chose to work more with Domersant's instead of the women's memories, although they had observed the actual killers or trigger pullers. One of them, up close as they crossed paths with her seconds after the murders.

"There is a date on the folder," Madigan tells him. "April 3, 2000… Now, let's go through it page by page. Can we do that?"

"Yes, sir."

On Leopold's screen in the control room, a sketch of the former taxi driver quickly dissolves into the photographic image of a twenty-something years younger man behind the wheel of the only vehicle in the country in worse shape than the Peugeot 304 parked in the lot at the Base. A passenger in the back seat is wearing a red baseball hat. That passenger is a friend and the owner of the vehicle. The image begins slowly to stream as vibrant live action. With a yellow shirt, the subject is behind the wheel, driving north on Delmas. He arrives at an intersection on the boulevard where two police officers intercept traffic and deviate it around the block.

Some vehicles coming from Petionville or higher Delmas make the U-turn before reaching the intersection. Some, perhaps, do so not to interact with cops, neither fake nor otherwise. Domersant hurries to take the red ribbon identifier for taxis off the rearview mirror as the cars slowly roll toward the intersection. He is somewhat presumptuous since he knows quite a few officers; he could, as in most cases, be allowed to drive through.

But those are no ordinary officers he finds out when two of them approach as he still fumbles to hide the broken ribbon in the glove compartment.

"My friend," says one of the policemen with his arrogance mistaken for authority, "this's not your route. What are you doing here?"

"No, officer. It's not my route," replies Domersant as he lets the ribbon drop to the car floor.

The other officer, with an eerie resemblance to the man in the yellow shirt, approaches and addresses him by his nickname.

"Dodo! What are you doing in Delmas this early in that clunker?"

"Mine is on the block ahead. I had a flat last night over there. What's going on around here?"

To this point, Domersant checks out. Indeed, the night before, a presentable woman who told him that she was an influential senator had hailed his cab. She had asked him to drive her to rendezvous around the city and in that section of Delmas. She identified herself to him as one Myrlène Luber, and she was conducting a Senate committee investigation that had required her to ride a taxicab as an ordinary citizen rather than being chauffeured around as usual, in an official automobile.

Immediately, what the experience of living in New York City does to someone kicks in the mind of the former B-2 visa overstayer. To make it in New York, the city itself will teach you how to develop a fast, sharp wit, to be always on your guards, on your toes, and on your game. And ultimately, you learn how not to accept and swallow any crap from anybody. In NYC, Domersant had seen the campaign inviting constituents to become acquainted with their representatives. Since he came back to Haiti for his parents' funerals, he has done just that. He followed politics, and he knew very well that there was no such name in the present legislature. He recognized her and bluffed as convinced that "fake ass" Senator Myrlène Luber was indeed on a bogus senate investigation and that she was up to no good. The money she offers sounds good, the cabbie is all in.

In his taxi driver's capacity, he is in it just for the job and for the money just like a mercenary. In fact, the passenger handsomely remunerated him after stops in Canapé Vert, Bourdon, Musseau, Juvenat, and a very brief stop in the Berthé section of Petion-Ville. The senator would stay in the vehicle where some men would come and converse with her in terms that he could not hear at the time. Through suggestion in 2023, he will listen to what was said as the men walked up to the taxicab. The patriarch who invented the MIM would use the words "props to a crime" to qualify the penniless or worthless individuals who approached and talked to the passenger. As an aide to the Warren Commission, the elder McLintaugh wrote a note in which he described Lee Harvey Oswald as such a prop. A close look at that particular event reveals to Madigan that in, at least two of these muffled conversations, the words "Major" and "Agree" are represented by related symbols. The last stop was precisely at that same intersection, where she got out to board a waiting Ford truck that slowly drove off in the middle of the road with its wheels on either side of the divider that was flat at the time. Nowadays, one almost needs a step ladder to go over the divider. The car finally got back on the right lane after drastically slowing down in front of the station. Domersant understood then that Myrlène was instead running some sort of scary errand.

With that much money in his pocket, Domersant had thought he could just go home for the night after Myrlène had exited his taxicab. Across the station, he realized he had been running on a flat and pulled over. Being closer to Petion-Ville, he went up and spent the night at his friend's, also a cabbie who would lend him a spare and give him a lift back to Delmas. He is even driving his clunker as the place starts to buzz with the day's activities a little before six in the morning.

As much as he would beg them and explain his predicament and even point to show them how close the vehicle was and that he had to return it at a specific time, the policemen would consider it lip service. The orders were strict that no car gets through.

"You know me, Dodo," says his look-alike officer. "I can see the car, but where it is, we cannot let you go there. The man is strict, and so are his orders. Anyway," he adds, "it's not going to be for long. Ten minutes top."

"Or you could just take a detour around this block," he adds as he points to tacitly remind him of that corridor around the neighborhood that will lead him straight to Mrs. Louis' place right across the station.

At a few steps down is the car. That's all. The officer reminds him not to venture out for the following twenty minutes. Instead, he suggests, Domersant should stop for breakfast at Mrs. Louis'.

Good idea. The vehicle drives on making a right turn. Domersant's friend, who is more familiar with the area, guides him. The clunker quickly turns left onto a new street, drives down, and stops mid-block. The men get out and meet behind the car, where the other man hits the trunk, which opens. Domersant takes the spare tire out. The friend points him to a small passageway right in the middle of the block that will lead right across the building of Radio Haiti on the main boulevard. The car drives away after spewing thick black smoke from its pipe, and Domersant rolls the tire across the street and into the corridor of about ten to twelve feet wide or less.

Domersant rolls the tire as he passes through a group of men dressed as Papa and Baby Doc's Tonton Macoutes with dark-blue clothes, dark sunglasses, and a red cloth around their collars walking in the opposite direction. In one of the small houses, a man, whom Domersant's mind labels as being himself, is shaving his beard in an open window with what he reads as a Thin Blade from Gillette in front of a small mirror that hangs on the side of the window frame. A little further, a woman makes coffee with a makeshift filter made of cloth which folks in the country call "Grèp" while a little boy, probably her son, awaits with a pot in his hand. Nearby, a little girl in school uniform grimaces as the woman behind her tries to run a comb through her thick nappy hair. A young man brushes his teeth with a cup of water in his other hand. He spits out and brings the cup to his lip. He rinses his mouth, swooshes, and projects the liquid far onto a skinny dog that quickly runs away. The young man runs and catches the barefoot toddler, dressed only with a T-shirt, dragging a toy car made of empty food cans as he tries to outrun Domersant and the rolling the tire.

In a pot of hot boiling oil, a relatively young woman, whom both Leopold and Madigan believe to be a younger Mrs. Louis, drops some vegetables or fries creating a column of vapor through which appears the antenna atop the building of Radio Haiti with the bullet holes on the façade wall. In the room and from the realm, he tells Madigan as he points to the structure that the bullet holes had been there for nine years since the army toppled President Aristide in 1991. The thuggish fringe thereof came to intimidate Jeando during that same Monday morning broadcast. He says that Dominique had probably made no effort to repair the front end of the building because the bullet holes were the scars that added to his accolades in the fight for justice and real change in the country. At the time, Jeando truly believed that his pal, the former priest could really deliver.

He stops and leans the tire against a stack of cinder blocks to buy coffee and bread that he quickly eats for breakfast. Then, disregarding the officer's advice, he continues on just a few steps toward the rented Daihatsu Charmant, his taxicab parked on the near side of the boulevard across the radio station still with the red identifier attached to the rearview mirror. He finally gets near the car. He drops the tire beside the right rear wheel and opens the rear passenger door. He bends inside the car and takes out the jack and the wrench that he left on the back seat before heading to Petionville in the middle of the night. It is at this point that the room, at the Base, really took on the three-dimensional aspect that the Method creates, "The Realm." It becomes what the boulevard looked like from 12:00 am to 6:30 am on April 3, 2000.

Time is kicking his butt. Domersant must hurry to return the vehicle to its owner, himself, another cabbie who must earn his daily bread and the monthly installment owed to the dealership. Most pressing, he wants to fix the darn flat and get the heck away from this place where all the red flags tell him some weird shit is about to go down. The caliber of his last passenger for the better part of the night and the reinforcement the policemen's presence at that particular intersection had helped his idea of what could be coming a short minute later. Right about here, the MIM flashes. On one of the screens, the symbols signal a "hearsay." The Americans quickly associate with it, the subject's ignorance. His ignorance of what is to occur despite being so close to its fomenting.

"Motherfucker!" Madigan hears in the intercom from Leopold. "Isn't that hearsay about former President Préval?" he asks.

"Sure is," Madigan replies. "They are some powerful ones too. The man has heard people say it. He thinks it is the truth and believes then President knew about that shit."

"In the fashion the symbols are sequenced," he adds, "I lean toward agreeing that this ignorance may regard the President more than it does Mr. Domersant."

"In my expert opinion, I believe that presumed ignorance also concerns someone else in the journalist circle. Take a look at that cluster down below."

"See that name in there?" Madigan asks.

"But," comes the reply through the intercom, "President Préval was his friend and was pimping him to be the presidential placeholder until the elections of 2005 that he won again, haphazardly."

"Woah!" says Madigan as the back-and-forth continues. "Another rumor is telling us that Rene—that was his first name, right? Well," Madigan adds, "he might not have won these elections fair and square. It is saying that someone else did."

"Manigat," Leopold says in the intercom, "Leslie Manigat won."

"But, Préval was re-elected, right?" Madigan inquires to make sure.

"Strange shit happened in this country," answers Leopold. "He was re-elected."

Meanwhile, in the realm, Domersant manages to loosen three, but the last lug nuts seem to present him with quite a challenge. As he tries harder, the wrench slides off the bolt and falls on his right hand. In the room at the Base, the cabbie presents with a case of stigmata. Like he did on that morning, the cabbie starts to bleed on the couch out of that scar on the back of his right hand. Domersant screams and holds his hand on the couch.

"It's alright," says Madigan as he wraps the subject's hand with a white towel. "You are doing well. Tell me more."

Within Domersant's memory on the boulevard, blood drips copiously from his hand onto the pavement as he repeats in pain.

Merde! Merde! Merde!

He leaves the spare tire, wrench, and the bolts. He gets in the car, spilling blood in the car as he crashes onto the back seat moaning in pain and he quickly falls asleep. He had earned enough last night to detail the car and pay an extra day to the owner. In the span of a few short seconds, he startles as gunshots awake him from his genuine pain and fatigue-induced nap. He carefully lifts his head to look outside as three men get in a car near the station. A woman also leaves the gate of the station. That woman, during her session, revealed that she went in to find out why her crush, Louissaint, had not stopped by for his usual cup of coffee. He is quick to go back to his nap in pain. Domersant did not see whether the woman had gone back to make sense of what had happened or crossed the boulevard in a hurry. Neither did he notice this other woman who would be on a botched collision course with her supposed rival. The car drives away as folks from inside the building start to gather around. Madigan sits up and quickly leans forward near Domersant's ear as that would be his initial attempt to invade and to distort. This was, in reality, what the cabbie witnessed and recollects from his being on the scene of the crime.

"No, Mr. Domersant," he softly insinuates. "No shots are fired yet."

At the other end of the hallway, Leopold abruptly bangs his fist on the desk.

"What are you doing, Madigan?" he asks in an upset tone. "Let him tell the story of what happened."

Madigan sets his papers down on the table near him, gets up, and leans over the couch. He kills the laser to stop all recordings at his end but makes sure he gets Domersant to go even deeper in his sleep.

"Mr. Domersant," he softly and calmly whispers, "your hand hurts very much… You are in the back seat, and you are soundly asleep."

Madigan leaves the room to walk down the hall because he thinks Leopold must understand that his work has not even begun. He frantically knocks. The door opens.

"Gee! McLintaugh," he exclaims. "Are you F'n nuts? Don't worry about what I do."

He could have talked to him over the intercom for only that, but there is something he thinks Leopold should learn about this "investigation." And, now is a perfect occasion.

"Son," he continues, "do you have a goddamn idea why Ekstroem sent you here? That prick wants you to fail so he can take Ed down and ban the MIM altogether. Since he became the Director, he's restricted most of it. Right? And, suddenly, he lifts all restrictions as you were coming in this cesspit?"

"Yeah!" concurs Leopold, "I wondered why."

"He baited," Madigan replies, "hoping Ed would bite."

"No. No, it does not end there," the scientist adds. "The word is Sosa is considering your father as the next FBI Director and the prick knows it. 'fucking loser still resents your mother marrying Ed instead of his vindictive ass… You think this is about Dominique? Ekstroem doesn't give a flying fuck about you, about Sosa, Lysius, or about the journalist. I came down here as a favor to Ed, who can't be here because of his closeness to the journalist. That prick Ekstroem knows that too. But he sent you. He sends his rival's fucking son. Think about that wrinkle, kiddo."

Leopold listens quietly and in shock to see Madigan that serious and mad lecturing him.

"Let him tell the story, you said? Well, I could, but if I do, your shit stops here, and you get nothing. All you have is the MIM discredited in Ekstroem's hands and two presidents who may get medieval on your case. Plus, Ed might lose Sosa's consideration. Worry about what you'd have on your fucking hands. Your father knows I did not come down here to play fair while Ekstroem isn't."

An awkward moment for Leopold. The head of an investigation to receive such a lecture as a child. Contrary to Jeando, whenever Madigan was in the McLintaughs' household, the youngster Leopold had always felt that sort of abrasive rigidity in the personage. Like a nagging father, he still comes back and sticks his head through the door.

"You know kiddo," he says but with a calmer tone, "'guy did some drugs around the time Nancy Reagan was telling kids to say no. His memory is like a New York City street under Mayor Giuliani. I must get in there and patch the potholes. When I get back in there, I will show you one of these holes."

Like a teenager after a scolding by one helicopter parent, Leopold feels that Madigan did not leave the room soon enough as he pulls out a sketch from a pile that turns into a bright still photograph of Domersant in a police uniform. The picture will dissolve into live moving images on the main screen when Madigan resumes his work at the other end of the hall. It is just randomly that Leopold chose to put this picture up. He had no idea that Madigan was going to resume by stretching Domersant's memory back a little at the intersection on Delmas. He must have already whispered the suggestion into Domersant's ear before Leopold hears his voice on the intercom.

"Take a look at the second officer who spoke to him at," Madigan says. (He gives the sequence, frame numbers, and the time as in the time it was when the memory was stamped and stored deep within the structure that yielded it to the Recog.)

Many scientists, including the late inventor, have subscribed to the concept that the place, the confine or structure where our human memory is stored up, may not even be in existence within the known universe. In one of his books, Edward McLintaugh Sr. suggests that the mere recalling of the very words we use as we speak calls for an unlimited number of rapid trips to and from that place wherever it may be. Madigan thinks that along the way during these trips, we shed some small yet significant details.

"That one policeman was his twin brother, for crying out loud," he says. "And they did not recognize each other at the intersection? And, approximately three million frames later, nobody dresses like Tonton Macoutes in the year 2000. Let me work, McLintaugh, and learn."

"Ten-Four," Madigan hears in the intercom.

Domersant remains asleep both in the back seat of the car and on the sofa.

CHAPTER 24.

The Assassination

The rear door opens on the cabbie sleeping in the back seat. Madigan gets in and sits next to him. As he looks around, Madigan only sees shapes of a grayish tone that move around. He should because this is not his own memory, but one he invades to do as he pleases, not to, however, cause any harm or wreak havoc. At the Base, however, he can wear a modification gargle that the inventor had called "Modi." With that, the image on the screen in front of him becomes a real representation of the boulevard. Madigan had self-hypnotized. Previously, he had attached to his skull and body the same wireless leads that run to and from the MIM on Domersant. The attachment is secured through a little device called "The Bridge" plugged into a USB port.

Like a person finds out he or she is not wearing a jacket after venturing out in the cold, Madigan returns from Domersant's memory. By the flickering of a switch, he needed to grab the corresponding version of the Modi that he must carry with him within the realm. When he returns in the car, Domersant wakes up after Madigan frantically shakes his shoulder.

"Shit's about to go down," he says. "Wake up, wake up."

At the wheel of his vehicle, Dominique drives past the policemen at the intersection without being stopped. At about the same time, Madigan turns Domersant's attention to the white car that has just made it through past the policemen in the intersection at the other end, north of the station. Dominique's car is stopped at the left of the Charmant's rear end, waiting to turn as the white car that had just driven through the other intersection presses on menacingly. Domersant raises his head to the level of the brim of the car door. The white vehicle with three men in the back abruptly stops, allowing the journalist to complete his turn and to enter the station's lot. The white vehicle pulls right as Dominique's car reaches the green steel gate of the station. Two armed men exit from the right side of their vehicle. The third man exits on the side of the road, and they all walk toward Dominique as he parks. The fourth man, the driver, stays in the car and pans the boulevard with his eyes from North to South. In a report from one judge and according to a witness, at that moment, employees and journalists inside the station have gotten the chill, panicked, and gave that alarming telephone call to Mrs. Jeando. Her husband was probably already dead before she hung up.

In the country's folktale, it is said that the same stick strikes both the black and the white dog. The taller assassin, in the middle, carries a long stainless-steel gun, a personal "gift" from either Dani or Tito. Should it be the former, this is probably, the same firearm Tito whacked Roger with nine years prior. The thug to his right quickly turns around, pans his eyes on the road, and focuses on Domersant's car for a short second. He thinks he has perceived some movement in that direction. The cabbie's stomach churns as he sinks his head lower, and the assassin presumes it's only an unoccupied car parked across the road.

"Dominique is getting out now," Madigan alerts Domersant though, in real time, the journalist is already dead as Jean-Claude is gasping on the ground.

The cabbie slowly raises his head as the assassin in the middle gets near Dominique's car. Without hesitation, he fires two quick shots at Jeando just as his second foot touches the ground. The thug shoots again as the journalist's brain orders his knees to muster up and support his body weight to walk out of the car. To this day, it is unclear as to what after or for Jean-Claude was running when the gunman on the left fired three shots to his chest. Jean-Claude falls and gasps on the ground before dying shortly later at a hospital. The assassin on the right shoots a round in the air as all three gunmen walk backward before they turn facing the boulevard toward their getaway car. They get in and take off as the boulevard rapidly becomes vibrant. The "policemen" at the two intersections have vanished. In his determination to push further, Madigan contacts Leopold from what is Delmas on that fateful morning of the year 2000, but within Domersant's memory at the end of January 2023.

"Hey, McLintaugh," he reaches out as he watches the white vehicle driving away. "From both intersections to the time the killers drive off, it's thirty-three seconds. And from the time the journalist turns into the station to them taking off, it's only eleven secs... I want to rerun it my way now in under twenty-eight, thirty-one seconds tops. The distortions," he continues, "should make it feel like four or five minutes."

Leopold looks at his reflection on the glass door, where the images on the screens, as reflected in the gargle, seem more distorted as he listens to Madigan's voice.

"So, they whacked him that fast," he asks.

"Yup! That's how it went down. Those guys," he adds, "were fucking good."

Madigan explains to the younger American that thirty-two seconds appears too long for such professionals and disciplined assassins to do that simple and easy job. Further, he attributes part thereof to the cabbies' substances ravaged mnemonics.

Leopold bends to reach below the desk and adds stacks of paper in the printer. His head tilts; the blond agent looks at the screen as Dominique's car drives down halfway past the policemen at that intersection with its left directional blinking. Madigan has already restarted the actions leading to the actual murder.

From inside the car, kept awake, Domersant looks on as Dominique, now with his pipe between his lips, prepares for the left turn. The white car that had driven unchecked through the other intersection just as Dominique's was overlooked at the junction to the South speedily race up the block. It pulls to the curb as Jeando completes his turn into the station's entrance. Contrary to the cabbie's authentic and undistorted mind recollection, the assassins' vehicle did not allow the journalist to turn first. Like typical Haitian drivers, the journalist was the aggressor here when he completed the left turn even though the thugs gave no sign of slowing down. Instead, they pulled over abruptly as would most Americans in road rage circumstances to engage in the verbal, even physical confrontation.

In constant communication with Leopold on the other side of the realm, Madigan watches the scene, unseen from the outside, through the left rear window. Madigan hurries Domersant as he keeps Leopold abreast of what is taking place on that immaterial boulevard. He tells Leopold that the two cars almost collided and thinks a fender bender might have postponed Jeando's assassination. Later in the boarding area, before his flight back to the US, he will confess that considering the mighty hands behind the crime, Dominique's lease on earth had well expired. The journalist would have been executed, if not, at the end of the month or sometime in May. For sure, he wouldn't have made it to even submit his candidacy for the December presidential elections. Then, it would have been obvious. The assassination would have stood for what it was intended. "A politically motivated slaughter," which will warrant such declaration by that professor as to why that particular microphone was ordered to be made silent.

"We must cross now," the American says.

With authority, he opens the driver's side rear door and grabs the Haitian by his collar. They cross near the rear end of Dominique's car. Standing by the driver's side door, the driver of the thugs' car seems to observe the two semitransparent silhouettes crossing the road behind the vehicle of the man they have come to whack. He visually pans the boulevard and lays his eyes on Domersant's car for a second longer. That car only appears unoccupied as per Madigan's rerun of the distortion. In fact, that is how it looked in the heat of the event in April of 2000. Domersant soundly slept on the back seat. No one saw him, and he did not know a thing either on that fateful morning. The cabbie's mind, nevertheless, Madigan argues, recorded even the most insignificant details of the crime scene.

Madigan and Domersant get to the sidewalk at the same time as Dominique's car front tires touch the curb. At that same moment, a woman wearing a yellow dress, not revealed in Domersant's initial memory account, dashes in front of

Dominique's car in the middle of the gunmen on the sidewalk in front of the station. The observant eyes of Madigan go to work in this sequence. During her session, the scientist couldn't help but acknowledge the superb chest of the woman on the couch and notice the beautiful pendant stuck in her cleavage. As though some red light goes on inside his mind, he stretches his subject's memory back to the middle of the road as he and the cabbie crossed the street as Dominique turned. He instructs Leopold to freeze the woman within Domersant's memory.

Would one take a bullet for one's boss or protect one's woman in the same fight?

Louissaint took three bullets, but he did not answer the dilemma. Before the complete freeze, perhaps for his pleasure, Leopold slows her to bask in the movement of her breasts. She runs out of the station's lot with Jean-Claude a bit far behind to catch her as Jeando parks and the assassins' approach. The young agent quickly reconsiders as he figures he was only thirteen when these puppies were flying ever so elegantly on that terrible April morning.

The gunman in the middle eyeballs her as she runs by and looks at them. Madigan is only interested in having a good look at the pendant bouncing on her breasts to determine if that pendant, the chest, and nipples have stayed the same over so many years. Of course, the American, at least, took a peek, an innocent one even. Jean-Claude, Leopold concludes, was only collateral. Breasts and pendant, checked. The dilemma, however, is in the air still.

Leopold accelerates the rerun from the middle of the street while slowing the thugs down so Madigan and Domersant could get near the station's gate first. They need to turn facing the road and look at their faces although Madigan is not at all interested in trigger pullers. The Haitian and the scientist are now between Jeando's car and the three gunmen. To kill the journalist, the thugs must go through them. Madigan turns his head to the right when he hears Jean-Claude's footsteps behind him which sound like these of a giant. The general acceptance is that the intendant only rushed out to open the gate for his boss as he does every morning. However, a different story took shape across the distortion of the two women's memories. Perhaps, he is running to redeem himself with the woman in the yellow dress who thought she had to come unannounced to the station on a groundless jealousy mission. She had to confront Louissaint for his sexual infidelities. Madigan, an hour earlier, would debunk Louissaint's infidelities as horrible hearsays or ill-meaning gossips. As Madigan whispers in Domersant's ear to have him look at the men's faces, the thug in the middle walks through them, aims, and fires at Dominique. The man on his left fires at Louissaint as he emerges running out, possibly after the woman who just runs through the assassins briefly eyeballing them. Unlike in Domersant's original version, the three gunmen did not walk backward to their car. Instead, the taller one in the middle walked forward. The others flanking him lingered a step back, with one firing in the air to ward off any potential hero shit from the employees inside the station.

Leopold remotely listens to Madigan as he looks at the image of a scared dog running past the three gunmen on the sidewalk near the getaway car. A white woman in a red dress walks by the men. Seemingly an out of place item within the images that emanate from the realm. If not, she probably is a tourist or an NGO employee. Later, during a telephone conversation, Leopold would learn from his father that the woman was really a decoy, or a glitch embedded in the system ever since the first trials when he was not even born. This glitch had evolved until it had morphed permanently into this form from that of a crawling baby. One may never know what exactly crossed his mind at that instant. He decides he wants to be part of the action on the boulevard within the man's memory. After he tells him of his intention, he undoes the bridge, and Madigan wakes up, and they execute the switch.

"You sure about this, buddy?" Madigan asks as he adjusts the bridge and the Modi.

"You're not going after these puppies, are you?" Madigan inquires sarcastically, aiming the lazer at the frozen frame on the screen.

Mullins' Recog crew took that shot right at the gate facing the boulevard. That image depicts what took place on that scene twenty-three years ago with, in the background, Jeando and Louissaint on the ground in pools of their own blood. Domersant is between the two men on the ground and the killers going back to their car in the foreground. The woman in yellow is frozen in front of the gunmen at whom she seems to stare. A woman in red walks southward on the sidewalk as one scraggy dog leaves the frame.

Less interested in the disposables that populate the cabbie's memory at the crime scene, Leopold's thought process would have him swim upstream and run against the distribution of tasks in the crime. Reports from different officials who had worked on that case assume the commonality of having many suspects declare that they had received X amount of money to silence the journalist. The man died after letting the cat out about the plot to kill Dominique. However, he suggested that roles were distributed from levels higher than that of that foot soldier who had enlisted the cabbie's service the night before the assassination. Although she ranked higher, the folks in top places entrusted the passenger with this footwork. Leopold wishes that Mullins had a chance to have footage of the taxicab to recreate a three-dimensional realm to place Domersant's recollection of especially his last flag down for the night.

"When I get on the other side," he tells Madigan, "run it from the frame where he finishes his coffee. And," he adds, "don't bother with the rest. I'll let you know."

After Madigan inserts the bridge into the port and quickly hypnotizes Leopold, he sends him off to Delmas and walks out to the control booth. Domersant stands by the tire near the cinder blocks. A cup in one hand, he is finishing a small flat and round buttered bread that mostly Haitians in the capital call "little butter" (word-for-word translation). After he chugs his last bit of coffee, he tends a twenty-five-gourde bill to the woman who complains. Her body language translates that she had not sold anything this early to give him any change back. Since Myrlène had paid him generously, he had to spare and enough to leave the whole bill.

He is now, possibly, at his second try to undo the last lug nut when the hand of a Caucasian man grabs him by the arm as he runs.

"Oh! Look at a white (creolism)," he says. "Where he comes from?"

"Run, get out of here," Leopold hurries him. "They are coming to whack Jean Dominique." "They'll kill you too. Let's go."

"Let's run to the intersection," he tells him. "Maybe your brother could protect you."

"My brother?" the cabbie inquires.

"Yeah, that officer up the road at the intersection. Let's go! Leave the fucking car, man!"

"Drag the motherfucker if you have to," Madigan yells from the booth. "But we must not distort all the time fragments within his memory at the same time."

"Madigan!" replies Leopold as he grabs the Haitian's arm, "You don't call him that. But I'll drag the son of a bitch's ass."

Madigan plays with the knobs on the panel while he guides Leopold as they rapidly run. He distorts the time on all fronts so they could get to the intersection fast and first as all else move relatively slow. The white car hauling the assassins is approximately at a slightly longer distance to the north intersection than is Dominique's to the South driving down ever so slowly, Madigan's courtesy, of course.

"Buddy!" Madigan says, "All this buys you only four-and-a-half seconds to do what you must at the intersection and be by the journalist's rear bumper as he turns."

Four-and-a-half seconds in the realm. That equates to three eternities on our plane of existence. Leopold remembers that these short eternities go by in a blink of an eye where his partner sits, and he is out to get some valuable information regarding the intellectual minds behind the assassination. Poor Dormersant. It would not be as easy. The former wide receiver at Michigan State literally carries him. Had the other American not advised him otherwise, he would not have the cabbie interrogate Wilner, his twin brother, on a lot of things. Sensing that any information from Wilner may be sensitive and politically damaging, Leopold instructs Madigan to upload it as is. Later, he will include that into the final report that he must hand to Lysius. His brother, he tells the agent who drags him, is not a cop. Domersant bluntly tells Leopold that the fake police officer is a car thief. Wilner, he discloses, usually supplies stolen vehicles for operations such as Jeando's assassination. Hence, the stalled white car before the intersection to the North of the radio station.

In such crimes, as was probably the case for JFK in the United States, and for attorney Mireille Bertin in Haiti, roles are distributed to different agents or cells by layers of importance. As for the assassination on Grassy Noll, the layer that whacked Bertin or the one on the boulevard of Delmas, is that prop layer that will be physically eliminated one by one by one. Serial killers clean to remove pieces of evidence after usually murdering prostitutes of whom no one will readily notice the disappearance. Jean's assassin in chief will have cowardly and mercilessly disposed of the human accessories to the murder. He will get rid, in a sense, of worthless nobodies that no one would care about. For sure, the empty sacks of shit pulled the triggers, but they did not have the money to purchase the bullets. Higher layers would do the actual logistical footwork. The top mastermind of Dominique's assassination had constituted a vast and complicated web or labyrinth of criminal accessories with the same orders and with different higher-ups that would warrant the logistics. The mastermind made sure that some kind of misunderstanding or rift exist among the members of the organization. The promises made to them about the distribution of the gain to be had after the kill was most certainly, coldly calculated. Leopold arrives at the intersection dragging the brother to the middle of the road. No pun intended. Wilner's brother.

"He'll not see or hear you," Madigan says, "but have his brother ask him on whose orders he is at the intersection."

Leopold unnoticeably pays attention to the policeman answering his brother's remote query from Madigan. Back in the control booth, the scientist had discovered a small cluster of recollection symbols. Insignificant at first, these had progressively gotten more and more visible as the agent and the cabbie were approaching the intersection. Domersant's memory apparatus had gotten near enough the stimulus it needed to recall that one specific event. That stimulus is the location, the spot where he stands to converse with his brother within the realm. Leopold suggests that Madigan exerts the time distortion horizontally parallel to the X-axis of the spectrum with the slightest distortion toward the N(XY) corner. He believes that so doing will allow Domersant to see all of the truck that the senator got into after exiting his taxicab.

"I could do that," Madigan comes back, "but something's got to give. Either Dominique or the assassins lose their slow speed or worse, we ruin the man's memory pudding at the limbic level. What's your gamble?"

Leopold lets the scientist know of his option by telling him to open door number 4. This choice entails that Madigan leaves the control booth and make the suggestions into Domersant's ear to freeze both vehicles at their respective distance. In the Hallway, on his way to the other setting, he could not help but give credit to Leopold's wit.

"Well, why didn't I think of that," he reflects so loudly that the two women in the waiting area hurry to fix their sitting postures, their hair and chest thinking he was coming toward them.

He enters. Leopold, on the nearby chair, and Domersant, on the couch, are hypnotized and far out there. Once he makes the suggestion that freezes the two vehicles on the boulevard, Madigan returns to the booth to change the axis on the time distortion graph, as Leopold had suggested. Instantly, the entire truck presents itself only to Domersant's vision inside the realm. The cabbie recounts to Leopold what he is recalling of the things he did not see after he parted with his last flag down at the intersection. Relatively to the Haitian, in his hippocampus, these events occurred only last night. When Mrs. Jeando rushed out, after the telephone call from the station, probably without her morning wash, she had never noticed the men in the car parked across her home. They also saw Jeando leave alone when he did, and they radioed it. To whom? The MIM determined that communication went to a layer higher than that of a Tito or even the senator. Had Jeando and his wife left together in the same car, for sure, she would have been, at the very least, severely wounded. If at all better, not to suffer his absence, she would have died at her husband's side. Domersant recalls that in a mental void, he pulled up to that yellow Nissan sedan a little across the journalist's residence. Early in the morning, in an eerie blankness, as she rushes out, Mrs. Jeando did not even realize that the yellow vehicle followed her.

"Does that truck have a license plate?" Leopold asks. "Describe it," he adds.

"No," Domersant replies. "No. Instead of the legal license plate in the back, it is one of Skull and Bones."

"What about in the front?" Leopold asks.

As Domersant walks the half-circle around his brother, Leopold leans a little to follow him. From the perspective of the policeman and if he could see Leopold, his brother has perhaps turned gay, and his blond companion is checking out his ass. He reads out the license plate number. Here again, President Josaphat's modernizing efforts pay off. Madigan plugs in the license plate number into the country's motor vehicle database and voilà.

That twin cab truck, Madigan reports back to Leopold, belonged at the time, to one Tito Massim. I looked him up.

"Do you know Tito Massim?" Leopold asks Domersant. "And what's happening now?"

"Yeah, that's him behind the wheel. He's opening the door for my last passenger. In his left hand is his shiny gun."

Later, at the place the order originated, Tito would hand that gun to a tall baby-faced thug telling him that he had always wanted to whack the son of a bitch. Still, the chief and the plan called for him to do it. Anyway, Tito knew he'd get his gun back since, in the overall program, he and Dani are slated to later dispose of that one specific human prop. Leopold has had this same feeling earlier in the afternoon, yet he doesn't know the significance thereof. Now, under hypnosis and bridged into someone else's memory, the agent thinks that the next higher layer is in that pickup truck. And, right above, Leopold believes lies the mastermind of Dominique's whacking, He continues with the pressure, asking Domersant if other people were riding in the rear cabin.

"Yes," he answers, "Toumain and somebody else are in the back seat."

Well, Madigan thinks to himself, *at least, someone from the mastermind's layer would have found the balls to physically come on the boulevard.*

Leopold grabs Domersant, and they start to run in the other direction on the divider after Madigan informs him of the time remaining, as the cars on opposite ends start moving again. As they run, Leopold asks Domersant why he keeps on looking back behind them.

Saddam's truck is right behind us, Domersant worriedly warns him. Tito's truck.

"What fucking truck?" Leopold yells out, forgetting that he asked for its license plate just one eternity ago.

They are already right in front of the station. They dashed before Dominique, and the assassins get there. In the meantime, the truck speeds up to move from over the divider into the proper lane. Domersant turns around as the pickup truck plows through them.

"That fucking... The truck drives through them... truck," yells Domersant.

Leopold stands and smiles as Domersant pats all over his body, surprised that he is still alive.

"Did you ask your brother who killed him?" Leopold asks, as they cross the boulevard.

"No," Domersant replies, "he never came back since a Dany picked him up that night."

"Dany, who?" inquires Leopold.

"His wife said she heard him say 'Oh! Dany, it's you.' We know a few people with that name. That is why we do not accuse anyone," Domersant says. "But," he adds, "the shit is out there. Everyone talks about it. They took him to a hospital with a bullet in his ass," he adds. "He later died from some other weird shit."

The car forcefully makes that short stop, and the journalist completes that quick turn in front of the assassins' vehicle. However, this time, instead of crossing to the right of Jeando's car, they pass on his side, perhaps to save precious fractions of a second. The assassins' car pulls over, Leopold also pulls Domersant a little to the left so when the driver opens his door to survey the surrounding while the others walk toward Jeando, they get a good look at their faces. When this occurs, Domersant finds himself face to face with his neighbor. The top of the vehicle's door is the only thing between the cabbie's and the assassin's snouts. Domersant owes money to Chapo, who many believe, by way of gossips, drove that night with this Dany character to Wilner's home. He might have even shot him in the ass and gone to finish him later at the hospital. Face to face unexpectedly with that mean motherfucker, Domersant freaks out and freezes with terror.

"Do you know him?" Leopold asks.

"Yeah!" he answers as he slowly takes a step back away from the thug's beak, ready to fire that nerve impulse across the synapse to a nerve muscle and flee.

Leopold grabs him firmly as Chapo looks right through them. In that short time, the woman in yellow runs out through the gunmen, meeting the skinny dog walking calmly in front of the woman in red. The canine runs away as the shots that killed Jeando are fired. The journalist is already dead as Jean-Claude Louissaint gasps on the ground. Paralyzed with fear, the woman in the yellow dress turns around. She just stands on the sidewalk, looking at the bloody scene and ogling the escaping killers. Later, Leopold would understand why Madigan worked with the memory of somebody who did not see a thing as opposed to the woman. The strange emotion of jealousy, coupled with the intense fear that paralyzed her on the sidewalk, would have rendered all of Mullins' work unusable. He learns that the amount of dense fog these two elements create in a person's life would also erect a cathedral of cloud in the realm. The three-dimensional recreation of Radio Haiti's edifice and its surroundings would not yield useful data to the system. The stretching and distorting may have reached their peak as Domersant's figure in the realm seems to enter a phase of disintegration.

"Take him off," Leopold hurriedly tells Madigan who himself was about to alert him of the effects of the last bit of distortion and stretch. "Flick his bridge. Now!"

As they return to the car, freaked out and weak, Domersant observes the look the killers give the woman as they appear to be moving toward him. Fearing for his life, Domersant cocoons on the sofa, turning his back to Leopold on the boulevard by the crime scene and to Madigan's empty chair in the room, shielding his face with the palms of his hands. In a short burst of somniloquy, he yells out loud, frightening the two women in the waiting area who also hear the uproar.

"Oh shit! They are coming to kill me."

"It is okay," Madigan who had sped out of the control booth, softly reassures the cabbie. "You are quickly and calmly fixing the tire, and nothing happens on the boulevard. No shots were fired, and you did not see a thing."

He nears the taxicab and drops the borrowed spare. He opens the rear passenger door, takes his tools. Right before he hurts his hand, Leopold arrives on the scene just as a passerby. This time he is dressed like a jogger on his early morning run.

"'Guess you need a hand with that," Leopold tells him.

Leopold had already disengaged from the bridge and unplugged the Modi from the port. Domersant comes through on the couch from the realm and from the confinement of his memory. Little by little, Mrs. Louis, who had taken over the kitchen at the Base, had the hospitable idea to prepare dinner. For now, she has ordered the maid to arrange a fruit platter. Of course, these are not raised in the so-called "agricultural country." Like most other items of necessity, these tired fruits transited through the Dominican border. The sort of facts the President-elect finds aberrant as then senator Geffrard argued to get rid of this metastasizing cancer. "We must agree to part with a limb or two or even a few organs." He would shake the Senate chamber, declaring that among his colleagues, there are these limbs and organs that have prospered with the shameful practice that goes on at the border. Never mind the fruits or where they come from. The banana split that Madigan prefers comes from Florida.

The three men, the Haitian and the Americans, get out of the room and arrive in the waiting area where Domersant first notices the wide bloodstain on his light blue shirt. Since he knows he has no wound to explain it, he starts to wonder whether this couple of "whites" had performed some alien-like shit on him. The women get worried as well and likewise begin to wonder what else they might have done to him and to them. They then turn the burden over to Leopold and Madigan to worry about never knowing why one after the other, the locals run into the restrooms.

In there, the women would search and inspect all the parts of their anatomies. They now worry even more about what they don't find: nothing strange or unusual. However, as typical Haitians, they shy away from raising their concerns. But, when they are at the table, Domersant leans over to his left, and his inquiry is audible to all.

"Mr. Leopold," he says, "I've got no wound. How come there's blood on my shirt, sir?"

Madigan has started to compliment Mrs. Louis on her cooking when the question drops. He cuts.

"Well. If you are a Christian," Madigan quickly replies, "we'll call that 'stigmata,' Mr. Domersant. Some memory you have in there," he adds, pointing to his head.

Madigan does not speak the language well, and the extent of Leopold's French does not allow for an in-depth explanation of the word. The women who were expecting that explanation find comfort when Leopold reassures the cabbie that he has to worry about nothing. That is exactly what the two women found in the restrooms: zilch, nada.

The old beat-up Peugeot pulls in front of the door as Domersant gets distracted when some white pigeons fly nearby and above the lot. The women are not into the birds, and they hurry Domersant inside the car that drives away. At half a block down the road, after leaving the compound, a car that was parked nearby makes a U-turn and drives in pursuit.

After the group left and before Madigan heads out to catch his return flight, they set out to review all they have. Leopold looks lengthily at the digital corkboard, where the still images generated during the different sessions flash randomly. On his desk, he realizes that the notification light on his telephone blinks. That message had been there since the first minutes of the hypnosis of Mrs. Louis's session. The notification is about a photograph that one of Christiane's friends had snapped of her and Leopold the day they arrived in the country. Well, Christiane sure has other things on her mind also. At her age, these are the kinds of stuff she indulges in, and hopes Mr. Toumain, her father, does not ever find out.

Looking at the stills on the screen, Madigan is standing over his shoulders when Leopold rubs two fingers on his telephone screen, and air draws a full square. Within the square, the life-size screen appears. He taps on the mail icon. A pre-recorded video message from Christiane who is doing her sexy or seducing walk wearing a bikini near the swimming pool. In the background, the look on the gardener's face still puzzles Leopold and now Madigan, who has never seen such a blank stare. And he would be right if he thinks that he is seeing a Haitian zombie.

Madigan makes an inaudible "Wow!" with his lips and fans his face with his hand. He tries to keep a straight face as Leopold slightly turns around. This is, perhaps, Madigan thinks, why this young cracker thinks he is a local. The scientist just experienced the feeling that King Solomon had when the young queen of Ethiopia emerged in his chamber from inside that rug. Leopold abruptly turns to him, and he looks away a little. The truth, Christiane, is that hot a chick. With reason, that older couple on the airplane is adamant they would not exchange her appeal for Ivanka Trump's peculiar stiff face and alien-like demeanor.

On the screen, the photograph that Christiane sent shows Leopold walking toward the suburban where a young uniform marine officer holds a door open. A group of Christiane's girlfriends had captured the photograph with, in mind, to have her tell them everything that women talk about. And lately, during that stay in the country, she had gotten a few tales as chatting materials. The hotel room, the woods in Kenskoff, the suburban, and of course, the beach at the Duvalier's old property at Carriès. Also, on the photograph, walking toward the airport's entrance is a bald-headed older man in a yellow suit on either side of whom is a Massim twin. Leopold is about to dismiss the picture as inconsequential when Madigan intervenes. With the noise that tongue, teeth, and palate make, and wiggling his finger, he beckons him not to delete it so fast.

"Before you do that," Madigan says, "perhaps you could ask why, the heck, the man in the middle was in Haiti. Apparently," he adds, "he is leaving."

"Who is he?" Leopold asks.

Madigan slides his fingers on the telephone screen, and he executes a throwing motion that sends the projected image onto a full screen, thus enlarging the faces of the men in the photograph.

"Meet the fallen angel of the old CIA, Joseph M. Chipp. Many say the 'M' stands for Mengele, but others think it fittingly stands for 'Manchurian.' He was let go by the agency. Now, he goes to places such as here to plan assassinations. Son, meet Joe Manchurian. An excellent friend of your boss'."

Madigan starts to walk away but quickly turns around and adds…

"Something you should remember, kiddo… 'If I'm God, that sorry ass, son of a bitch is the fucking devil.'"

Within the country's collective psyche, Jeando was killed not for his politically salty editorials or for holding to the fire the feet of few deceitful politicians and connected wealthy businessmen. S. Pierre Etienne, a die-hard politician, declared under oath that Jeando had gotten whacked only because he was presidential. By God, Jeando would have won it fair and square. With his declaration, the professor would have Madigan postpone his flight. Then, it would be incumbent to President Geffrard to make sure that each and every one who took part in the 2000 presidential elections lay their ass on that couch. Everyone. Whether you count yourself among the many losers in these elections or you were "just" lucky to be the winner thereof. Considering what goes on in this country's elections politics, like in November of 1987, January of 1988, or December of 1990, though it'd be a given that the candidate can win on merit, the fraud machinery is put in place anyway. Be it for safety or by instinct, René Préval would cheat his ass off for his friend, although Jean Dominique was such a man who would have said, "René, I will win. We don't need that shit."

Jeando is dead. Then what. The strict political overtone of that potentially serious contender's physical elimination warranted one crucial aspect. The party to profit from it needed to carefully plot their escape from under the clouds of suspicion. Their fog clearing narrative on the path to the presidency consisted of unabashed flattery and outright hypocrisy. That poor woman suffered it all and, allegedly, the journalist himself had had a hand filled with hypocrisy tended him sometimes before his "silencing." The assassination of Dominique was in no way the first rodeo for the minds and mastermind behind it. Put a good chunk of the population as a representative sample on Madigan's sofa, for crying out loud, the results will prove that the defense would have to motion for a change of venue. The accused, as perceived in the public opinion, will not have a fair trial. Rest assured. The physical person(s) who dragged his/her ass(es) to Delmas to whack the journalist was/were already killed, himself or themselves, for that matter. The criminal pattern of the serial killer, at that juncture, usually demands the removal or destruction of evidence. Jeando's, like many other such crimes before it, called for the physical elimination of hot-blooded human props. The notion that to cover just one lie, a person needs seven other myths that each will need seven others, seems to find a home here. It holds correctly and firmly in that strange criminal sphere of Haitian politics. It indeed stuck in the United States throughout the four years before David Sosa became president.

Still, the result will also justify the opinion that will have justice elude the journalist even after fifty or sixty years. The party responsible for such an idea clarified, for he is well aware of the other acts the cowards who planned the crime have been on.

He cited several assassinations and disappearances that have rocked that rich little country. That stupid and blind whore has never said a word for Bertin, Malary, and the list goes on and on. So many folks have died unnecessarily.

The frantic rush to clean up any prop that could lead to the mastermind and close circle began rapidly. The presidential aspirants needed to immerse full fledge into campaigning mode polishing and sharpening their slogans. Such slogans that would prove ineffective with Jeando in the race. Probably, the assassination was deemed too much to be implicated in while vying the highest office in the country. The consensus, therefore, may have been to delegate the elimination process to a criminal contractor. Enter Tito Massim and Daniel Toumain. Two individuals who could explain the presence of Joe Manchurian in the country in 2023 as a new president threatens to turn the paradigm on its head. The days and weeks after the death of Dominique, a suspicious pattern developed. One by one, suspected individuals from, perhaps, that prop layer, are taken into custody only to get mysteriously released and be found dead. Domersant's brother, who supplied stolen vehicles for such operations, died of a "malpractice." The bullet that was intended for his head burst instead in his buttocks. But he succumbed to some utterly unrelated shit. Then, it seems that the cabbie's last passenger was instead crossing off items on a long criminal grocery list.

"McLintaugh!" Madigan says. "Forget the presidential candidates in the 2000 elections or whoever won. I want that woman, that senator on the couch."

"James," Leopold replies, "she has never responded to an invitation to cooperate. She has been the entire time in the United States."

"If your boy, Lysius," Madigan says, "can arrange it, I will bring the couch to her, myself. Tell him to get Sosa on it fast," he adds as he turns to point at the picture, "if that man was in the country."

"Who are these guys with him?" Madigan adds. "I want to know."

CHAPTER 25.

A Protective Exile

In Washington, DC. Leopold would turn the temperature on high. Here in Haiti, the Tropic is abundantly generous. Everything is free. The ocean, the breeze, the sun, and the heat; everything, even the sex, is free. Well, sort of. He always enjoys hot, steamy and sweaty, loud sex. Her long, natural hair makes slush with the sweat down her back as she rolls onto the pillow. Her moaning fills the room. Her hands slide up and down Leopold's sweaty back. She turns onto the pillow, jumps, and sits on his stomach. By now, Leopold knows that his cowgirl is about to go to work. She pinches his nose, leans, and initiates a kiss then buries her face in silence at the side of his neck. Abort. No ride, then something is wrong.

"Is there a problem," Leopold asks.

"I don't want to leave," she answers.

"Whatcha talkin' 'bout Willis?" he asks, imitating Gary Coleman whom he enjoyed watching in his child days as he lifts her face up in front of his.

Christiane sobs as she tells Leopold of her father's immediate plan for her in a calculated urgency. Folks in the know in that country do this. When some trusted contact let them in on something that is to happen with the potential to disrupt life, they make sure their children are on a plane away from the hole. Lysius brought up the subject in the Senate, saying that most of his colleagues have no interest in fixing the education or health system, anything. Their kids, their wives, he said, are somewhere else. In fact, they are here alone in the country with their concubines. Some of the colleagues, he accused, engage in the coercing of our young girls, young women in the shameful practice of "Madan papa." Most in both chambers hold a green card that they maintain by flying every six months as proof of residency and eligibility to some benefit like food vouchers and "shit." In a general assembly session, he cited the example of one "lawmaker" in that very legislature who was in talks with a cousin hoping to arrange a marriage and obtain that ever elusive green card. Christiane and her brother are ordered on the next plane two days before Lysius officially becomes president.

Leopold gets out of the bed and walks away while tying the robe around his waist, and on his way to the bathroom, he restores the fresh air. It does not take much; the trip to the toilet is enough to morph Leopold back into his agent mode. When he walks back into the room where the young woman has turned on the television, he is dressed up. As he fixes himself, he thinks of asking Christiane the one question he had many times hesitated to ask. The occasion had rarely presented itself. In fact, the photograph that Christiane had sent him and what Madigan told him about Joe Manchurian preoccupy him. He understands now. With what she has just told him about her father's desire, it is "ask now or forever, hold on to your 'piece.'" If Christiane obeys, he may not readily know how her father feels about the future president and the investigation aware of his partner Massim's open disapproval of Lysius. The rift had existed between the two since Lysius first ran for the Senate practically fresh out of Yale against Tito's brother. The future president specifically accused Tito of a failed attempt to assassinate Lysius Geffrard, the elder.

"You know, I'm not sure," she answers. "I remember when I was younger, daddy used to enjoy watching him as a young athlete. But now, Lyzou is a politician, things have significantly changed."

"How about his friends and business partners?" he asks.

"Gosh!" she sighs. "They are different. Fat Jacques works for Lysius. But Mr. Massim and the twins have always hated Lysius. 'Don't know why besides they were accused of trying to assassinate his father."

That naked brown-skinned woman still wrapped in the sheets was indeed too young. She could not know or even remember what had really occurred between the Geffrards and the Massims during these senatorial elections. She may also be unaware that it was her father who recommended Cyprien to President Josaphat, who blindly swallowed and bought into Toumain's treachery. Leopold pours coffee into two cups and brings her a cup. He sits next to her on the bed. As he drinks, he runs his fingers through her hair.

"Coming here," he tells her, "the only advice from my old man and another old man was not to trust the calm here. He's giving you all that money," he adds as he looks at his watch. "Go to Geneva and come back to DC. In one week, I should be there."

Leopold steadily looked at his watch. That afternoon after driving Madigan to the airport, he went straight to the people in charge of Lysius' security. Leopold had the impression that the man who received him there actually tried to play him for a fool. In the poorly furnished room with only a cheap desk, a folding chair, and a telephone, the man appeared to the agent to be making mocked calls. McLintaugh did not buy into any of it at first, but he was wrong. The information that he relayed was authentic. Indeed, the only person whom he needed to see was still away from the capital with Lysius. The president-elect had not yet returned for his inauguration. Thus, two days and one hour for Leopold to report to President Geffrard with the findings of the investigation. He had left the modest office, however, with the solemn promise that Cyprien would contact him within the hour of his return.

"President-elect Lysius Geffrard," the TV reporter announces, "now has another nickname. By sarcasm, the people call him 'The Kangaroo,' who, instead of a pouch, has a fanny pack where he carries his former rival Nickesse Duvalier. At just hours away to officially become the country's president, Lysius and his not so fortunate former opponent, Nickesse Duvalier have finally returned to Port-au-Prince. The two men have embarked on a month-long journey around the country to meet up close with Lysius' new bosses, and potentially Duvalier's in the future."

"He is back," Christiane elatedly says as she spills some coffee on the white sheets. "Will you be ready to meet him at the time he told you?"

Leopold quickly walks around the bed to answer his vibrating telephone on the night table as he tells Christiane that he first needs to see Cyprien, who must call him by now. And, yes, it is Fat Jacques as the employee at that front office had promised.

"McLintaugh!" he answers as he blows an air kiss to Christiane.

"Forgive me, sir." Leopold hears through the receiver. "Before you left your card with my office, I was calling you McIntosh."

"And you are?"

"Cyprien, Jacques Cyprien, chief of security for the president-elect. Well," he adds, "soon to be president for one day."

"You mean President 'in' one day, sir," he tries to correct Cyprien, who offers no other response but a dry laugh.

"Were you calling me McIntosh? Ha!"

"I don't know you personally, but this country's a small-town and…"

He has not gotten all day. He left Christiane naked in the room, where she remains on the bed. She contemplates her forced exit from the country no later than the afternoon as far as Mr. Toumain is concerned. Leopold buys into a salad of a story. He agrees to rendezvous with Fat Jacques on a small road near "The Belvedere" overlooking the town of Petionville and the capital at a longer distance. The two men look at the city far down. Cyprien hands the binocular to Leopold, who pans East–West a couple of times before resting on the presidential palace that looks finished from the perspective and ready to receive its next occupant. What he cannot see is the business around it as the preps are underway for Lysius' big day with history.

"I am the biggest man in it," Cyprien says as Leopold looks at the palace through the binocular. "Not even the President-elect," he adds, tapping on his chest. "Everything must go through 'I.'"

With a smile, Leopold brings his index and middle fingers to his eyes and opens his arms very wide. In a sarcastic, cruel gesture about the mountain of adipocytes in front of him, Leopold blunts out.

"Ah! 'Me' see."

"I was in Washington with the president," replies Cyprien, who instantly takes in the fat quip and swallows some of his saliva before adding through the squeaky noise of a vehicle arriving behind them.

"Your name simply evaded me."

No one in this gathering is aware the agent is already familiar with the name on the side of the car. "MASSIM PHARMACEUTICALS" are the words on the door that opens as Chapo gets out. Jimmy shuts the passenger's side door and runs around the front of the car. Both he and Chapo pull out their gun.

"Ladies," Chapo shouts, "put your hands in da ahh… Eh! you the hippo. Put it down. What's under your jacket?"

Cyprien takes out a small caliber revolver.

"Now," Chapo orders, "put it on the ground… Kick it to me…"

"Forward," shouts Jimmy. "Paws on the car."

"Frisk 'em," Chapo orders his criminal apprentice as Jimmy rushes first to Leopold to search him. Of course, looking for the gun that he still covets. However, Jimmy is having a second thought. He steps back, deciding he will get to Leopold afterward. Meanwhile, Leopold is thinking about the rat he smells in all this. After all, Fat Jacques is no pushover. This immovable object puts his weight behind everything he does, even in his smile, which he does not do very often. Cyprien is known to have never taken chances on his duties. In fact, this characteristic figured high on Toumain's recommendation of him to President

Josaphat. The man in charge of the security of the president would never rendezvous guilelessly in that secluded road. On the way, Leopold had spotted his detail at various locations. The one he remembers as the most noticeable was in front of the former François Duvalier High school of Petionville, where they could observe the small road by The Belvedere.

Leopold came to the meeting to inform Cyprien on things he already knows and of which he is part. The all-embracing opposite of James Madigan was in the country, and everywhere Joseph Chipp sets foot, important people die. On the other hand, to satisfy the desire of the son of his boss Tito who offered him a few dollars more, Chapo must deliver Leopold to Qusay. Dany, Tito, and others want to eliminate the agent physically. Since the blond man had gotten into the landscape, Qusay has been holding it in his hand, and Christiane has stayed the hell away. Whereas the police officer at the Belvedere entrance deviated other cars, Leopold drove through as Jeando did by Domersant's brother on April 3, 2000. Fat Jacques was already there, seemingly alone when Leopold arrived. The FBI agent was aware but showed up anyway with confidence.

Since their interaction on the beach at Carriès, Chapo, and Jimmy have not seen much of Leopold. Qusay had ordered them instead on lingerie details, pretty much to stalk Christiane's back-and-forth to the Base or the hotel. When he learned of it, Saddam was not thrilled about his son's decision.

"Chapo, you remember this dude from that fucking beach?" Jimmy asks as Leopold smells his nicotine breath. "I'll be back, sweetie," tapping on the agent's cheek. "But first…"

Jimmy slides his hands around Leopold's waist and grabs the gun as Chapo looks on and shakes his head.

"Fucking thief," Chapo whispers to himself as Jimmy pats Leopold's cheek and goes over to Cyprien, saying 'the hippo first' as he starts frisking the fat man extending his arms around him.

"Shit! It's like huggin' the fucking planet."

He gets his hand inside his jacket and comes up with a breath spray and a roll of crisp bills. He puts the money in his pocket and waves the breath spray in Cyprien's face.

"Ah!" he says. "'Fuckin' hippo got bad breath?"

He throws the spray to Chapo.

"Here! Also good for penis' breath," he says sarcastically.

Chapo is not happy as the spray falls in his hand, eyeballing Jimmy, who turns and walks to Leopold, who looks at him with these eyes from hell. Jimmy tears into him also with the kind of looks he learned at Rikers Island. Leopold is not intimidated. He knows Jimmy is bluffing, for he gives him credit that he would not do anything stupid in front of Cyprien. Wrong. Out of the blue, he lands a mighty punch that shakes Leopold a bit. They ordered them into their car and drove to the other twin's home, where the setup is best for what Qusay has in mind.

Near Fort-Jacques, once in the house, after they led Leopold downstairs on an awning-covered veranda overlooking the city, it is time for Cyprien to claim his belongings from Chapo and Jimmy. By now, the agent knows that Cyprien is in on any plan this gang has for the coming days. First, he needs to break out of this place where Cyprien and the other two left him attached to a chair, not knowing who will show up. The only thing he has going for him now is the beautiful view of Port-au-Prince from the balcony.

Chapo comes forward and places the breath spray in Cyprien's hand. Jimmy reluctantly puts some bills in Cyprien's hand.

"Hurry up!" he orders him. "All of it. I don't have all day."

Jimmy goes to another pocket and places some more bills in Cyprien's hand. The fat man throws a stiff punch that sends the younger man to the floor, asking him whom he was calling a hippo. All to Chapo's amusement who always wants to rough him up.

"Take me to my automobile, you idiot," he tells Chapo.

At first, following Cyprien, who walks out behind Chapo to the car lot, Jimmy gave the eerie impression he was going to retaliate and strike the fat man. It turns out that he manages to have him give the money back to him after he sucks up to him on his sucker punch. Cyprien smiles in agreement and pulls the bundle out and gives it to the young man who closes the car door as Chapo drives out of the gate.

Jimmy sits behind the wheel of his cousin Khalil/Uday's expensive, German luxury car admiring and kissing Leopold's gun. He lowers the seat and lays back, caressing the weapon on his chest. The shiny barrel of his cousin's stainless-steel gun slowly approaches and kisses Jimmy on the left cheek. It's Leopold whose dirty clothes tell a story. He comes from a big fight with Uday, who could not wait for his twin brother more capable of handling the massive chunk of muscle the agent is.

"Say Ah! Open that pie hole," Jimmy hears.

"Yo, Khalil!" Jimmy says. "Don't fucking play like this, man. I see your piece in the mirror with blood on your hand. You skinned that cracker who's boning your brother's bitch?"

"He did," Jimmy hears again as Leopold masks his voice.

Jimmy rolls his eyes toward the rearview mirror and is shocked to see it's Leopold, who now inserts his cousin's gun into his mouth.

Gun. Telephone. Wallet. Put the seat up…

He quickly gets in on the back seat behind Jimmy.

"Drive!" he orders him.

On his way back to the residence, Chapo spotted the sports car. But he thought it was Khalil going down to Petionville for whatever reason. He could not have seen Leopold deep in the back seat with his gun pointed at Jimmy. He also thought that the white man was securely attached where they and Cyprien had left him. When Chapo arrives in the parking garage, it is hushed and, Jimmy is nowhere around. He looks for him all about the house.

"Hey! Young man. Deported, where are you?" Chapo calls out repeatedly as he goes from room to room around the mansion. He goes down a couple of flights of stairs and down to the basement calling him.

"Hey, thief!" he calls. "I saw you kept the fat man's money. Get the fuck out! Damn it."

As he nears the bottom of the stairs, a squeaky noise becomes audible. It is coming from outside, from the open terrace where they left Leopold while Khalil was busy with other things. He sticks his ear on the door and listens as the squeaking gets louder to him. Chapo opens the door and gets the shock of his life, although he has personally killed many with his own hands. He has never been that shocked in front of such a scene. The terrace looks like the path of a tornado. The chair they sat Leopold in is reduced to fragments. The plants are all or most broken and tottered on with the dark soil scattered all around. Chapo contemplates the scene in torpor, resting his eyes on what used to be the armrests of the chair. He identifies the cheap yellow tape they had used to tie up his wrists.

Walking slowly and cautiously through the chaos, fearing that the "white" they left here could jump him at any moment, he intuitively looks to the side, investigating the origin of the screeching noise. With the city far away down in the background, the swing set oscillates and squeaks. Like a giant pendant, the seat of one of the swings is attached to Khalil's neck with the chain around it, and he hangs as blood drips from his mouth with a still wet urine stain in his pants.

Meanwhile, near The Belvedere, Jimmy had parked his cousin's car next to the Suburban, who backs up and takes off slowly. At the intersection with the road to Kenskoff, making that left turn like a Haitian driver, the same way Jeando executed his before the assassins' car, Leopold's attention is drawn to the minivan before which he turns that did not even try to stop instead of smashing on the horn. The agent must now rush to the airport, where Toumain will be making sure his children leave the country. He has promised them to board the aircraft and personally put them in their seats.

While turning, the ignition key he took from Jimmy slides from the left to the passenger's side of the dashboard and flies off the car onto the pavement.

Oh, well, Leopold says, pulling from his pocket the smart telephone that he also seized from Jimmy. He throws it away to the side of the road where a young man makes the gravest mistake of catching it. Even the last of his life when he later answers that call from Chapo. In only a few minutes, this heartless criminal will come out of the house in a rage, determined to revenge the death of Khalil, one of his little bosses, the son of his big boss Tito. He ignores that Jimmy is sitting all tied up in a car with no key in the ignition. It had probably been rendered useless as hundreds of vehicles have run over it on the road. While driving toward the primary road, his instinct was to look for Jimmy before alerting Tito. No question of notifying the authorities. When he gets on the main road, he recognizes the minivan that the agent nearly crashed into at the entrance near Belvedere. He decides to execute an illegal U-turn to follow the minivan since he is in charge of that mission of which the van's driver is supposed to report.

In the early days after Jeando's assassination, the heavyweights who stood to profit the most from it needed to get back or to immerse in the real object of the profit. The Massims were losing a considerable of money and credit each time Dominique associated their laboratories with the tainted medications, alcohol, or ethanol that were marketed around the country. They lobbied for the cleanup and silencing job. They had proven to be very prolific and ruthless. Folks have disappeared, died, and fled, and more importantly, besides her supposed blindness, the bitch has also been mute and shy. In that country by tradition, to the attributes bestowed upon the Roman Iustitia or to the Greeks Themis and Dike, powerful and power-angry political hacks have added these of cheap whores with short and flimsy arms. What justice, one may wonder. The institution of which the short and frail arms won't bother to reach out and grab those hacks by the collar and land a boot at the seat of their pants.

Oncoming traffic is at a standstill. The Northbound vehicles traveling from higher up the mountains have no choice. Road rage is not those Caribbean folks' cup of tea. The ones who have gone and seen it overseas, in the United States in particular or those who have watched it on television may push an issue from time to time. The real rage is, for the most part, repressed and contained. It quietly occurs when officials order their chauffeurs to turn on their sirens and just drive against the flow oblivious to the other users of the road. Many an occasion, the chauffeurs abuse this feature for no apparent reason running their own errands. Chapo, at first, thought of doing that but waited in traffic until he pulls right behind the minivan waiting for the massive dark green iron gate to open, thus still impeding the flow of traffic from Kenskoff.

As the gate finally opens, to the outside, it seems as though electricity has finally reached the mechanism to move this mountain of steel. The look has again deceived, all onlookers find that out when the four security guards become visible as they push the large structure open on its rails. They had to wait that long because it took two of the guards close to two minutes to come and help the others. From the entrance, the minivan and Chapo after it must drive another four minutes to Tito's parking garage where that delivery is expected.

Tito Massim looks at his reflection on the side of the black window tainted minivan. He is a little amused to see himself as that small, bulky image. The driver gets out and opens the sliding door before he addresses the boss. He dramatically does this as, without a word, he shows Tito what is inside the vehicle. The two women from the hypnosis session at the Base are blindfolded. The driver drags them out. From behind the car emerges, blindfolded as well, Domersant whom another man pushes forward. They hit and force them inside the house.

"Very well," acknowledges Tito. "Very well."

CHAPTER 26.

Inaugural Crowd

The dark and outsized hands of Toumain sandwich Christiane's soft, feminine, and of-a-lighter-appearance delicate hand as he caresses and taps on it. In the back of the Mercedes, nobody is in the mood for small talks. This morning, Mrs. Toumain reminded her husband that the children had lived through and survived the terrible times of the frequent assassinations when his friend ruled the country at the beginning of the millennium. Why, oh, why is she forced to accompany her grown-up children who have traveled many times on their own? Junior has not turned his head a single time looking at his side of the road through the car window. Christiane did not plan to part so soon with her erotic encounters at the hotel or the Base. She is thinking of something and someone, but her father presumes that he has an idea what and who it is. He has not paid as much attention as he should have to Chapo's report of her at Carriès with the "white."

"We've arrived, sweetheart," he tells her. "The money in Switzerland is yours. All of it. Then you could stay in Washington. Kharim will visit you all the time."

"Kharim?" she protests in disgust.

As everyone in the back of the car is taken aback by Christiane's subtle objection, the luxury car rolls slowly onto the tarmac and stops near the airplane. The driver gets out to open the rear door, and another man from a vehicle behind rushes with a machine gun and stands guard at the foot of the airstair already in place on the right side of the aircraft. In the boarding area upstairs, Leopold had managed to find a spot near the gate to make sure he follows the family. From the glass window, he watches as Toumain holds Christiane's hand, walks up the steps until they are out of view.

Christiane gets herself comfortable in her seat, fastening her belt as a good child. Her father sits next to her while she looks through the window at the guards near daddy's vehicle.

"Well, honey, that's as far as I go. A kiss for daddy?"

They hug while Dany hugs mom, and they swap parents.

"Good girl," he says. "Take care o' yourself."

Christiane still observes through the window as her parents walk down the last steps and get inside the car that drives away. In the waiting area, her brother had met an old classmate, also leaving the country after similar confidences to his folks. He does not pay any attention to his sister as he chats with his friend. Her father might, at this minute, be thinking that he got rid of her for now. In her head, her noodles boil as her eyes roll about. And, her heart rate increases as she keeps check on her brother and everyone around her. She has a plan, and she knows that she must not fail.

Before Toumain's car drove off the tarmac, Leopold had already left the airport compound, en route to meeting with Dr. Pierre in the commercial center where they met the first time. Leopold chose to see the old man this day, at this time before the inauguration instead of earlier during the morning hours, which he spent fighting for his life up in the mountains near Kenskoff. Earlier, at the airport, the agent had thought of postponing the meeting but now needs to rush it and clear his mind of

Christiane's involuntary and impromptu departure. The old man has insisted that it be before he meets with the new president. Later in the evening, as per his mental note, he still plans to go over the dossier that he must submit to the sworn-in head of state. Although the age difference between him and Lysius is rather slim, Leopold reckons he must not give any ill-prepared dossier to this hardcore politician.

"Tick-tock, tick-tock, Leopold," he repeats to himself as he pulls the Suburban up near the Park's entrance thinking of the fast-approaching deadline he agreed on with Lysius. He climbs the few steps leading to the outdoor food court. As the old doctor comes within his view under his habituated umbrella, two men exiting the court with Tito following them at a distance, deliberately bump into Leopold. He quickly looks at them and turns around to find himself staring into the eyes of Tito. Leopold had become familiar with the feeling he experienced in the early minutes during History's hypnosis session. He convinces himself that he had that same feeling in front of the truck parked at the intersection during his stint into Domersant's recollection of the events from 12:19 a.m. to 6:17 a.m. on the 3rd of April 2000.

"Please forgive them," Tito softly tells Leopold with a smile. "They are savages."

By now, Tito is probably aware of whom killed his son earlier in the day, but in no wise did he expect to run into him this casually in this setting. He, too, has a deadline, and the hours are not long enough. Tito Massim has been around death too long to lose precious time over even that of his son. He realized who it was only after walking past him as he briefly pauses and turns around. Any other place, he thinks in his mind, he would have whacked the sucker cold. Leopold and Tito looked into each other's eyes for a brief second as Tito walks after the two men, and he walks toward Dr. Pierre, who welcomes him with a smile and relief.

"Huh! You are finally here," the old man says.

"I've got your message. Are you okay, Doctor? Your bag. It is a mess. What happened?"

"They took it," he complains.

"Who took what, Dr. Pierre?"

It is all technology here, and anything not medical flies right over the old man's head. In the morning, as he listened to the newscast of Lysius return to the city for his inauguration, he was about his hobby. Since he was a young man, Dr. Pierre understood that gardening is one sure way to renew with mother earth and release stress. This morning, Dr. Pierre was ready as he thrust his hand into his gardener's glove to perform some pruning of his plants. Some strange and small object fell from the sky right into his bag that he usually keeps next to his old Tandberg Solvsuper 4 radio receiver on his patio table. Dr. Pierre ran to investigate. He is relieved that the object did not damage the radio receiver he inherited from his grandfather, who died in the late 1970s.

"Hmm, he said as he curiously inspected the strange object."

He concluded he'd drive to the Base and show it to Leopold. Perhaps the laws of genetics had decreed Kharim also to be insensitive to the death of his brother and be about his father's criminal business. With their own approaching deadline, they have delegated things to a relative. They ought to stay busy with executing a dry run that involved flying their drone over essential sites in the city hence over the doctor's residence this morning. When the news of his brother's death reaches him, Kharim is monitoring the drone's flight while he drinks and makes out with some women. The mixture of boobs and booze reacts severely to the emotion from the news. Apparently, that was when he lost the device that spontaneously spiraled down to the ground. In this case, into the doctor's bag. That explains the handheld device recovery console in Tito's hand when his henchmen, in communication with him, bump into the agent as they flee.

At Tito's instructions as he monitors the flashing green and yellow arrows in the drone's GPS recovery device, the two men have approached Dr. Pierre's table. They spilled the content of his bag on the table and confiscated the object that even they did not know what it is. Tito stepped in like a hero to ease the old man whom he knows very well. Besides Jimmy, who, in the country, does not?

"Put everything back in the bag," he ordered his men, one of whom had already gotten hold of the drone. "And leave him alone," he added as he winked at the doctor.

"Hello, Doc," Tito added with sarcasm.

"I wanted to show it to you," Dr. Pierre says after telling Leopold what had happened in the morning and what just occurred a minute ago. "Perhaps you'd know what it is."

Leopold stands quietly over Dr. Pierre's shoulder and looks at a photo in the newspaper on the table, under his bag. In the picture, American President Sosa and Lysius get off a helicopter, a photo taken during the president-elect's visit in the US. The agent looks at the worried and shaken doctor's face and wishes he could stay a little longer with him or even drive him home. But, tick-tock, tick-tock. He understands time is not on his side though he feels ready to meet with the president and deliver what makes him, not even Madigan at this point if he had not told him, the "only" person on "earth," besides almost everyone in the country, who knows who indeed ordered the journalist's microphone be silenced for good. And perhaps, President Geffrard stands as the next person. Is not that the buffer line the Massims' thuggish and criminal enterprise was contracted to reinforce?

After he parts with the old man, Leopold returns to the hotel where a delivery awaits in the form of a photograph inside a canary envelope. The stars on the photo are Domersant and the two women at the hypnosis sessions, badly beaten and mutilated. Leopold has somehow failed to notice the envelope in his rush to hit the shower and calm the heat before delving for the last time into his job at hand. He had planned to stay in all the rest of the day and part of the night. The events that are to follow will have him settle differently for how the rest of the day unravels.

In the hallway, the envelope is picked up from the floor, and there is a frantic knock on door 18 N. It's Christiane dressed as a man with her hair under the straw hat she had on at Carriès. These pieces of her brother's clothes were the only things inside the single carry-on she always travels with. As far as her father is concerned, this young woman is illegally in her own country. Chatting with his classmate, her younger brother never realized he has been traveling solo until the layover at JFK, where he gave a call back to the parents. By the time of that call, life will have drastically changed. Shit will have blown. She probably knows he'd call them, and they would be looking all over, and that is why she dresses this way.

The door slowly swings open, and she gets in.

On the opposite side, Leopold welcomes her with his gun drawn.

"Who the heck are you?" he asks.

Christiane slowly takes off the hat and turns around as her beautiful hair falls on her shoulders. Leopold stands down.

"*Mon Dieu*, Leopold! Calm down. It's me."

"Gosh!" he says as he lowers the gun. "I almost smoked you. Careless," he blames her. "And crazy too," he adds.

"Leo. I am crazy and in love with you."

"I love you too. But—"

Christiane gets close and hugs him. They passionately kiss.

"And the envelope?" he asks.

"'Twas in front of the door," she answers without taking her head off his chest.

"How so?" he asks as he opens the package.

He looks at the blue shirt Domersant wore to the Base, but now in the photo, the stain from the hypnosis session is covered. The blue shirt is drenched in his blood. After the trip up the mountains in that minivan, another vehicle had dumped them near the American Base and the photo was taken.

"Gee! Domersant! Poor women," Leopold comments.

And a note falls from inside the envelope. Kharim Massim, who signed it as Qusay, wrote that the agent owes him the price of the paper on which the photo is printed.

"I know the bastard," she says. "Kharim sent those guys to the beach."

She refrains from telling the whole story and letting Leopold know that besides being a criminal, the man is bent by jealousy on eliminating him physically. She ignores Leopold's run-ins before he went to watch her board the plane. Thus, Christiane may not be obligated to tell him the man he left dangling to his death this morning was Kharim's twin brother.

"When?" Leopold asks as she rambles on about the potentially dangerous fallouts.

"This morning, right after Khalil's death."

"Khalil?" he asks.

Leopold may not readily register the real name. But had Christiane mentioned the name given to him by the populace, he would have recalled their fight this morning in which he left Uday on the swing. He is, only now, learning that he had consequently died. As she engages in a lengthy narration of what the FBI had briefed him many times, Leopold thinks it was odd. The father of the man he may have killed did not even raise a finger when they chanced upon each other earlier at the Commerce Park. He concludes that the gang might be plotting something more significant than, perhaps, avenging the death of a son, a twin brother, a boss, a cousin, or a friend. Then all of it leads him back to his interest, Christiane, who will not dare go to her house. Toumain would not swallow or have any of it. As he turns around and starts his sentence to tell her that she can't stay at the hotel, a vast explosion startles them and the whole city. Instinctively, they get in each other's arms.

"*Mon Dieu*!" Christiane yells. "What was that?"

They run out to one end of the balcony and look up into the distance.

A giant mushroom of smoke and dust goes up in the sky. The explosion is heard as far as the town of Leogane at 29 km

West of the capital. It will claim the lives of the nearly thirty-five hundred men who worked around the clock to have the presidential palace ready for the inauguration. The country's president, Josaphat, may not, at this instant, have any information as to what had happened. But as Leopold and Christiane return to the room under pulverized pieces of concrete falling from the sky, a message comes into the agent's phone. He quickly reads it.

"Gosh!" he exclaims. "The presidential palace has just exploded."

"With all the people working there?" she asks as she turns, forgetting that she wanted to run straight from the balcony into the bathroom."

Leopold turns the television on as Christiane comes to stand next to him.

REPORTER

Well, that building, as we know, has been destroyed in the earthquake of 2010. Pierre-Richard, we do not have any more information. Maybe the camera could make a 180 to show you what is coming our way.

Swift responses. In the distance, a mob advances while shouting and accusing the people most likely to commit such horror.

REPORTER

Pierre. That sea of humanity is the crowd of Lysius' supporters. They have followed him everywhere since he and his pal Nickesse Duvalier stuck to his sleeve or "fanny pack," have returned to the city this morning, for the inauguration. Yes, it is menacing, Pierre, as it moves toward us. The 4 1 1 communicates to us that the crowd chants accusations against Tito and Qusay

Massim, respectively, the father and twin brother of Khalil, known as Uday found dead in his home earlier today. The man on the street believes it is still the work of the same hands behind the assassination of journalist Jean Dominique. Those powerful hands, Geffrard's supporters say, are bent on foiling the investigation the future president will order reopened once sworn in.

No one would ever imagine that the investigation had already ended. Not even the willing participants, who have paid the ultimate price, really understood what was happening, on a couch, of all places. Tito and Dani, the high-priced criminals contracted from the early days to oppose any investigation, have no clue. And even latecomer Cyprien and many others, all are still waiting for "Leopold McIntosh" to make his initial move and start it after the new President would order it. Characteristic of Fat Jacques, who does not take chances, he had suggested that Tito remedy the people who volunteered to go at the Base. This mob of angry protesters carrying bats, clubs, car tires, machetes, and all sorts of weapons as they chant is as organic as spontaneous. Lysius, who wield extraordinary convoking powers, had not called his followers into the streets. That crowd that already individualizes the minds behind what had happened has already reached their verdict. They are not shy to chant that Tito, his son, and Toumain must taste what one of the former Presidents once told his supporters. Ah, the appalling odor of burnt rubber and barbecued human flesh! In 1991, Leopold's grandfather told Ed that "some fuck must be sick in his rotten mind to admit that's the fragrance he loves."

With ownership of more than 70 percent of the businesses, Tito and the pharmaceutical elite very early start to feel the consequences of their thoughtless actions. They become unhinged as the first makeshift Molotov cocktails are thrown at store windows around the capital. Amid the flames, the name "MASSIM" and others suggesting a Middle Eastern (Syrian, Lebanese, etc.) ascendance go down with shoes, car tire, medications, drugs, clothing, etc. When Massim Auto Parts, the largest of its kind in the Caribbean, is broken into by a couple of healthy muscled men with sledgehammers, it morphs into a haven for looters. Those folks have nothing to do with the politics of the times or a desire to avenge the senseless explosion of the presidential palace that killed thousands of the country's impoverished citizens who volunteered to help rebuild it. Most come out only to steal shit. Glued in front of the TV, Christiane nervously squeezes Leopold's hand as Lysius intervenes by telephone.

"Pierre-Richard," he says, "that mass of concrete, which is crumbling at our feet, can always be rebuilt as it has just been since some thirteen years after the earthquake. What will never be replaced are the thousands of lives lost today. Counting our losses, that is the real loss for the country and for us as a people. With our little finger, we can crush an insignificant ant to have the illusion and give the impression of being a higher power, a superior species. But the true power, Pierre, would be to blow life back into that fucking ant."

"Lyzou, do you accuse like your supporters are already doing?" the anchor asks.

"I always called the people to calm in similar situations. I will not do it this early, today. In 1986, after Nickesse's father left the country, I was only a child when the people swallowed General Namphy's curfew. Today, I say it is the sacred right of the people to express their anger and let it out of their system after their husband, father, brother, cousin, or a simple friend have volunteered and sacrificed so much to rebuild their house. I also believe that this is a wise people, but I'll grant myself a bit more wisdom by not accusing now, today. Way too many crimes have been committed in this fucking country. For example, the deaths of Luc Innocent, Mrs. Bertin, Izmery, Volel, and, of course, as I promised during the campaign to find and bring to justice the real assassins or 'assassin' of Jean Dominique. Pierre-Richard, a handful of wealthy and powerful thugs view my presidency as an end to their impunity. Well, so be it should I, too, lose my skin in this damn shit. My life would've been worth that of the great Jeando. For now, my friend, and now only, I neither accuse nor condemn."

As Lysius speaks, Leopold's phone rings. He leaves Christiane by herself in front of the TV. He now paces around the room. The young woman feels she needs to hear the conversation or, at least, try to guess what it is about. She subtly lowers the television to listen in, and Leopold does not care at this point. He is pissed.

"Mr. Ekstroem, sir," she hears along with other bits of short unfinished sentences or answers. "You sent me here to fail and to die. Yes, I have. I've been. Now, I tell you that the president-elect wields sharp swords each time he opens his mouth."

Christiane looks at him in a mirror across the room as he rolls his eyes and briefly listens between his short answers.

"Madigan. I know, sir … "The lady, sir, is Mrs. Luber." … "Yes, sir," he adds. "No, sir," .... "His security is hugely compromised … "From within, sir," he angrily says as his voice tone changes. "See what you can do' is not good enough... Your shit storm is now brewing and will blow up in your face, Ekstroem."

Confusing. The young woman reads into the change from Leopold saying, "Mr. Ekstroem, sir" to only "Ekstroem." Christiane understands she cannot stay glued to the TV as the journalist thanks Lysius.

"Get ready, sir. I'll be taking the storm to Washington with me… And, there's no telling how your ass will turn out."

Leopold hangs up and turns to Christiane.

"If you don't want to go home, you're not safe here. Let's get out of here," Leopold hurries her. "Paperboy's coming back."

Without her car now, she relies on Leopold, who, of course, will not leave her behind. Before crossing, Leopold remotely turns on the ignition as they dash toward the suburban parked alone on the other side of the lot. The SUV is about to start moving when Leopold spots Chapo in the rearview mirror suspiciously entering the hotel. From the gloves compartment, Leopold pulls out a gun and offers it to Christiane.

"Can you use this?" he asks.

"Hah!" Christiane laughs.

"Stay here."

She adjusts the interior rearview mirror and follows Leopold as he gets inside the hotel. Then she perceives a movement behind the car in the driver's side mirror. She opens the gloves compartment and dons the brass knuckle that she saw when Leopold opened it to get the gun. She looks in the mirror again and sees nothing, so she thinks she would instead be fixing her lipstick and hair while wearing the knuckles. Meanwhile, at the hotel desk, as Leopold runs past the service desk, the clerk is on the phone with Chapo, who had gotten a card from him to enter the agent's room.

"Incoming," Chapo hears through his earpiece.

Leopold finds the door ajar and pushes it with the tip of his gun and walks in. Chapo surprises him from behind, hitting him in the back. Leopold quickly turns around only to receive Chapo's uppercut that sends him flying. The fight progresses into the bedroom. Yet another blow and a combination; he falls on his back on the bed and looks up at Chapo, who slides his tongue on his gold maxillary incisors as he pulls his machete. This man still wears the same hat that he swears Papa Doc Duvalier himself placed on his head as a young lad. It is, therefore, possible that this blade is the same he used in the massacre at Rue Vaillant. What happens within Leopold's mind is lightning fast and is nothing short of creepy as the sparkle from the blade in the lights hits his retina. To Leopold, the imagery is poorly defined as a male human form wields a machete-like weapon of which the edge sparkles in the sun as he charges at a pregnant woman's silhouette. Leopold is baffled, but he has no time to delve into the logic of what had just flashed through his mind.

CHAPTER 27.

It's The Fight In The Girl

At the end of that eternity that lasted from the instant Chapo's raised the machete to before Lysius' official inauguration, Leopold finds himself still on his back. He knows he must not stay there. On the flip side, the older criminal fathoms his obligation to keep this young pack of muscle mass off his feet to stand a chance in the fight. Although the momentum favors him to connect blow after blow, the agent still attempts to get off the bed and on his feet. He finally reads the rate and sequence of the older fellow's punches. He intercepts one and powers up to propel Chapo up against the wall.

After his back hits the wall, the machete Samurai lands on his feet and charges again at Leopold with the blade above his head. And like a minute before, the blurry imageries come flashing again in Leopold's mind. This time, it's as though he sees from the perspective of the pregnant woman's midst. The long shiny object (the machete's blade) penetrates. A red liquid expands and slowly wipes the image out. Leopold quickly moves, and the weapon is plunged into the mattress. A kick to the side of the head disorients Chapo. Leopold follows through with his own series of punches and a superkick that sends the Haitian flying and falling into the chair that always receives Christiane's first pieces of clothing.

After punching Chapo in the jaw, Leopold pulls the machete out of the mattress. At that same moment in the hotel parking lot, from behind, Jimmy's hand grabs and covers

Christiane's mouth as the gun falls off her hands onto the car floor. He drags her through the window out of the vehicle along a wall as he starts unzipping his pants. Christiane grabs and pulls his thumb off his grip on her mouth. She pulls it back. With her dominant foot heel, she stomps hard on his toes. He lets go, and she turns around, landing a knee in Jimmy's crotch, and he bends in front of her. Christiane pulls off his bandana and sends a brass knuckle straight punch to his jaw. He falls to the ground in agonizing pain, and she beats him to an inch of his life.

"'Want to have your way with me?" she asks. "Rape this. Motherfucker."

She kicks him again and again.

"Take that for your sorry-ass cousin," Christiane tells him as she steps on his balls and twists.

Leopold is not interested in coming back to the hotel. He won't even check out. The American is just taking off. As he walks out through the open door, behind him, Chapo sits as one bloody pulp in the armchair with the half-open eyes of a dying man. The machete is plunged in his stomach and pierces through the chair as blood drips from the tip of the blade onto that famous hat Papa Doc Duvalier buried on his big head.

When Leopold arrives near the SUV, Christiane is not there. He turns around and sees her at the other end of the lot where Jimmy had dragged her. She stands towering over him, who is in pain on the ground. Leopold distracts her as he calls her out. She turns around. Jimmy quickly gets up and hits her in the back of the head, but she turns swiftly with a kick to his head, and he falls.

Leopold backs the car up toward her as she limps away from Jimmy. He gets out and walks toward her while Jimmy stumbles but gets up and attempts to throw a knife at her. Leopold fires a shot the sheer power of which lifts Jimmy in the air. His back hits the wall before he falls, crushing his balls atop a fire hydrant.

"Poor kid," Leopold says. "He had always wanted this gun."

They get in the car and take off. The Suburban drives slowly behind a crowd of protesters as Christiane plays the role of the GPS lady. "Turn here! Turn there! Go straight down a block," she would say, making him drive on streets and corridors he had never driven since he's been in the country. They need to get to the Base before the crowd in front of them meets and merges with other groups making it practically impossible for any vehicle to move. The crowd moves forward and clears up a street.

"Turn right here," she quickly orders him.

Once at the Base, the SUV pulls up and stops abruptly. Leopold gets out and sprints around to help Christiane.

"Ouch! Easy."

Tito monitors all of their moves through the images sent by the drone. Cyprien had informed him and Toumain about a deadline the president-elect had supposedly given Leopold. Still, the fat man could not precisely state the object thereof. On his screen, Tito gets a snapshot of Christiane's face as Leopold carries her out of the vehicle. Tito pulls out his phone and speed-dials.

"Dani, you have a problem."

Leopold sits in front of the 3D touchscreen computer, pulling up and moving files of the data from the hypnosis sessions. From Madigan, he had received the records on Mrs. Luber, whom the Kansas native met in an undisclosed location and without the FBI's stamp of approval. Thus, he literally brought the couch to her with his portable MIM and a few supporting gadgets. Extremely protective of the McLintaugh Investigation Method, James Madigan would not play fair and chose to bypass any approval from Ekstroem. Earlier, during the telephone conversation, Leopold had to reveal the name of the senator in Domersant's taxicab to Ekstroem, who somehow, possibly from Chipp, got word of Madigan's undertaking. The lady was a class, and James, a charming gentleman. Leopold had wished that Madigan had the sophistication of Mullins' crew. The senator knew quite a lot, and like flies over shit, the expert went at it all as she spilled it under hypnosis.

Christiane had entered another room probably to fix herself up following her fight with Jimmy in the hotel's lot and to grab a cup of coffee. She leaves the room with an envelope also. She is unaware that the agent had already gone about the message thereon. On the envelope is the note Dr. Pierre has left earlier with the officer who received him at the Base. When she walks into the area where Leopold works, a photograph of Jeando's face on the screen catches her attention. As Leopold moves and saves the files, the faces of people she recognizes come up numerous times. A series of photos and sketches that turn into photographs come on as he types the folder's name as "Assassination of Jean L. Dominique." Christiane's radar goes off. Her friend with benefits, she thinks, had never really told her everything, though.

Organizing the last photographs of the people involved in the crime, Leopold does not pay much attention to Christiane behind him. She is reading over his shoulder. Like Chaz Palminteri in the movie *The Usual Suspects*, both her jaw and her coffee drop. Leopold had gotten to the central suspects' names and pictures that include her father's. He turns around after the cup hits the floor. Christiane holds her emotions with her hand to her chest. Nothing. It's just a lousy cup that fell. Leopold resumes his work. On the screen, the photograph of the one individual that everybody knows as "the biggest fish of all" to whom the findings would ultimately lead. He had needed that be kept "confidential" until he meets with the new President. So much for this concealment, now. Christiane is not the only person. It is not as though this biggest fish is not already a familiar and loathsome kitchen item in the collective minds of the people. Because most of the worthless human props who went to Delmas were either physically eliminated or allowed to flee, the population at large, may not readily know them. Besides the names of her father and Tito, most folks will be right as they guess that other photograph and name Christiane realizes on the screen over Leopold's shoulders. He thinks he needs some privacy with the matter. Too late, Mr. McLintaugh, sir. The young agent ignores that though her father has always swum along with criminals, Christiane is part of another sample. That of History Channel and to a lesser degree, that of Morgan Freeman, the police officers.

"You need some rest, Chris," he suggests.

"I'm 'right," she contests. "The old doctor wants to see you. You know him?" she asks.

"'Met him earlier today," Leopold says with no elaboration.

When prompted, from inside a small silver box, Leopold pulls out a ring with an open-mouth lion's head sculpted and prong-attached to the gallery. He puts the ring on his finger and places his hand into a slot on the desk. Data are projected into the mouth of the figurine through bursts of laser-like green rays.

"He's the oldest doctor here," she says.

"He sure looks old," Leopold agrees as the data transfer is underway with his hand inside the machine.

As the process nears the 97 percent mark, Leopold starts to tap on the desk with his fingers and knuckles as he, out of the blue, whistles to the tune of what the students sang when Dr. Pierre, Dorothy, and he visited the schoolyard of Argentine Bellegarde. Christiane is impressed as she thinks that what he is playing sounds like notes from the country's. He stops as they hear two knocks on the door from the hallway. It is Mullins who inserts his head through the door.

"You got the ambassador on 5," he tells Leopold, who picks up with his free hand.

Christiane renews briefly with the chopped and incomplete sentences or answers as Leopold starts the unanticipated part of the conversation with the diplomat. When they begin to engage in the meaty matters of it, Christiane understands the look he gives her and leaves as Leopold silently thanks her. Perhaps, President Josaphat has reached the point where he can no longer handle this pressure cooker that is ready to blow any minute. The agent learns that the diplomat is walking out of a spur-of-the-moment meeting that Josaphat had called. The President had summoned to the makeshift palace within the last half-hour various senators, some other members of the parliament, and diplomatic missions in the country. True. Leopold could hear the diplomat's footsteps in the receiver. Now, he is convinced that things are moving really fast when he hears the doors of a vehicle slam shut. Along with his French counterpart, the diplomat is on the way to fetch Lysius to whom Josaphat has decided to pass the power within the hour instead of the officially scheduled date and time. Of course, the diplomat, before Leopold, was on the phone with Lysius, who also adjusted things requesting through him that the dossier be with him, in his possession as he takes the hurried oath.

With the data transfer complete, the agent's left hand is free and can serve another purpose at this time. He waves to Christiane the invitation to come back in sensing that the diplomat has told him almost enough.

"I will be ready, sir," Christiane hears as she comes in, and as Leopold looks at the blinking green light inside the ring on his finger.

A frantic pace begins, and he hurries her again as he did out of the hotel room. His mind was set about meeting with Lysius in two days and one hour, but suddenly, that must be within less than an hour. He quickly picks up a few things and his gun.

"Let's go," he tells her. "It is happening in an hour. 'Must give that ring to Geffrard beforehand."

"Who? The President?" Christiane asks in the sudden commotion. "What is happening in an hour?"

"No, his father," Leopold says. "I'll tell you in the car. Hurry!"

Tipped by Tito, Toumain knows very well he could not win in a shootout with the security detail near the American Base. He shows up anyway, but with a posse. A line of cars approaches slowly in the middle of the street. Maybe one of the few roads not yet congested after what had transpired earlier in the day. Two men concealing their weapons walk behind Toumain toward the

Base's entrance. He looks for no trouble. In his mind, he comes to have his daughter and deal with her insubordination at home later. From somewhere in his mind, he is about to regurgitate Chapo's account about Christiane at Carriès with "the white." The "white" who came with his daughter to his Vondelpark. Leopold follows Christiane as they run out in the hallway. The last turn offers her the view of her father and his men walking toward the Base's entrance. She stops cold on a dime. To avoid the confrontation and not to waste the little time they have, Leopold and Christiane opt for a smaller vehicle and drive out via a narrow alley on the other side of the Base. The relationship between Tito and Toumain could very well have the former avenge the death of the latter's son right there and then. Kept posted on the progress of the investigation, the ambassador had guaranteed the agent's presence at the embassy from where Lysius will monitor the events after he takes the oath of office.

Leopold drives around circling the block in a half-moon before getting back on the main street where the Base is. Neither Toumain nor his men pay attention to whom was in that small vehicle. In their understanding, the parked Suburban inside is enough proof that Christiane is still at the Base with Leopold, who just drove right under their noses. The live images from Tito's drone, after all, still show that vehicle.

"What's with the ring?" Christiane asks. "To the President or his dad?" she persists.

"To Mr. Geffrard," Leopold replies. "It contains the findings into Dominique's investigation."

"Urgh!" Christiane reacts in frustration. "The father or the son?"

Leopold smiles and stays quiet.

“I must propose to the son.”

Christiane asks no more questions.

CHAPTER 28.

President Josaphat Hurries

Sensing that the cooker "country" could explode on his watch, President Josaphat abruptly decides to stick that shit around Lysius' neck and get the fuck out. The President's thought process as shared with his wife. "Let me drop that 'gombo' in his fucking hands. He asked for it. After all, that is why the son of a bitch ran for President." The outgoing President looks forward to entering the elite club of Préval and Martelly to have completed their full term. *Terms* in the plural for the latter. And, as for himself, the only man in that nation's history to eagerly look forward to leaving the office. Not long ago, a few senators had literally cried blood and thrown fits when it was time to part most of them with the privileges and others, the immunity incentive of the office. President Josaphat hurries the proceedings, allowing no extra time for shit he deems not necessary enough. But he will warrant time for Lysius unshakable demand to have Nickesse Duvalier present since the US ambassador had begged Sosa to reconsider traveling to this ticking bomb. While in the car with the French diplomat, ambassador Johnson called President Sosa to explain the situation and dissuade him from visiting even long after the hasty inauguration.

"Mr. President," the ambassador said, "you want to be here in support for your friend. I respect that."

The French diplomat wishes he could be telling the same to his President, who was not scheduled to attend the inauguration.

At the Elysée, Lysius is likened to someone who could breathe new life into President Aristide's claim. Lysius is one hundred times more political and diplomatic than any of the country's presidents. Moreover, should he press on, it is a given. President Geffrard will have President Sosa's full and unconditional support. That backing will come even after Lysius had already told his American buddy he would also be coming after him concerning the country's agriculture.

"Sir," the ambassador continued. "I begged you as a friend, and as a diplomat. Now, I am warning you as an American citizen mindful of the safety of his President. Some bad folks here are aware of the shit you and the new President thought of together at Yale. Do not travel to this fucking jungle."

"You really think he will come here?" asks Christiane ignoring that Josaphat had given no time for anything else.

The diplomats drove Lysius directly to the shack that had served as the national palace since after the quake. This detail is why Christiane and Leopold have had to sit at the embassy for that long. The agent could understand it, and he is more at home here.

"He will," Leopold says, "but not as a President-elect."

"What do you mean?" she asks.

"He is taking the oath of office now, as we speak. That's what's happening."

Leaks. That sucks. Josaphat understands that this one day out of his term will send him down like a pathetic coward in more than just a few minds. In the minds of the same people who, perhaps unjustly, hang Jeando's assassination around somebody's neck with, of course, probable cause. His think tank took great pains to craft the narrative around his decision to rush things following the explosion. Supposedly, the hasty presidential oath-taking was to remain in the hush realm until all were on board for a special event live television broadcast from the US embassy. Shit leaks by officials telling a concubine who is a friend to the concubines of some other officials who had pulled strings for some friends of their friends. The diplomats did not board the automobile that Tito and Toumain, who was on his way to the Base seeking after his daughter, were already informed of Josaphat's decision. It is obvious where that chapter of the leaking originates. In this country, rumors, silent rumors, or administrative pillow talks seem to propagate faster than sound.

Moïse Josaphat, the man, apparently read into the terrible event of the mid-afternoon wisely weighing cause and consequences. He chose to cut a day off his term, perhaps to avoid a clash and protect the supporters of Lysius, who already are in the streets accusing Toumain and Massim. Those two, the President thinks, would not hesitate to butcher a crowd to corner the new President into walking back the idea of reopening Dominique's case. They are paid to protect their own asses and that of the mastermind, whoever that may be who engineered the journalist's assassination. Considering other aspects of the narrative, neither the outgoing President nor his advisors have any idea the investigation is complete. Moïse Josaphat, perhaps, like everyone else, still awaits a full-blown and dragging traditional probe.

In the rush and hush to install Lysius in the presidency, the protocol had almost disremembered the president-elect's single guest for whom they had sent a chauffeured limousine. Josaphat and his successor were already face-to-face when Duvalier arrives. After the formalities, ambassador Johnson rides with the new President to the US embassy where Leopold and Christiane await. The President is to deliver his first address to reassure the people that he now operates the shop and send a call to calm and restraint as only he could at this juncture. This is one instance where Moïse Josaphat's popularity deficit throughout his entire presidency shows the most and weighs the heaviest. Neither Duvalier's nor Geffrard's supporters would yield mindfulness to his words, and that's pretty much the country's population. Christiane had not understood the presence of the television crew at the embassy. Still, Leopold was aware since he is the one who suggested that the ambassador house Lysius and his family at his residence until the smoke dissipates.

"Mr. Ambassador, sir," Leopold said a week prior at the diplomat's residence, "I cannot find out whom Joe Chipp had programmed. I'd keep Lysius here if possible. He is a marked man."

Of course, Johnson tried again to convince Lysius during the ride to his inauguration. The French Ambassador witnessed his American counterpart dissuade one president and persuade another around the same matter. Sosa is as stubborn as Lysius, who refuses one half of Johnson's proposition for his safety. With the afternoon's destruction of the presidential palace, he accepts, however, to use the embassy temporarily. Ambassador Johnson welcomes the decision as he thinks once more about what he had told Leopold.

"It's not a perfect world, son," he said, admitting his fears of having Geffrard at his residence. His mob could set up camp around here 24/7 with the smell of burnt tires and barbecued human flesh.

"Dominique's killers," the agent replied, "who brought Joe Chipp here know that Lysius does not bluff. He is the target, sir. And, he added, I think you are mistaking the periods and the presidents. Lysius will get in his detractors' face himself. He never encouraged this type of mob violence."

The rumors have reached the uninvited guests, the crowds that start leaving the other protests, in the streets since the afternoon, to congregate around the makeshift presidential palace and the United States' embassy. At a distance on the avenue, the crowd starts to gather. By the time the ambassadors come out with the new President, it will have grown pretty sizable. When the motorcade reaches the US embassy, where it meets the denser crowd because the word has gone out down to its minute detail. Lysius' supporters knew he would go there afterward. So did Toumain and his men. Tito, with a special guest, also joins the party.

Claudine and her daughter did not make the trip to the embassy, as advised by Josaphat's wife. Anyhow, Lysius thought their presences were not necessary, and for what is going on in the streets, better shield the girls. However, Duvalier came along as Lysius insisted. As the vehicles pull up, the marines start to form their line of security to protect the ambassador and his guests, the country's new President, along with his former opponent. When he gets inside the embassy, his first action unwittingly confirms what Christiane had told Leopold on their way to the embassy. Despite his security, the President walks straight up to her with a surprised look on his face. Cyprien, who knows Christiane is supposed to be out of the country and is aware of Toumain's possible state of mind, eases his men as the President hugs her.

"Christiane! What are you doing here?" he asks.

"I am with a friend," she replies, gesturing to present Leopold.

"Ah!" Lysius exclaims. "McLintaugh! Has the country been kind to you?" he asks with a subtle wink about the young woman while he shakes hands with Leopold.

"You bet, Mr. President," answers the agent who registered both the question and the wink.

Amongst themselves, men understand this wordless language. The President pinches Christiane's cheek as he tells her that he and Claudine were talking about her just the night before. In fact, they were complaining of not seeing her as much of late. Probably since she has been in the country with Leopold. The new First Lady has taken a particular liking to Christiane, who had volunteered on one of her social projects as a senator's wife. The two quickly developed a stable bond. Lysius is aware that time is passing; the TV crew is ready for the President's *ad-lib* message.

"You know, we still have the same address," Lysius tells Christiane as the producer reservedly motions that his crew is ready.

On his way to the chair and desk waiting for him in front of the camera, he pulls the agent by the arm, silently inviting him to walk with him. Leopold did not anticipate him asking upfront for the dossier right away even though it is ready. After all, this is the reason he wanted to stop by the embassy before the ceremony.

Josaphat's time restraint did not allow that. Up to this point, Nickesse Duvalier may have felt like a fish out of water. Although everyone here knows who he is, he has no idea who is who in this company. He recognizes the busy television producer and only waves to him. In his rush toward the daughter of a man who may be plotting against him and the way the conversation led to Leopold, the President omitted to introduce his illustrious and only guest. Christiane is one pretty face that could enlarge Duvalier's chicks' base. He knows it and wastes no time. He walks straight up to her to introduce himself and gets her all smiling in less than a minute. A tiger's cub is not a cheep.

With the added boost of confidence that the ring on his finger allows him, the almighty *ad liber* delivers like no one else, but former president Aristide was able to. However, although with soft-spoken words, Titid spewed hatred and shit most of the time. He touches on an array of issues ranging from the country's problems, his campaign promises, and of course, the events of earlier in the day. At the center of his promises, he makes sure he sounds as though he breathes life into an investigation of which the findings are already in his hands, on "his ring finger." He is poised to make sure a lot of people go away for a long time. As he speaks, he remembers the crowd of his followers outside, hoping to have at least a glimpse of him. When both the French and the American ambassadors ride together in the same automobile with your President, you may have matters about which to be jittery. Kidnapping or shit like that. The people, in fact, start thinking of that, as previously in their recent history, Lysius believes he should step outside, be it for a short minute. Assuredly, these are his supporters. When the President runs this idea by his security chief, the fat man simulates disapproval before he changes his mind after a short and quick trip to the restrooms. He asks Geffrard to excuse his bladder issue. Treason shit.

For the first time, Nickesse Duvalier declines an invitation to be alongside his ex-political opponent since his victory. The President invites him to take a short ride with him on the avenue. A strong message to the rest of the world and to put the people at ease, assuring them that the diplomats did not kidnap him. More importantly, he thinks of sending a declaration that he will not fear anything and anyone. Duvalier considers he should not partake for this is his moment that he is supposed to share with his wife, daughter, and his supporters. Aware that half of the massive crowd out there is Duvalier's supporters, Geffrard insists. He begs and lures Nico to take part. Lysius is convinced that this message to the world, to their political equals and posterity, would be even more powerful should they share and bask. Nickesse Frederique Duvalier would not budge.

"Is this because of her?" the President asks his former rival. "You just met her. And, she is McLintaugh's girl, you know," he adds slanting to the agent to whom he has not yet introduced Duvalier.

When Cyprien walks out to the street with a few of his men, he is supposed to come back in and let Lysius know that all is in the clear in a perfect world. Since the day began, it has not been an ideal world. Thousands have senselessly lost their lives, and among the crowd, not everyone waits for Lysius to come out and be happy. Everyone knows that this is the most secure road in the country, if not in the region. The ambassadors do not disapprove, and Lysius steps out following Cyprien, who is permanently talking to his wrist. The job obliges. He secures the President all along the avenue. However, on the way back, things have changed. The crowd near the embassy is a bit modified. Joseph Chipp, aka Joe Manchurian, is not physically here, but just two words will make his presence felt in the crowd, in a matter of seconds. At only a few meters, the President could simply walk past the first marines at the gate of the embassy after he gets out of the vehicle.

Cyprien and two men walk right behind the President's SUV as it passes by a group of supporters wearing his campaign T-shirts. Lysius sticks out a hand so the people could touch him. The vehicle rolls to a stop near the two marines at the entrance. Lysius does not allow his bodyguard to open for him. He does it himself, gets out, and does not walk past the marines and into the embassy. The President goes to the right toward the rear of the car with the crowd to his left. What magnetizes him is the beautiful smile of a young woman wearing an artist's depiction of his face on a T-shirt. Feeling the supporters, he walks as far back as the third car behind the one he was in.

At one or two meters from where the newly sworn-in President interacts with the supporters, vociferous in that instant, someone sleeps. Not literally, but the formerly staunch Geffrard supporter stands unemotional, waiting for something. He has no idea what it is. Perhaps he does not even know where he is. If Lysius is John Lennon, this sleeper is the country's version of a Mark David Chapman with a long-sleeve shirt and unenthused, waving a miniature Haitian flag. Many vegetate in that dull state after they had two meetings with the dark angel of the CIA.

Chipp had brainwashed and programmed them into the sleeping killers they have no idea that they have become. The Dominican national holds a telephone in his ear. Next to the taxi driver who took Mr. Chipp across the border from SDQ in Punta Caucedo, the Haitian stands like a zombie. After one close encounter with Chipp, he does not even know why he is in that crowd. He is, however, aware that he awaits a communication to be spoken into his hear. The Dominican will whisper in the Haitian's ear who will unleash hell till he gets the intended target. Like an unsuspecting prey to its patient predator, Lysius could not get any closer. From the dark minivan where Toumain had joined Tito, who monitors the aerial images, the Syrian silently utters the trigger words that the Dominican hears through his telephone receiver. At his end, he slowly leans toward the former Geffrard's supporter, now a stone-faced Manchurian.

"Yellow tulips!" he shouts loud enough into the Haitian sleeper's ear that the President could hear as he startles a bit. Without a second utterance of these two words, it is like Caesar with his thumb up and the President lives. He repeats them softly, clearly, and almost silently into his Haitian companion's ear.

The Manchurians drop their telephone and flags. They step out of the crowd and draw their guns, as all seem to come to a halt. The only movement is from Lysius and the assassins converging toward the President. The driver of the nearest vehicle is the first to see them. As he yells, "Assassins!" he gets a bullet from each of the men. He falls back in his seat as his blood sprays onto the dashboard and windows. Lysius is already falling after he receives a bullet in the chest and another one in the head. The Manchurians drop their guns and stand there with their hands in the air. They could flee by just blending with the crowd. Or otherwise, would they pull a copy of *A Catcher in the Rye*? They do neither. They freeze on the spot like suspiciously the President's security does during the immediate seconds of the chaos. Not a single order from Cyprien for these long and eternal seconds.

Panicked, Christiane runs out of the gate and through the marines at the checkpoint. She passes Fat Jacques and his men toward Lysius, who gasp in a pool of his blood near the car. Leopold comes out surrounded by the marines and runs after Christiane. Is he running to prevent her from venturing any further? Another group of heavily armed marines now doubles up the security at the embassy's entrance blocking access to the embassy where the ambassador stands at the door looking at the development in the street. Nickesse Duvalier also comes out running past the ambassador and through his security.

"No! No!" Christiane cries, nearing the wounded President. "Not him! O, God! Claudine!"

As Nickesse arrives by Leopold and Christiane, who has Lysius' head on her laps as she is knelt down on the pavement, the mob seizes the two men. A second or two earlier, Leopold had already taken care of what he ran out to do. At the same time, the people dragged the Manchurians more toward the middle as two car tires move from hands to hands over the horde toward its center. Following by drone, Tito and Toumain high-five each other. The aerial images from the drone focus on Christiane with her arms extended toward the sky. The crowd chants demanding death to the two men and those responsible for the explosion of the presidential palace. They do just that and quickly. The

Manchurians die very fast as well. Before his very last breath, Lysius complains of the smell of their burning flesh. That image of Christiane with Lysius' head on her lap, her hands to the sky, will go around the world as a symbol of the country in mourning. A double courtesy of Tito Massim as he leaks his images to the international press.

After Leopold had gotten near Lysius, Duvalier may have entered the agonizing President's field of ill-defined view. Leopold feels the weakest pull on his hand from Lysius. He deciphers it as if the President wants to say something to him in private. His complaint about the smell of burnt flesh was *res publica* and known to all. The agent leans to the President's lips but could not understand his last words.

At the Base, the digital clock marks 1:21 am… Christiane sits on the bed with her legs crossed under the jersey of the University of Michigan football team she had borrowed from Leopold. No escape. She surfs with the remote control as every TV station reports on the assassination. The door opens and closes with the sounds of footsteps. She startles. Like a snake, she slithers to a drawer and pulls out a gun.

"Still up?" Leopold says. "Awake?"

She jumps off the bed and into his arms as he enters the room. She beats on his chest as she tears up.

How? How? She wonders. "How? The palace explodes with thousands of my people. My friend's husband," she complains, "dies on my lap a few hours ago… And then, sleep? Leopold?" she asks. "How?"

"Yeah," he says caressing her hair. "It's hard on you. We leave tomorrow. I'll have you see someone in DC."

He picks her up and carries her to bed.

"Try and sleep now," he tells her as his mind travels back to what he has been thinking about during the whole time he spent at the embassy. With his team and the ambassador, he spent hours reviewing the images from the surveillance cameras throughout the area. This is the Eureka moment except for the last wish of a dying President baffles Archimedes. Did Lysius ask him to give the ring to his former political opponent, Nickesse Duvalier? If Nickesse is not, according to "hearsays" that had entered the country's folklore, the family is familiar with the notion of a ring changing hands at the time of somebody's passing. On one such occasion, the condition of the exchange would not warrant Nickesse to be born of his mother. According to the legend, Nickesse was born out of his father's disobedience to a warning. "That's a load of beef shit!" the older officer would say.

9:04 am. The telephone buzzes and vibrates, as Leopold and Christiane are still asleep in each other's arms. He turns around and reaches.

"McLintaugh," he answers.

Now awakened, Christiane could hear the ambassador in the receiver. "McLintaugh," he says, "I am sorry to disturb you so early after keeping you up so late."

When Leopold comes down in the lobby wearing sweatpants after the ambassador has summoned him to manifest as he was, he finds him sitting with the commissioner next to him. On his way down, the diplomat and the agent continue to talk. The ambassador hangs up when he turns around and sees Leopold approaching.

"I know your mission here is over," the diplomat says. "Before you leave today, I wanted you to brief the commissioner here, who has yet to formulate a definitive statement."

"Mr. Johnson, sir, the commissioner's statement is simple," Leopold replies. "The men lynched in the afternoon by the mob did not kill the President." On the way to the projection room, he reminds the two men that after some people have attained a certain level or stature in life, just one person cannot kill them. Most, however, may not welcome the notion that it takes an organization to assassinate such men as Malcolm X, JFK, King, and, for that matter, journalist Jean Dominique. The mere mention of Jeando's name strikes a chord. Twice upon a former President's short shifts in the office, the commissioner was on his payroll and is still a loyal groupie.

"This assassination, Mr. Commissioner," Leopold continues as he starts projecting the images on the screen, "bears the fingerprints of this man. One Joseph Chipp, aka Joe Manchurian. He is photographed here with the Massim twins."

Ever since out of school, Daniel Toumain sponsored this man into strategic posts throughout different administrations. Before long, Toumain and ultimately Tito will learn that the FBI is already on to them in the killing of Lysius. Leopold recalls the need-to-know clause and refrains from saying more when the commissioner appears more interested in Jeando's case rather than what is at hand.

CHAPTER 29.

Fallout

Along the narrow pathway that serpents in around the dilapidated houses that the images from Tito's drone depict as a labyrinth of misfortunes, three car tires roll. This time around, it is not by a man sleeping on a couch. The man who walks behind these tires is a professional barricade erector. After the departure of Nickesse's father in 1986, people have tried to fend for themselves in any way possible. For over thirty-five years, there have been more streets protests days, more walkouts days, etc., than there school days or even jobs in the country. The floods of worn-out clothes, shoes, chicken and turkey wings, expired and spoiled Frankfurters, etc., have done away with a plethora of professions. Many folks depended on these to care for their households. Resourceful, the people find and create other means for their survival. They call it "The Stir," or as they term it in their creole language, "Brasé." The people's got to do what the people's got to do to make ends meet. It is cheap. The political hacks know it, and they take advantage of it.

The barricade he is building must block all traffic leaving the capital by this route. The boy assisting him drops the chair he was carrying to aliment the fire. The man stops the tires and walks straight toward a luxury car that had pulled up across the street. The dark window rolls down halfway. Kharim Massim tends an envelope to "the barricader" who opens and peeks with a smile as Kharim executes a K-turn and drives off.

Although Leopold abstained in time from much talking, the diplomat has not been that circumspect. Well, the Commissioner gathered enough information to vaguely suspect the existence of an item that perhaps Lysius was supposedly about to receive. The Commissioner also learned that the agent's work is complete and that he is leaving the country by mid-afternoon. This barricade mainly must prevent Leopold from reaching the airport if Tito's plan A fails. In normal circumstances, that part of the program would engross Chapo and Jimmy. These are not ordinary circumstances. Tito has never learned or tried to trust anyone besides his loyal Chapo and most recently his nephew. In just one day, his son, his crime buddy, die, and his nephew can only lay down on his stomach on a hospital bed like Forrest Gump with no one to bring him ice cream. Massim knows he must avenge. At times, he regrets not having done anything when he bumped into Leopold at Commerce Park. Retrieving the drone seemed assuredly more important than his son.

This section of the city seems to rejoice in the passing of the new president and to be numb to the other terrible event earlier the day before but not necessarily so. Most people out here have been paid to be in this crowd. Their protest does not seem organic. For the most, in this country, folks don't even know the nature of their protests. Just like the setting up of the barricades, they do it for a living. During the presidential elections that Josaphat won, it was evident that the crowds bore uncanny resemblances. One day, they would protest against or in favor of this Moïse, the next, the other Moïse as the booking allows. They oppose on demand. Meanwhile, Mullins, the last agent still in Haiti with Leopold, is thanking the maids who have cared for them at the Base before he boards the car with Leopold and Christiane.

The city is in chaos taken over by high flames, thick black smoke, and the asphyxiating smell of burning rubber. Some gatherings accuse a former president of sponsoring the assassination of Lysius and associate him with Dominique's murder and the death of thousands of citizens in the explosion of the presidential palace. At this particular barricade, a trap is intended. Behind the flames and smoke, the criminals await the diplomatic car transporting the agents and Christiane. The car arrives. The fellow who received the envelope from Kharim acts as an official at a checkpoint. After comparing a photograph that he received from the surviving twin, he looks at Leopold's face. He warrants the other occupants of the vehicle to pass through since their license plate, as he tells them, indicates that they are indeed diplomats. He then signals to his crew to open the fiery barricade.

The SUV drives through the smoke. But it is only to abruptly stop mid-block behind what is left of a tractor-trailer with no wheels in the middle of the street.

"And this shit?" Leopold questions.

On a secondary dirt road immediately after the barricade, sat in an ambush in a black minivan, Toumain and Kharim armed with a machine gun. They slowly roll onto the main road after the diplomatic vehicle.

"Ambush!" shouts Mullins, who had quickly surveyed the surroundings as the minivan now speeds about the corner, and armed thugs emerge from the narrow corridors. Behind them near the barricade, the man who checked them fires an AK-47, or long sleeve in the country, blowing the vehicle's rear tire. Leopold and Mullins shove Christiane down into the deep of the back seat as the marines on either side in the middle back row rapidly spray the men appearing out of the corridors. In this hail of bullets, Mullins is hurt and won't make it. With the numbers against them, the marines and the agent cannot win. They were, however, holding their own, each on his side of the vehicle, dropping the inexperienced local gunmen one by one. When he, Toumain, drives close enough, Kharim becomes able to take both of them out with only a shot for each.

Cornered in the middle of a street with a dead driver in a car with blown-out tires, the agent can't put forth much resistance. Kharim quickly gets out of the minivan, wipes the black off his face, and points his gun at the back seat.

"Out! Get out!" Kharim shouts. "Hey, hey! You! The honey!" He orders Christiane. "On this side… Leaving with your new boyfriend?" he asks her as she walks in front of him.

Covered with Mullins' blood, Leopold and Christiane meet behind the car with their hands up as Kharim frisks Leopold and takes his gun.

"Hmm!" he says in awe of the agent's piece. "Jimmy was right," he audibly thinks glancing at the weapon.

Toumain gets out, walks straight to his daughter, who does not recognize him at first. He throws his hat angrily at Christiane, who did not expect to see him here.

"Father!" she instinctively exclaims.

Filled with rage, Toumain slaps her very hard.

"You betrayed your father?" he tells her.

Furiously wigwagging, Toumain's gun goes off and accidentally shoots her in the chest. Toumain is surprised. She falls and gasps as Kharim's phone rings.

A young man on a motorcycle, comes around by front wheel up and making a lot of noise. He rides through the smoke to let the leader of the blockade know that he had spotted the other marines arriving their way as back up. But the two marines in the SUV had already taken the leader out. The young man circles the bike around his corpse and debris on the pavement, and all that distracts Kharim a bit. Leopold quickly charges at Toumain, tackling him. He takes his gun and shoots him. Kharim recovers on time and dishes Leopold a kick and hits him on the head with the butt of the machine gun knocking him out.

"Killed my brother, you fucking fagot?" he says. "You can have that dead bitch," he adds… "I would whack your ass right now if father didn't want you alive."

As the young man on the bike circles around the vehicles, the noise he makes annoy Kharim, who summons him to stop and help him. He orders him to grab the keys from Toumain who never leaves keys in the ignition. The young man hears the directions but has another idea. He goes into Mullins' pocket and takes his wallet as Kharim impatiently yells at him.

"The other fucking dead man!" he screams without taking his eyes and gun off Leopold.

"Can you, fucking thief, drive?" he asks the young man.

The young man hesitates to tell him that he can only ride and does not drive sticks. In his left hand, he has Leopold's gun pointed at him; he reaches and gets the machine gun with the right one. He pulverizes the kid's motorcycle.

"Now, motherfucker, you do drive sticks. Hop on," he orders the youngster as he pushes Leopold inside the minivan.

By rage, out of jealousy and heartlessness, Leopold suffers the brunt of Kharim's visceral ferocity in the minivan during the trip to his father's basement. There, he sits unconscious on a wooden chair designed to look like an electric chair, and he's attached with handcuffs on either armrest. Meanwhile, Tito lays out torture devices on a table. He looks at him in the mirror on the wall and between each item that he places on the table and bits of visions that come flooding his mind each time. The forensics scientist Madigan would put these visions circa 1987 when the young woman therein sets a table in a spacious dining room.

Kharim enters the room, leans over, and with malice, pulls Leopold's ear.

"'Fucked her on that beach? Now fagot, we fuck you up."

Kharim slaps him and gets a jar from the table. He opens and places it under Leopold's nose, and he starts to wake up. Finally, Leopold's eyes open with a rumble of thunder in them. Taken aback and frightened, Kharim falls back on his butt. Also startled, Tito turns around with his jaw ajar, locks eyes with Leopold, and experiences another flash from his past where he forcefully fuddles the breasts and buttocks of the maid. The young woman turns around, pushes off him, and he falls. With a knife and a fork in her hands, she sternly warns the younger Tito.

"Hah!" Tito shrugs off that most extended bit of the vision as a spark flies when he strikes an electric cable to one pole of the car battery he uses as a power generator. The light bulb hanging over Leopold flickers on and off. Kharim rushes out of the room to get to the ringing house telephone as Tito approaches Leopold, who eyeballs him head-on, straight in his eyes and without blinking. Quite a stare.

"Hah! You got the eyes of the devil," he tells him as he gets washed away into yet another flashback sequence. In this one, he revisits his younger recently married self raping the young maid on the marital bed right below a photograph of his wedding with his wife. In Leopold's blank and thunderous stare, Tito recollects the powerless young woman who could only shred him with her eyes and take it without any emotion. At the time of the rape, she rendered herself numb to his sexual brutality.

To Tito, who has not seen much action for a long time or experienced even a morning wood, that tiny part of his perverse fantasy acts like the magic of Viagra. Twice he tries. Once, the first time, he fails to summon these imageries of him sexually assaulting the woman in his mind. Over and over, he tries to relive the abuse he inflicted as he tries to block the sequence from the domestic dispute that had followed with the suspicious Mrs. Massim. Leopold, meanwhile, sticks to what is happening in 2023, circa one day prior. He replays in his mind before reenacting how he freed himself at Khalil's house before leaving him on the swing set. As Tito mentally tries to erect a dead part of his anatomy, Leopold intensifies his strength. And suddenly, he stands, lifting the chair up with him and backs up to the stone wall with a Herculean strength as Tito freezes in shock.

The chair breaks, but the two armrests remain attached to him by the handcuffs. Grabbing the armrests, Leopold charges at Tito, who reaches for a carpenter's hammer and quickly turns around. The pointy edge of one armrest perforates his chest spraying his blood over Leopold. With the other armrest, Leopold strikes a blow to Tito's head. Massim falls powerless at his feet. Leopold finds the handcuffs' keys in Tito's pocket and he rids himself of them. He picks up the hammer from the floor and tiptoes out of the room with sprinklings of Tito's blood on his clothes and face. Leopold saunters up to the stairs as he hears Kharim's laugh through the walls and pinpoints from which room his voice is coming.

The laughter comes from that room, the agent concludes. He looks through the peek hole. There, Kharim is admiring Leopold's gun. At the same time, he listens on the telephone sitting facing the glass window overlooking the swimming pool right below and the city of Petionville close by, and further still, the capital city of Port-au-Prince, then the bay in the distance.

"No, no, no," he says as he gets up. "I tell you what. I must be in Columbia tomorrow. Let's meet in Miami. At the airport."

Kharim slowly walks to the wall near the door behind which Leopold peeks through, eavesdrops and anticipates the event it opens. Kharim unhooks a car key off the wall and turns the holder ring with his finger. It is subliminal when he opens the door and takes half a step only to turn around still on the phone. Leaving the door ajar, he walks back in. Kharim' half action through the door takes Leopold by surprise. He takes a deep breath but bangs the back of his head on the wall behind him. He now holds his breath. As he slowly walks and listens on the phone, the small noise of Leopold's head banging the wall startles Kharim a little. He stops, looks around, and again sits down, facing the magnificent view through the sliding glass window.

"Oh, that guy?" Leopold hears as Kharim laughs. "Father's fixing him his afternoon breakfast, as you call what he'll give him."

As Leopold quietly enters through the door, Kharim places the gun on the small table next to him, picks up his glass, and takes a sip.

"He's enjoying some good stuff now as we speak," he says.

"Psst!" calls Leopold, who had crept behind him

Kharim turns around very surprised. He tries to reach for the gun. Leopold throws the hammer that hits the younger Massim's hand and the weapon that falls off the table and into a corner on the floor.

As the Syrian quickly gets up, Leopold charges at him, taking him through the glass window, and while in midair, Leopold holds Kharim in a lock, head-butting him in the nose that starts to bleed. The calm surface of the water in the pool is disturbed when that first drop of blood falls right before the two men violently splash in. The splash creates a mini tsunami around the swimming pool that levels the small plants and flowers. Qusay is no Uday—he can hold his own. They throw and land punches at each other in the pool. Leopold swings Qusay ducks and seizes him by his shoulders. The Syrian pushes and holds him under the water as he gasps in exhaustion. For a brief moment, the water seemingly gets calm.

Suddenly, Qusay falls backward in the water as Leopold emerges, holding both of his legs by the ankles. Qusay tries to bend up from under the water, but Leopold quickly grabs him by the throat and powers him on the water's surface and holds on.

Qusay stops moving after a while. Leopold lets go of him and gets out of the pool.

The American is all wet and dripping when he appears in the doorway. He slowly walks in. He looks at a long and far-reaching bloody streak on the floor, going from one door to up the stairs. He cautiously ascends rolling his eyes around in all directions. The bloody stain continues onto the second set of stairs and straight past the living room's door. Leopold quickly gets into the living room and retrieves his gun from the floor in the corner near the small table and the broken glass window. He looks down at Kharim, who floats in the middle of the bloodied pool.

"Paperboy," he says to himself.

As he turns around, a gunshot brings the luxury ceiling lights down. Copiously bleeding and crawling on the floor, Tito clicks, and clicks out of bullet or his gun jams after missing its mark.

Leopold walks calmly toward the open door with his gun pointed at Tito, who is a frightened, bloody mess. Tito crawls backward in front of the gun to the edge of the stairs and stops as Leopold stares intensely, aiming the gun at his face. And for a brief instant, feels what he felt within Domersant's memory at the intersection on the boulevard near Radio Haiti. Leopold kicks him down the stairs and watches as Tito's broken and bloodied body rolls down and goes to rest on the bloodstained mat at the foot of the stairs. There, he farts and takes his last breath as Leopold turns around. He's got a plane to catch this afternoon. He leans in through the door and grabs all the cars' keys on the living room's wall and exits.

The minivan starts to move forward then stops. Leopold gets out and quickly runs to a Mercedes-Benz parked between a BMW and a jaguar.

He gets in but he seems distracted as he looks elsewhere, fumbling to find its ignition key. The twins' latest acquisition, the newest Ferrari model, sits under a covered parking space. Among the keys, he sees the remote key, and the Ferrari starts. He gets out of the Mercedes.

"Who says I was born in a poor country?" he loudly asks himself as the Ferrari speeds away on a long stretch of empty road.

The digital speedometer burns up the numbers as Leopold pushes the pedal to the floor.

"Fuck! The old man," he recalls.

He makes a U-turn and speeds off.

While the women try to calm their crying infants, they turn around all shocked to see the wet and torn clothes on this white man who enters the crowded waiting room. A young mother wraps her arms around the needle-phobic baby on her lap as a young nurse caresses the infant's cheek with one hand. In the other, she has some syringes, and the child, of course, fathoms that the nurse indeed has evil intentions. Leopold's attention goes to the young mother, reminiscing stories about his mother being as young when Dr. Pierre cared for her at Rue Vaillant. The women and even the babies who stop crying seem surprised to see Leopold, whom the old pediatrician has spotted the instant he barged through the doors. Doctor Pierre is not very surprised for he knows who this is. What does surprise him, however, is the state he is in.

“Hah! Mr. Leopold,” he says as he steps out of his office. “What happened, my son? I was beginning to think that you had left already.”

From the middle of the room, Leopold wobbles toward the old man, and a relatively old nurse walks out to meet him.

The old man and the nurse help him inside the office and seat him as Dr. Pierre gets around and sits behind the desk. The nurse gives him one green scrub pants and a white medical blouse that are very short on him. They belong to Dr. Pierre. When he appears in the room with a band around his forehead, he gets on an exam table and sits.

Dr. Pierre comes in, stands in front of him, pulls the blouse, and applies a dressing over one of the larger bruises on his shoulder. As he later thanks the old man for treating him, he tells him of his surprise to see that he still can handle such a busy and demanded practice.

“I'm grateful for that,” he says as he kisses his thumb. “Other faculties, I have no more. “Today,” only one exchange seems fair to me,” the old man tells the agent … ‘These babies' cries for my coffin.'”

“Take care o' my bruises before that exchange, young man,” Leopold jokingly tells the doctor.

“After birthing the likes of you and of Lysius they killed yesterday, I say it is time,” he complains.

“My mission here's over,” says Leopold, who feels a little pinch as the doctor touches a bit deeper. “I leave today. 'Guess if you come to DC, my parents would be honored to receive you.”

“Before it's too late,” adds Leopold as he sighs and sits straight up. “They think they are getting too old, too fast.”

"You remember my mother, don't you, Doctor?" he asks.

The old man recounts to him the story of his birth one more time, perhaps for the older nurse to hear it again. This time in the presence of the actual man who played the role of that blond baby boy in that school yard. He tells of Dominique's investigative work, about which the journalist had kept him informed, in search of his biological father. He tells him about that domestic dispute at the end of which his biological mother gets thrown out with nowhere to go.

"After Ed and Dorothy left with the young girl's baby," Dr. Pierre continues pointing to Leopold, "Jeando investigated into her life until he discovered his biological father… And the last time I saw Ed was at Jeando's funerals. Dorothy came back once."

If he wobbled in the clinic, he is likewise leaving, but this time, it is not physically. While the doctor talks, Leopold mentally journeys back inside the brain and memory masses of both History and Morgan attempting to view the pregnant girl he saw on the MIM's monitor. He believes she stared into the officer's eyes for his purpose. He is somewhat disconcerted by what he has just heard from the old man, especially after what had transpired about an hour ago. As he is about to leave, they shake hands. The hand of the old man appears gigantic to the agent while he feels the rest of his body as being tiny and far away. The infants' cries echo from far away in his ears, and the room seems to spin around him as he wobbles out of the door and hears the echoing voice of Dr. Pierre.

"These babies' cries for a coffin."

"Yes, son. I birthed you in that courtyard among dead bodies…"

"I birthed Lysius."

"I birthed your brothers, the twins."

"Tito Massim is your biological father as Jeando found out."

Leopold throws himself behind the wheel and pauses in disbelief. A flashback of his brief encounter with his biological father plays out in his mind. In Commerce Park, as the old doctor comes within his view under the umbrella, the two men bump Leopold as they exit the court with Tito following them. He sees himself quickly turn around to stare into the eyes of his biological father, according, of course, to the stories stemming from Jeando's investigation. Over and over, he hears Tito say: "Savages. Please, forgive 'em."

"Forgive 'em."

"Please forgive the savages."

He quickly relives his fights with Tito and both his brothers. Still, very quickly, he snaps out of his dreamlike state, shakes himself off, takes a deep breath, and speeds away to the airport.

The Commissioner, along with uniform officers, walks out with Cyprien in handcuffs as he was attempting to flee. They are helping his head down into a police vehicle when the Ferrari stops behind the officials' car. As Leopold gets out, a young police officer blows his whistle and runs, hoping to intercept Leopold as he rushes toward the entrance.

"No, no, no!" yells the officer. "Doctor. Your car will be towed."

Leopold keeps running and throws the Ferrari's remote key at the officer who catches it.

"You don't need to," he tells him as he runs past. "Keep it."

For a second, the officer hesitates. He looks at the key in his hand, then at Leopold running away, and he looks at the Italian Jewel of a car from Maranello. The officer runs to the vehicle. As he presents at the boarding gate, the overhead television silently broadcasts the news of Tito's death with captions. Collectively, those paying attention and who knew who Tito was, react as though his presence on the planet affected them all be it for good or evil. As the agent reads the caption "TITO–QUSAY DEAD" on the screens, he understands that he is leaving the country with baggage of different feelings. Feeling of having conducted a thorough investigation into Dominique's assassination that unmasks the real killers of the journalist and the mastermind. He knows that he'll be on this earth for a time, with James Madigan and his father Ed McLintaugh, the select few who agree with the declaration of the professor with balls the size of grapefruit. "Jeando was murdered," Professor P.E. said, "because he was dignified, confident and that, around the year 2000, Dominique's bearing and demeanor befitted a president." A praiseworthy bundle of feelings to leave the country with until another one rapidly cancels it out. There is no one in the nation to act on the findings. Leopold thinks that Lysius' wish at the time of his death could only jeopardize Duvalier's life. Nickesse would become a marked man should the rough players around him become aware of the existence of such a ring and his inheritance thereof. The data therein contained are but damaging information regarding many of them still politically active and that one ruthless "big fish." The plane finally takes off, with onboard Leopold's heart as the most cumbersome luggage carrying his knowledge of having killed his brothers, father, and powerlessly witnessed the death of his love interest, Christiane.

***

The mood in the living room is quite festive. As the two men await the girls, Leopold sits across from Ed, who moves the newspaper to the side clear his face as he leans.

"Do tell, son," he says to him, alluding instead to matters regarding his roots. "What did you find out?"

"Not that I have a biff with it," he answers, not registering Ed's real interest. "Same-sex union, father, not my cup o' tea."

"Where are you taking this, son?" Ed asks under shock.

"A bad omen, father. I placed a ring on a man's finger. Ten minutes later, he's dead."

At the same time, Leopold's daughter runs and giggles in the hallway.

"Daddy! Daddy!" she cries as she runs into his arms. Dorothy and Teresa arrive after her.

Placing the girl on his lap, he sips a bit from his glass, visibly happy to notice his wife.

"I was devastated when they killed Lysius. Stubborn," he adds, "with a big mouth, though foul at times, he was an exceptional man."

With his daughter in his arm, Leopold walks over to the women.

He kisses Dorothy and locks in a long and passionate hug and smooch with Teresa.

Filled with joy, Dorothy joins her hands together. She lifts her eyes up as her lips silently give thanks.

"Thank you, Lord," she says.

THE END

AFTERWORD

After the death of Lysius, the transitional government is housed in a mansion donated to the state by his father. To honor his wish, Nickesse Duvalier accepts his nomination as ambassador to the United Nations and serves honorably. Through the years, he and Leopold befriend each other purposefully on the part of the FBI agent who later claims the Haitian nationality. Duvalier ultimately runs again and wins the elections fair and square with the overwhelming support of his and Lysius' coalitions. However, that will earn him a host of new detractors. Allied to Moïse Jean-Charles, *(Old Moy*), some former followers' turncoat because of Duvalier's integrating Geffrard's politics, embrace what the people sarcastically call DBP "Dessalines' Bastards Platform."

President Duvalier makes sure all the people connected with the cowardly events of April 2000 and February 2023 are sent away for a very long time. He secures restitution from the fortunes of the most influential folks who have masterminded these criminal events.

However, Jeando's family will have respectfully declined to accept restitution from the fortunes of some on the ground that more than half of their wealth was stolen from the Haitian people who did not kill the journalist.

How ironic and what are the odds? A Duvalier delivering justice for Jean Leopold Dominique?

ABOUT THE AUTHOR

Ene'es ELIGREG or HZ2999QHWS1H, as he's known in the dimension, is of Haitian and Extraterrestrial origins with a 1:9 ratio. Mr. ELIGREG is the only being without a birthdate. He was not born. His alien ancestors devoted over 80 years to perfecting and finalizing the faceless humanoid infant form that they entrusted to a Haitian family around the early 1970s. The face he now has is of entirely human skin tissue the Aliens received from the Haitian couple's combined genome. Hia look is identical to that of the human couple's ninth child. The humans' task consisted of cultivating a great leader for the Virtuals' civilization, and they did not fail. At the terrestrial age of eleven, Ene' es ELIGREG became the first part-human President of Virtual Haiti and, at the same time, the perpetual leader of all the civilization. He ruled as President until 2017 when he stepped down to care for the education of his human daughter. He now resides partly in Kenskoff, Haiti, and the Bermuda Triangle. He spends time flying around the galaxy on board his UFO-like vessels.

According to legends, the African slaves in Saint Domingue did receive extraterrestrials assistance in their quests for freedom. The Aliens, males, and females knew many of the darker-skinned humans in the biblical sense. They all left with their new families in February 1804, after the battle of Vertieres in 1803 and the Declaration of independence of Real Haiti as the first black free nation on the planet. They established a civilization that waxed strong in the Bermuda Triangle in a submarine Country that emerges sporadically from the deep. ELIGREG came to prominence in the human realm during the vacuum created with the departure of President Michel Martelly at the end of his term in office in 2015. The ETs and human ancestors of both Real and Virtual Haiti asked for his leadership in the real country. Contrary to HE217T56, the current President of Virtual Haiti who would support a Duvalier run in 2022, ELIGREG never hides his friendship and support to every current Real Haitian President. As he says, "get elected and I'll support you."

Let us stop right here. Ene' es ELIGREG is actually the pseudonym adopted by the author and copyrights' claimant. In the introduction of this book, he tells of his love for storytelling. This is his actual given first name as it would be spoken by the Virtuals in the complex language he has them speak within the concept he's created. Remember, Virtuals are the descendants of the African slaves, and the Aliens who helped them found the nation of Haiti that they called "Emaenema'n" or "Motherland" or "Real Haiti."

The author writes in both English and French and hopes your purchase will help further develop the many concepts he has thought of throughout the years.

GRATITUDE

The author hopes you enjoyed this story, although the real events that inspired it are by no means amusing. They were, and are sad, very sad. And, he really felt the same sorrow that the character of President Geffrard experienced in the dorm room at Yale. He is very grateful that you acquired the book. Your purchasing his book does make a difference. At the same time, you help bring his other concepts to life in literary form and perhaps beyond.

Thanks again for your support!